"Good afternoon, l̶_____ brings you here to enjoy our hospitality?"

Those brown eyes of hers flashed at Sam. "Good afternoon, Captain. I am in jail because one of your policemen invited me."

"I see." Sam's grin widened. She was not as cool as she pretended. Underneath all that poise Miss Randolph was mad as a wet hen. "Would that be the one who found you at the courthouse refusing to allow the children to go back to work when they were told to do so? And what did you hope to gain by such behavior?"

Mary's head lifted. "A doctor's orders that the children were not to work in such heat. Which I accomplished." A look of pure satisfaction spread across her face.

Sam gave her a mock stern look. "Miss Randolph, what am I to do with you?"

She flashed him a cheeky grin. "Pay my bail?"

Dorothy Clark
and
Renee Ryan

The Law and Miss Mary
&
Hannah's Beau

HARLEQUIN® LOVE INSPIRED®CLASSICS

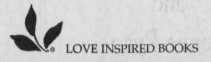

LOVE INSPIRED BOOKS

Recycling programs for this product may not exist in your area.

ISBN-13: 978-1-335-47359-2

The Law and Miss Mary & Hannah's Beau

Copyright © 2019 by Harlequin Books S.A.

The publisher acknowledges the copyright holders of the individual works as follows:

The Law and Miss Mary
Copyright © 2009 by Dorothy Clark

Hannah's Beau
Copyright © 2009 by Renee Halverson

www.Harlequin.com

Printed in U.S.A.

CONTENTS

Award-winning author **Dorothy Clark** lives in rural New York. Dorothy enjoys traveling with her husband throughout the United States doing research and gaining inspiration for future books. Dorothy believes in God, love, family and happy endings, which explains why she feels so at home writing stories for Love Inspired Books. Dorothy enjoys hearing from her readers and may be contacted at dorothyjclark@hotmail.com.

Books by Dorothy Clark

Love Inspired Historical

Stand-In Brides

His Substitute Wife
Wedded for the Baby
Mail-Order Bride Switch

Pinewood Weddings

Wooing the Schoolmarm
Courting Miss Callie
Falling for the Teacher
A Season of the Heart

An Unlikely Love
His Precious Inheritance

Visit the Author Profile page
at Harlequin.com for more titles.

THE LAW
AND MISS MARY

Dorothy Clark

For the Lord seeth not as man seeth;
for man looketh on the outward appearance,
but the Lord looketh on the heart.
—*1 Samuel 16:7*

This book is dedicated with appreciation
and affection to my extremely talented editor,
Melissa Endlich, who knows how to make each book
the very best it can be. Thank you, Melissa.
It is a pleasure to know you,
and an honor to work with you.

And a special thank-you to my wonderful friend
Jean Mallery. It was Jean who first learned, all those
many years ago, that I was secretly writing a book,
and encouraged me to follow the Lord's call.
If it hadn't been for you, Jean, I wouldn't be
working on my seventh novel. Thank you
for your faithfulness, encouragement and love.

*"Commit thy works unto the Lord,
and thy thoughts shall be established."*

Your word is truth. Thank You, Jesus.

To You be the glory.

Chapter One

St. Louis, 1840

Mary Randolph shifted her gaze from the muddy waters of the Mississippi River flowing under the steamboat to the scratched and gouged promenade deck rocking gently beneath her feet. In spite of the sun shining overhead, both river and deck were dull, lusterless. The same as she. Tears flooded her eyes. She blinked them away and squared her shoulders, refusing the thought, determined that no remnant of the past would cloud this first glimpse of her future.

The tempo of the engines driving the paddle wheels slowed. A raucous blast from the boat's whistle split the air. Mary gripped the rail with both hands and peered out at the city of St. Louis, thankful for the sudden downdraft of wood smoke from the steamer's tall stacks that made her eyes smart and water, giving her an excuse for any betraying, glistening tears.

The *Fair Weather* gave another blast of her whistle, slipped into a berth and nosed up to the bank. Cobblestones paved the incline from the river's edge that leveled off in a street that formed the city's front door. Mary crowded closer to her brother in the sudden press of passengers along the rail and studied the area. Steamboats and other river craft of all descriptions lined the sloping bank, taking on or unloading passengers. Smokestacks belched plumes of acrid smoke into the warm, moist air. Whistles blew, announcing arrivals and departures. Ships' mates shouted orders to their crews. Chains rattled and ropes squeaked with tension as cargo was taken aboard or lowered to the dock. Hammers pounded as repairs were made. And beneath the din hummed the constant murmur of voices.

Mary blinked the moisture from her eyes and took a step back to use her brother as a windbreak while she adjusted her new hat. "I did not expect such a hustle and bustle of activity in a frontier city." She shook out the long tails of diaphanous fabric streaming from the base of her top hat down her back, and moved forward again to stand at the rail. "There must be at least twenty or twenty-five steamboats docked along this shore, James."

"I make it closer to thirty, perhaps more. It's difficult to tell." James leaned over the rail as far as he was able and looked up and down the shoreline. "There are so many smokestacks it looks like a forest growing out of the river." He pushed himself erect and placed his mouth close by her ear. "And only six of these steamers are ours—including this one. I shall write Father of the stiff competition immediately."

Mary released her hold on the rail, stared at the flecks of peeling paint on her gloves and lowered her voice to match his. "Do you suppose Father knew of the neglected, weather-beaten condition of the ships before he bought the line? If the *Fair Weather* is any indication, the vessels of the Mississippi and Missouri steamer line are in very poor condition."

"He knew. Wilson had all the information when he came to St. Louis to make the deal in Father's stead." James leaned closer to her. "And Father knows why. His agent had reported someone has been letting the ships fall into disrepair while they skimmed off the profits. I am to discover the culprit."

Mary stopped brushing her hands together to rid her gloves of the paint specks and looked up at him. "So *that* is the reason for our secrecy."

"Exactly." He turned his mouth back to her ear. "If anyone learns our father is the new owner, the thieves will cover their tracks and disappear. We must be cautious and trust no one with that information until I uncover the truth."

"You are warning *me* to silence?" Mary shot him a look of disbelief. "Surely you do not think anyone will learn our father purchased the line from *me?* Why, if I were a devout person, I would be on my knees this very moment giving thanks to God for our secrecy. This is the perfect situation for me." Her face tightened. "Of course, if it were not for God, I would not need anonymity from Father's wealth and status." The words came hissing out in a bitter whisper. She pressed her trembling lips together and turned away from the flash of sympathy in her brother's eyes.

"Mary, listen—"

She shook her head. Wind gusted over the rail, snatched the long, flowing tails of fabric on her hat and whipped them forward again. She brushed the filmy fabric from her face and swallowed the tears that threatened to expose her heart.

"Mr. Randolph?"

"Botheration!" James sucked in air and held it. She glanced at him through her lowered lashes, saw his frown. The threat of tears fled. A smile tugged at her lips. She, Sarah and James all used the "hold and count" method to gain control when they were upset or annoyed. It was one of the gems of wisdom their mother had taught them. *Mother.* Homesickness washed over her like the river water whispering along the shore.

"We will discuss this later." James whispered the words into her ear and turned. "I am James Randolph."

Mary watched a heavy-set man, garbed in a black suit, shoulder his way through the milling crowd of passengers to stand beside them. She straightened as the man peered at her, his gray eyes magnified by the wire-rimmed glasses perched on his slightly bulbous nose. He dipped his head in a polite bow and looked back at her brother. Surprise—no doubt at James's youth—flickered across his face, quickly replaced by an expression of polite respect.

"Eli Goodwin at your service, Mr. Randolph. I am the bookkeeper of the Mississippi and Missouri steamer line. Captain Lewis sent word of your arrival, and I have come to escort you to the manager's residence. Mr. Thomas, the former manager, vacated the premises when he was dismissed from his position. You need not wait for your trunks. I have arranged for them to be delivered."

"How good of you, Mr. Goodwin. My sister and I have had a long journey and are most eager to get settled into our new home."

The man nodded. "I trust your accommodations aboard ship were comfortable and your journey a pleas-

ant one. If you will follow me?" He turned toward the
stairs leading down to the main deck.

James stepped back from the railing, creating a small
space in the press of people. Mary gathered close the
long, full skirt of her dark blue gown and stepped into
the void he had created. Urged forward by her brother's
hand at the small of her back, she followed in Eli Goodwin's wake.

Samuel Benton stood at the edge of the river, narrowed his eyes and drifted his gaze over the *Fair Weather*'s main deck. A few frowns, a few curt nods revealed
that his purpose in coming to the levee had been accomplished—the crew knew the law was present and
watching them. Perhaps it would be enough to discourage anyone who might intend to damage the ship. Though
it could be that such danger no longer existed since the
line had changed owners.

Sam scanned the deck again, paying particular attention to the firemen and engineer. He did not believe the
mishaps on the three previously destroyed or heavily
damaged boats of the Mississippi and Missouri steamer
line were all accidental. Boiler explosions and shipboard
fires were common occurrences on the river, but not to
three of one line in such close succession. He had a hunch
someone had helped the "accidents" along. And, after his
talk with Thomas last week, it had seemed possible that
the new owner of the line had a hand in it. It would not
be the first time sabotage had been used to drive down
the purchase price of a business. And the secrecy of the
buyer's name was a possible indication of his involve-
ment in the crimes. As Thomas said, what other reason
could the new owner have for keeping his identity hid-

den? Of course, being replaced as manager of the line, that could be Thomas's anger talking.

Sam frowned and raised his gaze to the steamboat's promenade. He would have a clearer picture of the situation after he talked with James Randolph, the man taking Thomas's place as manager of the M and M line. Randolph was somewhere in that milling throng of people and he wanted to meet him, find out what sort of man he was. But first he wanted to ask Captain Lewis who, if any, of the crew Randolph may have met with during the trip. And it would be interesting to know who Randolph would speak with on his first afternoon in town.

Passengers began to file down the *Fair Weather*'s gangplank in a steady stream. Sam glanced their way, automatically checking faces for known criminals or gamblers with bad reputations. A flutter of blue on the promenade deck caught his attention. He looked up, saw a woman brush at the material adorning her hat. His policeman's mind registered facts—the woman was taller than average, and thinner, with dark hair. Not particularly pretty—at least not in a conventional way. But there was something arresting about the woman, about the way she held herself.

He watched her wend her way toward the stairs leading down to the main deck, noting her graceful, but purposeful way of moving. There was nothing simpering or clingy about her. And he guessed she did not need the protection of the man guiding her through the crowd. She looked quite able to manage without an escort. The way she followed in the wake of that man in front of her, bespoke—

Goodwin! Why was he here? To meet the new manager? Sam scowled. He had been wondering if Goodwin had a hand in the M and M steamer disasters, though Thomas said no. He tracked the progress of the three of them with new purpose. Yes, the woman was definitely staying close to Goodwin. So the fellow with her must be the new manager. Thomas had not mentioned James Randolph was married. Sam shifted his focus to the man, catalogued the facts. Tall, dark, well-groomed. Fit, but on the slender side. He could not see his face. The three disappeared in the crush of people at the top of the stairs.

Sam pivoted and loped toward the gangplank. He would talk to Captain Lewis later. "Pardon me, sir." He gave a polite nod to the fellow coming off the walkway, stepped in front of him and held out his hand to stop the couple beside him. "Pardon me, please." He hurried past them, leaned against a wagon loaded with firewood and riveted his attention on the flow of people. It would be interesting to see if anyone other than Goodwin disembarked with the Randolphs. Or if someone was waiting to meet them.

Sam gave the area another quick scan, frowned. It was odd Thomas wouldn't meet his replacement. A twinge of unease reared. He quashed it. Thomas could be waiting at the office. Or he could be angry enough that he refused to meet Randolph and help him settle into his new position.

Three men and two more couples filed past. Sam glanced up. Eli Goodwin was at the top of the gangplank, the Randolphs at his heels. He studied James Randolph's face, looking for clues to the man's character, trying to decipher if he was expecting to meet someone. Randolph was young, very young, for such a responsible position. He looked to be no more than nineteen or twenty. Half Thomas's age. Sam shifted his gaze for a quick look at

Randolph's wife and peered straight into her eyes. Brown eyes. Not dark. Medium—like her hair. And challenging.

Sam stiffened, told himself to look away—knew it was already too late. She had spotted him studying her husband. He watched them descend, let Eli Goodwin pass and stepped around the wagon into the path of the young couple.

"Mr. Randolph?"

"Yes?" The man stopped, looked up at him, dark blue eyes posing a question.

"I am Samuel Benton, Captain of the St. Louis police." He glanced at Randolph's wife, saw the coolness in her eyes, gave her a polite nod and looked back. "I bid you and your wife welcome to our fair city." He offered his hand, received a firm clasp in return. "I will be calling on you tomorrow. There are a few rules, regulations and other matters about running a steamboat line in St. Louis that I want to discuss with you."

James Randolph nodded. "I shall await your visit with interest, Captain." He turned to the woman and grinned. "Come, dearest, Mr. Goodwin is waiting to show us to our new home." He took hold of her elbow.

The woman laughed, changing her countenance from cool and austere to fond and amused. Her lips, which had been pressed into a firm line, curved upward in a soft smile. Honey-colored flecks sparkled warmth into her large, brown eyes fringed with long lashes. Sam stared, taken aback. How had he thought her not particularly pretty? She was—

"Stop it, James. Captain Benton cannot know you are teasing."

Her voice was low-pitched for a woman's, soft and easy on his ears. A bit husky. Intriguing. She glanced up at him from beneath her hat's stiff brim and discovered him looking at her. The warmth in her eyes cooled.

"You have erred in your conclusion, Captain Benton. I am not James's wife. I am his sister."

"Forgive me, Miss Randolph, I assumed—"

"There is no apology or explanation needed, Captain. It was a natural assumption and of no import. I merely wanted to correct your error." The river breeze blew the fabric adorning her hat into her face. She frowned and pushed it back, looked up at him again, all trace of warmth and humor gone. "Now, if you will excuse us—I am weary from the journey and anxious to reach our new home. And to remove this ridiculous hat."

Her frosty demeanor killed his smile. "Of course, forgive my poor manners in detaining you." He glanced over at her brother. "Until tomorrow, Mr. Randolph." He gave them a polite nod and headed for the gangplank. If he hurried he could still catch Captain Lewis. James Randolph seemed open and friendly enough, but that did not mean he was above a little unscrupulous behavior. Perhaps on behalf of his boss? He would keep watch on his movements the next few days. As for his sister...what did that "ridiculous hat" comment mean? Women did not wear hats they considered ridiculous. Had she worn it by way of identification to Goodwin? Or as some sort of signal to someone else?

Sam frowned, stepped onto the *Fair Weather*'s main deck and turned to look out at the levee. Eli Goodwin was leading James Randolph and his sister up the incline to Front Street. No one had joined them. He scanned the area but could spot no one paying the Randolphs any particular attention.

He watched a moment longer, then satisfied he had

missed nothing of importance, turned and strode toward the stairs leading to the captain's quarters on the hurricane deck. He would not only ask about James Randolph's activities on the journey, he would ask about Miss Randolph's activities, as well. It was quite possible—in spite of that forthright look in those beautiful, brown eyes of hers—that she would help her brother if he was involved in this steamboat sabotage business. He took another quick glance over his shoulder at the tall, slender figure in the dark blue gown, then gripped the railing and, bucking the flow of the departing passengers, started up the stairs.

Chapter Two

❧

Mary walked beside James, taking in the hubbub of sound and motion around them. Workmen streamed in and out of warehouses, carrying filled burlap bags on burly shoulders or swarmed over huge stacks of crates or barrels. Laborers loaded carts with firewood and hauled it to their boats. Animals, in gated farm wagons, lowed and snorted. Others grunted and squealed as they were forced up gangplanks. Chickens squawked while barking dogs circled their cages. Mary had never seen or heard anything to compare with it. It was organized bedlam.

"That is our warehouse, Mr. Randolph." Eli Goodwin paused and pointed. "The one you see overtop the roofs of these smaller storage sheds. It was built on the higher ground because of flooding."

Mary's stomach flopped. She glanced from the large, brick building with "Mississippi and Missouri Steamer Line" sprawled in large, faded-white letters above the fourth-story windows to the muddy river, and was suddenly very thankful for the rising levee bank they were climbing.

"Does the river flood often?"

James's question brought a flash of the flat, rolling land along the river's banks into her head. Mary glanced at Mr. Goodwin.

The man nodded. "You can count on it in the spring. And if there are heavy rains upriver throughout the year, she will flood again. And there is no telling how high the river will rise. But business goes on. When floodwater covers the levee, the captains run their steamers in and moor them to the warehouses."

"You jest!"

James's challenge of the story gave her hope. It died when Eli Goodwin shook his head and started walking again. Mary tossed her brother a look of dismay, then followed the bookkeeper as he wove his way through the various piles of merchandise to the street at the top of the levee. Carriages, carts, drays and wagons of all sort rumbled over the cobblestones. Mounted men added to the traffic flow.

"This is Front Street. And that is Market Street across the way." Eli Goodwin indicated an intersecting road a short distance from them. "And there, on the near corner, is the company office."

Mary looked over at the narrow, two-story stone building. An oval sign bearing the company name held its place between a door and two mullioned windows painted red.

"A bank on one side, and an insurance company on the other corner. An excellent location."

Mary smiled at the satisfaction in James's voice. "And it is only a few steps away from the warehouse on the levee. Surely that is of benefit."

The bookkeeper nodded and shoved his glasses higher on his nose. "Do you wish to visit the office now?"

James shook his head. "No, tomorrow will be soon enough. For now, I want to get Mary settled in our new home. Is it far?"

"No, sir. It is only two streets away. We will cross here."

James's hand closed on her elbow. Mary pulled close her long skirts to avoid horse droppings as they followed Eli Goodwin across Front Street, dodging between a farm wagon full of produce and another loaded with squealing pigs to reach the walkway area in front of the stores. "Gracious me!" She jumped out of the path of a honking, wing-flapping goose being chased by a dog. "I have never witnessed such…such…"

"Pandemonium?"

She looked up at James and laughed. "The very word I was searching for."

"It is much quieter away from the levee, Miss Randolph. We go this way." Eli started walking up Market Street. The din of activity fell away as he led them past an intersecting dirt road, then turned right onto the next one and stopped. "This is it."

Mary stared at the small brick house sitting square on the corner lot. A porch across the face of the cottage shadowed the two mullioned windows, one on either side of a centered door painted white. Wood shingles, bleached and curled by the hot Missouri sun, covered the porch and house roof. Two brick chimney stacks stood at the cottage's gabled ends.

The chain supporting a dangling cannonball squeaked in protest as Eli Goodwin pulled open the gate in the lime-coated picket fence that enclosed the property. Mary dipped her head, thankful her hat was wide enough to hide her face, and stepped through the gate and up the short, brick walk. James would surely laugh if he saw her shock. Although, from his silence, she was quite certain he was as stunned as she. The cottage was charming, but so *small*. Why, you could set the whole of it into one end of the stables at home.

"Mrs. Dengler cleaned the place, made up the beds fresh for you and such. And I arranged for Mrs. Rawlins to leave a meal for you. She was cook for Mr. Thomas, the former manager, and has agreed to cook for you if you wish. They will both call on you tomorrow morning to learn if you want them to stay on, or if you prefer to set about finding other help." A frown drew Eli Goodwin's brows together. "I believe that is all. Here is the key to the house, Mr. Randolph." He handed James a skeleton key, gave a curt nod. "I wish you a good evening, sir. And you, Miss Randolph."

"And you, Mr. Goodwin." Mary offered the man a polite smile. "Your thoughtfulness will make our first evening in our new home a comfortable one. Thank you."

"And you have my gratitude as well, Goodwin. I will see you at the office tomorrow." Once inside, James closed the door, hung his hat on the hat tree and followed Mary as she moved out of the narrow entry into the room on the right. "I wonder if Mr. Goodwin ever smiles?" He shrugged and glanced around the small parlor. "Well, here we are in St. Louis." His lips twisted in a wry grimace. "In a very *small* cottage. Are you sorry you came?"

Mary cast an assessing glance his way. "Now why was I certain you would ask me that very question as soon as the door closed behind Mr. Goodwin?" She lifted her hands and pulled out the pin holding her hat in place.

"There! That is much better. I *told* Madame Duval these long ties would be annoying. But she insisted it was the latest style."

James frowned. "And why did *I* know you would avoid answering me? If you are disappointed, Mary—if St. Louis is less than you expected—it would be best for you to return home now." He flushed beneath her steady gaze. "I mean, rather than to unpack and have to go through all that work again."

"How very sensible and considerate. But I had no expectations, James. Only an intense desire to leave Winston Blackstone behind. *And* every other man living in Philadelphia who knows father is wealthy, as well." Her facial muscles went taut. She hated herself for believing Winston Blackstone's lies. For opening herself up to be hurt by his perfidy.

She turned and dropped her hat onto the seat of a Windsor chair sitting beside the fireplace. It gave her a reason to turn her back on the sympathy in James's eyes. She should not have mentioned Winston. She hastened to change the subject. "And, in truth, I find St. Louis intriguing. Did you notice all those rough-looking, buckskin-clad men? And the Indians roaming about the levee mingling with the people? Do you suppose they are dangerous?"

"I am quite certain they can be."

She heard James move, listened to his footsteps draw close. She removed her gloves and tossed them down by her hat.

"Winston did not mean to hurt you, Mary. He did not mean for you to ever know about Victoria. He was doing the honorable thing and telling her goodbye."

Mary clenched her hands into fists. She had avoided

talking about Winston ever since the night of the party. But James persisted. Perhaps if she explained he would stop trying to make her talk about what had happened. And perhaps it would cleanse her mind of the memories, free her to move on with her new life.

She turned around and studied her brother's face. "Why are you so determined to discuss Winston, James? You have been trying to do so our entire journey. Did Mother and Father charge you with the task?" She squared her shoulders and lifted her hand to stop his reply. "No matter. I will bow to your wishes and we shall discuss Winston and the entire sordid situation—" she pointed one long, tapering finger toward the ceiling "—*once*. But do not *dare* defend him to me. Do not stand before me and call his actions *honorable*."

The word scorched her tongue, seared her heart. She took refuge from her pain in a sudden burst of anger. Allowed the heat of it to carry her words beyond the lump of hurt in her throat. "I saw Winston with Victoria in the gardens, James. And, I assure you, there was nothing lofty or honorable in their embrace. Nor did the ardor of his kisses speak goodbye—except to the announcement of our betrothal." She lifted her chin and hid her trembling hands in the deep folds of her long skirt. "At least I was spared the humiliation of a public betrayal. Although everyone present that evening did suspect the reason for the party was to announce our future marriage."

"Mary, I had no idea!" James hurried to her. "Why did you not tell us you had witnessed Winston and Victoria embracing in the gardens?" He reached to pull her close.

She stepped back and shook her head. If he put his arms around her, she would burst into tears. "And have all my family pity me even more? As you are doing now?"

She turned away, brushed a stray lock of hair off her cheek. "It changed nothing that I saw Winston's betrayal with my own eyes."

"I suppose that is true. Though it may make it more difficult for you to forgive him."

"Forgive him?" She pivoted, stared up at him. "You are not serious, James?"

"Yes, I am." He stepped closer. "Listen, Mary. When you refused to see him before we left, Winston came to me and explained the entire situation. He confessed it was only after losing you that he realized how much he cared for you. He begged me to plead his case with you. Of course, I refused. But he convinced me that he is genuinely distraught at losing you." Warmth from his hands penetrated the fabric of her gown as he took hold of her shoulders. "Mary, Winston loves you and wants you back. He wants you to come home to Philadelphia and marry him. It is *that* which I have been trying to tell you the entire journey."

"He— He said— And you—" Her throat closed on the words. Mary dug her fingernails into the palms of her hands, fighting a sense of betrayal that was not fair to her brother. He did not know the entire story. She took a breath, held it, released it slowly. "I know you wish only what is best for me, James. And I thank you for that. Truly. But do not be swayed by Winston's persuasive powers. His only regret is in losing the generous dowry Father offered for me. It would have cleared all his debts. I know, for I not only *saw* Winston with Victoria, I *heard* him as well." She lifted her hand and tapped his chest. "Winston's pocketbook chose me, James. His heart chose Victoria." She made herself look at him and forced the rest of it out of her constricted throat. "And, as he said to her, 'What man would not choose her petite, blond beauty and sweet nature over my dark, angular plainness and bold, forthright ways were debt not an issue?'"

Anger darkened James's face. His chest swelled beneath her hand as he sucked in air. She blinked the sting of tears from her eyes and shook her head. "Do not say more, James. Please. Do not make useless protests. Winston's words only confirmed what I have known all my life. I am aware of how I appear in comparison to other women. It has always been so. Mother and Sarah shine like golden jewels. But it is only Father's wealth that gives me beauty and luster in men's eyes. And I, like every woman, want to—to be a jewel in the eyes of the man I love. Me—not Father's money. I want to marry a man who loves and values me for myself. And I will settle for no less."

"You are *wrong,* Mary!" James tightened his grip, gave her a gentle shake. "You are a lovely and desirable woman. And Winston Blackstone is a fool! As am I for believing him. He does not deserve you."

She touched her fingers to his lips, saw the hurt for her in his eyes, and forced a smile. "You are a wonderful, loyal brother, James. But please, do not be concerned for me. Perhaps somewhere there is a man—even here in St. Louis—who will see me as a jewel. And with no one here knowing who our father is, should such a man declare his love for me, I will be certain he cares for me alone. That is why it is so perfect that no one here knows of our father's wealth. And if that does not happen—" she took another breath "—I will yet be glad I came. For I would far rather be a spinster than a bargain. Now... we shall never mention Winston Blackstone again." She raised her face, kissed his cheek and spun away. "Shall we explore our new home?"

"That shan't take long."

The wry humor was forced. Mary sent James a look of gratitude for accepting the change of subject and picked up her hat and gloves. "Shall we start with the upstairs? I want to put this ridiculous hat away."

Chapter Three

Her first full day in her new home. Mary heaved a sigh and looked around her. What was she to do with her gowns? Her dressing room at home was larger than this bedroom. And her bedroom was— No. No complaints. Not even to herself. She had begged to come to St. Louis with James, and her parents had granted her wishes. She would not turn into a whining scold because of a few lost comforts.

She marched to the cupboard built into the niche on the left side of the fireplace and opened the door. There was room for five, perhaps six dresses, plus her night-gown and robe. She turned, fisted her hands on her hips and nibbled at the left inside corner of her top lip. She would need her plainest day dresses. And a finer one for church. The rest of her gowns would simply have to stay in the trunks. But where would she store them? Another dilemma.

"What is all this?"

Mary turned toward the door, took one look at James's baffled expression and burst into laughter. "I am choosing gowns to keep here in my room. The rest must stay in the trunks. I have no thought as to where— James! The office. Do you suppose there would be room in the back to store my trunks?"

"Perhaps. I will know after I see the place. I came to tell you that I am going there now." A frown crossed her brother's handsome face. "I have been thinking about those Indians we saw yesterday, Mary. I am concerned about leaving you here alone."

"Oh, poof!" She waved his concern away and lifted her rose-colored cotton gown from a pile on the bed. The matching embroidered jacket would come in handy for cooler days. "I will be fine. Mrs. Rawlins and Mrs. Dengler will be coming soon for their interviews. And, meanwhile, if any Indians come in with intent to do me harm, I shall simply hide myself in one of these stacks." She laughed and swept her hand through the air, indicating the dresses heaped on the floor, draped over the open trunks and spread out on the bed. "They would never find me."

James laughed, then sobered. "You are certain?"

"Yes! Now go, and leave me to my work."

Mary sat on the settee, smoothed out her skirt and smiled at the women perched on the Windsor chairs. "I am impressed with the cleanliness of the house, Mrs. Dengler. I would very much like for you to continue to clean for us."

The German woman smiled and dipped her head. *"Dank."*

"And what is your given name, Mrs. Dengler?"

"I am called Edda."

Mary smiled at the older woman. "Are you prepared to begin work today, Edda?"

"I can do work today, *ja*."

"Wonderful." Mary held back a sigh of relief. "There are gowns in my bedroom that must be packed away in my trunks for storage. When you finish with them, I would like you to make the beds."

"*Ja*, Miss Randolph."

Edda walked to the stairs and Mary turned to the woman on the other chair. "The stew you prepared for me and my brother last night was delicious, Mrs. Rawlins. As were the rolls that accompanied it. Do you always do your own baking?"

"Yes, I do."

"And are you available to cook for us every day?"

"I am." The woman nodded. "I am a recent widow with children full grown and gone from home. I have no call on my time."

Mary's heart contracted at the sorrow on the woman's face. "I am sorry for your loss, Mrs. Rawlins."

The woman dipped her head.

"Are you able to take up your duties today?"

Relief spread across the woman's face. "Yes, Miss Randolph. And my name is Ivy."

Mary smiled and rose to her feet. "I have paper and pen waiting in the kitchen, Ivy. If you will tell me what stores you require and what foods you wish for today's meals, I will see to their purchase."

The sun overhead was bright in her eyes. Mary dipped her head slightly, using the shirred brim of her coal-scuttle bonnet to shade her face. The deep flounce running around the bottom of the long, full skirt of her green gown brushed against the cobblestones as she walked down Market Street toward the river, the basket she had found in the kitchen swinging back and forth in her hand.

The sounds of activity on the levee became louder and more distinct as she neared the river. Wind gusted, picked up dust and flung it about. She ducked her head against the onslaught, hurried around the corner toward the Mississippi and Missouri steamer line office building and ran full tilt into a muscular, lean body. "Oh!" She staggered backward. Strong hands gripped her upper arms, steadied her. She looked up to thank her rescuer.

"Captain Benton!"

"At your service." He released her arms. "Are you all right, Miss Randolph?"

The heat of a blush crawled across her cheeks. "I should ask you that question, Captain. Please forgive me. I assure you I am not in the habit of knocking into people. I was…well… I was hurrying to reach my brother." She gave a little laugh and straightened her bonnet that had slipped backward when she had bumped into him. "Our cook has given me a list and I am on my way to purchase needed stores and food for dinner. And, I confess, I am a little hesitant to brave the levee area without an escort."

She glanced up at him from under her hat brim. *Gracious, he was tall!* She was not accustomed to men tilting their heads to look down at her. "I am unfamiliar with Indians or mountain men, and I am not eager to meet any of them on my own. At least, not yet. Thus, I was on my way to ask James to accompany me to the grocer's." She was prattling like a silly schoolgirl in the presence of a handsome boy! Mary clenched her teeth together and tightened her grip on the empty basket.

"Very wise of you, Miss Randolph."

His calm answer restored her aplomb. "And why is that, Captain?"

"There are some rough and unsavory elements on the waterfront. We are working to clean up our city. But there is much left to do."

"I see." Mary hid the tingle of apprehension that slipped along her nerves and turned toward the office door. "Thank you for the information, Captain. Now I *know* I need James to accompany me."

A frown lowered his straight, dark brown brows. "I just called to speak with your brother, Miss Randolph. He is in a meeting."

"But Mrs. Rawlins needs—" Mary stopped, glanced at Front Street and took a deep breath. "Would you please direct me to the grocer's, Captain?"

"I will do better than that, Miss Randolph. I will escort you there."

"You?" Mary jerked her gaze to him.

He grinned, no doubt at her response. A slow, lopsided sort of grin that did queer things to her stomach. She took a step back, suddenly uneasy at the prospect of being in his company. The man was overwhelming. And why would he offer to escort her? "It is most kind of you to offer aid, Captain. But it would not be right for me to take you from your duties." She glanced up and down the street to choose her direction.

"The well-being and safety of the citizens of St. Louis *is* my duty, Miss Randolph. Allow me." He reached out and took hold of the basket. "If you are ready?"

His answer left her without argument, but did little to allay her unease. Mary glanced at him, then looked down at his hand gripping the handle. Unless she wanted to engage in a tug-of-war for the basket—a contest she was sure to lose since the man was twice her size—she had no choice. She released her grip on the basket.

"We need to cross Market Street." He held her elbow.

Mary forced herself to relax. She was being ridiculous. He had not offered to help her from some nefarious motive. It was a simple politeness. A duty. Not every man had a hidden agenda like Winston Blackstone. She walked to the curb beside him, tried not to feel delicate and protected as he guided her through the carriage traffic. But it was difficult not to feel that way with his tall, lean body shielding her, and his hand holding her so protectively. She gave a quiet sigh of relief when they reached the other side and he released her arm. She glanced around as they started down the walkway.

"Are you recovered from your journey, Miss Randolph?"

She nodded, gave him a polite smile. "Yes. Quite recovered, thank you."

"You are fortunate. Steamboats are a vast improvement on other river craft, but still, long trips can be exhausting." He smiled down at her. "If you don't mind my asking, where are you and your brother from, Miss Randolph?"

"Philadelphia" sprang to her tongue, but was quashed by another spurt of caution and suspicion. Why did he want to know? Did it have something to do with being a police officer? Well, she had no intention of telling him. That information might lead to her father's identity. The Randolph shipping line was well-known in Philadelphia. She glanced up, gave a graceful little shrug. "Why ever would I mind your asking, Captain? We are from Pennsylvania." She shifted her gaze. "Oh, look! A bookstore.

How lovely." She gave him another polite smile. "Do you enjoy reading, Captain?"

"I do. Though I seldom have time."

Some subtle change in the timbre of his deep voice warned her that he was aware of her evasion. She turned her head toward the two-story brick, stone and wood frame storefronts to hide her face from him. Those blue eyes were too observant.

A half-naked Indian, a pile of animal pelts folded over one arm, exited a leather goods store, then mingled with the people on the walkway and strode straight toward them. Mary froze, staring at the shocking sight of the Indian's bare torso. She had heard so many stories... His eyes, black as a night sky, bored into hers. She lifted her chin and crowded closer to Captain Benton, suddenly thankful for his presence. The Indian went on by.

"There's no danger, Miss Randolph. We've been at peace with the local Indians for many years. They come into town often to conduct business." He smiled down at her. "I know it is a shock to you Easterners at first, but their presence is a sight you will soon become accustomed to."

His smile and the calm in his deep voice eased her nervousness. She nodded, looked away from his disturbing, penetrating gaze. "I am certain I shall, Captain Benton." She started walking again. He fell into step beside her.

"The plains tribes are a different matter, of course. But you are safe in town."

A shiver slithered down her spine. She glanced at him, uncertain of how to respond. Up to now, hers had been a pampered life. She was not used to feeling afraid.

"Stop, you little thief!"

Mary jerked her gaze forward. A young boy, panic on

his face, was running toward them, a large man wearing a stained white apron in hot pursuit.

Samuel Benton leaped into the boy's path.

The boy tried to swerve, but the man behind him thrust out his hand, caught the boy's shoulder and yanked him to a halt. "Got ya! Now, you'll find out what thievin' gets ya!" He nodded at Samuel Benton and shoved the boy forward. "Throw 'im in jail with the rest of the thievin' jackanapes, Captain."

"Surely not!" Mary rushed forward, lifted her chin as both men looked her way. "He is only a boy."

"He's a *thief!* An' here's yer proof." The man grabbed the boy's right arm and jerked it upward. There was a crushed roll in his hand. A bony hand, attached to a pitifully thin arm.

Mary gasped. "Why, the boy's half-starved!" She glanced up at Samuel Benton. "He is hungry, Captain. Surely you will not arrest him?"

The captain's blue eyes darkened. "That is my job, Miss Randolph. He broke the law. The reason does not matter." He reached for the boy.

Mary stepped between them. "It matters to me, Captain." She stared up at him, at his darkened eyes, his set jaw and drew herself to her full height. "But I can see there is no room in your St. Louis law for mercy." She pivoted to face the vendor. "Unhand the boy, sir. I will pay for his roll."

Hope leaped into the boy's eyes. But the man in the apron let out a growl, tightened his grip on the boy's skinny shoulders and looked over her head. "You do yer job an' throw 'im in jail, Captain. There's too many of the rapscallions roamin' the streets an' stealin' from hardworkin', decent people now. Y' let this 'un go, an' the rest of 'em'll be swarmin' around our stores like bees o'er clover."

"There is no theft if Miss Randolph pays for the roll, Simpson." Samuel Benton's deep voice rolled over her shoulder. "Release the boy."

"Wait!" Mary winced inwardly as the hope faded from the boy's eyes, but he was going to run the moment he was free, she could see it on his face. And she saw something else written there, as well. Shame. And defiance. She fastened her gaze on him. "I need someone to carry my purchases home, and I thought perhaps you would do that for me, young man. In exchange for your services, I will buy you a thick slab of cheese to go with that roll. Is that agreeable to you?"

Pride replaced the shame. The defiance gave way to caution. The boy drew himself up straight and nodded.

"Very well." She handed the man behind the boy a coin. "You may release him now."

The man scowled, lifted his hands from the boy's shoulders and walked away, grumbling beneath his breath.

The boy stayed.

Mary let out a breath of relief and turned to Samuel Benton. "Thank you for your help, Captain. But I no longer require your aid." She did not bother to hide her disgust at his treatment of the boy. "If you will please give this young man my basket and tell me where the grocer is located, we shall be on our way."

He stared down at her for a moment, then dipped his head. "As you wish, Miss Randolph." He handed the basket to the boy, then returned his gaze to her and made a slight bow. "Good day, Miss Randolph. You have no need of my direction. The boy knows the location of the store. Mr. Simpson is the grocer." He turned and walked away.

Mary watched his lean, broad-shouldered figure disappear into a nearby store, chiding herself for the disappointment weighting her stomach. What did it matter what sort of man Samuel Benton was? The captain was nothing to her.

Chapter Four

Mary looked down at the young boy clutching her basket and smiled. "And thus, we are left on our own. Where is Mr. Simpson's store—" She shook her head and gave a little laugh. "I cannot keep calling you 'young man.' What is your name?"

The boy stiffened, his nostrils pinched slightly, his eyes narrowed and his mouth firmed as he stared up at her. Had she looked that wary when Captain Benton questioned her? No wonder he knew her answer was an evasion. She kept silent as the boy studied her. After a few moments, he relaxed a little, gave a small shrug. "Name's Ben." He pointed a bony finger down the street. "Yonder is the grocer's." He lowered his hand and gripped the basket handle. Probably to hide his trembling.

Mary started walking, letting out a quiet sigh of relief when Ben fell into step beside her. He had looked poised to run, and if he decided to do so, she could not stop him. Her lips twitched at the idea of her raising her long skirts and darting among the shoppers on the walkway chasing after the boy.

A puff of wind swirled up from the river, lifting a sour

odor from Ben. She held her breath, waiting for the gust to cease, and glanced down. Tears filmed her eyes at the close sight of Ben's grimy skin, the clumps of dirt and straw in his matted hair, his dirty and torn clothes. She guessed him to be nine, perhaps ten years old. So young. And so horribly thin. Had he no one to care for him?

Thoughts of the homeless children brought to her aunt Laina's orphanage in Philadelphia crowded into her head. The tears in her eyes threatened to overflow. Was Ben an orphan? She blinked the tears back, released her breath and focused on the situation. Ben needed help, not pity. And she needed information. It was possible he had parents—though his unkempt, half-starved condition made it seem unlikely.

She stole another look at the silent boy. He was so easily frightened, so ready to run. How should she start? *I always mask my questions with friendly conversation.* Of course! How many times had she heard her aunt Laina say that? Mary smiled, looked down. "I like the name Benjamin." She made her tone of voice light, friendly. "Is it a family name? Perhaps your father's?"

No answer.

She tilted her head to get a better view of the boy's face. His lips were pressed together and he was blinking rapidly. Her heart seized. "Ben—"

"This is the store." He shot across the walkway, stopped by a store's open door and looked back at her.

"Go away, you *ragamuffin!*" A woman loomed out of the darkness of the store, pausing in the doorway. "Urchins like you are not welcome around decent people! Go away, I say!" She made shooing motions with her hands, then drew her long skirts close so they wouldn't touch Ben before she started out of the store.

Ben cringed away from the entrance.

If that woman makes Ben run... Mary rushed forward, placed her hand on Ben's shoulder and pulled him to her side. She could feel his bones through his shirt. And his shaking. She straightened to her full height and gave the shorter woman her haughtiest look. "Ben is with me, madam. And he is very welcome." She ignored the older woman's gasp and, holding tight to Ben, brushed by her into the store.

The interior was cool and dark. Mary halted to allow her eyes to adjust to the loss of sunlight and to get her bearings. Silence fell. She swept her gaze around the room, met varying degrees of shock or disgust on the faces of the store's patrons and lifted her chin. "Come along, Ben." The click of the heels of her shoes against the wide plank floor echoed through the hush as they crossed the room. She stopped in front of the grocer cutting meat on a chopping block at the far end of a long counter in front of the back wall.

"Good day, Mr. Simpson." She gave him a cool nod. Gave another to the waiting customer who had backed away at their approach.

A scowl drew the grocer's thick, black brows together. "Get that thief outta here. I don't—"

"Ben is here to carry my purchases, Mr. Simpson." There were startled gasps behind her. The grocer's scowl deepened. She ignored a flurry of whispers and stared straight into the man's angry eyes. "And I am here to open an account. My brother and I are new in town and must establish our trade somewhere." She watched his scowl dissolve to the level of a frown. "My brother is the new manager of the Mississippi and Missouri steamer line.

Of course, if you would prefer we take our custom else-
where…" She turned away.

"No need fer that. My wife'll serve ya."

The words were low, reluctant. Mary turned back.
The grocer inclined his head at a stout woman behind
the middle of the counter and went back to his work.

Mary headed toward the woman, another spate of
whispers accompanying her as customers moved out of
her path. She didn't have to urge Ben to come with her,
he matched her step for step, his head bowed, his gaze
darting about the room like a trapped animal.

"Come again, Mrs. Turner."

Mrs. Simpson's customer glanced at Ben, snatched
up her parcel and rushed away. Mary stepped forward.
"I should like to open an account, please."

"Of course." Mrs. Simpson smiled at Ben, looked back
to give her a welcoming smile. "And the name?" She
dipped her pen and poised it over a book.

Mary stared, taken aback by the cheerful attitude. She
returned the woman's friendly smile and let the hauteur
slide from her voice. "James Randolph." She placed the
list Ivy had given her on the counter. "These are the items
I need today. And also—" she took her basket from Ben,
placed it beside the list and indicated the crushed bun in
the bottom "—this bun and a thick slab of cheese." She
glanced down, caught Ben eyeing a large barrel, and
looked up. "And two pickles from your brine barrel."

Mrs. Simpson nodded, turned and began selecting the
items on the list from the shelves on the wall. Mary took
the opportunity to look around the store. She caught the
customers staring at her and Ben and gave them each a
sweet smile. There was a sudden bustle of activity as they
returned to their business.

"Will there be anything more, Miss Randolph?"

Mary turned, looked down at the filled basket and shook her head. "Not today, Mrs. Simpson."

The woman glanced toward her husband—who was wrapping a cut of beef in paper—then looked down at Ben, slipped her hand into a crock to pull out a piece of taffy. "I heard you tell Mr. Simpson that you and your brother are new in town, Miss Randolph. Welcome to St. Louis." She dropped the piece of candy beside the roll and the piece of cheese and slid the basket across the counter. "I look forward to serving you again."

"And so you shall, Mrs. Simpson. Thank you for the welcome, and for...everything." Mary smiled, met the woman's gaze in silent understanding, then handed the basket to Ben and headed for the door.

Sam turned the key in the lock, pulled the door open and stepped back. So did the man beside him.

"C'mon, Captain. It was only a little scrap."

Sam shook his head. "You pulled a knife, Hogan." He jabbed his thumb through the air in the direction of the cell.

"Yeah, but—"

"No buts. You know the rules here in St. Louis. You pull a weapon during a fight, you go to jail." Sam placed his hand on the laborer's beefy shoulder and applied enough pressure to move the man into the cell. He swung the door shut and shoved the key into the lock.

Hogan grabbed the bars. "C'mon, Captain. My boat leaves tonight. I gotta get to the levee and load cargo or Captain Rolls'll have my job."

"You should have thought of that before you pulled

that knife." Sam turned the key, yanked it from the lock and started for the outer room.

"How about we make a deal?"

"No deal, Hogan."

"Not even to find out what happened to the *Swift Water?*"

Sam stopped, turned and stared into the bloodshot eyes in the scrubby, whiskered face pressed against the bars. "What do you know about the *Swift Water?*"

Hogan grinned. "You gonna let me outta here?"

Sam walked to the cell. "That depends on what you know and how reliable your information is."

"I know one of the crew was paid to blow her up."

"Sorry. Everyone has heard that rumor." He turned toward the door.

"But they don't know who."

There was certainty behind the words. Sam looked back. "Who?"

Thick lips pushed a curved line through the grizzled beard.

Sam nodded. "All right, fair enough. How do you know? I'm not interested in rumors."

"It ain't no rumor. I seen him flashin' money and braggin' about it in a tavern. Tellin' around what a big man he was an' all."

"Who paid him?"

Hogan scowled. "Don't know. You'll have to ask him that yerself."

Sam nodded. The story had the ring of truth. "Do you know anything about the other destroyed M and M line boats? The *Clear Water* or the *Mississippi Princess?*"

"The *Princess* was an accident. Sawyer got her. Don't know about the *Clear Water.*"

"All right." He stuck the key in the lock, paused. "But the deal is this—if you ever pull a knife in a fight again, you'll do double time for it. Understood?"

Hogan nodded. "Yeah." He glanced down at the ring of keys. "The name's Duffy. He's a stoker."

"I know him. Do you know what boat he's working?"

"Last I knew he was up the Missouri on the *Adventure*."

Sam twisted the key and opened the cell door. "All right, Hogan. Get back to the levee. And don't forget— no more knives or I'll put you back in here and throw away the key."

Hogan nodded and hurried down the hall. Sam followed him to the other room, tossed his keys into the drawer, then grabbed his hat and dogged the man's heels outside. Now all he had to do was locate Duffy. And find out if the man had any connection to James Randolph, or the new owner of the M and M line. Maybe he could do that through Thomas, and not tip his hand.

He cut across lots to Olive Street, where Thomas had lived since vacating the manager's cottage, and knocked on the door of Emily Stanton's boardinghouse. He waited, wondering about the sudden sense of disquiet in his gut.

The door opened. He smiled and touched the brim of his hat. "Good afternoon, Mrs. Stanton."

"Why, Captain Benton!" Surprise widened the round eyes looking up at him. "What brings you here?"

"I need to talk with Mr. Thomas. If I could—" He stopped, staring down at her shaking head.

"You're too late, Captain. He ain't here."

The disquiet grew. "Did he tell you where he was going? I can catch up with him if—" The gray head was shaking again.

"He didn't tell me where he was going. Only packed up and left three days ago." A frown deepened the wrinkles in the plump face. "Late at night, it was. I heard someone on the stairs, peeked out my door and saw him leave. Sort of odd. Most times when someone goes sneakin' out the door in the middle of the night, it's 'cause they can't pay their bill. But he didn't owe me nothing."

"I see." Sam nodded, touched his hat brim again. "Thank you for the information, Mrs. Stanton. Good afternoon."

"Good afternoon, Captain." She started to close the door, then pulled it open and stuck her head out. "If you hear of somebody decent that needs a room, tell them I've got one empty."

"I'll do that, Mrs. Stanton." Sam trotted down the steps and headed for the levee. Now he had two men to track down. Duffy and Thomas. Queer, Thomas leaving like that. Could there be a connection between that and James Randolph's arrival? Seemed as if there might be. But why did Thomas *sneak* off? There was no reason for that, unless it was to keep his leaving a secret. And if that was so, who was he—

Sam's face tightened. Could it be *him?* Could it be Thomas didn't want *him* to know he was leaving town? Now why would that be? He tugged his hat down snug and let his mind play with that thought while he ate up the distance to the levee with his long strides.

"What is going on in here?"

Mary spun around, and gaped at her brother standing in the washroom doorway. "James! You are home."

He nodded. "Yes. That is what I do when it is time to eat. I come home. Why the surprise?"

She laughed and hurried toward him. "I did not hear you come in the house is all. As small as it is, I was certain I would. I am sorry. I should have been waiting to greet you." She touched his arm, gave a little push—a signal for him to leave.

He stood his ground, riveting his gaze on the scene behind her. *Botheration!* She had wanted a chance to explain before he saw Ben. Especially since the boy was wearing a shirt that had been in James's dresser drawer when he left the house that morning. Her heart sank as he frowned at her.

"Mary, what—"

She squeezed his arm, sent him the silent "don't ask questions" command with her eyes that she had perfected during their childhood years. Of course, that was when her demand usually involved keeping a secret from their parents. It was different now. He would probably ignore her signal. "I am finished here, James." She gave him another tiny push, then looked over her shoulder. "Edda, if you will launder Ben's clothes, please."

"Ja." The plump woman turned, lifted the small pile of filthy garments off the floor and plunged them into the tub of Ben's bathwater.

James's frown deepened to a scowl. Mary gave him another pinch. "Shall we go into the parlor and chat while Ivy prepares our dinner, James?"

His gaze fastened on hers. "That is an excellent suggestion."

This time he yielded to her pressure against his arm and stepped back. She sailed past him, hurried to the small parlor and turned to face him. The scowl was still on his face.

"All right, Mary. Why is our cook's son wearing one of my shirts?"

"Our cook's *son?*" She laughed and relaxed into one of the Windsor chairs. "Ben is not Ivy's son, James. He is a boy from the streets who carried my basket home from the market. And as for your shirt...what else had I to dress him in while his clothes are being laundered? I could hardly give him one of my gowns."

"An unknown, dirty boy from the streets is wear—"

"Hush, James! He will hear you." Mary surged to her feet, then closed the parlor door and whirled to face him. "And Ben is not *dirty.* I had him bathe as soon as we fed him and he agreed to stay awhile—Ivy even scrubbed his hair clean." She glared up at him. "And shame on you for your lack of compassion! What—"

"Whoa! Hold on." James held his hand up palm forward. "Before you castigate me for my attitude, I think you should at least tell me what is going on. How that boy got into our house and—"

"I *have* told you, James."

"No, you have not. You told me that he carried your basket home." He frowned at her. "I cannot believe the grocer would have a boy that dirty and unkempt working for—"

"James!" Mary launched herself through the intervening space into his arms. "James, you are a genius! What a wonderful idea."

She planted a kiss on his cheek and spun out of his grasp. "I have been trying to think of what to do to help Ben. He is such a proud young boy, and you—" She stopped, frowned. "Of course, Mr. Simpson will not care for your idea. At least, not at first." She paced the short distance across the room, turned and headed back. "But Mrs. Simpson… Yes, I am almost certain she—"

He reached out and caught her by the shoulders. "Mary, what you are talking about? What idea? And who are Mr. and Mrs. Simpson? What have they to do with this boy from the streets? And what has he to do with us?"

"Nothing. And everything." She locked her gaze with his. "Ben is an *orphan,* James. And half-starved. Would *you* have let him be arrested and taken to jail for stealing bread to eat?"

Her words were soft, but challenging. James released his grip on her shoulders and straightened.

"You ask that question of *me,* Mary? You *know* I would not."

She placed her hand on his arm. "I *do* know, James. And I meant no offense. I asked only so you would place yourself in my position." She gave him a wry smile. "Neither one of us would be able to face Aunt Laina again if we allowed such a thing to happen in our presence."

He nodded, and his lips curved in a smile that matched her own. "True. Nor Mother and Father, either." His smile faded. "But you still have not told me how you met Ben. Or—"

"Or what?"

He shook his head. "My questions will wait until after I hear your story." He draped his arm around her shoulders, then led her to the settee and sat down beside her. "I am all 'at sea.' Begin."

"Yes, of course." She tucked a wayward strand of hair in the loose knot on the crown of her head and looked over at him. "You know I had marketing to do this morning—food stores and such?"

He nodded, then grinned at her. "It will take some time for me to get used to the idea of *you* doing household tasks, but…yes, we discussed that last night, *Miss Housekeeper*." His grin widened.

She gave him her "big sister" look. "If you wish to hear the story, James, be serious!"

He tamed his grin to a smile and dipped his head in agreement. "I shall be."

"Very well, then." She angled her body toward him. "I was nervous about going to the levee alone—because of the Indians and mountain men—so I decided to go to your office and ask you to accompany me."

His levity fell away. He frowned. "Goodwin did not tell me that you came to see me."

"Because I did not." The memory of Captain Benton's grinning face flashed. Warmth crept across her cheekbones.

James stared.

Bother! Mary lifted her chin and gave him a look that dared him to comment about her blush.

He passed on the challenge. "Go on."

"At the front door, I chanced upon Captain Benton, who had called and found you busy in a meeting with some other gentlemen." She looked down at her hands. "He inquired as to my dismay at your unavailability and, when I explained, offered to accompany me to the grocer's." In spite of her effort, there was a tinge of defensiveness in her voice. She looked up.

James grinned. "So the *captain* is the cause of that heightened color in your cheeks. I shall have to remember to thank him for his kindness to you when next I see him."

She gave a little huff. "Stop teasing, James! It was

duty, not kindness that prompted the captain's actions. Now…as I was saying. The captain and I were walking along Front Street when Ben came running toward us, with the grocer giving chase. He caught the boy and told Captain Benton to throw him in jail with the rest of the thieves." She paused, taking a breath.

"And you intervened?"

"Well, of course I did! It was obvious the boy was half-starved and frightened out of his wits. I thought surely the captain would show mercy, but when I protested the arrest, he said the boy was guilty of theft and he had no choice but to take him to jail." She jutted her chin into the air. "So I told him I would pay for the roll, struck a bargain with Ben to carry my basket and informed Captain Benton I had no further need of his services!"

She expelled her breath in another huff, then gave him a smile of pure satisfaction. "And that is how I met Ben and enticed him to come home with me. I suspected from his condition he was an orphan. On the way home I managed to get him to talk about his past." She sprang to her feet.

James rose. "And did you find out about his parents? Is he an orphan?"

"Yes. Ben's mother died two years ago. And last fall his father sold their farm and made plans to come west in the company of some friends. They started their journey this spring. Ben's father was killed fighting river pirates on their way down the Ohio."

"Poor Ben!"

"Yes. Poor Ben. The friends brought him downriver with them to St. Louis, took his father's possessions as payment, then told him there was no room for him in their wagon." Anger surging, she paced across the room, then headed back. "They left him here with no one to care for him while they joined a wagon train and traveled on." She stopped in front of him. "How could they *do* that, James? How could they rob a child, then simply leave him like that?"

He shook his head. "I have no answer for such unconscionable behavior, Mary. But I know Aunt Laina would be very proud of you. As would Mother and Father. As am I."

"But?" She gave him a quizzical look.

"But... I see some difficulties we must find solutions for. What do we do with Ben now?" He lifted a hand and rubbed the back of his neck, peering down at her. "Have you given thought to that? Is there an orphanage—"

Mary threw her arms around his neck and squeezed with all her might.

He returned the squeeze, giving her a puzzled look when she stepped away. "Thank you. But what was that for?"

"The 'we.'" She smiled up at him. "There is no orphanage, James. But the most wonderful thing has happened! Ivy is going to take Ben home to live with her. She is recently widowed and her children are grown and gone from home. It is perfect. Ben will be well cared for, and Ivy will not be lonely."

"That *is* a happy solution."

"Yes. And now you have solved the other problem." She whirled away, turned back and clasped his hands. "I have been concerned over the cost to Ivy for Ben's care. *And* over Ben's feelings. He is a very honorable and proud little boy who wants to earn his way. Why, hungry as he was, he would not eat the roll and cheese I promised him as payment for his help until he had carried my basket home, for that was our agreement. Anyway…" She squeezed his hands. "Oh, James, I am certain your idea will work!"

"*What* idea?"

"Why for Ben to work at Mr. Simpson's store." She let go of his hands and whisked away again, her long skirts whispering as she moved across the floor. "Marketing baskets can become very heavy when you carry them for any distance. And I am certain ladies would be willing to pay for Ben to carry their baskets home. Oh, it is a lovely idea!"

"So is dinner." James laughed and slapped his growling stomach. "And I believe I hear Ivy carrying our meal in from the kitchen." He made a formal bow and offered Mary his arm. "Shall we discuss this situation further while we partake of whatever it is that is creating such a delicious smell?"

"La, it shall be as you wish, good sir." Mary lifted her skirts slightly, made him a deep curtsy, then laughed and slipped her arm through his.

James chuckled and opened the door. "I do not know if I have Ben or the captain to thank, Mary. But it is good to see you so animated again."

Chapter Five

"We are in agreement, gentlemen?"

Sam glanced around the table, noting the response to the mayor's question. All nine of the aldermen nodded.

"Excellent!" The mayor smiled his satisfaction. "Let the record show that final plans for the addition to the courthouse have been unanimously approved and we hereby direct the work move forward with all dispatch. Now then, on to the next piece of business. It is for this that I invited Captain Benton's attendance on our assembly this afternoon."

Sam gave a brief nod as the aldermen glanced his way.

The mayor cleared his throat. "Captain Benton, all of us here are aware that our city has enjoyed significant growth in the past two years. We now have a theater, a hotel, banks. A water company is in the works. And the long-delayed plans for a public school are being drawn. The vast numbers of new buildings and the cobblestone paving of many of our streets have changed the complexion of our city from that of a wilderness town. And the increased safety of our citizens is also a factor in achieving that goal. I wish to commend you, Captain Benton, on the excellent job you are doing in taming the wilder elements among us."

There was a general murmur of agreement.

"Thank you, Mr. Mayor." Sam acknowledged the commendation and waited. He had not been called to this meeting only to receive a compliment.

"Because of all this, there is much to recommend St. Louis to men and women of substance and refinement who are considering moving west, not to the frontier, but to an established place. We want to attract those prosperous elite to our city."

There was another murmur of agreement.

"However…"

Sam braced himself.

"There is a problem that must be addressed if we are to be successful in our pursuit of that objective." A frown drew the mayor's thick brows together. "The lowborn and penurious people pouring into our city in the hopes of joining a train heading west are becoming greater in number every year. And while the monies they spend to buy wagons and supplies, or for repairing or restocking their wagons, are prospering our businessmen, the orphans and runaways they leave behind are becoming a plague, a *blight* on our fair city's image. You can scarcely walk down the streets without seeing the dirty ragamuffins skulking around. Why yesterday, one of them made so bold as to walk right past my wife into Simpson's grocer!"

Sam stiffened. *The boy the Randolph woman had saved from arrest!* It had to be him. Most youngsters were too frightened to go into a store alone.

"The experience was too much for my wife's sensitive nature. She was quite undone when she reached home.

Levinia had a time calming her." The mayor scowled down the table at him. "This cannot be permitted to go on, Captain Benton! No person of wealth and culture will wish to set up business and make his home in a city that cannot keep its streets clean of such an ugly blemish. You do an excellent job of controlling the gamblers, drunks, mountain men, boatmen and others who frequent the more disreputable establishments on the levee. Yet these…these *street urchins* run amok among their betters. Have you an explanation for this deplorable situation, Captain?"

"I do, Mr. Mayor." Sam glanced around the table at each of the aldermen, trying to get a sense of where they stood on the issue. "The explanation is a simple one. I arrest lawbreakers. And there is no law against children walking the streets of St. Louis. Thus, unless one of these 'urchins' is caught stealing, or otherwise breaking the law, there is nothing I can do about their presence on our streets."

The mayor scowled, drumming his fingers on the table. "That is a most distressing answer, Captain."

Sam held his face impassive, tightening the grip on his hat that rested on his knee. *If this ruined his chance to court Levinia—*

The mayor stopped his drumming, glanced around. "Gentlemen, we must find a way to get these ragamuffins off our streets. We can hardly pass a law denying all children that right—we have children of our own. And the people we are trying to attract for permanent settlement must be made to feel St. Louis is an ideal place for them to rear their children. They must feel we welcome their children as future productive citizens of St. Louis society. Have any of you a solution to offer?"

The aldermen shifted in their chairs, knit their brows and studied the table. Silence fell.

Sam held back a scowl. It seemed Miss Randolph's interference with that boy's arrest had stirred up a pile of trouble. He turned his hat in his hands and waited.

Alderman Field cleared his throat, leaned forward and looked toward the mayor at the head of the table. "What if we pass a law to the effect that any child under the age of twelve who is not a citizen of St. Louis must be accompanied by an adult when in town?"

The mayor leaned back in his chair, rested the heels of his hands on the table and drummed his fingers. After a moment he nodded. "That might work, Arthur. If any outsider questions the law, we will explain it is for the children's safety. Yes. That might work." The mayor's gaze shifted.

Sam straightened.

"Would that law give you the authority you need to get these dirty, unkempt jackanapes off our streets, Captain?"

"It would. As long as they are not accompanied by an adult, Mr. Mayor."

"Excellent! *Excellent!* All in favor of such a law?" The mayor smiled at the affirmative chorus. "Let the record show the law passed by unanimous vote. Captain Benton, you are hereby instructed to procure posters giving notice of the new law and post them in plain sight at the fields outside of town where these wagon trains form. And that, gentlemen, should settle our problem."

"And create another, Mr. Mayor."

The mayor's smile dissolved into another frown. "And what problem is that, Captain?"

"What do I do with the children I arrest? Our jail is

meant for adults. There are no provisions for young—"
Sam stopped, stared at the mayor's uplifted hand and held his silence.

"Your concern is misplaced, Captain. Those urchins are accustomed to rough conditions. They need no special provisions. Jail will likely be an improvement on their present living conditions. Now…you have heard the law, and you have your instructions. I am certain you will carry them out in your usual exemplary fashion. And that concludes our business. This meeting is adjourned."

Sam unlocked the cell door and pulled it open. "All right, Larkin, time's up. You're free to go. And stay sober. You cut up another man and I'll lock you up and throw away the key."

The large, bearded man rose from the cot and swaggered toward him. "Your threat don't scare me, Captain."

"That's a shame. Because it should." Sam smiled, a quiet smile that carried a promise, and stepped back to let Larkin pass. The big man's boots thudded against the plank floor, fading as he crossed the outer room. The outside door opened, then slammed shut.

The jail was empty again. But for how long? Sam glanced into the vacant cells. Thanks to the mayor's ridiculous law they would soon be filled with children. And what would he do with them? Grown men he could handle. But youngsters?

He frowned, strode to the outer room and dropped into his chair. One of those cells would already be occupied by a boy if Miss Randolph had not interfered.

He scrubbed his hand over the back of his neck, then shoved his heels against the floor and rocked back on the chair's hind legs. The look in those brown eyes of hers when he had been about to arrest that little thief had made him feel lower than a worm's belly. But when she had looked at the boy...

Sam shook his head, laced his hands behind his neck and stared up at the crack in the ceiling. Why had she been so concerned about a boy she didn't even know? And what was she hiding? Why didn't she want him to know where she was from? Not that that was rare on the frontier. Plenty of people who came west didn't want their past known. Still, if it had anything to do with her brother and the M and M line...

Sam shifted his weight, rode the chair forward till the front legs hit the floor. It was time to pay that call on James Randolph. Maybe he would be more forthcoming than his sister.

Mary stepped back toward the edge of the street and scanned the storefronts. Shoes...candles...cigars...

"You look a little lost, Miss Randolph."

She gasped, and spun around to stare at a blue shirt. One with a badge pinned to it. She lifted her gaze to Samuel Benton's face. Blue eyes gazed down at her.

"I did not mean to startle you, Miss Randolph. Only to assist you—if I am able to do so." He smiled and indicated the package in her basket. "I see you are doing some shopping. I hope you are finding our stores compare favorably with the ones you left behind in..."

"I have only been in one shop thus far, Captain Benton. That is hardly enough to make any comparisons." Mary looked again at the storefronts. The man's presence scattered her wits, and she needed to keep her senses about her. That was the second time he had tried to find out where she had lived back east. "I was searching for an emporium. Or a haberdasher." She glanced up at him. "I need to buy some items for Ben. Suspenders and such. If you would be so kind as to direct me?"

"Miss Mayfield's Emporium is five stores down, just before the corner." He stepped out of the way of shoppers passing by. "I'm glad I happened upon you, Miss Randolph. You have saved me an embarrassment. I'm on my way to speak with your brother and I thought his name was James, not Ben."

"My brother's name *is* James, Captain Benton. Ben is the young boy I took home yesterday." She gave him a cool look. "The boy you wanted to arrest."

"You took that boy *home* with you?"

Mary stiffened. "You need not look so *shocked,* Captain. Indeed, I find it offensive that you deem me the sort of person who would leave a child to roam the streets starving and uncared for." She looked him straight in the eyes. "What else was I to do but take him home with me? Let him be jailed?" Her challenge hit the mark, judging from the darkening of his blue eyes.

"What *else*—" He stopped, stared at her and sucked in air.

A surge of satisfaction flooded her. The man looked quite nettled. Good. Perhaps he would not be so eager to arrest another helpless child. She peered at him and waited.

"I assure you, Miss Randolph, I meant no offense."

Her hope flattened. So he was not going to change his mind about arresting children. She gave him a curt nod. "If that is so, Captain, then I accept your apology. Good day." She whisked about with a swirl of her long skirts and started down the street, focusing her attention on the storefronts. She refused to acknowledge her disappointment or to look back in spite of the tense feeling between her shoulder blades that told her he was staring after her.

Sam fisted his hand and rapped on the partially open door. This interview should be interesting if James Randolph was half as exasperating as his sister. That woman was undeniably the most sharp-tongued, irritating—

The door opened. Sam wiped the scowl from his face.

"Ah, Captain Benton. Come in."

"Mr. Randolph." Sam closed the door of James Randolph's office, shut all thought of the man's sister from his mind and extended his hand. Randolph's gaze was straightforward and friendly, his grip firm.

"How may I be of service, Captain?"

Sam shook his head. "There is nothing in particular, Mr. Randolph. I am sure Goodwin has informed you of all the regulations concerning businesses and steamboats in St. Louis. I am here because I make it a practice to call on new businessmen in town to let them know who I am, and that I am ready to assist them if they have any problems of a legal nature."

"An excellent idea, Captain. I appreciate the gesture. I shall certainly call on you should the need arise." James Randolph smiled and indicated the chair in front of his desk. "Please, have a seat."

Sam noted the openness in Randolph's face and gesture. It was not indicative of a man with something to hide from the law. But appearances could be deceiving. He removed his hat and folded his long frame into a Windsor chair. "I stopped by yesterday, but you were engaged in a meeting. You want to be careful who you deal with, Mr. Randolph. St. Louis sits on the edge of the frontier, and that creates problems unknown in the cities back east. It is easy for a man to cheat someone, then simply up and disappear—though we have ways of tracking them down eventually."

Sam watched James Randolph carefully, hoping to detect the slightest change in expression or demeanor as he talked. The veiled warning seemed to have no effect on the man. Randolph was either dense, honest—or a good actor. He pushed on. "We are doing our best to tame the less restrained who come to town to celebrate after months in the mountains or a long and successful journey upriver. And, also, to maintain some control over the establishments they frequent and the undesirable… er…shall we say, *residual effects* of those visits. And then, of course, there are the Indians. They are usually quite a shock to those who come to St. Louis from the eastern cities." He stared into James Randolph's eyes. "I assume you had no Indians freely roaming the streets of your city?"

"Nary a one, Captain. And you are right—they were quite a shock. Especially to my sister. Mary was reluctant to face them on her own. As was I, to have her do so." James Randolph rose, stepped around the desk toward him and extended his hand again. "Thank you, Captain Benton, for your kindness in escorting Mary to market yesterday. You have my deepest appreciation."

Sam rose and grasped the offered hand. "No thanks are needed, Mr. Randolph. It is my duty to see to the safety and comfort of St. Louis's citizens." He quirked his lips in a wry smile. "And I am not at all sure your sister shares your gratitude. My services as her escort were summarily dismissed after an encounter with a young thief."

"Yes, I heard of that." James Randolph's smile matched

his own. "Mary can be a little autocratic when riled. And she has a soft heart for those who are downtrodden. Nonetheless, she is grateful for your assistance." The smile faded from Randolph's face. "Now, as you say there is nothing we need discuss, I must beg your pardon, Captain. The Mississippi and Missouri steamer line seems to have been run in a very slipshod manner by the previous owner and his manager, and I have much to do to set it aright."

Sam nodded. The disquiet was back. He filed away the two pieces of information he had learned from the visit. Thomas had run the steamer line in a careless manner, and James Randolph was hiding something. He had adroitly avoided the invitation to divulge the name of the eastern city of his origin—as had his sister. Perhaps it was time to tip his hand and shake Randolph up a bit, see what fell out into the open.

"I understand." Sam tugged on his hat and moved to the door. "Thank you for your time, Mr. Randolph. I make it my business to find out about the people who take up residence in St. Louis. And, if in the course of your familiarizing yourself with this business, you find that need for my services, do not hesitate to call upon me." He dipped his head and walked from the room, leaving James Randolph staring after him.

A steamship's horn pierced the silence. Another answered. Mary turned onto her back and sighed. She tossed the sheet aside, slipped her feet into her silk slippers and used the brilliant starlight to guide her to the window. Sleep was impossible. She was supposed to be in Philadelphia planning her wedding. Instead, she was at the edge of a wilderness in St. Louis, Missouri, facing an unknown future. How could she sleep when her whole life had gone topsy-turvy?

Her stomach cramped. She pressed her hands against her abdomen and took a long, slow breath to ease the pain of the nervous spasm. What would life hold for her? It was true she would rather be a spinster than some man's bargain. But that did not mean her desire to love and be loved, to marry and have children, to grow old with a beloved husband beside her was gone. It was all in her heart, and stronger than ever.

Tears welled. *Poor little Miss Mary. She'll have a hard time findin' herself a husband, bein' plain like she is. Now, if she was blessed with the beauty of Miss Sarah...* Oh, how true her nanny's words had proved to be.

Mary blinked the tears away and lifted her face toward the dark sky, the same questions that had plagued her all her growing-up years swirling in her mind. Why had God made her tall and thin and dark-haired? And, what was worse, given her the bold, forthright nature that was off-putting to men? Why had He not made *her* small and blond like her sister, with a golden beauty and gentle sweet nature that drew men the way nectar drew bees? The way Victoria drew Winston. Why did God not love her as much as He did others?

The familiar hurt squeezed her chest, made it hard to draw her breath. She opened the sash, then went to her knees, crossed her arms on the sill and rested her chin on them to catch any movement of air. Muffled sounds of revelry, from the direction of the levee, floated in on a warm breeze. A steamboat blasted its whistle. Another answered. The noise of the levee continued day and night. And it was all so strange and new.

Fear nibbled at the last shreds of her composure. The

tears she had held back slipped down her cheeks. What had she done? Was her decision to leave Philadelphia a right or wrong one? Should she have swallowed her hurt and her pride and accepted Winston as her husband even though she knew it was only her father's money he wanted? Was he her last chance for a family of her own? Was the pretense of love better than a life alone?

"Twelve o'clock and all is well."

The words came, muted but distinct. She grasped on to them like a lifeline. Twelve o'clock—the beginning of a new day. And all is well. Pray God it might be so.

Sam leaped back from the slashing blade, grabbed the mountain man's thick wrist and twisted. The double-edged skinning knife clattered to the floor. He grabbed a fistful of the cursing drunk's buckskin shirt and shoved him toward his deputy. "Take him to jail and let him sleep off his meanness. I'll run him out of town in the morning." He picked up the weapon and walked outside.

A roar of voices calling for whiskey or beer erupted behind him. Music started playing. The din mixed with the noise coming from the other saloons, the lapping of river water, the churning of paddle wheels and the blasting of steam whistles to make St. Louis's own peculiar sound of revelry.

"Twelve o'clock and all is well."

Twelve o'clock. Time to go home and let his lieutenant and the night guards take over.

Home. Sam snorted, adjusted his hat and started up the road. Home was a room in Mrs. Warren's boardinghouse on Walnut Street, handy to the jail and courthouse. True, it was a vast improvement over the broken-down hovels he had lived in as a kid. Or the open fields, hay mows and sheds that had been his only shelter after he had run away from his drunk of a father. But it was far from what he had planned. Still, he was getting close. He had made some smart investments that were swelling his bank account. And now, he was gaining entrance to St. Louis society by courting the mayor's daughter. Yes, he was getting close.

He turned onto Walnut, glanced up at the dark, star-littered sky and smiled with grim satisfaction. *Remember when I was seven years old and I begged You for some warm clothes for Daniel and Ma and me, God? Remember how I begged You for a house without holes in the walls and roof so we could be warm and dry? For somebody to come and help us?* A hard knot of resentment twisted in his stomach. *Remember how Danny and Ma sickened and died from the cold? I told You then I would make it without You. That I would be "somebody" someday, and no one would sneer at me ever again. Remember, God? Well, keep watching, because I am almost there.*

He threw a last disdainful look at the sky, took the porch steps two at a time, pulled open the door and went inside.

Chapter Six

"**My**, it is warm!" Mary dabbed her damp forehead, tucked her handkerchief into her pocket and glanced toward James. "I keep thinking of how lovely and cool it always is at home, even on the hottest of days."

"Hmm..."

"An astute comment."

James lowered the newspaper he was reading and gave her a sheepish look over the top of it. "Sorry, Mary. I did not mean to ignore you." He set the paper aside. "I know what you are saying. I have thought of home a time or two myself today. I did not realize St. Louis was so much warmer than Philadelphia." His lips curved in a rueful smile of commiseration. "Randolph Court stays cool because of its large size. I fear there is no hope of that in this small cottage."

"How cheering you are."

He chuckled.

Mary stuck her tongue out at him like when they were children and rose from the settee. "Do you suppose one gets used to the heat?" She lifted the strands of hair stuck to her moist neck, tucked them back into the loose knot on the crown of her head and sighed. "I think I will go outside and see if there is at least a breath of a breeze." She glanced his way. "Would you care to join me?"

"I would be delighted."

"Delighted?" She drifted by his chair and tapped his shoulder. "I think not. Agreeable perhaps. You would be *delighted* if I were a certain blond young lady named Charlotte Colburn." She threw him a smile over her shoulder and headed for the door. "But, alas, Charlotte is home in Philadelphia and you must content yourself with my company. At least for the nonce."

James grinned and shrugged into his jacket. "Charlotte is pleasant, but there was no understanding between us. And I am certain I shall meet equally pleasant girls here in St. Louis. And, while I do not deny I enjoy being with a young lady, my dear sister, I do not esteem their company more highly than yours. Only...differently."

"Indeed."

"Do I detect skepticism?" His grin widened. "For shame, Mary. I shall prove what I say is true." He lifted her hat from the hook on the tree and held it out to her. "Shall we go explore our new town?"

"What a lovely idea!" Mary took the wide-brimmed straw hat, knotted the filmy ties beneath her chin and moved out onto the porch. She waited until he closed the door, then stepped down onto the brick path and walked to the gate. "Which way shall we go?"

James pushed opened the gate and motioned toward the cobblestone street forming the right border of their fenced-in corner lot. "I suggest we walk up Market Street, away from the river. It is coming on to evening, and I think it might be best to avoid the levee area."

"Yes. That might be wise. I have no desire to run into

the 'unsavory elements' Captain Benton spoke of. Or the good captain, either, for that matter."

"Mary..."

She shot him a look. "Do not use that reproving tone, James. I know we are to be forgiving. But Ben is a *child*. The captain could have shown him mercy."

"He is a police officer. It is his job to arrest those who break the law."

"Yes, that is what he told me. And if the captain had had his way, that is exactly what would have happened to Ben." She stopped and faced her brother. "Do *you* think Ben belongs in jail?"

"Of course not, but you cannot hold it against the man for performing his duty."

Mary stared at him a moment, then turned with a swish of her long skirts and resumed walking. "My head tells me you are right, James. But my heart refuses to be sensible about the matter." She gave him a sidelong glance. "Homeless children do not belong in a jail. They belong in an orphanage—like Aunt Laina's. Alas, there is no orphanage in St. Louis. Nonetheless, the matter is well settled—despite the captain's lack of compassion."

They reached the corner and veered right. A steamboat's whistle blasted a strident note, then another. Mary glanced at James and laughed. "I believe I am becoming accustomed to the constant blare of those whistles. That time I only flinched instead of nearly jumping out of my skin."

He grinned down at her. "I am sure in a few more days we will not notice them at all. Or the Indians and mountain men. Though it is still something of a shock when one walks into the office and books passage on our ships. Particularly since they often pay their fare with *pelts*."

"Truly? I cannot imagine." Mary stopped and looked up at him. "How do you know what a pelt is worth?"

A frown creased his forehead. "I have no notion as to their value. I am learning to judge that. Meanwhile, I let Goodwin handle all such transactions while I watch. It is quite an art, bartering. The Indians are quite skilled at it."

Mary started walking again. "Have you found any information that points to whomever was skimming the profit from the line?"

"Not yet. Everything is too new—such as this trade in pelts. But I shall. I am watching Goodwin. There is something about the man I do not trust. It would not be hard for him to take advantage of my ignorance, so I am secretly keeping a careful accounting of all transactions, apart from the company records he keeps."

"And if you discover he is stealing from the line?"

"I shall have Captain Benton arrest him."

Mary snorted. "You mean if the good captain is not too busy arresting children." She turned her head and looked forward. The sun rode low in the sky, the bottom of the blazing orange orb hidden by the leafy canopy of a tree atop the rise they were climbing. She lifted her hand to shade her eyes from the glare of light and looked across the street at an imposing two-story brick building with a clock tower, topped by a pillared dome, in the center of the roof. A large park surrounded the building. Mary gave James a sidelong look. "Shall we cross over and see what that building is?"

He nodded and took hold of her elbow. They waited for a buggy to pass, then hurried across the street and walked up the wide brick pathway to climb the steps. The cooler air in the shade of the portico felt wonderful. Mary removed her hat, fanned herself with its wide brim and watched James stride over to a brass plaque on the wall beside the handsome double doors straight ahead.

"This is the courthouse, Mary. Rather small, I should think, for all—"

One of the doors opened and an elegantly dressed young woman stepped out onto the portico, almost running into James.

"Oh!" Light brown, delicately arched brows lifted and big, blue eyes opened wide as beautifully shaped lips parted in surprise. "Forgive me, sir. I was not paying attention to my path."

James smiled and made a polite bow. "Not at all, miss. The fault was mine. I should not have crowded the doorway."

"You are too kind, sir." Long lashes fluttered down over the blue eyes as the woman smiled, revealing dimples in cheeks tinged with a hint of pink.

Mary's chest tightened. The woman was petite, blond and beautiful. The same as Victoria. Everything *she* was not. She stopped fanning, raised her hat to her head and settled it a little forward to hide as much of her face as possible. The wide, gauzy ties she formed into a large bow to hide her small, square chin. There was nothing she could do about her height. Or her slenderness.

She glanced down, surreptitiously bunched the fabric of her long skirt at her narrow waist to make her frame look fuller, then looked back toward the woman and froze. So did the tall, blond man holding the door. Their gazes met. The heat of a blush spread across her cheeks, but Samuel Benton did not so much as flicker an eye. He only gave a polite nod, though she knew he did not miss the tiniest imperfection in her appearance, or her pathetic attempt to hide them.

Mary stood rooted in place, acutely aware of the sheen on her flushed face in comparison to the cool perfection of the beautiful, petite blonde. She felt like an ugly giant, but not for anything would she betray her discomfort to the woman giving her a keen, measuring look from under those ridiculously long lashes. Or to the captain, either. She squared her shoulders, lifted her chin and pasted a polite smile on her face.

Samuel Benton stepped forward. "Good evening, Miss Randolph… Mr. Randolph. May I present Miss Stewart." He looked down at the young woman. "Miss Stewart, Miss Randolph and her brother are two of St. Louis's newest citizens. Mr. Randolph has come to town to manage the Mississippi and Missouri steamer line."

James gave a polite bow. "Your servant, Miss Stewart."

Mary smiled and dipped her head, wishing she were seated. She was at least three inches taller than the woman. "Good evening."

Miss Stewart smiled in response, showing her dimples off to good advantage. "I shall have to tell my father of your arrival in our fair city, Mr. Randolph. I am certain he will want to meet with you. He is the mayor of St. Louis and very solicitous of its businesses." Her gaze shifted, chilled. "And my mother will want to make your acquaintance, Miss Randolph. She heads many of the charity and cultural events of St. Louis." She turned to Samuel Benton and gave him a dazzling smile. "You were going to see me home, Captain Benton?"

"Of course, Miss Stewart." He glanced in their direction. "Good evening, Miss Randolph... Mr. Randolph." He offered Miss Stewart his arm, then escorted her down the stairs and out to Market Street.

Mary stared after them a moment, then reached up and yanked undone the huge bow hiding her chin, cross with herself for allowing Miss Stewart's beauty to upset her.

"Shall we go on with our exploring, Mary?"

She took a breath and retied the bow...smaller. "Yes, of course, James." She forced a smile and tried not to think of how her heart had faltered when the captain's gaze had met hers, or of how lovely Miss Stewart had looked beside the captain, as James took her elbow and they descended the steps together.

It was no use. Thoughts kept tumbling around in her head breaking her concentration. Mary sighed, put down her pen and lowered the wick in the oil lamp until the flame sputtered and died. She would finish the letter to her parents tomorrow.

The wood chair creaked softly as she rose from the writing desk. A slight breeze rippled the fabric of her dressing gown as she walked to the open window. At least it had finally cooled off a little. That would make sleeping more pleasant. If only she could sleep.

Faint sounds of St. Louis's revelry drifting in the window were drowned out by the loud, persistent hum of a hungry mosquito hovering around her ear. She swatted the insect away and looked out into the moonlit night. Had Captain Benton spent the evening sitting on the mayor's front porch wooing Miss Stewart? Was he there still?

Mary frowned, leaned against the window frame and let the night breeze flow over her. Why was she unable to erase the couple from her mind? She was not normally so weak-willed. It must be the strong resemblance Miss Stewart bore to Victoria Dearborn that had her so…so… agitated. That, and the look of admiration in Captain Benton's eyes as he gazed down at the petite blonde. It was the same way Winston Blackstone had looked at Victoria.

Mary sighed, then shoved away from the window and walked to the four-poster bed. She longed to walk about, but the room was too small to pace. She sat on the edge of the bed, tugged a pillow from under the woven coverlet and reclined against it. The mosquito found her. Another joined it. She swatted them away, rose to her knees, yanked the gauzy bed hangings free of the bedposts and pulled them into place, making certain the edges lapped. That would keep the annoying insects away. If only there were a curtain she could pull across her mind to keep the unwelcome thoughts and images away.

She snorted and batted her eyelashes, dipped her head and looked up, ever so coyly, through them, as Miss Stewart had done while talking to the men. It was nauseating! Miss Stewart was an outrageous flirt, who was obviously dissatisfied lest she capture the admiration of every man she came in contact with. Why, Miss Stewart was flirting with James right under the captain's eyes! Why were men blind to such machinations?

Mary fluffed her pillow and sank down against it. *How would it feel to have a man look at you the way Winston looked at Victoria? The way Captain Benton looked at Miss Stewart? As if you were beautiful and delicate and precious? How would it feel to have a man love you?*

The stars shining beyond the filmy fabric blurred. Mary swiped the tears from her cheeks, grabbed another pillow and flopped over onto her side, hugging the fluffy softness close against her constricted chest. This loneliness was her portion in life. God had not seen fit to make her beautiful in the eyes of men. There was no sense in wishing for things that would never be.

Chapter Seven

❧

Sam relaxed in the saddle, at ease with the powerful ripple and thrust of his horse's muscles, the solid thud of hooves against the hard-packed earth. It was a nice day for a ride, and it had been a long time since he had been astride Attila. He did not get out of St. Louis often.

He ducked under a low-hanging branch, rested his free hand on his thigh and glanced up at the cloud-dotted, blue expanse above. Too bad he could not have enjoyed this excursion more. But the trip's purpose was not to his liking. Still, posting notice of the new law concerning emigrant children under the age of twelve was part of his job, and he had done it. Now, he would have to enforce it.

His face tightened. So did his stomach. He blew out a breath easing the constraint and returned his attention to the trail ahead. The thick band of trees that hid the wagon train gathering site from the city was thinning. He would soon be back to town. He frowned and eased back on the reins, slowing Attila's pace.

At least it was late in the season. The wagon train forming now would probably be the last for this year. The influx of emigrants should stop soon. And perhaps by the time they began gathering again next spring, the situation concerning orphaned children would be different. Meanwhile, he would do what he must.

Sam set his jaw, clamped a firm lid on his unease and directed his thoughts toward his goals. He had worked with a view to them since he was old enough to muck out stalls and help farmers plant and harvest crops. He was not going to give them up now. He would do his job. And he would fulfill his plan.

He closed his eyes and summoned the vision he carried in his heart. His house would be perfect. There would be no soot, no faded fabric, no chipped paint in the wood trim or gouges in the wood floors. He would have carpets in every room, fancy furniture and real paintings on the walls. And it was going to be big. Three stories high with lots of windows and tall white pillars holding up the high porch roof.

He frowned and opened his eyes. He was close. Very close. The lead mine upriver he had invested in was proving very profitable. And his other interests were doing equally well. His finances were secure. What he needed now was the land.

He knew the piece he wanted. It had a knoll, the highest spot around, where he would build his house to look out over the river. It would be the first place seen by people coming down the river to St. Louis. A real showplace. All he had to do was wait for Charlie and Harry Banks to come back to town so he could make the old mountain men a generous offer for their property. Maybe then they would stop mining for silver and live an easier life in town. And then, when his house was built, he would marry Levinia Stewart and they would become the young leaders of St. Louis society.

Sam smiled, leaned forward and patted Attila's neck. He had it all worked out. All he had to do was court Levinia and wait for Charlie and Harry. He closed his eyes again, pictured the way it would be. But for some reason he could not see Levinia in the house. He frowned and stopped trying to place her there. It was too early. That was the problem. He had only begun to court her. But he intended to marry her. The mayor's daughter was everything he needed his wife to be. She was the most beautiful woman in St. Louis, a fitting mistress for his showplace house. And she was the key to his full acceptance into society.

Sam shifted his weight in the saddle and let his mind drift back to the way Levinia had looked last night. She had been agleam with beauty, clearly outshining Miss Randolph.

Miss Randolph.

Sam stirred, jolted by the same sense of guilt that had hit him when he had met her gaze last evening. It was clear, from the look in her brown eyes, that she still felt he was wrong about arresting that young boy. But that was his job!

Sam jerked his thoughts away from the condemnation in Miss Randolph's eyes. He knew the desperate acts hunger drove one to, but he could not afford to feel guilty for performing his duty. His job was providing him with the means to accomplish his goals, and he would not give that up for anyone. Certainly not for a woman with a pair of accusing brown eyes. No matter how beautiful those eyes were.

Danny had brown eyes.

Sam sucked in air, fought the pressure in his chest. The approaching victory suddenly felt hollow. Danny and

Ma would never know he was holding fast to the promise he made them to be so rich and important nobody would ever sneer at any of them again. At seven years old, he had thought that promise could take the place of the food and warmth God never sent in spite of his prayers. He had thought the promise was strong enough to keep them alive—the way it did him. But Danny was too small, and his ma too weak. Their sickness got worse until it killed them. He had tried to take care of them, but he could not save them.

Sam's face tightened. He glanced toward the sky. *I failed you and Danny then, Ma, but I will not fail you now. I will keep my promise to make you proud of me.*

He emerged from the trees and reined south, headed for Chestnut Street and the stables behind the jail.

The jail.

The tight ball of unease returned to his stomach. What sort of place was a jail for a kid?

"I am certain it would work out well for your store, Mrs. Simpson." Mary gave the grocer's wife a warm, encouraging smile. "Marketing baskets can become very heavy before one reaches home, and I believe many of your customers would be willing to pay a small stipend for Ben to relieve them of that burden. I believe they would welcome such a service, and favor your store with their custom for offering it." She placed her hand on Ben's shoulder, drawing the stout woman's attention to the boy who was all shiny clean and dressed in clothes that had once belonged to Ivy's sons.

Mrs. Simpson glanced at her husband, who was stacking burlap bags in the corner, and shook her head. "You will have to gain Mr. Simpson's approval, Miss Randolph.

And I am quite certain he will refuse you." There was commiseration in her eyes.

Mary thought it likely the woman was right, but she would not give up without a fight. Ben had been so happy when she had explained this idea to him. "Very well. Thank you, Mrs. Simpson." She lifted her chin, turned toward the corner to speak with Mr. Simpson and almost bumped into a small, elderly woman. "Oh! Forgive me, madam, I—"

"The fault is mine, dear." The woman placed a blotchy, thin-skinned hand on her arm. "I overheard a bit of your conversation and moved closer where I could shamelessly eavesdrop on the rest." The woman smiled, and the creases and wrinkles in her face deepened. "My hearing is not what it used to be. But I heard enough to know you have an excellent suggestion, young lady. If you will permit me to help, I believe the three of us—" another smile included Mrs. Simpson "—can convince Mr. Simpson it would prosper his store. Do you agree, Martha?"

Mrs. Simpson nodded.

Mary stared, stunned by the elderly woman's offer, and doubtful of its value. Still… Mr. Simpson held no fondness for *her*. And Mrs. Simpson had agreed. She smiled at the tiny woman. "I should be most appreciative of your help, madam."

"Good!" The woman returned her smile. "Now, ladies, let us see to Mr. Simpson."

Mary grinned. She could not help it. The woman's faded blue eyes were fairly twinkling. She was obviously delighted at the prospect of a challenge. But how could she help?

The woman sobered. She slid her basket off her arm and set it and a small piece of paper on the long wood counter. "Here is my list, Martha. But, as I shall not have to carry my basket myself, add a quart of molasses, a bag of tea and a good portion of honeycomb. Oh. And two of those lemons—fresh ones, mind you. I must say, this is a most helpful idea. But tell me, what is the cost for this young man to carry my basket home for me?"

Cost? Mary took a closer look at the elderly woman beside her. How clever to persuade Mr. Simpson through his pocketbook. She should have considered that. But she had thought only in terms of a stipend for Ben. Mary held back a chuckle. The aged woman's face held an expression of pure innocence, yet she had raised her voice loud enough to be heard throughout the store, and was watching the result out of the corner of her eyes. Another good idea.

Mary wiped the smile from her face, lowered her lashes and shot a glance toward the corner. Mr. Simpson had straightened. He looked their way and a frown darkened his face. He brushed his hands together, sending some sort of dust flying into the air, and started toward them. Mary jerked her gaze back to the other women before he caught her watching him.

"You mistook my conversation with Miss Randolph, Mrs. Lucas." Mrs. Simpson lifted the hinged lid of a large wooden box and began to scoop tea into a small cloth bag. "Miss Randolph suggested that Mr. Simpson hire this young boy to carry baskets for our customers, but my husband has not agreed." She shook the bag down, dropped the scoop and tied the neck of the bag closed with a length of cord, then paused with the bag poised over Mrs. Lucas's filled basket. Her left eye closed in a quick wink. "Do you still wish these other items?"

The elderly woman sighed. "No, only the things on my

list, Martha. Put the tea back and take the others out, for they will make the basket too heavy for me."

Heavy footfalls thudded across the plank floor and stopped. Mr. Simpson scowled at his wife, took the package of tea from her hand and placed it in the basket. "There's no need for that, Mrs. Lucas. I ain't heard nothing about this boy carrying customers' baskets, but it sounds all right." He placed the wrapped piece of honeycomb his wife handed him in the basket and added the lemons. "The cost'll be ten cents."

"Nonsense!" Mrs. Lucas's eyes narrowed. "I came to buy groceries, not to be robbed, Elijah Simpson! I shall pay five cents."

The grocer added the molasses to the filled basket, then crossed his thick arms over his burly chest and stared down at the diminutive woman. "Seven."

There was a rustle of movement behind her. Mary took a quick glance over her shoulder. The customers had stopped browsing and had drawn close.

"Stand your ground, Isobel!" A thickset woman with a jutting chin snapped out the words. "I should very much like someone to carry my basket, but I will pay no more than five cents. As you say, anything more is outright thievery!"

There was a chorus of agreement.

Mr. Simpson's scowl deepened. He raised his hands. "All right, ladies. All right. The cost'll be five cents."

Smiles spread over the faces of the assembled women at the grocer's growled words. They gave each other small nods of satisfaction and turned back to their shopping, chatting over their victory as they went.

Mary could have hugged Mrs. Lucas and Mrs. Simpson.

"Pick up that basket and get moving, boy!" The grocer snarled the words and turned away.

Mary's elation flew. "Wait, Ben." She took hold of Ben's arm as he reached for the basket, and pasted a polite smile on her face as the surly grocer pivoted around to glare at her. "I think you are forgetting that Ben is not yet in your employ, Mr. Simpson. Shall we discuss his wages?"

Sam leaped off the gangway, turned and fastened his gaze on the steamboat as the *Independence* gave notice of its departure with three quick blasts of its whistle. He ignored the movement of the laborers around him, and held his place. The danger point would come when the *Independence* swung around to head upriver. She would be close to the *Washington* then, and an agile man could jump from the deck of one steamboat to another, if given enough reason to do so.

Sam tensed and focused his attention on the narrowing distance between the two boats. He figured the money Frank Gerard had been systematically winning from his victims at cards was reason enough for him to ignore the warning he had been given and try to make his way back to the table at the Broken Barge. But the gambler was trouble—he won too often, and by questionable means. He would not be allowed in St. Louis again.

The *Independence* finished the swing and straightened on its course. The muddy waves splashed lower on the cobblestones, then ceased and merged with the river on its way south to New Orleans. One more problem gone. But there still seemed to be an endless supply of them.

Sam tugged his hat brim lower and started up the slope. He stepped around a wagon loaded with crated shoats and angled toward the *Cincinnati.* She was leaving for parts north this afternoon and this would be the first departure of one of the boats of the M and M line since Randolph had taken over its management. It was likely he would be on hand. And that made this a perfect time for an "accidental" meeting with him. He knew the man and his sister were hiding something. And he intended to find out if it concerned the vandalism of the line. And he would look around to see if Duffy was among the crew.

"Thank you again, Mrs. Lucas."

"Hush, dear." The elderly woman patted Mary's arm and smiled at Ben, who was holding her basket. "The two of you have thanked me enough."

"But it was so *clever* the way you suggested Mr. Simpson hire Ben."

"Not clever, dear…necessary." The woman's faded blue eyes twinkled up at her. "I should be the one thanking you. I have not enjoyed myself so much in years. People look on you as useless when you get to be my age." A wistful look replaced the twinkle. "Now… I must get home. I am beginning to tire." She turned to go, then looked back. "You are a lovely young lady and I should like it very much if someday you have time to call upon me."

Mary smiled and nodded. "I shall come to call in a few days, Mrs. Lucas. After I am more settled."

The elderly face crinkled into a return smile. "I shall look forward to that, my dear. My home is on Chestnut. Ben will know the way. He can escort you and we shall have a proper tea!"

"Lovely."

Mary watched Mrs. Lucas walk away, Ben beside her

carrying the grocery-laden basket. It did not seem too burdensome for him. Indeed, he looked proud and happy. They disappeared behind a group of women on the walkway and she turned to scan the storefronts. James had asked—

"Let me go!"

Mary snapped her gaze in the direction of the frightened wail. A young girl was crouched behind the rain barrel at the corner of Tanner's Ladies Shoe Store, trying to tug her arm out of the grip of a policeman. The officer bent over the barrel, grabbed the girl by the shoulder and hauled her out onto the walkway.

"Please!" The girl hung back, grabbing for the rim of the rain barrel. "I ain't done nothin' wrong. *Honest.*" Tears ran down her face, making tiny paths through the grime on her cheeks. Sobs shook her small, skinny body.

Mary's heart swelled.

"Another of those filthy emigrant children!"

"Something should be done about them, Clara. Can you not speak to Robert about the situation?"

"Indeed, Clara, you must! It is disgraceful the way they are let to roam about the streets disturbing good folks!"

Mary whipped around. Three women, their faces pinched in distaste, were giving a wide berth to the child and the policeman. And no other person in the area seemed to be paying any attention to the small girl's plight.

The unloved and unlovely of this world are often invisible to those of affluence. Her aunt Laina's words rang in her head. Anger stiffened her spine. Mary whirled back and marched forward. "What is the trouble, officer?"

The policeman looked up. "No trouble, miss. Takin' this one off to jail."

The girl seemed to shrink before her eyes. The poor little thing was shaking like leaves in a windstorm. Mary began to shake herself—with growing anger. She fought to keep her voice pleasant. "And what has she done to warrant such treatment?"

"Nothin', miss. 'Tis the law now, is all."

A shadow fell over her. Mary turned and looked up, straight into the eyes of Samuel Benton.

The captain gave a polite dip of his head. "Have you a problem with one of my men, Miss Randolph?"

"I do indeed." Mary drew herself up to her full height. The man's size was intimidating. "This officer says he is taking this little girl to jail, though he admits she has done nothing wrong."

"I told her it was the law, Captain."

"All right, Jenkins. Continue your patrol, I will take over here."

"You want me to take this 'un to jail?"

Mary stepped closer.

"No. I will handle this." The captain grasped the sobbing girl's shoulder and the policeman strode down the walkway.

Mary lifted her chin and prepared to do battle.

"Have you ever been hungry, Miss Randolph?"

The question, posed in a conversational tone, stole the starch from her spine. She eyed him with suspicion. "Of course I have."

The captain fastened his gaze on hers. "I am talking about starvation hunger, such as these street urchins suffer."

Street urchins! Her anger came surging back. She drew breath.

He raised his hand. "You need not answer. Because if you had known such hunger, you would know that being fed every day would be a blessing to them."

"In jail, Captain?" Mary clenched her hands at her sides and looked him full in the eyes. "Is that what you tell yourself to soothe your conscience? That you are doing these *children* a favor by putting them in jail? Would *you* exchange *your* freedom for a meal?" His expression did not change one iota, but there was a tiny flicker in the depths of his blue eyes and she knew her words had stung him. She pressed her advantage. "There are other ways to feed a child, Captain Benton. And, as this child has done nothing wrong—by your own officer's admission—you have no right to jail her."

"You are wrong, Miss Randolph. Mayor Stewart and the town council have passed a new law that went into effect today. It is now illegal for any child under the age of twelve, who is not a citizen of St. Louis, to be on the streets of the city unless accompanied by an adult."

She gaped up at him, held mute by astonishment. But only for a moment. "You are going to jail *children* because they are alone on the street?" Her voice was soft, lower and more husky than normal. "What of orphans like Ben? He is to be jailed, not for any wrongdoing, but because his parents had the bad fortune to *die?* That is absurd!" Her fingernails dug into her palms. "It is ludicrous. *Preposterous!* It is…it is…"

"The law, Miss Randolph."

The captain calmly inserted the words when she sputtered to a halt. She glared at him.

"And I am sworn to uphold it. Good day." He picked up the girl, eliciting a wail of terror.

"Wait!"

He tightened his grip on the struggling child and looked at her.

She cleared her throat. "You cannot take the girl to jail. She is with me."

"Miss Randolph—"

"You said children under twelve who are not with an adult!" Mary lifted her chin and held out her hand. "I am an adult, and she is with me. Please put her down, Captain. I want to go home."

A frown pulled Samuel Benton's dark brown brows together. His blue eyes darkened. Mary squared her shoulders and lifted her chin a notch higher. Their gazes locked. And held. She refused to look away. She was right. And he knew it.

He looked down and lowered the child to the ground.

Mary released a shaky breath. *It has only been a moment. Surely it has only been a moment. It only felt like forever.* She leaned down and took the girl's small trembling hands, rough with scratches and ground in dirt, in hers. "It is all right, now. You have nothing to fear. You are going home with me. And we are going to get you something to eat." She glanced at the small, dirt-caked bare feet, then at the grimy little face and smiled. "You shall have a bath. And we shall get you a pretty new dress and some shoes to wear. Would you like that?"

The child stared up at her out of green eyes awash with tears. A sob broke from her throat and she threw herself against Mary's legs, buried her face in the fabric of her skirt and nodded.

Mary rubbed the little girl's bony back, blinked tears

from her own eyes, then straightened and cleared the lump from her throat. "Come now, you cannot walk if you are crying. Take my hand." She gave the small hand that slipped into hers a reassuring squeeze and turned toward Market Street.

"You cannot save them all, Miss Randolph. There are too many of them."

The captain's soft words brought her to a halt. She turned back and looked up at him. "I would not be able to sleep at night if I did not try, Captain. But if what you say is true, then I shall need help. Would you care to join me?"

She left the challenge hanging there and walked off, shortening her stride so the child pressing close against her could keep pace. At the corner, she could resist no longer—she glanced back. Captain Benton was still there on the walkway, looking after her. No doubt wishing she had never come to St. Louis.

Chapter Eight

She felt him looking at her.

Mary lifted her head. Her brother was standing in the doorway, a grin on his face. "I amuse you, James?"

"Yes, indeed." The grin widened. "I never thought to see you mending clothes."

She wrinkled her nose at him. "I am not mending the dress. I am altering it. And it is about time all that instruction in fine needlework bore fruit." She looked down and took another stitch along the seam. "Callie is so thin, there were no dresses in the store to fit her. And I refuse to burden Ivy with this extra work. She is already doing so much, taking Ben and Callie in as she has. What a blessing it is that she was the cook for—" She stopped midstitch and gave a wry laugh. "Gracious. I sound like Mother—seeing God's hand in a *coincidence*." She gave a little shake of her head, completed the stitch, then poised the needle for the next, using the thimble on her finger to push it through.

"Speaking of God…"

She slanted a look up at him. "Were we?"

"His name was mentioned."

She did not return James's smile, merely shrugged and worked the last few stitches of the seam as he walked to the chair opposite her.

"Do you realize tomorrow is Sunday, Mary?"

She did indeed. "And…" She jabbed the needle into the soft cotton fabric and tugged the thread through as she had countless times under Miss Spencer's tutelage.

"And…" James lowered himself into the Windsor, stretched out his long legs and crossed his ankles. "I went to the levee today when the *Cincinnati* departed. Captain Benton was there."

The needle stabbed into her finger. *Bother!* Mary yanked her pricked finger out from under the blue dress and stuck the tip of it in her mouth. "Captain Benton seems to be everywhere. Especially when innocent children are being arrested."

"I asked him about a church. He told me of several and gave me directions to their locations…though I got the distinct impression he did not himself attend any of them."

"That is not surprising. The man has no conscience!" She huffed, finished off the seam, then reached into the small sewing box her mother had insisted she bring along to the wilderness.

"I went to see the pastor of one of the churches. The service begins at nine o'clock, the same as at home."

She snipped off the thread and placed the scissors back into the box. "*There.* I am finished." She stuck the needle into the pincushion and tossed it after the scissors.

"Mary?"

She shot him a look as she shook out the small dress. "I heard you, James. I will be dressed in my finery and ready to go by half after eight in the morning. But I shan't like it." She flicked the lid of the box closed and secured the small latch. The little blue dress dangled from her other hand. She brushed the five narrow bands of darker blue fabric that circled the bottom of the skirt into place and sighed. "James...do you remember what Aunt Laina says, that 'the unloved and unlovely of this world are often invisible to those of affluence'?"

"Yes..."

She glanced at him, saw the question in his eyes. "I never truly believed that until these past few days." She draped the dress over the arm of her chair, then rose and crossed to the window.

"Perhaps that is because you were never before confronted by situations that proved it to be true."

Mary nodded. "Yes. That must be the reason. Mother and Father and, of course, Aunt Laina and Uncle Thad care about the downtrodden. And they befriend those who share their feelings. I have never before seen people who...who are so selfish and uncaring."

There were soft footsteps on the carpet. James appeared beside her, leaned a shoulder against the window frame and looked at her. "We all played with the children at Aunt Laina's orphanage. And you and Sarah helped there when you got older. But none of us ever witnessed Aunt Laina's struggle to establish it. We only heard bits and pieces of the story as we were growing up."

A buggy rolled into view. She watched until it was out of sight, then turned to face him. "I never realized how courageous Aunt Laina is. I shall never forget the disdainful disgust on the faces of the customers at Simpson's market when they looked at Ben. Or the hard-heartedness of those three women on the street today. They looked at Callie as if she were some loathsome creature instead of a child. And everyone else on the walkway either glanced at her and the policeman and walked on or averted their gazes completely. They simply did not care about the child. And as for Captain Benton…" Her face tightened. "He does not bear speaking about."

"Mary—"

"Do not tell me again that the captain is only doing his duty, James. He is *wrong* to take those children to jail and he knows it. I saw it in his eyes. I do not know how the man sleeps at night. I hope it is poorly!" She gave another huff, walked to the small piecrust-edged table stand and picked up her sewing box to put it away in the corner cupboard. She turned to pick up the dress, gasped and spun about to face him.

He straightened. "What is it?"

"I only know of Ben and Callie, James! How many children do you suppose are already in jail? And how am I to prevent the arrest of more of them? I cannot patrol every street and watch every policeman." She stared at him, nibbling on the left inside corner of her upper lip while her mind circled the problem.

He pushed away from the window and gave a little shrug. "True enough. Of course, if the law was revoked—"

"*James.* The law—" She laughed, rushed forward and threw her arms about him in a fierce hug. "Thank you, James. You are so very, *very* clever. That is the answer. I shall have that ridiculous law revoked!"

He had selected the right woman to be his bride. There was no doubt about it. Sam leaned against a pillar and let his gaze travel over Levinia Stewart as she spread the long, silk-flower-trimmed skirt of her yellow gown and seated herself on the swing. Yes, she was the perfect choice for his wife. That was exactly the way she would look gracing his porch. He would be able to picture her there now.

Levinia glanced up at him from under lowered lashes, gave him a dimpled smile and pushed one small, silk-slipper-clad foot against the floor to set the swing in motion. "You must not look at me so intently, Captain Benton. It is not seemly."

He rose to the coquettish cue. "Forgive me, Miss Stewart. But your beauty draws my eye as candlelight draws a moth. I find it impossible to resist looking at you. As, I believe, would any man."

The quick flash in her blue eyes before she lowered her long lashes told him that she had been well pleased by his compliment.

"You flatter me excessively, Captain."

Her tone told him that she wanted more. He took the hint and fed her another morsel. "That would be impossible, Miss Stewart. My tongue cannot find words adequate to describe your beauty."

He was rewarded for his effort with another dimpled smile.

"I see you are not a man who accepts reproof, Captain Benton." Levinia's small foot peeked out from beneath her skirt to push against the porch floor again. The swing moved gently to and fro. "The evening is pleasant."

So the flirting was over for now. It was time for small talk. "Yes. The cloud cover has cooled things a bit. It will most likely rain tonight—and tomorrow."

"Oh, I hope not tomorrow. I have a lovely new dress to wear to church." A flirtatious, coaxing look came his way. "Shall I see you in church, Captain?"

Sam's face tightened. Church was the last place he wanted to be. But if he were to win Levinia and be accepted within the social elite of St. Louis, he would have to play the part. *Does this amuse You, God?* He pasted a smile on his face. "I will be there, Miss Stewart. Though with you seated in the congregation, it will be hard for me to concentrate on the sermon."

Her small laugh rippled softly on the cool, evening air. "Gracious, Captain, you must desist from paying me so many compliments or you will quite turn my head!" She lifted her gloved hand and toyed with one of the blond curls dangling at her temples. "Mother is very pleased with this new law Father passed to clear our streets of those filthy urchins. She was quite undone the other day when one of them entered Simpson's market. He almost *touched* her gown!"

A delicate shudder. Planned, not real. And another of those feigned coaxing looks. *Does she practice?* He couldn't imagine Miss Randolph acting in such an affected way. He squelched a frown.

"I hope you will arrest them all soon and get them off our streets. They are a most unpleasant sight, and quite ruin a lovely day of shopping."

You are going to jail children because they are alone on the street? Because their parents had the bad fortune to die? Sam shook his head, studied Levinia's face to rid himself of Mary Randolph's voice in his head. "I shall uphold the law to the best of my ability, Miss Stewart."

"Oh, I did not mean to suggest you would do less, Captain. Father says he can always depend on you. He says you will go far." Levinia's pink cheeks dimpled in another smile that did not quite disguise the appraising look in the widened blue eyes. "He says with his guidance and support you may even be mayor of St. Louis one day."

Sam dipped his head to hide his elation. "I am pleased to hear your father thinks well of me." He looked up and locked his gaze with hers. "And may I hope you feel the same, Miss Stewart?"

"Why, Captain—" Light flashed across the dark clouds on the horizon. Thunder rolled in the distance. "Oh!" Levinia placed a hand on her chest and rose from the swing. "I fear your prediction of inclement weather is coming true, Captain Benton." There was another flash of light, a low rumble. "I dislike storms. Forgive me, but I must go inside before the rain begins."

"I insist you do, Miss Stewart. I would not want you to take a chill. Please, allow me to assist you." Sam stepped forward and opened the door for her.

"Thank you, Captain Benton. I shall look forward to seeing you at church tomorrow." She gave him a quick smile and rushed inside. Sam tugged on his hat and trotted down the porch steps.

So the mayor thought he would go far. Maybe even be the mayor of St. Louis someday. Well…maybe he would. A smile split his lips. Levinia would be the perfect wife if he went into politics. And judging from her actions tonight, along with that measuring look she had given him, she was considering that possibility herself.

Rain pattered on his hat, splattered against his shoulders and danced on the hard, dry ground. Sam glanced up at the roiling clouds overhead and frowned. He was in for a good soaking before he reached home. But the courting call he had made on Levinia was worth it. He had found out his plan was going forward even better than he had anticipated.

The wind picked up. Rain pelted his back, plastering his shirt against his skin, but nothing could disturb the warm glow of satisfaction inside him. The only thing that could make this evening better was if he had ridden Attila. He smiled, pulled his hat brim lower and stretched his legs out into a ground-eating lope. Church tomorrow. It seemed God was going to help him achieve his goals after all.

Was that thunder? Mary laid her book aside and crossed to the open window. Black clouds were tumbling across the sky. The ends of the branches of the elm tree in the backyard dipped and swayed in a rising wind. Light glinted across the horizon and her thoughts darted to her sister. She leaned on the windowsill and looked toward the northeast. Sarah was terrified of thunderstorms since she had seen lightning strike her fiancé dead aboard a ship they were sailing.

Mary shuddered and wrapped her arms about herself. If two sailors in a dingy had not spotted the skirt of Sarah's dress caught on a broken-off piece of the ship when she fell in the water, her sister would have drowned. Mary looked up, watched the black clouds filling the sky, shutting off the evening light. *Oh, Sarah, I hope the sun is shining on you in Cincinnati.*

The wind gusted, blowing the skirt of her dressing gown against her legs. Rain slapped against the raised window, coursed down the small panes and flowed off in rivulets. The candle on the washstand beside her bed guttered and died.

Mary shivered and stared out into the dark. How many young children were out there in the storm? Where did they take shelter? *You cannot save them all, Miss Ran-*

dolph. There are too many of them. Captain Benton's words flowed through her mind. They bore a frustrating truth. Doubt assailed her. She brushed the rainwater from the sill with her hand, closed the window and stared out into the stormy night.

Should she request an audience with Mayor Stewart? Or was Captain Benton right? If she was successful in presenting her petition to have this law removed from the city charter, what then? Who would feed, clothe and shelter these young, orphaned children? She had no room in this tiny cottage. And she could not ask Ivy to take in more of them.

The lightning flashed brighter. The thunder rumbled closer, and the rain drummed on the roof over her head. Mary sighed. It was too big a task for her alone. But she would do what she could. Tomorrow she would write and ask her father to increase her allowance. And to allow any more orphaned children she found to sleep in the warehouse. It was not enough, but it was a start. And she *would* call at Mayor Stewart's office on Monday. She could not help a child who was in jail.

Jail.

Her thoughts returned to her confrontation that afternoon with Captain Benton. *If what you say is true, then I shall need help. Would you care to join me?* Mary frowned and unfastened her dressing gown as she crossed to her bed. Anger had pushed her into challenging Captain Benton—but why did she get so angry with him? She knew he was only doing his job. It *was* his duty to uphold the law. And he had been gentle when holding Callie this afternoon, unlike the other policeman. But—

Mary shook her head and hung the damp dressing gown over the back of the desk chair to dry, then kicked off her slippers and crawled under the covers. She arranged her pillow, rested her head on the downy softness and closed her eyes. It did no good. The truth hovered in her heart, waiting to be confessed. She wanted him to be better than that. She wanted him to help the children instead of arresting them. She wanted to admire him.

The admission brought warmth rushing to her cheeks. She was attracted to Captain Samuel Benton, more than she had ever been to any man—including Winston Blackstone. Though why she should be was beyond her understanding. The man made her uncomfortable. Simply being in his presence was…disturbing. And today, when he had looked at her—

Mary snapped her thoughts away from the memory. She did not want to examine too closely how she had felt during that long, uneasy moment. That way led to more hurt. She was well aware of her shortcomings in men's eyes. Especially men like Captain Samuel Benton who courted petite, beautiful blondes like Miss Stewart.

Chapter Nine

Mary adjusted the long wrap that matched her amber, watered-silk gown and walked down the center aisle beside James, looking neither left nor right. Why did he always choose a pew close to the front of the church? She would much prefer to hide in the back, and he knew it.

James stopped beside a pew on their right and Mary slipped in, grateful for the opportunity to sit down. At least now her tallness would be disguised, not that anyone present could have failed to notice it as they had made that long walk! And thank goodness it was still overcast. The cool, stormy weather gave her an excuse to wear the dress with the high collar that hid her thin neck. And its matching bonnet, with the amber silk flowers clustered on both the inside and outside of the wide brim made her face look a little softer, less…angular.

Angular. How she hated that word! But it had stuck in her head ever since she had overheard Winston use it to describe her to Victoria. It was unflattering…but true. Her cheekbones were— No! She would not think of her shortcomings.

Mary frowned and spread her skirt, then again arranged the lavish fabric of the wrap to make herself look a little heavier. It was the best she could do. She fixed her gaze on the pulpit, and by sheer dint of will, held Winston's words at bay. Soon she would have to rise to sing the chosen hymn and everyone would be able to see she was at least two or three inches taller than most of the other ladies assembled. That was enough to have to think about. Oh, why had God made her so—

The organist hit a chord.

Mary set her jaw and joined in the rustle and stir as the congregation rose. She knew the words to the hymn by heart, but her thoughts froze, arrested by the sight of the tall, blond, broad-shouldered man sliding into a pew across the aisle. Her pulse quickened. James was wrong. Samuel Benton did attend church.

She dipped her head to hide her face beneath the brim of her bonnet and watched the captain. He nodded and smiled at someone. She followed his gaze to see the object of his attention and looked straight at the mayor's daughter. The young woman's long lashes fluttered down over her blue eyes and two dimples appeared in her pink cheeks in a coy response to the captain's greeting.

Oh, my! Perfectly done. Mary let out a quiet sigh. The woman had flawless flirting abilities *and* beauty enough to draw any man's eyes—to turn any man's head. She dropped her gaze to the petite blonde's softly rounded shoulders and arms bared for all to see—and for the captain to admire. Not that *that* mattered. It was only the unfairness...

Mary yanked her gaze back to the front of the church, squared her shoulders and mouthed words, the familiar, acrid taste of bitterness in her mouth as she pretended to sing.

* * *

"I am reading today from the book of Isaiah." The pastor's voice rang out into the silence.

Mary sat erect in the pew and turned inward to think her own thoughts. God loved her less than those He blessed with beauty and charm; she did not owe His word her attention.

She rested her hand on the open Bible in her lap and slanted another glance at Samuel Benton. He seemed at ease. But less than attentive. She frowned and tapped the toe of her shoe on the floor beneath the concealing hem of her skirts, the sound deadened by the multiple layers of fabric. Were young, helpless children being arrested and jailed while she sat here in church watching one of their captors stealing secret looks at Miss Stewart? And where had the woman bought that snippet of a hat that showed her blond curls to such advantage? She had never seen one quite like it. She would have to explore the shops of St. Louis this week and see what they had to offer. A hat like that would be a perfect birthday gift for Sarah. It would set off her delicate beauty the same as it did for Miss Stewart.

"'…he hath no form nor comeliness; and when we shall see him, there is no beauty that we should desire him.'"

No beauty? Mary glanced up at the pastor. Who—

"'He is despised and rejected of men; a man of sorrows, and acquainted with grief: and we hid as it were our faces from him—'"

Mary stared, her attention riveted on the words. Why, the pastor could be speaking of the orphaned children. That is exactly the way the people in Simpson's grocer and on Front Street had treated Ben and Callie. They did not care that the children were alone and frightened and half-starved without parents to care for them. They despised and rejected them because they were dirty and unkempt. They would not even look at them. Or else they wanted to *jail* them.

Mary shot a look across the aisle at Samuel Benton. Did he see the similarity? Had he heard the pastor's words? It appeared not. The captain's gaze was fastened on Miss Stewart, not the pastor.

Mary drew in a long, slow breath and blinked her eyes to control a sudden rush of tears. She stared down at her folded hands, the words the pastor had read ringing in her head—*there is no beauty that we should desire him.* She bit down on her lower lip and blinked harder, furious that the words made her want to cry. Why should they? It was not anything new to her. She knew beauty made people desirable to others—and that a lack of beauty brought rejection. She should. Winston had rejected *her* for lack of beauty. That was a grim truth she carried in her heart. Carried and accepted. But…

She lifted her head and looked across the aisle, unable to stop herself, though the sight of the mayor's daughter made the ache in her heart swell. Oh, why had God not loved her enough to make *her* petite and blond and beautiful? Rejection would never happen to Miss Stewart. A woman as lovely as she need never fear that. With her beauty, any man would desire her…as Captain Benton did.

The line of departing people ahead of them was barely crawling forward. *Another* reason she preferred the back of the church—one could exit quickly. And all she wanted was to go home and hide. She refused to cry—no matter how her chest ached. Mary inched ahead, stopped and tapped her foot, finding relief in venting her irritation. Did *everyone* have to shake the pastor's hand?

The short, plump, elderly woman in front of them, who had greeted them earlier, looked back over her shoulder. So did the woman's husband.

Mary pasted on a polite smile and stilled her foot.

James looked at her.

The pressure in her chest increased. They were too close—knew each other too well. She could read the silent "What is wrong?" in his eyes as clearly as if it were written on his forehead. She gave a slight shake of her head, mustered a smile she knew would not fool him and turned away from his close perusal. Her emotions were too raw at the moment for brotherly sympathy. It would break her down.

She stepped a bit to the side to see how close they were to the door and gave a soft sigh of relief. Only two more couples. The young man speaking with the pastor glanced her way and she looked down in maidenly modesty. A ridiculous subterfuge she affected upon such occurrences in order not to see the look of disappointment in the man's eyes when he got a good look at her face or realized her height and slenderness.

The line moved.

Mary stepped closer to James, adjusted her wrap to better cover her shoulders and waited.

The line moved again. The elderly couple spoke to the pastor, shook his hand and stepped through the door. A flash of sky, people drifting down the walk toward the street. *Finally!*

"Greetings, Mr. Randolph. I am so glad you joined us this morning." The pastor beamed a smile at James, then glanced her way. "And is this young lady the sister you spoke of?"

"Yes, she is." James's hand tightened on her elbow and drew her forward. She summoned another polite smile.

"Welcome, Miss Randolph. Thank you for coming to join us on this lackluster day." The pastor shifted his gaze to include James and offered his hand. "I hope you will both come again."

"We shall, Pastor Thornton." James released the pastor's hand and stepped back for her to precede him through the door.

At last! They could go home. The pressure in her chest eased. Mary took a deep breath, drew her wrap more closely about her and looked toward the street. She came to a dead halt, staring at the trio standing near the end of the brick walk. For one foolish moment she considered spinning about and running back inside the church. Instead, she moved forward. *Only nod a greeting and walk on by, James. Please walk on by. Do not make me stand there and be compared to—* He stopped. Had her hand been on his arm, she would have pinched him.

"Good day, Miss Stewart… Captain Benton." James dipped his head. Received a nod from the captain and a dimpled smile from Miss Stewart in return.

"And good day to you, Miss Randolph." Samuel Benton rested his gaze on her briefly, then indicated the young woman standing beside Miss Stewart. "May I present Miss Stewart's cousin, Miss Green."

James bowed. "Your servant, Miss Green."

A farm wagon, with the faint smell of a barnyard about it, rolled to a stop on the road beside them and an older man tipped his hat their direction. "Afternoon, Levinia… Captain. Time to go, Rebecca."

The young woman gave them a friendly smile. "It was nice to make your acquaintance. Please forgive me for rushing off. But we have to hurry to reach home before dark." She turned to the others. "Do you want a ride, Levinia?"

"Gracious no!" There was the slightest crinkling of the small, narrow nose. "You go on, Rebecca. Captain Benton is escorting me home."

"Very well." Rebecca Green moved to the wagon.

James stepped forward and offered her a hand up. She took her seat, smiled and waved. "Good day, all."

"Good day." Mary returned Rebecca's wave and joined James on the walkway.

Levinia Stewart slipped her gloved hand through the captain's arm and dimpled up at him. "Shall we go, Captain Benton?" She turned the smile on James. "So nice to see you again, Mr. Randolph." The residue of the smile came her direction. "And you, Miss Randolph. Good day."

"Good day." Mary returned Miss Stewart's smile in kind.

The captain tossed a nod their direction and the two walked off, with the wagon lumbering its way up the road ahead of them.

Mary glanced up at James. He was staring after them, a bemused expression on his face. She gave a quick tug on his sleeve. "Shall we go home?"

"What? Oh. Yes, of course, Mary."

She turned and started off. He fell into step beside her. "Please try not to look as besotted as the captain, James. I know Levinia Stewart is beautiful, but—"

"Miss *Stewart?*" James looked over at her and shook

his head. "Miss Stewart is pretty enough. But Rebecca Green is beautiful."

Mary gazed up at him, her mouth agape. "Rebecca Green? James, Rebecca Green has *freckles!*"

"I know. I saw them." He grinned. "Did you notice they look darker when she blushes?"

"No. I did not even—" Mary gave him a suspicious glance. "When did she blush?"

"When she put her hand in mine to climb into the wagon."

Mary laughed. "You sound very pleased that you caused that blush."

"I am." He leaned down and pushed open their gate. "I wonder where Miss Green lives. And if she goes to church every Sunday. I think I will ask the captain the next time I see him." He shoved his hands in his pockets and whistled his way up the walk.

Mary stared up at him. Had he lost his mind? How could he think Miss Green lovelier than Miss Stewart? Why, she could point out a dozen flaws that made her less attractive. But it was obvious James meant what he said. She stole another sidelong look at him and shook her head. Absolutely besotted!

"You'll be all right, boy. There's no reason to be afraid." Sam motioned the silent boy into the cell, locked the door and walked away. He had learned that was best. The kid was so scared he could hardly walk or talk, but the others would take care of him. There were four of them in there now. And a girl in the cell beside them. A little girl…seven, maybe eight years old.

The muscles in his face drew so taut his skin hurt. He tossed the ring of keys in the desk drawer, grabbed his hat off the hook beside the door, then went outside and drew in a deep breath of air. Free air. All the prisoners he talked to said the air was not the same when you were locked in a cell. And for the first time, he understood what they meant. When he locked those kids in, they were so frightened they could not breathe right and his own lungs labored to draw in air for them. Air that was stale and thin and unsatisfying.

Sam tugged his hat into place and started down Chestnut Street toward the levee. A steamboat whistle blew news of its arrival. He quickened his steps. Maybe Duffy would be working this boat. Or perhaps there would be a gambler with a bad reputation, or some other unsavory character onboard he could arrest or continue out of town. *Something* that would make him feel like a law officer doing a worthwhile job again, instead of a bully picking on kids. If it were not for his goals…

Mary Randolph's face popped into his head. He gave a low growl. The woman was becoming a major annoyance. She made him feel like a criminal, though he was the one upholding the law. But all the same, he admired her spunk. The way she lifted that small, square chin, ready to defend a child she did not know…. Amusement tugged his scowl into a smile. He had no doubt she would fight *him* if she had to. She was a born she-bear, that one. The thing was—that was one fight he had no real heart to win.

Chapter Ten

"Excuse me, Miss Mary." Edda stood in the doorway, her eyes wide, her hands buried in her apron. "There is a policeman come to see you, *ja?*"

"A *policeman?*"

Edda's head bobbed. *"Ja."*

Captain Benton. "All right. Thank you, Edda. I will be right down." Why would the captain come to see her? Mary frowned, put away her pen, placed the stopper in the ink well and then rose to look in the mirror. As usual, wisps of hair were escaping at her temples and down her neck from the knot on the crown of her head. *Why could she not make them stay in place?* She lifted her hands to tuck them where they belonged, then shrugged and headed for the stairs. What did it matter? The captain was not paying a social call. All the same, she tugged the bodice of her gown more smoothly into place as she walked down the stairs.

"Good afternoon, Ca—" Mary halted, stared at the swarthy policeman standing beside the front door, then moved forward again. "I am Mary Randolph. You wished to speak with me, officer?"

"Yes, Miss Randolph." The policeman whipped off his hat and dipped his head. "Captain Benton sent me to bring you to the jail."

"To the *jail!*" Shock tingled through her.

"Yes, miss. I am to escort you."

"But…"

"And he bids you hurry."

Mary gaped at him, then gathered her wits and shook her head. "Officer, I do not know why the captain sent you to arrest me. But I have done nothing wrong, and I am not go——"

"Oh, no, miss, you have it wrong. I am not here to arrest you. It's about the child."

Relief turned her knees to jelly. She placed her hand against the door frame to brace herself. "The child?"

"Yes, miss. The young girl. She's took sick."

"Oh. I— A moment, officer."

Mary turned and headed for the kitchen. Why had the captain sent for her? She— Did it matter? A child was sick, and she was wasting time. She quickened her steps, pausing at the kitchen doorway. "Ivy, I am going to the jail to see about a sick child. Please explain to James if I am not home in time for dinner."

"The *jail?*" Ivy stared, then shook her head and nodded. "I will tell him."

Mary whirled about and rushed to the front of the house. When the policeman had broken the news to her, had she looked as shocked as Ivy? Her lips twitched. Probably so. She sobered, grabbed her straw hat off the hat tree and settled it on her head. "All right. I am ready, officer."

"Yes, miss."

The policeman opened the door. Mary stepped onto

the porch, grabbed the long, gauzy ties of her hat and knotted them under her chin as she followed the policeman down the steps to the gate.

"Captain Benton is waiting inside, miss." The officer opened the door of the square, one-story, stone building and stepped aside for her to enter.

Mary took a deep breath and stepped into the dim interior. Gray stone walls supporting the room's dingy, plastered ceiling absorbed the light from the two front windows on either side of her. The door behind her clicked shut. Movement drew her eye and her stomach flopped as Samuel Benton rose from his desk chair and strode toward her.

"Thank you for coming, Miss Randolph. I apologize for bringing you here, but—"

"I prefer an explanation to an apology, Captain Benton. Why am I here?" Mary stared up at him, not caring about her rudeness in interrupting him. "I understand there is a sick child. But what do you expect from me?" His face flushed. He was no doubt angered by her tone, but she cared not a fig for Captain Benton's feelings. Any man who would arrest children was not worth polite consideration.

"I had Doc Patterson look at the girl. He says she needs nursing care, and the mayor refuses to—" He stopped and cleared his throat. "I thought perhaps you would be willing to—"

"Volunteer my services as a nurse?" Another flush. Was he embarrassed about the situation? Good! "Where is the child?"

"In a cell in the back. I'll take you to her." He grabbed a ring of keys from a desk drawer. "This way."

"A moment, Captain." It was obvious Samuel Benton was in a quandary. Mary squared her shoulders, looked him straight in the eyes and shamelessly took advantage of his dilemma. "If I nurse the child, it will be on my terms."

He stared down at her a moment, then nodded.

Mary followed him through the doorway on the inside wall and paused, taken aback at the sight of the barred cells that lined both sides of a short, dark corridor. She had never been in such a dismal, cheerless place. A raspy cough from one of the cells started her moving again. She hastened after the captain into the darker region, keeping her hand firmly anchored to her side, though she wanted to clamp it over her nose. A musty, sour smell mingled with the odor of human waste permeated the place. She took shorter breaths and regretted having to breathe at all.

The captain stopped. Keys jingled. Metal scraped against metal. There was a loud click as he unlocked one of the barred doors. "In here, Miss Randolph." He stepped back to allow her room to pass.

The cramped cell received light from a single barred window high in its outside stone wall. Mary swept a quick glance over the interior. A painted stand with a crockery wash bowl on its surface stood beneath the window. A metal pail covered with a wooden plank sat beside it on the slate floor. On either side, their heads jammed against the stone wall, were two narrow cots. In the cot on the right lay a little girl, her thin body barely causing a lump in the striped blanket that covered her.

Mary glanced at the captain, wanting to take the girl and lock *him* up in her place. "What is her name?"

"Katy Turner."

She brushed by him into the cell and knelt beside the

girl's cot. The small, dirt-streaked face was flushed, the eyes closed. "Hello, Katy. My name is Mary, and I have come to take care of you. How do you feel?" She placed her hand on the small forehead. It was hot and dry. The girl's eyes opened at her touch. Tears rushed into the blue eyes bright with fever.

"M-my th-throat hurts." The girl's voice was thick, raspy. The tears overflowed onto her grimy, gaunt cheeks. Cheeks that should be round and pink.

Mary nodded, anger welling until it pushed the breath from her lungs. "You will feel better soon, Katy. I promise." She looked toward the cell entrance. "I shall need your help, Captain Benton." Her voice was as frigid as the girl's forehead was hot.

Samuel Benton's face tightened, but he made no protest, merely stepped to her side.

Mary tucked the blankets around the little girl, then stood, tipped her head back and looked up at him. "I am taking Katy home to care for her, and she will *not* be back, Captain. I will find her a home or she will live with me. Now, as she is too ill to walk, you must carry her for me. Please lift her carefully."

"Miss Randolph—"

"Those are my conditions, Captain." Her voice was quiet, her tone implacable. Mary set her jaw and met Samuel Benton's scrutiny without so much as a flicker of her eyes. Something flashed deep in his. She did not bother to try to define it, merely turned and strode to the door of the cell. Her heart jolted. Across the corridor, six young boys of various sizes, dressed in dirty, tattered clothes, clung to the bars of their cells, staring at her.

There was movement behind her. The captain's footsteps drew near. Mary blinked tears from her eyes, smiled at the boys and hurried down the corridor toward the doorway and freedom, with the faces of those small boys seared into her heart and mind.

Mary's hands shook so she could hardly hold her scissors. She could not remember ever being so angry. Not even when Winston had betrayed her with Victoria.

She cut a hole in the seamed end of her embroidered cotton pillow slip, cut two smaller holes high in the side seams, then grabbed a long piece of ribbon from her dresser drawer and headed toward the dressing room. She paused beside Edda, who was on her knees tucking the ends of a sheet under the pile of folded quilts on the floor beside the end wall of the bedroom. "Is the pallet ready, Edda?"

The housekeeper fluffed a pillow and placed it on top of the sheet. "*Ja.* 'Tis ready, Miss Mary." She spread her short, thick fingers wide and patted the pile. "And 'tis nice and soft, *ja?*"

"It is exactly what I wanted." Mary smiled her appreciation and hurried to the dressing room. "How is Katy doing?"

Ivy looked up. "I think she is feeling some stronger, thanks to that broth she managed to swallow before her bath."

"Good. I have her nightgown ready." Mary looked at the skinny little girl in the tub. Her eyes were closed. "Poor little thing, she looks exhausted. Help me get her out of the tub so I can dry her off and get her into bed." She hung the pillow slip over the edge of the washstand and slipped her hands under Katy's thin arms. Ivy slid hers under the child's skinny legs. Mary nodded and together they lifted the little girl from the tub.

"I—I'm c-cold."

"I know, but you will be warm soon." Mary grabbed a towel, wrapped it around Katy, then went to her knees and began to dry her. "Thank you for your help, Ivy. Please go finish that sage tea concoction now. And be sure to add the honey—it helps to hide the taste of the vinegar." Thank goodness she had helped at her aunt Laina's orphanage. At least she knew what to do for a sore throat.

She finished drying Katy and pulled the pillow slip over the child's damp hair. The little girl shivered. She tied the ribbon around the tiny waist, pulled her close, gave her a quick hug then took her by the hand. "Come along, Katy. Edda prepared a lovely bed for you so you can rest and get better." She led Katy to her bedroom, helped her onto the pallet and tucked a blanket around her fragile, shivering body. Katy's eyes closed.

Mary stood by the bed watching until she was certain the child was asleep, then stepped over to the writing desk they had shoved into the corner to make room for Katy's pallet and took her seat. She pushed aside the letter she had been writing to her sister Sarah when the officer arrived and pulled a clean sheet of paper forward. There was a tiny *clink* as she removed the stopper from the ink well and dipped in the pen.

Katy moaned. Mary glanced down at the sleeping child. Soft, black curls tumbled around the bony face that was flushed with fever. *How could anyone jail such a child?* Mary's spine stiffened. She wiped the tip of the pen against the neck edge of the ink well. She needed help and she knew exactly where to find it. She touched the pen to the paper and began her letter.

Dearest Mother and Father,

"What are you going to do with her when she is well, Mary?" James looked from the child on the pallet to the furniture shoved close together along the walls of the cramped bedroom and shook his head. "She cannot stay here. There simply is no room."

"Shh, she might hear you, James." Mary motioned for him to follow her out of the room. She grasped the banister and started down the narrow stairs, then glanced over her shoulder at him. "There is no need for you to concern yourself over Katy. I have everything planned."

James gave a soft snort. "I have no doubt of that. You are a very resourceful young woman when you want something, Mary Randolph."

She stopped, turned to face him. "I could not leave Katy in jail with no one to tend her, James. And I cannot send her back there when she is well."

"I know that, Mary. And it seems Captain Benton knows it, also."

"He does now!" She gave a little huff and spun around to walk into the parlor.

"What is happening here, Mary?"

"What do you mean?" She walked to the settee and turned to face him.

"I mean you act awfully prickly whenever Captain Benton's name is mentioned." He fastened a brotherly gaze on her. "Do you really dislike the man that much? Or is the opposite true?"

"That is ridiculous!"

"Is it?"

"Yes. It is. And stop smiling."

"All right." He walked over beside her. "What is this plan of yours?"

"Well, Katy will stay here where I can tend to her until she is well. Then she will share Callie's bed at Ivy's house." She sighed. "That takes care of the sleeping arrangements. But it still leaves meals…and clothes…and schooling…" She shoved a strand of hair off her forehead, then smoothed her hands over her hair, which only resulted in more of her wild, dark hair falling free.

"And have you a solution for those, as well?"

She seated herself on the settee and looked up at him. "I believe so. Of course, Ivy cannot afford to provide for the children. And *I* am responsible for bringing them into her life—therefore, they shall take dinner and supper here. And my allowance is sufficient to provide the necessary clothing for them—at least for now. And I will school them while Ivy is cooking our meals."

"And if you save another child?"

She shook her head. "I have no idea what I will do if that happens. I shall have no trouble if, when Father reads my letter, he agrees to increase my allowance. If he does not…well…" She gave a tiny shrug.

James sat in a chair, leaned forward and looked her straight in the eyes. "Mary, you cannot spend every bit of your allowance on these children. You have needs, also."

"Yes, but—"

"There is no 'but,' Mary. I will help. But even with my help… Even if Father does increase your allowance… You will not be able to sustain the expense of three children for long." He took her hand in his. "*Think,* Mary. Children grow. Their needs increase. And if you save another, and another… It will be impossible for us to provide for their needs."

She gave another long sigh. "I know, James. I have thought of nothing else all afternoon. And I know what you say is true. But I cannot turn my face away and pretend I do not see their suffering. I cannot simply leave these children to their fate, which is to be jailed for no reason other than they have no parents to care for them! I cannot do that, James. I cannot!"

She pressed her lips together. Blinked. Blinked again. He squeezed her hand. She looked up at him. "When I was at the jail today, there were six boys—" She lifted her hands and wiped away the tears on her cheeks. "I know I cannot care for all of these children, James. I *know* that. But if you had seen them holding on to those bars and looking out…" She drew her hand from his, rose and then walked over to look out the window. "I shall simply have to think of something."

"Thank you for carrying my packages home for me, Captain."

"My pleasure, Miss Stewart."

She smiled up at him. "I am so glad you happened by Virginia's house as I was leaving. It gives me the chance to tell you how very pleased Father is that you have so quickly rid our streets of the disturbing presence of those filthy urchins. Mother and I are pleased, as well. It was most pleasant shopping today. I did not see *one* of those dirty creatures lurking about."

Sam nodded. "You won't see them from now on. They are afraid to be on the streets in the daytime for fear of being arrested. They come out at night, hoping the darkness will hide them." *Because of him.* He frowned. "And it may be that some of them are ill. A little girl I had in jail is sick. Doc Patterson said she needed care, but your father said there was no money for such expenses."

"Well, of course not. Gracious! That care would be very expensive. And all of Father's plans to improve and beautify St. Louis are costly." Levinia gave a toss of her head, bouncing the golden curls spilling from the back of her bonnet. "And why should the good citizens of St. Louis pay for the care of those disgusting urchins? If they were not so dirty, they would not be sick." She stopped, gasped. "Oh, my! I certainly hope they do not pass on their filthy diseases to the rest of us." She took a step back. "Are you quite well, Captain?"

Did the woman never think of anyone but herself? Sam squelched a bubble of irritation at her total lack of sympathy for the orphaned children's plight. "I enjoy excellent health, Miss Stewart. I would not allow myself the pleasure of your company did I not." The compliment soured on his tongue.

"But if you are around this sick…" She gave a helpless little wave of her hand.

"Girl," Sam supplied, keeping his tone pleasant. "You need not fear, Miss Stewart. The child is no longer at the jail. Miss Randolph has taken her to her home to care for her." The image of Mary Randolph leaning over the child in the jail swam before him. The concern on her face, the kindness in her voice. He pushed it away, bent down and opened the gate to the mayor's house with his free hand.

"Miss Randolph? Who— Oh, I recall her now. She is that tall, thin, *plain* woman we met on the steps of the courthouse last week. And again after church on Sunday." She gave him a coquettish glance from beneath her long lashes.

It was an invitation for him to pay her superior beauty

a compliment. He knew it as surely as if she had spoken it out loud. Annoyance rippled. Something in him turned stubborn. He nodded. "That's right. That is Miss Randolph. Though I don't know as I would call her plain." *Not with those eyes, and that proud little chin.*

Anger flashed across Levinia's face. "You find her attractive, Captain Benton?"

Careful, Sam. He smiled down at her. "You know who I find attractive, Miss Stewart."

She tilted her head and sent another of her dimpled smiles his way.

She hands those smiles out like a reward. His annoyance surged again. Sam scowled. What was wrong with him? "Here we are." He took her elbow, helped her up the steps to the porch, then released her arm and handed her the packages. "Good evening, Miss Stewart."

She gave him a sharp look. He sucked in a draught of night air and pushed his vexation aside. "One could hope that Virginia Weller lived at a greater distance." He forced a smile. "Our walk would have been longer."

"Yes. That would have been pleasant, Captain." She flashed her dimples at him. "Good evening."

Sam opened the door, watched Levinia enter the house, then hurried to slip through the gate toward Chestnut Street, headed for the stables. He needed a ride. A long ride on Attila over the plains outside of town to clear his head and get his thinking straight before he sabotaged his own goals. But all the same…

Mary Randolph, plain? Sam snorted. Not to his way of thinking!

Chapter Eleven

Another steamship whistled its arrival. As a horse trotted down Front Street, Sam glanced over his shoulder, automatically taking note of the rider. A buggy rumbled over the cobblestones and he peered into the night, but it was too dark for him to see its occupants. He didn't recognize the horse or the rig. Probably someone come across the river from Illinoistown on the ferry.

He faced front again as James Randolph tucked the key to the door of the Mississippi and Missouri steamer line office building into his pocket and opened the door. Sam followed Randolph inside and closed the door. The noise of the activity on the levee was reduced to a muffled din by the building's thick, stone walls.

"The ledger is over here." Randolph lit an oil lamp on the table by the window and crossed the room with it, splotches of yellow light bobbing across the plank floor as he walked.

Sam followed him around a table to the high bookkeeper's desk and pushed aside the stool.

"Here are my tallies." Randolph handed him a sheet of

paper covered with neat columns of numbers, then held the lamp so the light fell over the desk.

Sam focused his attention on the figures, shifting his gaze between the company ledger and the paper in his hand. There was a sizable discrepancy between the totals. To the company's deficit, of course. He closed the ledger. "The bookings for passage recorded are certainly less than those you have written down, Mr. Randolph. And they can be easily proven. What about the pelts you have listed? Where are they?"

"In the back room." Randolph headed toward the rear of the office. "I apologize for bringing you here this late at night, Captain Benton. But the pelts are to be shipped to New Orleans tomorrow. Tonight was my only chance to prove my suspicions are correct."

Randolph opened the door to the back room and lifted the lamp high. "Over here." He moved forward and light splashed on bundles of pelts stacked at the end of a long table against the far wall.

Sam strode over to them, put the paper down on the table beside the first stack and began to count. He watched Randolph out of the corner of his eye. The young man was mad as a hungry bear, but handling it well. "You're short, all right."

Randolph nodded. "I figured if Goodwin was the one skimming the profits from the company, he would in some way take advantage of my ignorance of the value of pelts. I would not know the difference in value recorded in the ledger and true value. That is why I kept count of the ones he accepted as payment. And, as I suspected, he has made off with a portion of the pelts. That is another reason I brought you here at this late hour. I believe Goodwin may be leaving town tonight."

Sam studied the young man's face. "Goodwin has likely been stealing company profits for quite a while. Why do you think he is planning to run tonight?"

"Because of this." Randolph picked up the piece of paper on which he had carefully recorded all the transactions of the past week and started back to the front office. "I keep this in the top right drawer of my desk, hidden between two papers in a folder. When I went to get it tonight, it was between the wrong two papers."

An expression of disgust swept over Randolph's face. He closed the door of the back room. "I leave the door to my office ajar, so I can hear and record all the transactions. The hinge squeaked a bit this morning and when I looked up, the opening was a bit narrower. Someone had bumped the door. I believe it was Goodwin."

The young man shook his head and placed the oil lamp back on the table. "He must have seen me writing down information and suspected I was on to him. When I came back tonight to check on the pelts, I saw the list had been moved, which meant he must have searched my desk after I went home for the evening. So I counted the pelts, confirmed my suspicions were correct and set out to find you."

Sam moved to the front door. "It looks as if you have proof enough, Mr. Randolph. Do you want to press charges?"

"Yes."

Sam nodded. "All right. You hold on to that piece of paper—and I will go pay a call on Goodwin. If we get lucky, I may catch him with the pelts." Another steamship whistled news of its departure. He looked in the direction of the levee. "But my guess is—since he learned you now know—he has already left town." He opened the door. The sounds of activity and nighttime revelry poured in.

"I will come with—"

"No." Sam shook his head. "This is my job, Mr. Randolph, and I'll handle it. You have done your part. I'll be in touch." He stepped out into the night and turned north. Goodwin lived on Olive Street. Near the boardinghouse Thomas had stayed in. Sam frowned and hurried his steps, even though he was sure the man had already caught a steamboat out of town.

Mary stooped to feel Katy's forehead. The summer savory herb Ivy had given her seemed to have broken the fever. The little girl felt cooler. And she had stopped moaning and thrashing about in her sleep.

Mary let out a sigh of relief, and stepped over to the window. It was too warm in the bedroom for her comfort, but she did not dare open the window and expose Katy to the cooler air. She glanced back at Katy. The little girl was sleeping soundly. It would be all right to leave her for a few minutes.

Mary snatched up her dressing gown and tugged it on as she went downstairs and out onto the porch. The sounds of St. Louis's revelry drifted to her on the breeze flowing from the river. She lifted the thick, heavy braid off the back of her neck and moved to the steps. It was so late. Why did James not return? And why had he gone back to his office tonight? Had it something to do with his suspicions of Eli Goodwin?

She dropped the braid and placed her hand against the post beside her. Could James be in danger? She glanced up at the star-sprinkled sky. *Please, God, do not let any harm come to James.*

A steamboat whistle blew three short bursts.

Mary jerked her gaze down from the sky. Why had she prayed? It was useless. Her family believed that God loved them, watched over them and answered their prayers. But she was not one of God's favored. Why would He care enough to answer her prayers? Tears filmed her eyes. In spite of her mother's teachings, *her* prayer was simply an ingrained habit, not an exercise of faith.

Footsteps sounded. The gate creaked. Mary started, slipped behind the post and looked toward the street. The dark form took on shape and features. "James!"

Her brother stopped, looking up at the porch. "Mary? What are you doing awake and outside at this late hour?"

She smiled down at him. "Waiting for you to come home. *And* catching a breath of cool air. It is warm upstairs and I did not want to open my bedroom window. I thought a breeze might harm Katy."

He nodded and started up the steps. "How is she doing?"

"Much better." Mary smiled at him as they crossed the porch. "Her fever has broken. And she is sleeping well."

"That is quite an improvement." He opened the door.

"Yes." Mary glanced up at him as she walked into the house. "What has kept you so late, James? Has it something to do with your suspicions of Mr. Goodwin?"

"Yes. I now have enough proof to press charges."

"Those secret records you have been keeping."

James scowled and nodded. "Yes. But Goodwin found them. That is why I had to take care of things tonight. Captain Benton has gone to arrest him—if Goodwin has not left town."

"I see. At least the matter is solved and you can now

turn your full efforts into making the steamer line the best in St. Louis."

"I am not certain it is solved, Mary. I believe Captain Benton thinks there is someone other than Goodwin involved. I could be wrong, of course."

She watched him hang his hat on the tree. "Speaking of Captain Benton, James…"

"Were we?" He glanced down at her and grinned.

She knew immediately he was thinking of their conversation last Saturday evening. She wrinkled her nose at him. "His name was mentioned." Her dressing gown floated around her slippered feet as she moved into the parlor. "I have been thinking about those small boys Captain Benton has in his jail. Their faces are haunting me." She lifted her chin and turned to face him. "I cannot leave them there, James. I have to get that horrid law revoked, then go to the jail and bring them home." Her pose of bravado collapsed. "Will you come with me?"

James shook his head. "I cannot, Mary. With Goodwin gone, I have to stay at the office."

"Oh, of course. I had not thought…" She brushed at her hair and glanced around the small parlor. "If I bring those boys home, I have no idea where they will sleep…"

James stepped closer, draped his arm about her shoulder and squeezed. "You get those boys free, Mary. We will find a way to take care of them."

Chapter Twelve

Mary made a slow pirouette and studied her reflection in the mirror. Today she wanted, *needed* the confidence of looking her best, and she had chosen to wear one of her finest gowns. The light, ecru pongee with cinnamon-colored lace trimming the collar, the puffed sleeves and long, three-tiered skirt flattered her dark hair and eyes. At least, that is what Madam Duval said. And it must be true, for her mother agreed.

Mary turned her back on her image, then picked up the matching gloves of cinnamon lace and pulled them on as she walked out of the dressing room.

Her only regret with her choice of gown was the matching hat. If one could call it that. Mary frowned and lifted her hand to touch the wide band of matching fabric, shirred to stiffness and trimmed with flowers made of the cinnamon lace. The band circled the thick, loose knot of hair at her crown. There were no bows to hide her neck or chin, only the narrow ribbons that slid alongside her coiled hair and tied in the back. And there was no wide brim to hide her face. She glanced at her everyday straw hat hanging on the hat tree, but rejected the idea of wearing it instead of the minute confection. The straw hat would not do today. Elegance suited her purpose.

She sighed and walked to the kitchen. "I am leaving now, Ivy."

Ben slipped off a stool at the table and gaped up at her. "You look pretty as a flower, Miss Mary!"

"Why, thank you, Ben." She laughed, leaned down and gave him a quick hug, then straightened, glanced at Ivy, who had paused from her work of kneading dough, and gave a little shrug. "It is the fancy dress." She looked down, ran a cinnamon-colored lace-gloved hand over her skirt, then glanced back up. "I wanted to tell you, Edda will stay upstairs with Katy. And that I told Callie she must come downstairs soon. I do not want Katy tired. Oh! And please make sure Katy has more of the sage tea concoction every hour for her throat. It does seem to be helping." She tapped the toe of her foot and nibbled at her lip. "I believe that is all. I will return as quickly as possible."

She turned with a swirl of her long skirts and started back through the dining room. "Wish me well!"

A chorus of well wishes from the kitchen and from upstairs followed her to the front of the house. She laughed at Ben's and Callie's exuberance as she stepped out onto the porch, and closed the door. With another swish of her long skirts she turned and hurried down the front steps.

"Good morning."

"Oh!" Mary jolted to a stop and looked up. Her breath caught at the sight of Samuel Benton. She pressed her hand to her chest and stared at him.

He stared back.

Warmth spread through her, heating her cheeks. She had no hat hiding her face. No wonder he was staring!

Her fingers twitched. She wanted to lift her hands to hide her foolish blush, but refused to do anything that might call his attention to it. She could, however, do nothing to hide the deep breath she must take or swoon. She drew in air, expelled it, drew in more. It helped. She was less… shaky. She lowered her hand to her side, wished he would look away and when he did not, lifted her chin. Let him see her plainness! "Did you want something, Captain Benton?" *Good!* Her voice was steady.

The captain nodded, then cleared his throat. "I had to speak with your brother this morning. I was on my way back to the jail and thought I would stop by and see how Katy Turner is doing."

"How *Katy* is doing?"

"Yes." The blue eyes looking down at her darkened. "In spite of your poor opinion of me, I am not a monster who hates children, Miss Randolph. I am a policeman doing his job. If I did not care about Katy Turner, I would not have sent for you when the doctor said she needed care."

Embarrassment sent the heat flowing into her cheeks again. And, once again, she refused to hide the flush. She deserved his poor opinion. "You are right, of course, Captain Benton. Please forgive me. I am grateful you sent for me when Katy became ill, and I hope you will do the same for any other children you may find in the same condition." She mustered a smile, then moved forward when he turned toward the street. "Katy is doing much better. Her fever broke last evening, and her throat is much less raspy and sore this morning. We have been giving her sage tea with honey and vinegar."

The gate squeaked. She looked down, uncertain as to

what she should do. But he was holding it open for her. She smiled her thanks and stepped through.

"Which way?"

"I beg your pardon?" She looked up, but looked down again. The directness of his gaze was disconcerting. It was no wonder she felt discomposed! She reached up to pull the brim of her bonnet farther forward to hide her face, then remembered her hat had no brim. She brushed an imaginary hair off her temple and lowered her hand.

"Which way are you going? Toward the levee?"

Gracious, he had a deep voice! "No. I am going to the courthouse. To pay a call on Mayor Stewart." She shot a quick glance at him to see how he took that news. He merely nodded.

"I am headed that direction, if you would accept my escort?"

Poor man, trapped into offering because of good manners. And she could not refuse for the same reason. "That is most kind of you, Captain, thank you."

They walked the short distance to the corner and turned uphill. A slight breeze played with the dangling ends of the thin ribbon bow that held her hat in place. The sun warmed her back. She sighed, grateful that her features were now in the shade.

"Are you becoming accustomed to St. Louis, Miss Randolph? To the clamor and din of the steamboats and levee? To the sight of Indians and mountain men roaming the streets?"

There was a smile in his voice. Mary met his gaze. The memory of that moment when she had seen her first Indian and crowded close to him for his protection flashed between them. And then she remembered Ben, who she had also met that day, and looked away. "I am indeed,

Captain Benton. I no longer jump every time a steamboat blows its whistle. And I am no longer wary of going shopping without escort. But I despair that I shall ever become accustomed to the sight of the Indians."

He chuckled, and the sound seemed to bounce around in her stomach, causing it to quiver and tighten. She took a breath to ease the sensation. "You said you had to speak with James this morning. Were you successful in arresting Mr. Goodwin?"

"You know of that?" He took her elbow. "We cross here. Mind the step down." He waited for a passing wagon, then guided her at an angle to the other corner. "I'm afraid Goodwin escaped. When I got to his boardinghouse, he was already gone. I made some inquiries on the levee and found he had taken passage on a steamboat headed downriver. There's no telling where he'll go from there. To join Thomas, likely."

She looked up at him. "The former manager of the line?"

He nodded, took her elbow again and guided her onto the brick path that led to the courthouse. "That's right. I figure they had to be working together. Otherwise Thomas would have turned Goodwin over to me, same as your brother did."

They reached the courthouse steps and he offered his arm. She stared at it, remembering the image of the petite Miss Stewart clinging to it. Comparing that to her own tall self soured her stomach. But there was no help for it. She slipped her hand through and rested it on his forearm, aware of the firm, muscular strength of it as they began to climb.

"I have come to know your brother quite well since you arrived in St. Louis. He's a fine man."

"On that we agree, Captain Benton." She drew her hand from his arm as they reached the portico and forced a smile. "Thank you for escorting me, Captain. I am grateful for your kindness."

He gazed down at her, and the heat crawled into her cheeks again. She had not meant it to sound like a dismissal. He crossed to the double doors, opened one and gave a polite little bow. "My pleasure, Miss Randolph. The mayor's office is the first door on the right."

"We have no money for an orphanage, Miss Randolph, and I will not have those *urchins* roaming our city, stealing from our shopkeepers and cluttering up our streets with their dirty, unkempt presence! They are offensive to our finer citizens!"

Finer citizens? Mary took a breath, held it, then slowly released it. Clearly appeals to the mayor's conscience would not work. Perhaps he would be moved by financial considerations? "Mayor Stewart, when these *children* are arrested and jailed, the city must provide them with meals and a place to sleep—the same as would be done in an orphanage. Surely there is a building available to the city where—"

"*Miss* Randolph—" The mayor's palms slapped against the top of his desk. He rose to his feet. "I have tried to be patient, but my patience is at an end. In an orphanage, the city would have to pay people to care for these urchins. In jail there are already keepers to—"

"*Jailers,* Mr. Mayor."

The man's face flushed an angry red. "Those ragamuffins stay in jail! As for meals and a place to sleep—they will *earn* their keep. There are jobs they can do on the additions to the courthouse, and on the public school we are to begin constructing."

Mary shot to her feet and looked him straight in the eyes. "And did your daughter help construct the private academy she attended, Mr. Mayor?" The words flowed from her mouth sweet as honey.

The mayor's eyes narrowed. He rested his palms on his desktop and leaned toward her. "You have a bold, sharp tongue, young woman."

"Better a bold, sharp tongue than no heart, sir! Good day!"

Mary whirled about, took two steps and faltered at the sight of Captain Benton standing beside the open door. She raised her chin, her back ramrod straight, and marched on. When she reached the door, she shot him a glance that told him what she thought of men who would treat helpless children in such a fashion and stormed out into the corridor.

"Miss Randolph, wait!"

She turned, her entire body quivering with anger, and watched him walk to her. "You might have warned me of the mayor's plans to make laborers of the children, Captain. You might have warned me that my visit to his office would be futile."

His face flushed. But his gaze held steady on hers. "I did not know the purpose of your visit, Miss Randolph, or I *would* have told you. And I heard of his plans to use the children as laborers the same time as you, when I stepped in that office minutes ago. The mayor does not inform me of his plans."

"I see." Sadness swept over her. Unreasonable, unwelcome sadness. She believed him, but it made no difference. "Well, you know now, Captain. What are you going to do about it?"

She pivoted and walked to the front doors. And this time she did not look back.

Mary moved about the store, anger driving her steps. She may not be able to get those boys out of jail at the moment, but she could do something to make their lives a little brighter until she could think of a way. How anyone could be as heartless as the mayor when it came to children was beyond her. And Captain Benton was little better!

She frowned, picked up a ball, turning it in her hand. That would not be a good choice, as the cell was far too small to allow for throwing a ball. And if it rolled out of the cell, who would retrieve it for the boys? She put the ball down and moved on.

To be fair, the captain *had* sent for her when Katy took sick. But he should not have jailed her in the first place! Of course, if Katy had been on her own on the streets, what would have happened to her when she became ill? She would have had no care.

Mary paused. How many other children on the streets were sick or injured in some way? The possibility of their suffering made her ill. And angrier. There had to be some way to provide a home for those children! And she would find it.

She glanced at the shelves in front of her. Smiled at the sight of a gaily painted kaleidoscope. That would be perfect. If it were light enough for them to see through it. It had been so dark and dank in that cell! She put the toy in her basket, added another for the children at home and moved on. What else? She needed six toys. One for each of those boys, so they could be busy, have something to do. Tops!

Mary added two of the wooden toys to the basket and wandered over to another table. A game of checkers caught her eye. That would entertain two of the boys at once. She picked up the wooden box and a smile touched her face. She and James often challenged each other at checkers. Sarah was not as much fun to play with. She was not as competitive. What else? Jackstraws! Yes, they would do well. And perhaps one of those wooden cup-and-ball games. And paper dolls for Callie. There were several to choose from. She made her selections and went to the counter.

Sam sat deep in the saddle, the wind blowing in his face, the thunder of Attila's hoofbeats in his ears. The chestnut loved to run and Sam gave him his head, exalting in the power and strength of the horse's legs beneath him.

He needed this. He needed this wild gallop out here on the open plain to clear his head. He needed time alone. Only he and Attila…running.

Sam's face went taut. He leaned forward, patting the thrusting neck. "Ease up now, boy. Ease up."

The chestnut slowed. Sam held him to a canter and rode on trying to escape his own thoughts…his conscience…the memory of Mary Randolph's accusing eyes. Those *eyes!*

Sam glanced to his left. The sun was hanging low in the western sky. He reined Attila into a big sweep toward the right, and headed back toward town.

What *was* he going to do? Why did Simon Stewart have to come up with this scheme for using these kids for free labor? It was…it was *wrong*. Plain wrong. And there was no way to put a good face on it. What kind of life was that for kids? Up in the morning, marched to a job— And what sort of job would it be? Picking up rocks? Sifting sand? What? Then marched back to their cells, fed a supper of scraps from the restaurant—half of it not fit to be eaten—and then laying down their hurting bodies on hard cots and sleeping behind locked, barred doors until the morning when it would start all over again?

Sam swept his gaze over the waving grasses on the plain, on the band of trees he was approaching. He was free to go where he wanted—but not those kids. They were locked up in cold, dark cells away from the sunlight and fresh air. And they had done nothing wrong. Nothing to deserve such treatment. It was all because they had no parents. No one to care about them.

No one but Mary Randolph.

She had brought them toys. Things to make their days a little brighter. And what a fighter, that woman! A smile tugged at his lips. Taking on the mayor of a city to fight for kids she didn't even know. The smile died unborn. Sam stared into the distance—saw the past. What would his life have been like if there had been someone like Mary Randolph to care enough to fight for him? And what of Daniel? Maybe Daniel would have lived if there had been someone like Mary Randolph to take him into her home and nurse him when he was so sick.

Sam's stomach knotted. He yanked his thoughts from that path. That was a dangerous, *costly* road to travel down. The past was dead. There was no help for the boy he had been, but there was plenty of help for the man he was determined to become. Help from the mayor and Levinia, to achieve all he'd dreamed of. He tried to summon her face but Mary Randolph stayed stubbornly in his thoughts.

She was a pretty woman. He had known that from the first time he saw her laugh, but he hadn't realized *how* pretty until today, when she came hurrying out of her house with her brown eyes sparkling, her lips curved in laughter and her dark hair shining in the sun. It was the first time he'd seen her without a bonnet. She was beautiful. And when she smiled…

Sam blew a long breath of air into the twilight and shook his head. He'd had all he could do to stop staring at her. And when she had taken his arm… She sure fit well at his side.

He scowled, turned Attila onto the path toward town and slowed him to a walk. He had no business thinking about Mary Randolph. He was going to marry Levinia Stewart—even if she seemed less admirable than he had thought. He could be wrong about her. But even if he wasn't, he was not going to give up his plans. All he needed was the deed to the land he wanted for his house. Then he would ask for her hand.

But what about those kids?

Sam reined in the horse at the stables and dismounted. He pulled open the door and led Attila inside, the comfortable sound of the horse's hooves thudding against the puncheon floor easing his tension. He undid the cinch strap, reached for the saddle and froze.

He narrowed his eyes and absently scratched under Attila's mane, examining the idea that had popped into his head from all sides. The argument might hold water. Maybe there *was* a way to help those kids.

Chapter Thirteen

Sam closed the door and turned to face the portly man behind the desk. "Thank you for seeing me, Mr. Mayor."

"Not at all, Captain Benton." The mayor waved him toward a chair. "What is this meeting about?"

"These street children." Sam winced inwardly as the mayor's eyes narrowed. If this cost him—

"What about them?"

"Well, sir. They present a problem I did not, at first, anticipate."

"And that problem is?"

"Sickness." Sam removed his hat and took a seat. "It has been worrying at me ever since Ka—the girl took ill a few days ago."

"She's worse?" A scowl darkened the mayor's face. "You told me you would handle the problem, Captain."

"I did, sir. When you refused money for the nursing care the doctor ordered, I had Miss Randolph brought to the jail. She is nursing the girl." No need to tell him that he had allowed Mary Randolph to take the girl home.

The mayor's scowl deepened. "You would do well to

keep that woman away from the jail, Captain. She is a busybody! Now, what is the problem?"

A *busybody?* Because she helped the children? Sam frowned. "Quarantine."

"What?" The mayor jerked forward in his chair. "The jail is under *quarantine?"*

That had got his attention. Sam shook his head. "No, sir, it is not. But I have been pondering what would happen if one of the street children we arrest has some sickness that would bring that about. Consider what would happen if the jail, and my men and myself, were all placed under quarantine."

"Unthinkable!" The mayor stared down at his desk. His short, fat fingers drummed against the smooth mahogany surface. "That would be an impossible situation."

Sam held his silence, let the mayor's imagination picture the situation and the resulting chaos in the city. The man lifted his head, looking at him.

"That cannot be allowed to happen, Captain."

"I agree, sir. That is why I came to you." Sam tightened his grip on his hat. "The city must open an orphanage to house the children. There is a building on Spruce Street—"

"Nonsense! An orphanage costs money!" The mayor rose and strode to a window to look outside. "There are more roads to be paved. The city water works must be completed. And the courthouse is to be expanded. And the park." He pivoted, paced back to his chair. "These are the things the finer citizens of this city expect me to provide for them, Captain. Not an orphanage for the children of emigrants who die on their way west."

Sam's face tightened. It was becoming harder and harder to hold his tongue. To swallow the mayor's callous attitude. He drew a calming breath. "They also expect police to protect them from the wild and unsavory elements of this town, Mr. Mayor. And if the jail were under quarantine, that service would be halted. The boatmen and mountain men would make the levee unsafe."

"I am aware of that, Captain Benton!"

"Then, sir, you agree the children must—"

"Do not speak to me again of an orphanage, Captain! I will not be known to the fine citizens of St. Louis as the mayor who wasted their money!"

Wasted? Sam's hand clenched. His hat brim curled beneath his fingers. "Then what is your solution, sir?" The question came out sharper than he intended.

The mayor narrowed his eyes. "Do I detect a spirit of insubordination, Captain?"

"Only concern, sir." Sam rose and clapped on his hat, using the time to get his temper under control. "I am concerned that this practice of housing these street children in the jail may one day interfere with my ability to perform my job."

"I see. Well, concern yourself no more, Captain Benton." The mayor leaned back and smiled. "There is a simple solution that will prevent such a scenario as you present from ever happening. From this time on, you and your men shall not arrest any child that shows signs of sickness."

Mary wielded the eraser, then chalked different numbers on the slate she had bought that morning. A lock of hair fell onto her forehead. She brushed the hair back, held the slate up for the children to see and smiled encouragement. "Three plus three equals…"

Ben scowled.

Callie looked down, her lips moving silently as she pressed the tips of her small fingers one at a time on the table. Her right hand shot into the air. "I know, Miss Mary."

Ben's scowl deepened. "That's 'cause you cheated."

"Did not!"

"Did to! Countin' on your fingers is cheatin'. Ain't it, Miss Mary?"

"*Is it not.* We do not say 'ain't,' Ben." Mary looked across the table at Ben and Callie and struggled to keep a smile from her face. It had been such a short time since she had rescued them, silent and afraid, from the streets, and already they acted like brother and sister. "And we do not argue, children. It is impolite and—"

She stopped. Listened—heard Edda going to answer the knock on the door—and returned to her work with the children. "Callie, I know it is easier to count on your fingers—" Her pulse stuttered. Was that Captain Benton's voice? She chided herself for her foolishness and focused her thoughts back on the business at hand. "But it is better if you memorize the answers to—" She glanced up as the maid came to stand in the dining-room doorway. "Yes, Edda?"

"Captain Benton to see you, miss."

Her foolish pulse stuttered again. Picked up speed. "Thank you, Edda." She put down the slate, then ran her hands over her hair. "I will be right back, children. You think about the answer to the problem while I am gone."

She hurried to the front door, paused to collect herself and then opened the door. Samuel Benton stood on the porch, his big hands resting on the shoulders of the small boy who stood in front of him. She swept her gaze from the boy's frightened, grimy face, to his scratched and dirty hands, over his ripped overalls and shirt to his dirty feet. Another arrest. Her anger flared. She looked up at the captain.

He gave a slight nod. "Forgive my intrusion, Miss Randolph. I don't mean to disturb you. But I think this boy may be ill."

"Oh." Concern overrode her anger. Mary leaned down and peered into the boy's blue eyes. They were shimmering with unshed tears, but clear. She smiled. "I am going to feel your forehead for fever, young man. All right?" She stretched out her hand.

The boy jerked his head back and glared defiance at her. "I ain't sick!"

The captain's hands tightened on the boy's scrawny shoulders. "Miss Randolph is only trying to help you. Let her feel your forehead, son."

Son? Mary shot her gaze to Samuel Benton's face. He looked…different. She pulled her thoughts back to the boy, slipped her hand under the matted lock of hair hanging down over his grimy forehead. It felt normal. She saw no sign of illness. "Captain, I do not know why you believe—"

"I know my bringing the boy to you is an imposition, Miss Randolph. And I apologize for it."

She glanced up, shocked by his interruption. She had never known the captain to be rude. Obstinate and heartless, but not rude.

"I had a meeting with the mayor this morning—about the possibility of an epidemic at the jail that would result in a quarantine."

"A quarantine!" Mary shot up straight. Stared at him. "But that's…that's…" *Ingenious.* Why had she not thought to use that argument? And why was he telling her about his meeting? Did he think she cared if his jail were shut down? She would rejoice!

"Yes. A terrible possibility." He shook his head. "As you can imagine, that would be an impossible situation for the city." He stared straight down into her eyes.

Something in her stirred—went on alert. He was telling her this for a reason. "Yes. Impossible." She struggled to follow. Where was this leading?

"Because of that possibility, the mayor decreed my men and I are *not* to arrest any children that may be sick. However, I am no judge of such things. So I brought the boy to you."

"Oh. *Oh!*" Understanding flashed between them. A smile birthed in Mary's heart, rose to her lips and eyes. She could have hugged the man! She leaned down and touched the boy's forehead again. "I do not believe the boy has a fever, Captain Benton. But his eyes *are* unnaturally bright." She straightened again, looked full into Samuel Benton's eyes. "Perhaps it would be best if you leave him here with me—in case." Something flickered in his eyes. Relief?

"Perhaps that would be best, Miss Randolph. With your permission I will take him inside."

The boy leaned back, dug in his heels. "I ain't goin' in there!"

Samuel Benton turned the boy around, held his skinny upper arms and then squatted on his heels in front of him. "Listen to me, son. It is this, or jail. Do you want to be locked in a cell?"

Mary stared at the captain, at the look of concern and compassion on his face—the firm but gentle way he held the boy as he talked with him—and her heart got caught in her throat. What had happened to the cold, heartless policeman that did his job without regard to its consequences?

The captain looked up. Their gazes met. And held.

The boy stirred.

The captain cleared his throat and rose. "The boy is ready to go in now."

Mary nodded and stepped aside—fought to regain her equilibrium as the captain herded the boy into the small entrance hall.

"The answer is six, Miss Mary. Three plus three is *six!*" Ben came running, slate in his hand, Callie on his heels. Both children came to a dead halt when they saw the captain…backed up a step…then another.

Mary stepped forward and placed her hand on the new boy's thin, bony shoulder. His wiry body tensed at her touch. "Ben, would you and Callie please take this young man to the kitchen and ask Ivy to feed him? I will be along in a minute."

Ben shot a wary glance at the captain, then nodded. "Sure, Miss Mary." He motioned to the boy. "C'mon. Ivy's making cookies." He headed toward the kitchen. The boy stole a glance at the door, glanced up at the captain, then followed after Ben. Callie trailed off in their wake.

Silence fell.

Mary glanced at the captain. He was looking at her. She dropped her gaze and smoothed at her skirt feeling crowded and knowing it was foolish. How could a room get smaller? "Thank you for bringing the boy to me, Captain." She made herself look at him and noticed he had removed his hat. "I will take good care of him."

"I know that." His voice was soft, low-pitched. His gaze held hers. "I've seen—Ben, is it?—carrying grocery baskets for the customers at Simpson's store." He shook his head. "Whoever would have thought such a thing would come about. I hardly recognized him, he looks so happy and well."

"Ben is a very proud little boy and wanted to earn his keep. We let him think he is doing that." She glanced toward the kitchen, then drew her gaze back to Samuel Benton. "It was James's idea that he work for Mr. Simpson." A smile played at her lips. "I thought it was poetic justice."

He chuckled, and her stomach did that funny little flutter.

"It's good for a boy to feel he's helping out. From what I see, Ben looks pretty busy. Maybe this new boy can carry groceries at Simpson's, too."

So she was right. He had brought her the boy instead of arresting him. And he intended the boy would stay in her care. Happiness bubbled. She tamped it down. What had brought about this change in him? Was it real?

The captain slid his hat around in his hand, glancing around. "Where is Katy? Is she doing well?"

Mary nodded, as she brushed at her hair. "Katy is much better. But she still needs rest. She is upstairs napping." She glanced up. He was staring at her again. She stiffened. "Is something wrong?"

He shook his head, reached toward her hair, then drew his hand back and made an awkward little gesture. "Chalk."

Oh, no! Mary turned her hands palms up. The finger and thumb of her right hand were covered with the white powder. *That* would never happen to the elegant and beautiful Miss Stewart. But what did it matter? The captain was here on business. She brushed her hands together and forced a laugh. "We were having school."

He nodded. "I saw the slate in Ben's hand." He took a step toward the door. "Well… I have to get back to my patrol. Thank you for taking the boy, Miss Randolph. Good afternoon."

She pressed back against the wall to let him pass. "Good afternoon, Captain Benton." She watched him tug his hat on and walk down the porch steps, then closed the door, squared her shoulders and headed for the kitchen ignoring the wobble in her legs. She had a young boy to take care of.

Now what did the mayor want? Why had he sent for him this time? What couldn't wait until morning? Sam climbed the steps to the Stewarts' porch, knocked on the door and stepped back as it opened.

"Captain Benton, how nice to see you again. It has been awhile." Levinia stepped out onto the porch, dimpled up at him. "I have been waiting for you. I am afraid Father had to leave suddenly."

"The mayor is gone?"

"Yes." She pouted up at him. "Are you not going to greet me, Captain?"

"Yes, of course, Miss Stewart. Forgive my bad manners." He made her a slight bow.

She smiled up at him. "You are forgiven." She drifted toward the railing, glanced up at the sky. "What a lovely evening."

Sam braced himself. He was beginning to recognize Levinia's smiles. This one meant she was after something. No doubt another compliment. He was beginning to tire of the demand. The woman's vanity was never sated. He searched around in his head and mustered something appropriate. "The beauty of the evening cannot compare to your loveliness, Miss Stewart."

"You flatter me, Captain." Another dimpled smile, followed by a pretty little pout. "But you seem...quiet. Father said you had a little disagreement this morning. Is it troubling you?"

Ah! So *that* was what she was after. The mayor had set Levinia to bring him to his knees. And arranged this meeting to bring that about, no doubt. Was the man inside waiting to hear if Levinia made him change his mind? "Disagreement?" Sam reached up and adjusted his hat to hide his irritation at being "handled."

"Why, yes." A wide-eyed look of innocence. "That is what Father called it. He felt you were...annoyed... with his refusal to spend city funds on an orphanage for those horrible street urchins. Naturally, he is upset by your stance." She moved back to stand close to him. "He thinks so highly of you, and feels he could help groom you to take his place as mayor when he leaves office."

Was that a threat? Sam looked down at Levinia, tried to discern what was behind her smile.

"Now truly, Captain—" This time the dimpled smile was accompanied by a slight pressure on his arm from her dainty hand. "Do you not agree the money would be better spent in completing the water works for the comfort of St. Louis's finer citizens, and building a lovely new courthouse with a beautiful park where..." a demure lowering of her eyes "...a lady and her *beau* could stroll and enjoy each other's company?" She lifted a coy gaze to him. "Or perhaps attend outdoor concerts together? And even plays?" A long sigh. "I would so enjoy such evenings."

She seemed so guileless. Could he be wrong about her intentions? Perhaps her lack of concern for the children was because she heard only her father's opinion of the situation. "I'm afraid the pleasure of such an evening would be marred for me by the knowledge of the children who would be sitting in jail weary and sore from being forced to work on those public buildings and parks."

Anger flashed across her face, quickly hidden by a flirtatious smile. But not quickly enough. He had been right. Her purpose for the tantalizing promises was to bring him into agreement with her father. Though perhaps that wasn't her only purpose. An odd stillness came over him. Sam tried to close his mind, to reject the thought, but it persisted. Perhaps Levinia was grooming him into what she considered to be a worthy husband for her. Perhaps she didn't consider him good enough as he was.

"How can you feel thus, Captain? Those lowborn urchins are accustomed to working for their food. After all, they are the spawn of the filthy poor who swarm into our city from those horrible wagon trains." Her voice coaxed, cajoled. "Why, you would be doing them a favor by arresting them. A bed in jail would no doubt be a *luxury* to them. And at least they would be under a roof that does not leak."

The words speared straight into his memories. Sam clenched his jaw so tight the muscles along it throbbed. He had spent many a night cold and shivering in a bed soaked with rain or covered with snow. But at least the bed had been *his,* and he had been free to leave it whenever he chose. He took a breath, reminded himself it could be she simply did not understand. "The children would have the same sound roof over them in an orphanage, Miss Stewart. And in an orphanage they would not be forced to perform hard labor. Nor would they be under lock and key. They would be free to go outside into the sunshine and fresh air."

She looked up, shaking her curls in a sad little way. "I believe you err in your loyalties, Captain. An orphanage would be a tremendous drain on the city's coffers. And what of the children of the better citizens who may have to give up a park to fund such an institution?" She dimpled up at him, though he noted that it looked slightly forced. "Do you not agree you would do well to save your sympathy for those who are worthy of it?"

Worthy. There it was, bald and bare. Insults, slights, sneers from his childhood flooded his head. Sam stared down at Levinia, and for the first time, he fully and truly saw beyond her surface beauty to the utter selfishness and meanness of her nature that mirrored her father's. He felt a chasm opening between them that he was not sure he could bridge.

"I do indeed, Miss Stewart." The ambiguous answer was the best he could offer, but it was clear it only angered her further. There was a sudden glitter in her eyes, a straight, hard-pressed line where her coaxing pout had thrust her lip outward.

She removed her hand from his arm and stepped to the door. "Perhaps you need to think the situation over, Captain. I am certain, when you have done so, you will reconsider your position concerning these urchins. When you have, I will be pleased to have you call on me again. Good evening." She opened the door and went inside without a backward look.

Sam strode across the porch and down the steps, Levinia's threats ringing in his ears, anger percolating. She had made herself clear. Either agree and support her father's plans or lose her father's backing for his political future, and his chance to win her hand. He had to choose. The Stewarts or the orphans.

Sam sucked in a deep breath of the cool evening air and stepped through the gate. Why had this situation with the orphans arisen, anyway? It made him see truths he did not want to see. Now he was forced to make a decision he did not want to make.

He traveled down the road toward the jail, the sound of his footsteps echoing in his head, dissolving into the night. He was so close to attaining all he had dreamed of. To achieving the purpose that had kept him alive and fighting through all the shame and degradation and poverty and hardship of his childhood—to fulfilling the vow he had made all those years ago. How could he throw away his goals he had worked toward all these years? How could he give them up now that they were within his reach?

How could he not?

The thought brought him to a dead halt. What had he become? Was he a man willing to sell his conscience to pay for his dreams? Sam clenched his hands at his sides, fought the inner stirring, the awakening of truth that made the wall he had so carefully erected around his heart crumble into useless rubble. His face tightened. He stared up at the darkening sky, the knots in his stomach as hard as the clenched fists at his sides, the pain, the longing for love and acceptance that had become the driving purpose of his heart bared. Anger ripped through him. *Why now, God? Why now?*

Mary tiptoed across the bedroom and opened the window. Katy was so much improved, surely the night air would not harm her. A breeze flowed in the window, warm, and so slight she could barely feel it on her bare arms.

She sighed and tiptoed back to bed. There was little hope the room would cool off, but at least the air was fresh. She plumped her pillow and rested against it, then pulled up the long skirt of her nightgown to her knees and wiggled her bare toes. Did Levinia Stewart perspire? Probably not. She seemed impervious to the heat. At least, she had looked cool enough that day on the courthouse portico.

A mosquito buzzed around her ear. She swatted it away and reached for the bed curtains, then remembered Katy. She could not let the little girl be eaten alive so she could have fresh air. She slipped back out of bed and hurried over to close the window. The corner of the roof of the small shed out back caught her eye. What was in there? Could it be cleaned out and made suitable to sleep the boys? She would look tomorrow.

Ben had pleaded with Ivy to let the new boy, Will, come home with him and sleep on a pallet on the floor in his room. But if the captain brought another child… And she was quite certain he would. Gracious, that was clever of him to bring up a possible quarantine! And then, when that…that *heartless* mayor declared they simply were not to arrest any sick children, to use the declaration to keep the children out of jail….

He had looked so different—so tender and caring while reasoning with Will—talking him into staying with her. Anger spurted through her. Why did he have to do that? It was easier to deny her…her *attraction* to him, when she believed him heartless. But when he had squatted down and taken hold of Will's arms, the look on his face…

Oh, how had this happened? She did not even like the man! Mary wrapped her arms about her chest, holding in the hurt. Yes. Yes, she did. That was the problem. There was no use denying it. She had been attracted to him before he had been concerned over Katy. Before he had brought Will to her. She had been attracted to him from the moment he had grinned and took hold of her shopping basket that first day. But now…now she *liked* him. What a fool she was, to allow herself to become attracted to a man like Samuel Benton. A man who courted a beautiful woman like Levinia Stewart.

Mary wiped a spate of tears from her cheeks, crossed the room and climbed back into bed. She had tried not to care about the captain. She had truly tried. But it seemed her heart had a mind of its own.

Chapter Fourteen

"Oh, James!" Mary clutched the letter in her hand to her chest, jumped out of her chair and whirled about the room, the long skirt of her blue gown ballooning out around her. "Father says he will not increase my allowance, but he will send an *equal* allowance for the support of the children! Oh, how wonderful! Now I shall have *double* the funds to spend on them."

James laughed and shook his head. "I do not believe that was Father's intent, Mary."

She stopped whirling and dropped back into her chair. "I know, but they have so many needs and I want for nothing. Oh, my. Only think, James! I shall be able to buy new shoes for Will—he does not say so, but I know his are too small and hurt his feet. And another dress and nightclothes each for Callie and Katy. And Ben needs a new shirt. And they *all* must have good clothes to wear to church. And then, of course, more school supplies. I shall go shopping tomorrow!"

She looked over at him. "But I do not mean to ignore your news. What do Mother and Father say in your letter? I mean beyond Mother's avowal to pray and their declarations of love. Did you tell them of your growing interest in Rebecca Green?"

"I mentioned it…casually."

She wrinkled her nose at him. "That will not fool Mother. She will know you are more than 'casually' interested in Miss Green."

"I know." He shot her a suspicious look. "Have you mentioned my interest in Miss Green in your letters home?"

She laughed and leaned back in her chair. "I may have *casually* mentioned that I spend quite a few evenings home alone when you call on Miss Green."

"Mary…"

"It is only the truth, James." She waved her hand toward the letter he held. "What does Father have to say?"

He gave her a last exasperated look and glanced down at the letter. "He speaks about business, of course. He agrees with my opinion that it would be more profitable to scrap the *Journey's End*—" He glanced over at her. "That is one of our steamboats. An old stern-wheeler that is small and in very poor condition. Stern-wheelers are harder to maneuver, and her small size is not conducive to high profits per run. So, as I was saying, Father agrees it would be more profitable to scrap the *Journey's End* and build a new, large and luxurious side-wheeler, rather than to invest money in repairs. I estimate a new ship such as I envision will pay for herself in four runs."

"You did not tell me of that, James." She pursed her lips, nodded her head. "It sounds very sensible. You are turning into quite the businessman. You are certainly learning about steamboats. *And* you caught the man who was stealing the profits from the line—though he escaped the law. Wait until Father and Mother learn of that! They will be even more proud of you—as am I. Truly." She smiled at him. "You will have this line turned around and making huge profits in no time."

He laughed and tapped his letter. "I had better. That is what Father sent me here to do. And speaking of profits... I need your help, Mary."

"*My* help? Whatever for?"

"The line has been so neglected, we have to do something to improve our reputation. You have excellent taste, and I want your advice on decorating the main hall and passenger cabins of this new luxury steamboat I picture. I want this steamer to be the very best boat on the river!" He frowned and leaned forward. "I have been trying to think of ways to make it different—better than the competition, so people will swarm to book passage with us."

"That is easy." Mary laughed and smoothed the wrinkles from the letter she had crushed in her excitement. "All I have to do is remember our journey here to St. Louis. I was longing for a well-prepared meal. And a greater selection. I became very tired of the fare offered. And those narrow beds! Why, I almost rolled out of mine every time I turned over. You should put regular double beds in each cabin. *That* is luxury! And—"

She stopped fiddling with the letter and stared up at him.

He waved a hand. "Go on, Mary. Those are excellent ideas. What else have you to suggest?"

She shook her head, trying not to be too excited by the thought that had occurred to her. "James...you said you were going to 'scrap' the *Journey's End.* Does that mean you are going to...to *discard* it?"

"Yes, of course. Why?"

"And everything on it?"

His gaze sharpened at her eager tone. He nodded his head. "Yes, everything is old and, as I said, has been neglected. Why?"

"Then I can have the cots for the children!" Mary jumped to her feet again, too excited to remain seated. "I have been wondering where we can sleep any more children—I am certain there will be more now that—well... now. And I thought perhaps we could make use of the shed out back. But, of course, we had no beds. And—"

"And now we have them."

"Yes."

"And you have been praying for beds?"

"Yes, but it is only a coincidence, James." *Was it?* She folded her letter. "I should like to accompany you the next time you go to the levee. I would like to see the *Journey's End*. I may find other useful items aboard."

"Very well. We shall go tonight, directly after dinner. Before nightfall, but after the heat of the day has begun to wane. But now, I must return to the office. I have hired a new bookkeeper to take Goodwin's place and I am keeping a sharp eye on his accounting!"

"It is such a pleasure to have your company, Miss Randolph."

"Please, call me Mary, Mrs. Lucas."

The elderly woman beamed a smile at her, then went back to pouring their tea. "Thank you, I shall. Cream, dear?"

"A little. No sugar." Mary accepted her cup and placed it on the table in front of her. "I am sorry it has taken me so long to pay my promised call. But I have been so busy I find it difficult to find time for social calls."

"Yes, I can imagine." Mrs. Lucas added sugar to her

tea and stirred. "How many children have you taken in now, dear?"

Mary gaped. "You know of the children?"

"Oh, yes. Ben keeps me informed. But my lumbago is acting up again, so I have not been to Simpson's in a few days." Mrs. Lucas made a face that caused her wrinkles to deepen. "A nasty inconvenience, lumbago. It interferes with my gathering of the latest news." She gave a hearty chuckle.

Mary's own lips curled in a wide responsive grin. "How many of the children do you know of?"

"Hmm, let me think. There is Ben, of course. And a young girl of eight years named Callie—" her face squinched in thought "—and another little girl named Katy, who, I believe, was ill. How is she doing?" Mrs. Lucas picked up a tray and held it out to her. "Cookie, dear? There are ginger and plain sugar ones."

Mary smiled and put a ginger cookie on her plate. "Katy is doing fine. Her sore throat is healed, she is able to eat and is putting on some weight. But you are behind one child. We—my brother James and I—"

"Yes, I know about James. I believe he is courting Levinia Stewart's cousin, Rebecca Green." The faded blue eyes brightened with interest. "I also know about your cook, Ivy. And your maid, Edda. But you were saying...?"

Mary choked back laughter. "Our newest child is a young boy of ten, named Will. You may, perhaps, see him the next time you go to the store. He, like Ben, wants to earn his way. And I thought perhaps he could join Ben in carrying baskets for Mr. Simpson's customers. Actually, it was Captain Benton that suggested he do so."

"Ah, Captain Benton." Mrs. Lucas's wrinkled face

flooded with satisfaction. She placed a cookie onto her plate, set the tray down and smiled. "And is this Will of yours a nice, handsome, blond young lad like Ben?"

Mary jerked her thoughts back to the children. "No. I mean, he is very nice, but there is no physical resemblance between Will and Ben. Will has dark eyes and brown, rather curly hair, a long nose and a wide mouth." She watched in fascination as Mrs. Lucas broke off a piece of ginger cookie, placed it on her spoon and lowered it into her cup of tea. A moment later the woman lifted the spoon to her mouth and ate the bite of cookie.

"The boy sounds a mite homely."

There was nothing mean about the words, only factual. But still, Mary bristled. She knew how it felt to be unfavorably compared to others. She took a sip of tea, put down her cup and broke off a piece of cookie, giving herself time to form a calm response. "I suppose some would see Will that way. But that is only his outward appearance. He has a wonderful, kind heart. And a gentle manner with the girls, who absolutely *plague* his steps. And when he laughs, you cannot help but laugh with him. Everyone in our home adores Will. I find him quite beautiful." She put the bite of cookie in her mouth to keep from saying more.

"He sounds right pleasant to be around." Mrs. Lucas soaked another bite of cookie in her tea. "Do you suppose he would be willing to do some chores for me? Nothing too hard, mind you. Only fetching in stove wood and such like. I'd pay him well."

There was a wistful quality in Isobel Lucas's voice. Mary peered more closely at her smiling eyes. There was a shadow of loneliness in them. Her heart swelled. "I am sure Will would be pleased to come and help you. Would it suit if I send him around tomorrow morning? We have school in the late afternoon—before supper."

"Morning will be fine." The old woman's eyes sparkled across the table at her. "And if there is anything I can do to help you with these children you take in, you let me know."

Mary peered at her, remembering her influence with Mr. Simpson. "Can you get this ridiculous law about arresting orphans under the age of twelve revoked?"

Mrs. Lucas shook her head, fluttering the gray wisps of hair escaping from the knot on her head. "I'm afraid not. Nobody can change Simon Stewart's mind when he gets ahold of an idea. But what won't go in a front door can be carried in the back. An' I know most everybody in this town—an' all their secrets, too. So if you have a problem…you come see me. I'll be pleased to help. It'll give me somethin' to do."

"It is kind of you to offer, Mrs. Lucas." Mary finished her cup of tea. "I am afraid I must be leaving. I am going with James this evening to see a steamboat that is being scrapped. I hope to salvage a few of the beds." She sighed and ran her hands over her hair. "We are running out of space to sleep the children, and I am considering turning the shed in our backyard into a dormitory of sorts for any more boys that come our way. It is very small, but it shall have to do as the mayor will not consider establishing a city-funded orphanage."

"You asked Simon Stewart to build an orphanage?" The elderly woman chuckled. "I can imagine his answer." She shook her head. "Simon's nose is so high in the air he can't even see the ground. He's plumb lost his way. Still…there's always that back door." She brightened again. "If you need some help with supplying the needs of those orphans…you know…blankets, clothes, shoes an' such, you let me know."

The sun was still shining, the golden rays bathing the *Journey's End*. But nothing on the steamboat reflected the bright light.

Mary lifted the front of her long skirt and walked up the gangway onto the scarred deck. The white paint of the railing was chipped and peeling, and the paint on the sides of the boat was little better. Everywhere she looked there was dirt or soot. The cabin windows were dulled with dust.

"This way, Mary."

She turned and followed James to the stairs that led to the boiler deck. He stood back and let her precede him. The steps were worn, but sound, the railing firm. She stepped off the stairs into the main cabin and looked around. There were four round, wood tables, each with six chairs, clustered about a heating stove with a round chimney pipe that rose straight through the ceiling. At the far end was a similar heating stove in the middle of a grouping of furniture—a couch and two chairs with dirty, torn fabric—sitting on a threadbare carpet.

"Goodness, James. I thought the *Fair Weather* was in poor condition. Has this boat been running in this state?"

"Until a few weeks ago, yes." He looked around and shook his head. "I told you that we needed a truly luxurious steamboat to repair our reputation."

"My, yes!" She turned and opened the door to one of the passenger staterooms that lined both side walls. The room was small, narrow and deep, with a single bed covered with a faded woven coverlet, a stand beneath the window in the outside wall and a horizontal board, with double hooks every few inches along its length, spanning the wall opposite the bed. Everything looked dusty and dingy. She could not decide if the paint on the walls was faded and dirty, or if it was the quality of light coming through the thick dust on the window. But that did not matter. It was the bed she wanted.

She lifted the hem of her gown clear of the door sill and turned. "James, how will— Oh!" She pressed her hand to her chest and stared at the figure at the top of the stairs.

James pivoted—smiled. "Good evening, Captain."

Samuel Benton nodded, then looked her way. "I did not mean to startle you. I thought I saw movement through the windows and came to investigate." He strode toward them.

Mary glanced down at her gown, brushed at a spot of dust clinging to it. Was there any on her bonnet? She glanced back over her shoulder, but it was impossible to see her reflection in the filthy window.

"As long as I am here, may I have a word with you, Mr. Randolph? About that business you told me of this morning."

Mary shot a glance at the captain, then looked at James.

"You may speak freely in front of Mary, Captain. I discuss these things with her. She knows the M and M line lost three steamboats to questionable 'accidents' shortly before the line was purchased and I took over as manager."

"Very well." The captain glanced at her. "The buyer kept his name a secret, and for a while I suspected him of arranging the 'accidents,' but—"

Mary jolted. "You thought m—the new owner arranged to have the steamboats destroyed?" She caught the captain's quizzical look at her and hastened to cover her shocked slip of the tongue. "Gracious! Why would anyone do such a thing?"

"There are a lot of reasons. But none of them matter for your brother proved me wrong." The captain smiled. "He would make a good policeman."

She looked at James. "What did you do?"

He shrugged. "When the captain told me his suspicions about the 'accidents' to the steamers, I searched back through the company books and found there was insurance purchased by the line for the cargos that were lost, as well as insurance on the steamers, but there was no record of any payments received. I showed the captain what I found this morning."

"And I went to talk with the manager of the insurance company."

"And…"

James's word hung in the air. She looked at the captain.

"And they paid the claims to Mr. Thomas, the former manager. The new owner and…anyone else new to the company…is cleared of any complicity in the staged accidents. If you press charges, I'll fill out warrants for his arrest and send them around to the towns downriver."

Anyone else new to the company? Mary stiffened. Did he mean James? *How dare he!* She drew breath. James touched her shoulder. She glanced at his face and held her tongue.

"I will come to your office and do that tomorrow, Captain. I am glad that mystery is solved and I can now expend all my efforts in improving the line." James smiled. "And it is good to know you are quick to check into possible trouble—though I am surprised you bother with a steamboat that is about to be scrapped."

Mary stared at James. How like their father he was, so calm and controlled. Pride coursed through her.

"I've chased many a drunken mountain man or idle laborer—even Indians—from abandoned boats, Mr. Randolph. Fire is always a threat, and they treat them like a boardinghouse. Figure they can sleep in one of the cabins and no harm done. But—"

"A *boardinghouse!*" Mary stared at the captain, looked at James and laughed. "A *boardinghouse*. Of course!" She whirled around, marched to the center of the room and turned in a slow circle, counting.

"What are you doing, Mary?"

"There are twenty-four staterooms, James."

"Yes…"

She hurried back to his side. "Oh, James, do you not see? It is perfect!" She looked up at Samuel Benton, saw understanding flash in his eyes. And doubt. She lifted her chin. "How many children have you in jail, now, Captain?"

"Children in— Mary! Have you gone *mad?*" It was a roar of disbelief.

She reached out and gave James's arm a soothing pat. "How many, Captain?" He grinned—that slow, lopsided grin that did queer things to her stomach.

"Six boys and two girls, Miss Randolph."

Sam strolled down the street letting his presence keep things on the levee under control. A smile tugged at his lips, which broke into a full-blown grin. He couldn't help it. He had been grinning all night. Every time he thought of Mary Randolph standing in the middle of the *Jour-*

ney's End main cabin, jabbing the air with her finger and counting staterooms.

He detoured toward the river to check on the activity at the various warehouses. He couldn't help thinking about her, either. That woman could out stubborn a mule! There was no give in her. At least, not where the orphans were concerned. The mayor had refused her request that the city fund an orphanage, now here she was, figuring on turning that scrapped boat into one. But how would she manage it? Even a scrapped boat was worth something. Of course, with her brother as manager of the line...

How many children have you in jail?

Sam shook his head, watched some laborers loading up their ship with wood. He had been stunned by her question. Still was. Even more by the determined look in her eyes when she had lifted that little square chin of hers. No, she was not giving up. She was going to get those children out of jail and make a home for them on top of it. Quite a difference between Levinia Stewart and Mary Randolph. One was determined to keep the orphans in jail, and the other was determined to get them out.

"One o'clock, the weather is fair, and all is well."

The words sounded clear as he scaled the incline back to the street. Time to go home. Sam frowned. All was not well in his life. There was no open friction with the mayor, but it was obvious he was no longer in favor. And Levinia had turned her back and walked away when he had seen her in front of the dressmakers this afternoon.

His frown deepened. He lifted his hand and massaged the taut muscles in his neck and shoulders. The message sent by Levinia's behavior was clear. Either change his stance on the orphans and support her father, or any hope of a future between them would be gone. It did not dis-

turb him as much now. He was growing to accept the
demise of his goal for a future in politics with Levinia
at his side. In truth, he was beginning to look on it as
a fortunate escape. Levinia was not the person he had
thought her to be. The woman had no heart to her. And
he would not accept her terms. Not even to have his
dreams. A man didn't amount to anything if he didn't
have his self-respect.

He yawned, then turned onto Walnut Street. *Don't you
worry, Ma. You sit tight, Danny. I will keep my promise. I'll be somebody. You have my word on it.* Sam set
his jaw. He would gain his goal without the Stewarts'
help. He would do it the same way he had achieved all
he had so far accomplished—by honest effort and hard
work. And all was not lost. He still had his plans for his
showcase house.

He tried to summon the vision, but for some reason it
would not appear. All he saw was the knoll, the grassy
fields around it and the river. He must be too tired. It had
been a long night. Three drunks jailed. He hated putting
them in the cell beside the boys, but he had no choice.
It was a good thing Miss Randolph didn't know about
that. A smile curved his lips. Mary Randolph. She sure
had a cute little chin.

Chapter Fifteen

"Mary, I understand your desire to help these children. *I* want to help them! But this…this *plan* of yours is…is…"

"I believe *ludicrous,* or perhaps *preposterous,* is the word you are searching for, James."

He scowled down at her. "They are both apt! And I should add *costly!*" He snatched his hat from the hat tree and slapped it on his head. "And I am not speaking only of money. You are investing too much of your heart into these children."

Mary nodded. "Perhaps. But someone has to care about them, James. And I have no husband or children of my own to spend my love and care on."

James's face softened. He stepped toward her. Mary frowned and turned away. She had not meant to let that bit of bitterness be bared.

His hands gripped her upper arms. "Forgive me, Mary. You hide your feelings so well, I forget about your pain over Winston's betrayal. But, please, do not be discouraged. The Lord will send you a man who will love and cherish you as you deserve. One whom you will love with your whole heart. And you will have children of your own. As many as you wish."

Mary sighed. If God wanted her to have a husband who would love and cherish her, He would have made her beautiful and gentle-natured and appealing. But dear James would never admit that. He was such a wonderful, caring brother. And he meant well. It was not his fault the words he spoke to encourage her only deepened her sadness. His vision of her future would not come true. She had accepted that. But she would have to do a better job of guarding her tongue, to protect her brother's tender heart. And she would have to pretend she believed what he said was possible. She forced a bright smile and turned to look up at him. "You may be right, James. But, meanwhile, there are hungry, hurting children who need care."

"I know. But you give your heart so freely, and I do not want to see you hurt or disappointed, Mary."

He did not add the word *again,* but she heard it in his voice. She swallowed back tears and kept the smile pasted on her face.

"Please, do not become too excited about this plan to turn the steamboat into an orphanage. There are so many obstacles." He frowned and shook his head. "The boat has to be renovated—which is expensive and time-consuming. And even should you, by some miracle, accomplish that, you have no land to place it on. And then there is the cost of maintenance. And of feeding, clothing and—"

She touched his lips with her fingertips, unable to listen to more without breaking down. "I know, James. Truly. I know. But, for some reason, I feel…compelled… to save these children. I know what it feels like to…to receive scorn." She blinked away tears. "I cannot give less than my best for them, James. And if that means my heart gets bruised—well—" she gave a small shrug "—it has been bruised before." She forced another smile and gave him a little push toward the door. "Be off to work, now. I have a full morning with lists to make and shopping to do."

"All right, Mary. But we will talk more tonight about this plan of yours for salvaging the *Journey's End* to use as an orphanage."

She stood in the door until he reached the gate, then gave a final wave, closed the door and leaned back against it. If only James's wishes for her would come true. But they would not. Not for someone as plain and *angular* as she. Those dreams were for the Sarahs and Veronicas and Miss Stewarts of the world.

Poor little Miss Mary. She'll have a hard time findin' herself a husband, bein' plain like she is.

Mary lifted her chin and shoved the memory of her nanny's voice back into the dark recesses of her mind where she had carried it since she was five years old. She pushed away from the door and squared her shoulders. That was enough of feeling pity for herself. She may never have a husband who loved her, but she had children to care for.

"Don't forget now—slow down when you are in town. You don't want to run someone over and hurt them." Sam fastened a stern gaze on the boys sitting astride their restless mounts. "You save your racing for out on the plains—hear?"

"Yes, sir, Captain Benton."

"All right. If I have to speak to you again, I'll get your fathers to sit in on our conversation. Now, be on your way. And give your parents my best."

"Yes, sir."

The boys rode off at a fast walk. Sam grinned and shook his head. That would probably last until they turned the corner. He started back up the street, then halted. Levinia Stewart was coming out of Sanderson's Hats and Gloves. She was garbed in an expensive gown that flattered her petite form, and a hat that revealed her blond curls and the beauty of her face. Her pink cheeks were dimpled, her mouth curved into a smile as she chatted with her friend. He watched her, waited for the disappointment, the sense of loss to hit him. But there was nothing. Not one little stirring. No desire to go and speak to her. Only an irritation that he had succumbed to the beauty she used as a weapon to win her way.

He moved forward again, saw when she spotted him. Watched the beguiling smile she put on, as other people would don their clothes. Using it as an instrument to win him over. He touched his hat brim in polite greeting as he approached. "Good morning, Miss Stewart... Miss Weller."

Levinia started to turn her back. He did not pause or slow his pace. Shock swept over both women's faces. Levinia's smile died. A glitter appeared in her blue eyes, which sharpened her gaze as he continued his purposeful stride. The lovely features contorted into an expression of fury at his lack of submission. Levinia Stewart did not like to lose. The woman was spoiled, pampered and willful. How had he ever thought her beautiful?

Excited chatter drew his attention. Sam glanced ahead. A young boy and two smaller girls, all carrying paper-wrapped packages tied with string, stood around the doorway of Nicholson's Shoes and Boots. He took in their clean, smiling faces and shining hair and smiled. All that remained of the gaunt, filthy, fearful children Mary Randolph had taken under her care were the neat patches applied to the boy's clean dungarees, which sported new suspenders. The girls both wore new dresses, one in yellow and brown checks, the other in blue. And the boy had on a pair of shiny, new work boots.

His heart jolted. How he had yearned for a pair of boots when he was a barefoot kid.

"Children, do not block the door, it is impolite." Mary Randolph stepped out of the store and moved to the side. The children crowded around her. "Do you all have your packages?" Wind gusted off the river, flipped her bonnet backward. She grabbed for it, dropping one of the packages she carried. She leaned down to pick it up, and banged heads with the boy who had done the same. Laughter bubbled out of her, echoed by the children's giggles.

Sam rushed forward and scooped up the package. "You seem to have your hands full, Miss Randolph." Brown eyes with honey-colored specks aglow with laughter looked up at him. The laughing lips whispered a soft "Oh," and a deep rose color crept along delicate high cheekbones. He stared. The rose color grew deeper. Long, thick, black lashes swept down over the brown eyes, and a narrow hand raised to pull the bonnet forward.

"Thank you, Captain Benton."

Her voice was softer, huskier than he remembered. He filled his suddenly air-starved lungs, became aware of the children's silence and looked down. They had all taken a step back—moved a bit closer to her. Shame hit him. These children thought he was some sort of ogre. So did Mary Randolph.

He smiled and dipped his head at the girls. "You young

ladies are looking pretty today." That won him a timid smile from each of them. He glanced at the smaller of the two. "It is good to see you well and able to enjoy such an outing, Katy."

He shifted his gaze to the boy and held out the paper-wrapped parcel to him. "You look a good strong boy, and a gentleman always carries a lady's packages."

The boy's eyes flashed with pride at the compliment. He took the package, tucked it under his arm, then reached out for the two smaller ones Mary Randolph still held.

She inhaled to speak, glancing up at him. He gave a very small shake of his head. She exhaled and handed the boy her packages.

Sam smiled down at him. "Good man."

The boy grinned.

He heard a softly indrawn breath, looked back at Mary Randolph and read the approval in her eyes. And something more. But before he could identify it, she looked away.

"Thank you again, Captain. It was kind of you to help us. Now, we must be on our way. It is almost time for dinner." She smiled at the children. "Please lead the way, Will."

He watched them walk away, Will and the older girl in front, Miss Randolph and Katy behind. A hunger grew in his heart, spread to every part of him. They looked like a family. And he didn't even know how to be a part of a family. But he wanted one.

The thought jolted him.

He stepped to the side, out of the flow of shoppers and stared after Mary Randolph and the children. He hadn't thought much about it before. He'd been too busy planning his road to financial and social success, but he wanted a family. A whole houseful of healthy, noisy kids. Maybe he'd even have one that looked like Danny.

The yearning deepened, followed by hard, swift relief—the kind he felt when he had evaded a mountain man's knife or a laborer's hard fists. He shot a quick glance up the street the other direction. Levinia Stewart was entering Miss Mayfield's Emporium. The relief hit him again. If she had not given him that ultimatum over the orphans... If he had not been forced to face his own heart...

Sam returned his gaze to Mary Randolph and the children. She was holding Katy's hand and laughing. He could not fit Levinia Stewart into that picture. He could not imagine her as a mother, holding a baby in her arms, wiping away a toddler's tears. Levinia would have a nanny to care for her children. He frowned and shook his head, remembering the night of his parting from her. He had blamed God for it. If that was true, he owed God his gratitude, not his anger.

Sam snorted and turned to cross the street. That was a new thought. One foreign to everything he had believed all these years. But he could not shake his feeling of relief. And if God had saved him from making a mistake in marrying Levinia, perhaps— No. That was going a stretch too far. He'd give it some thought later.

Right now he needed to visit the *Golden Fleece.* He had heard two of the furnace stokers were there who had been part of the crews of two of the M and M steamboats that sank due to explosions. They might know something about Duffy or Thomas and those "accidents." And if he could get them to tell him what they knew—

"*Captain!*"

Sam spun back, saw Will running empty-handed toward him and jerked his gaze down the street. Mary Randolph was standing, packages in hand, girls beside her, looking his way. *What—* He looked down as Will skidded to a stop in front of him. "What is it, Will? What's wrong?"

"Ain't nothin' wrong, Captain. Miss Mary sent me back to ask if you ain't patrolin', would ya like to come… er…join 'em…fer supper tonight? She said t' tell ya they eat shortly after Mr. James comes home—'bout seven o'clock. And she apologizes fer the short notice."

It took him a moment. He looked back at Mary Randolph, saw her smile and give a single nod. What had prompted her invitation? He looked back down at Will and nodded. "Please tell Miss Randolph I will be pleased to accept her gracious invitation. And don't forget to carry those packages for her."

"Come in, Mary, come in!" Mrs. Lucas beamed a smile at her. "I did not expect to see you again so soon. Have you come for tea?"

"No, I truly do not have time for tea, Mrs. Lucas. I have a very busy afternoon ahead, and a guest coming for supper." Mary stepped inside and closed the door. "But you asked me to tell you about the children, and I am so excited I wanted to share my news with you."

The elderly woman's eyes lit with interest. "Well, come in and sit down."

Mary followed her into a lovely parlor. A large floor clock ticked off the minutes, making her even more aware of the pressing time. Mrs. Lucas took a seat in a chair covered with tapestry and indicated the one facing her. "Now tell me your news. Have you another child?"

Mary took her seat and shook her head. "No. But I believe I have discovered the answer to providing a home for them all." She removed her bonnet and smoothed her hands over her hair. "You know my brother, James, is the manager of the Mississippi and Missouri steamer line?"

"Yes. And I hear he discovered Eli Goodwin had been cheating the company and set the law on him. Everyone speaks most highly of your brother. But what has that to do with an orphanage for the children?"

"James has recommended that one of the older steamboats be scrapped—"

"The *Journey's End*."

Mary laughed. "Yes. Truly, Mrs. Lucas, I am astounded by how much you know about what goes on in St. Louis!" She leaned forward. "Do you already know what I am about to tell you?"

The elderly woman's face crinkled with laughter. "I promise you, I do not. But if you give me a day or two, I will."

Mary grinned. "Very well. Here is my news. I am going to renovate the *Journey's End* and turn it into a home for the children!"

Mrs. Lucas's eyes went wide, her mouth opened—closed—then turned up into a wide grin. "Why, what a…a…simply perfect idea! You are truly an astonishing young woman."

"Oh, it was not my idea—well, it was—but only after Captain Benton mentioned that mountain men and idle laborers often use abandoned steamboats as boardinghouses. When he said that, it suddenly seemed the perfect answer for the children's needs."

"Captain Benton?" The faded blue eyes sharpened.

"Yes. He happened by as James and I were looking

over the steamer. He thought we were mountain men or something."

"I see." The older woman's lips twitched.

Mary frowned. "What is it?"

Mrs. Lucas waved a hand through the air and shook her head. "Nothing at all, dear. When you mentioned the captain, it made me remember he and Levinia have hit a rocky patch is all."

Her heart lurched. "A rocky patch?"

Mrs. Lucas nodded. "Yes. But you were telling me about your idea."

"What? Oh. Yes, of course." She rose and began to walk about the room. Mrs. Lucas was studying her face far too closely. "There are twenty-four staterooms on the steamer—each quite small, but more than adequate for a child. And the beds are there, though they will need painting and new bedding. And the main cabin will do wonderfully well for a school *and* a play area." She made her way back to her chair. "Of course, everything is dreadfully dusty and dingy. The entire boat needs a good cleaning and painting. And the curtains must be replaced. And—"

"And have you funds to do all of this?"

Mary sighed and resumed her seat. "Not yet." She squared her shoulders. "But I will *find* a way. I simply have to get those children out of jail."

"I'm sure you will, dear." Mrs. Lucas leaned forward and patted her hand. "And I will think about what I can do to help."

Mary rose, then leaned down to give the elderly woman a hug. "Thank you, Mrs. Lucas. Now, I must be going." She picked up her bonnet, put it on and began to tie the ribbons. "If I am too busy to come myself, I will send news of my progress by Ben."

"You do that, dear. And may the Lord bless you. This is truly a wonderful, charitable thing you are doing, and—"

Mary stayed her hands, looked down at Mrs. Lucas. "And what?"

"Oh, nothing, dear. Nothing." She started to rise.

"Please, Mrs. Lucas. Do not trouble yourself. I can see myself out."

"All right, dear." The woman relaxed back in her chair. "Come again, Mary. I shall look forward to your next visit."

Mary walked to the door and glanced back. Mrs. Lucas was sitting in the chair with a wide smile on her face, looking very pleased.

Chapter Sixteen

He was coming to supper. Oh, why had she extended that invitation? When would she learn not to be so *impulsive*? Mary pulled her ecru pongee from the cupboard, then put it back again. The captain was not coming to call on her, and that was her best gown. She certainly did not want to give him the impression that she had meant more by her invitation than— Than what?

Mary shut the door on the cupboard *and* her thoughts and walked away. She would not treat this supper differently than any other. Her green gown was good enough. She marched to the dressing room, peered into the mirror, smoothing the lace collar and straightening the cameo pin at its juncture.

Against her will her gaze lifted to her face. She could not wear a hat or bonnet in the house. He would see her as she was, in all her plainness. Of course, he had seen her that way before, on the day he had escorted her to the courthouse, and again the day he had brought Will to her.

The argument did not help. None of it helped. Not the sensible reasoning, or the foolish reassurances. She had asked the captain to supper because of the children.

Because he had treated them so kindly and made them smile. Because he had made Will feel so proud and fine. She had wanted to thank him in a way that would let him know she recognized his change of heart toward the orphans. But now *her* heart—her foolish, *foolish* heart—wanted to make something of this supper that it was not.

Mary lifted her chin and tucked away the locks of hair that had, once again, fallen from her knot. Plain brown hair. And plain brown eyes. And those horrible high cheekbones!

She sighed and turned from the mirror. She hated mirrors. Had hated them since she was five years old. Every time she looked in one she heard again Nanny Marlow's words and realized she was one of the unlovely of this world. Not ugly, but not beautiful like Sarah, or Veronica, or— *Veronica, my beloved, what man would not choose your petite, blond beauty and sweet nature over Mary's dark, angular plainness and bold, forthright ways?*

Mary clenched her hands. What was she thinking? Why did she allow her heart to even pretend there might be something more to this supper than appeared? Because she *wished* it to be so? Winston's words and actions proved the folly of such a desire. And her appearance mattered not a fig's worth! The captain was courting the beautiful Miss Stewart—even if they had hit a…a rocky patch!

The thought crushed the last of her resistance. Tears welled into her eyes. Mary whirled and rushed out of the dressing room, away from the mirror that stole all her hopes and dreams.

Sam stopped short of the gate, straightened the cravat at his throat, tugged his vest in place and shrugged his shoulders to loosen the constricting feel of his coat. He had worn his good clothes for the children's sake. They would be more comfortable with him out of his uniform. His lips twitched. "You keep telling yourself that long enough, you might come to believe it, Sam."

He frowned and shrugged. He might as well admit it. He wanted Mary Randolph's approval. He held the woman in high esteem. And he had been the object of her challenging looks and words long enough. He wanted her to know he had risen to her challenges. And—

Sam stiffened, stared at the cottage as if he could see through the walls. Mary Randolph was the one who made him examine his own heart concerning the children. It was *her* challenges that made him realize he could not comply with the mayor's plans. And today, it was the sight of her with the children that made him realize how much he wanted a family of his own. How much he wanted—

The truth slammed into him. He stood there, astounded, *dumbfounded* and not a little disgusted by his own stupidity. Why had he wasted time courting Levinia? He was in love with Mary Randolph.

A steamboat whistled. A dog barked. Sam shook his head, pulled himself together and pushed open the gate. Mary Randolph considered him a cruel, heartless ogre. How would he ever prove himself worthy of her love? The cannonball on the end of the chain rose, then fell again, closing the gate when he stepped through. He strode up the brick path, climbed the porch steps and paused with his fisted hand ready to knock on the door.

Peals of laughter sounded from inside the house, Mary's low, musical laugh among them. It was the most wonderful, the most inviting, the most terrifying sound he had ever heard. He was twenty-seven years old and had never in his life, since he was seven years old, been around a family. And never a happy one. And that was what was inside that house. A family. Perhaps not of blood, but a family, nonetheless. And Mary was its heart.

He took a deep breath, reaching to knock. The door burst open and a laughing boy crashed into him, followed by two giggling girls. "Ugh!" Sam staggered back a couple steps, instinctively closed his arms about the children to keep them from falling and grinned at Will, who skidded to a halt, went up on his toes and wildly circled his arms like a windmill to keep from pitching forward onto the others. He opened his arms. "You want in, too? I am strong enough to hold all four of you."

There was a chorus of giggles and laughter. The children righted themselves. Katy reached out and snatched the bonnet Ben clutched in his hand. "Told you I could catch you!"

"You didn't catch me, *he* did!" Sam found himself the target of Ben's pointing finger.

"Well, I *would* have!" Katy yanked on the bonnet so hard it came down over her face, which set off another gale of laughter.

Sam chuckled, then raised his face to the tall thin woman who appeared in the open door. "I'm sorry, sir. They didn't know you were here." The woman wiped the smile from her face. "Children, apologize to Captain Benton and we'll be off for home."

There was a flurry of apologies. Sam acknowledged them with a smile as the children filed off the porch. At least he thought he did. He couldn't be sure. His attention was riveted on Mary, who now stood at the open door, laughter lighting her face and warming her eyes.

"I apologize for the overly exuberant welcome, Captain. Please come in." She stepped back.

Sam removed his hat and crossed the threshold, his palms moist, his mouth suddenly dry as dust. If God *was* involved in all that had thus far happened, may He grant that the invitation would be into Mary's heart.

"Oh, what a lovely cool breeze." Mary stepped through the door the captain held open for her onto the porch, and fought back a rising disappointment. Supper was over. The captain would make his excuses and leave now. And James—

Was standing before her putting his hat on. "If you will excuse me, Mary... Captain Benton. I have an engagement."

"With Rebecca Green?"

James grinned at her teasing. "No other. Well, I am off. Enjoy your evening."

Heat rushed into her cheeks. She could have shaken him. He made it sound as if the captain were courting her!

James's grin widened. He gave her a wink, tipped his hat to a jaunty angle and then trotted down the steps to the road. His merry whistle floated back to them as he hurried away.

Mary stared after him, vowing to make him pay for that bit of embarrassment. She sucked in a breath, lifted her hands and smoothed back her hair. She might as well give the captain his opening to leave, then go and help Edda with the dishes. "Would you care to relax here on the porch a moment, Captain Benton?"

"That would be pleasant. After you, Miss Randolph." He bowed her toward the porch furniture.

Was he not leaving? Mary masked her surprise,

stepped over to the new porch swing James had hung and seated herself. She watched from under her lowered lashes as the captain propped his shoulder against one of the roof support posts and crossed one ankle over the other. He certainly did not look as if he were in any hurry to leave. Her heart thudded. She plucked an imaginary piece of lint from her skirt to gain time to compose herself.

"I know you have not had much time, Miss Randolph, but have you thought over your original intent? Do you still plan to use the *Journey's End* for the orphans?"

"I do indeed, Captain. Though I have not as yet determined how I shall accomplish my goal." Is that why he stayed? Was he trying to discover her plans for some reason? Perhaps for the mayor? Her stomach twisted with disappointment. Were his acts of kindness toward the children for a nefarious purpose? *Oh, God, if You care for these children, please, please, let it not be so.* She pushed her toes against the floor and set the swing in motion.

"I have been giving the matter some thought."

"Oh?" Her disappointment swelled. She braced herself to argue her position.

"Yes. The steamer can stay in the dock while it is being renovated, but, of course, it cannot remain there permanently." His gaze fastened on hers. "Have you any notion where you will locate the boat when the work is finished?"

"No." Her mind raced. Why was he asking? "I know only the land shall have to front on the water. I should imagine it would be very difficult to move the boat inland any distance."

He nodded. "It can be done. But it would be costly. As will any land on the river. Those parcels are highly sought after by men of business. Millers and such. And you won't want the children close to the levee area." He stared off into the distance, the hat in his hand tapping against his thigh. "There is talk of expanding the levee both up and down river."

Her heart sank. If she could not use the steamboat, what would she do? She looked down at her lap. Smoothed a wrinkle in her skirt. So much for prayers.

"Still, there are a few possibilities..."

She lifted her head and stared up at him, trying not to show her confusion at the statement. "Possibilities?" Was this some sort of snare she could not perceive? Perhaps she should make him give her facts. "If you would be so kind as to tell me the location of those possibilities, I shall look into them immediately." She lifted her chin. "And perhaps you could draw me a *map* so I might find my way? Oh! And—forgive my ignorance, but I have never been involved in these sort of transactions before. Where does one go to find the cost of these land parcels?"

He grinned.

She stiffened. "May I ask what it is you find amusing, Captain? Is it my questions, or my behavior? I realize it is unseemly for a woman to be so bold in her requests, but—"

"I do not find it unseemly, Miss Randolph. I find it delightful. That is the reason for my smile." He sobered and his gaze fastened on hers. "I applaud your enthusiasm in your quest to help these orphaned children. And I hope you will accept any help I am able to offer you."

Her mind stalled on the word *delightful*. It took her a moment to accept the term as a politeness. She was not accustomed to the captain in a social capacity. He was quite good at turning a polite compliment, for whatever his purpose. She composed herself and looked at him. The time had come to stop this charade. "You wish to help?"

"I do."

He sounded so earnest. "Truly?"

He nodded.

Mary stared, then looked down at her hands. She wanted so much to believe him but she dare not trust her judgment.

"I know we have crossed swords over the children in the past, Miss Randolph. But I am the captain of the police and it is my job to uphold the law. I hope, however, that I have demonstrated to you, by calling upon you for help when Katy took ill, and by bringing Will to you, that I am not heartless or uncaring of these orphans' needs. And that I do not agree with the mayor's plan to use them as free labor on city projects." His voice was deep, quiet, persuasive. "And, while I still must do my job, I will continue to do my best for all of these children, and to prove myself honorable to you. I only ask you grant me the opportunity to do so."

Mary looked up at him, her head cautioning her to be careful, her heart telling her to trust him. She wanted to. With her whole being she longed to trust him. But Winston had seemed honest and sincere, also. He had looked straight into her eyes and made his declarations—and every word he had said to her had been a lie. And this time, it was not only her heart that could be hurt. It was the children, as well. She took a deep breath. *Almighty God, please, if I err in my judgment, do not let the children suffer for it.* "I will be glad of your help for the children, Captain."

He nodded. "Thank you for your trust, Miss Randolph." He shifted his position as he sat on the railing. "Have you made plans beyond housing the orphans on the steamboat?"

"What sort of plans?" She flushed at her skeptical tone, but he seemed not to notice it.

"Well, for instance, who will be with them to watch over them? Do you plan to hire someone to oversee the orphanage? And where will they live on the boat?"

Mary rose, walked to the railing and stared out at the twilight sky. "I have not had time to consider all you ask, Captain. But I believe I can answer your queries." She gave him a sidelong glance as he rose and stood beside her. "James has grown fond of Miss Green, and I believe she feels the same fondness for him. Therefore, as James is quite persuasive and disinclined to tarry once he makes a decision—*and* as this cottage is very small—I am quite certain I shall, at some time in the not-too-distant future, need to find another place of residence. In a way, I shall be orphaned, too." She gave a small laugh and smoothed her hands over her hair. "Therefore *I* shall be with the children, and, of course, live in one of the staterooms." *How would she ever manage?*

"Housing for the children's caretaker is one of the things I have been pondering, Miss Randolph. And I believe you may find my suggestion acceptable, even favorable. But the hour is late. May I call again? To go over my thoughts about the renovation of the steamboat with you?"

Mary looked down at her hands gripping the railing and tamped down the tingle of excitement caused by the thought of spending more time in his company. He was not asking permission to make a social call. It was for the orphans. She looked up at him and smiled. "I shall look forward to hearing your suggestions, Captain."

"And I to the pleasure of your company, Miss Randolph. Perhaps I could escort you to the *Journey's End* Sunday afternoon, around two o'clock? It may be easier to explain my ideas there."

"Very sensible, Captain."

He made a slight bow. "Until Sunday, Miss Randolph."

She smiled and nodded, then made herself turn and go into the house. She did not want him to look back and find her watching him walk away. All the same, when she reached the door, she could not resist one quick look over her shoulder.

He was standing at the gate watching her.

Her cheeks flamed. But he could not see from that distance. She dipped her head in a polite farewell, thrust open the door and hurried inside.

Sam strode up Market Street, cut across Fourth Street and headed along Walnut toward the boardinghouse, his long strides eating up the distance. What did that little glance Mary Randolph had stolen mean? Dare he hope it meant the same as the look he had stolen at her? How could it be? She was so cool, and defensive and…and prickly around him.

And why wouldn't she be? They had clashed so often over the children, how could he even expect her to trust him or hold him in any sort of respectful regard? He was a fool! Why had he taken so long to see the truth?

Sam pivoted, crossed back over to Market and headed for the stables behind the jail. Forget the suit! Forget the dark! The moon was out. The road out of town hard-packed and free of holes. And he needed a ride. An all-out, no-holding-back, ground-eating, hoof-pounding ride!

Chapter Seventeen

Sam stared up at his deputy. "So Goodwin is dead?"

Jenkins nodded. "The New Orleans police got a record of it. He was cut up and robbed outside of a gamblin' hall. They found his body the day before I got to New Orleans with the warrant for his arrest."

"And Thomas got away."

Jenkins nodded. "The police found the boardinghouse he was living in, but he was gone when they got there. He left the same night Goodwin was killed, on a ship for London."

"Probably with Goodwin's money on him. All right, Jenkins. There's nothing more we can do now. But we'll be waiting when he comes back. Go home and get some sleep."

"Yes, sir."

A murmur, low and restrained, ebbed and flowed from pew to pew. Glances, surreptitious and angry, rode its crest, broke over Mary, drowned the pleasure of bringing the children to church for the first time. It had started from the pew occupied by the mayor, his wife and his daughter, swelled to include the front section on the left side of the aisle and rippled through the rest of the congregation.

Mary stared at the vacant pew in front of them, could feel the emptiness of the one behind. She glanced at James, read the message of support in his eyes and sat straighter. She lifted her chin higher and smiled at the children lined up in the pew, though anger tingled from her head to her toes. How could people be so cruel? Had the children noticed? Did they realize the looks and the mutterings were about them? They were so quiet and still, only their gazes moving across the congregation then returning to her.

She touched Callie's shoulder, received a soft smile that made the girl's rather plain face a thing of beauty. Gave Ben and Will smiles of reassurance, got a cheeky grin from handsome, blond, blue-eyed Ben, and a wink from the irresistible, dark-haired, dark-eyed Will in return, and patted Katy's hand. Timid Katy, who nonetheless had a quick temper. The boys delighted in teasing her. And she gave back in kind, her blue eyes snapping, her black curls trembling, and more often than not, her small finger shaking in her tormentor's face as she corrected them. She was a beautiful child. They all were beautiful, in their own way. And so well-behaved on their first time in church. Goodness, she was proud of them!

Tears stung the backs of her eyes. Had she done wrong by bringing the children to church? She had expected a few shocked looks, but she had not anticipated such ostracism and anger. The children had already been hurt by people on the streets and she did not want them suffering rejection again.

She listened to the church filling, all but the pews in

front and back of them, and blinked back tears. Should they leave? *Almighty God, please, please, do not let these children be hurt by my decision to bring them here today. Please. Amen.* A calm settled over her. It was odd how often she prayed these days. She had not prayed for years. But while she still questioned God's love for her, she was quite certain God cared about these orphans.

The door opened at the back of the church. A woman's soft footsteps came down the center aisle. Mary heard Ben whisper to Will, "It's Mrs. Lucas." She lifted her head to look. The elderly woman passed by two partially empty pews on the left and turned toward the pew in front of them.

A woman on the left aisle seat whispered something. Mrs. Lucas turned back, nodded and smiled. "Yes, I know, Rose. Miss Randolph and the children are friends of mine." The elderly voice broke the silence. Drew glances. The woman snapped upright, gave a toss of her head and faced the front.

Mrs. Lucas smiled and stepped toward their pew. James rose, motioning for the boys to do the same. Mrs. Lucas's faded blue eyes twinkled up at him. "My! You are a handsome lad."

Color rushed into James's face. It was the first time Mary had seen him blush in years. But he rose to the occasion. He smiled and winked at the elderly woman. "And you, madam, are a lovely woman of impeccable taste."

Mrs. Lucas laughed and motioned for him to lean down. "Rebecca Green is a very lucky young lady." Mary heard the whisper, had to clamp down on her lip to keep from laughing at James's shocked expression. "Now take your seat, young man. I shall sit up here." Mrs. Lucas turned toward the pew in front of them, then looked back.

"With your permission, I should like these two young gentleman to sit with me." She beamed at Ben and Will.

"Of course." James stepped aside, and the boys filed out and into the other pew, one on either side of the small, elderly woman.

James took his seat and they all slid closer together. Closing ranks. The thought was not a happy one.

The murmuring began anew.

Please, God, do not let Mrs. Lucas be hurt because she has befriended us.

The organist struck a chord. Mary rose with the congregation to sing the opening hymn, swelling with pride at the sight of Will and Ben rising to stand straight and tall beside Mrs. Lucas. The singing started and the children joined in. She glanced down at the girls, then exchanged a smile with James. Callie had a beautiful voice, true and clear. Katy was not as fortunate, but sang with great enthusiasm, all the same.

There was a general rustle and stir as people resumed their seats when the singing was over. The pastor strode to the pulpit, looked down and gave a small nod. Mary watched as Mrs. Lucas gave one in return. She frowned and took her seat. That was more than a casual greeting. It was a bit of silent communication. And the elderly woman's face now bore that same pleased expression she had worn at the end of their visit.

Silence settled.

"Almighty God, bless these Your people with 'ears to hear' and open hearts to receive Your message of truth this day. Amen." The pastor opened his Bible. "I take my text today from the book of James, chapter two. 'My brethren, have not the faith of our Lord Jesus Christ, the Lord of glory, with respect to persons.'"

Mary smoothed a wrinkle from her skirt and settled herself to listen.

"'For if there come unto your assembly a man with a gold ring, in goodly apparel, and there come in also a poor man in vile raiment; and ye have respect to him that weareth the gay clothing…'"

Mary snapped her attention to Pastor Thornton, looked at Mrs. Lucas, who was sitting, gaze fixed forward, hands folded in her lap, a beatific smile on her face. Is that what— Had she—

Mary darted a look across the aisle at the Stewart family. The mayor was scowling, Mrs. Stewart was looking at her husband, and Miss Stewart was staring at the pastor, looking displeased.

"'But ye have despised the poor.' And in doing so, you commit sin." The words rang out.

The mayor went rigid. His face turned a frightening shade of purple. He turned his head her way.

Mary stared at him, alarmed for his health. He seemed to be having trouble breathing. Mrs. Stewart said something and patted his arm. And Miss Stewart— Mary stiffened. Miss Stewart, like the mayor, was glaring at her. She stared at the woman's face, at the features suffused with anger, at the glinting blue eyes, the lips curled with disgust and felt the animosity aimed their way.

She reached her arm around Katy, pulled her close, then looked down to reassure Callie. Her breath caught. Plain little Callie sat listening to the sermon, a soft glow warming her brown eyes, a small, gentle smile on her mouth. Tears filmed her eyes. Callie was not plain. The child was beautiful. Truly beautiful.

"In the book of Samuel, it says…'For the LORD seeth

not as man seeth; for man looketh on the outward appearance, but the LORD looketh on the heart.'"

Mary looked from Callie to Miss Stewart and the truth, bright and glimmering, shining in all its glory, burst upon her. To God, Callie was truly beautiful. As beautiful as anyone. Because God did not look at golden curls or dimpled cheeks—God looked at a person's heart. And if that was true, then— Tears welled into her eyes. *Oh, God, I have been so wrong! Forgive me, for doubting Your love for me. And please let my heart be pleasing unto Thee.* She blinked hard, reached for the embroidered, linen handkerchief she carried in her reticule and dabbed her eyes.

The pastor stepped out from behind the pulpit, looked out across the congregation. "My brethren, in light of this message, I urge each of you to examine your hearts today. Do you value others because of outward appearances and worldly successes? Do you 'despise the poor,' to your discredit? Or do you, as does the Lord, look upon a person's heart and character? May the almighty God help us all to follow as He leads."

At the last amen, the mayor rose and stormed up the aisle, his wife in tow, his daughter at his side. Several others rose and followed them. Mary clutched her handkerchief and watched them go. Miss Stewart turned her head, shot them all a venomous look, then stuck her nose into the air and swept on by.

For the first time in her life, Mary looked at a petite, beautiful, blond woman, not with envy, but with compassion. She turned and gave Mrs. Lucas a hug. "Would it be possible for you to join us for dinner, Mrs. Lucas? The children and I would be delighted with your company. James has other plans."

"Yes, I see." Mrs. Lucas twinkled up at him. "I believe your 'other plan' is dawdling by the door, Mr. Randolph. I suggest you hurry to her before Rebecca runs out of reasons to tarry."

James chuckled. "I believe I am going to enjoy getting to know you better, Mrs. Lucas." He leaned down, gave her a peck on the cheek, then waved a hand to the children and rushed off up the aisle.

Mrs. Lucas smiled and looked up at her. "Your brother is a delightful young man, Mary. The two of you are a wonderful testimony to your parents. As these children will one day be to you. Now, let us depart. I am afraid I am too weary to accept your kind invitation, but you all may see me home."

The sun beamed down on the *Journey's End,* its brightness creating the contrast of deep shade. Mary welcomed the coolness of the shadows, the slight breeze coming off the river. She raised her hand and lifted a strand of hair off the nape of her moist neck, and tried not to think how every suggestion the captain offered made more clear the enormity of the task she had set for herself.

"And now about the kitchen."

Mary nodded and followed him into a dismal room, took one quick look around and gasped. The place was a disaster. "Oh, my." She closed her eyes, took a deep breath and opened them again.

The captain grinned. "Cooks on steamboats are not known for cleanliness. But if you look beyond the dirt and grime…"

"Yes." She took a closer look. Iron pots and pans littered a brick hearth along the far wall. Large, long-handled spoons and two-pronged iron forks, along with other implements, hung from cut nails pounded into the rough beam mantel and in the brick beside the bake ovens. Pewter trenchers and goblets marched in broken formation down the length of the mantel, and porringers formed piles at the end.

Overhead, sooty oil lamps hung from a joining of two long iron hooks. Along the wall to her right was a large dry sink holding a copper basin full of pots and pans, and a tall cupboard—one door hanging askew from its hinges—full of crockery and pewter dishes. The wall on her left was formed by a deep pantry she assumed held the food stores. Nothing could have induced her to open one of the doors to see if she was correct.

A long table with a thick, scarred top, stained with something she did not want to examine too closely, marched down the center of the room. And behind her, on both sides of the arched opening through which they had entered were barred cages. Feathers mixed with dried dung in the bottom told of their purpose. She took a breath, albeit a shallow one, and shrugged. "It seems to be well supplied. And, I suppose it…has possibilities…"

The captain threw back his head and laughed, a deep-chested, full-throated laugh.

She stared at him.

He shook his head, knuckled tears from his eyes. "I apologize, Miss Randolph. But if you could see your face…"

Her own lips twitched. "I suppose I do look rather undone. I confess, I am feeling a bit overwhelmed by the vastness of this undertaking. I did not realize…" She shook dust from the hem of her old blue gown and squared her shoulders. "Nonetheless, I shall manage. Somehow. What is next, Captain?"

"The cargo storage area of the main deck. That is the open area we walked through to reach the kitchen." He led her back through the arched opening. "As you can see, there is a wall at the outer edge of the boat opposite the kitchen. That was meant to keep perishable cargo dry." He stepped to the end of the long wall, then walked toward the center of the boat at a right angle, drawing the toe of his boot along the floor to make a line through the dust. He strode to the other end of the wall and did the same, then made another line connecting them. In the middle of the long rectangle, he drew two more lines, stopped and faced her. "I told you the other night that I had a suggestion for where the overseer of the children can live. This is it. If we build walls where I have indicated, there will be a dressing room—" he pointed to the square he had drawn in the center "—and two spacious bedrooms. One for the overseer and, I thought, perhaps one for the cook." He indicated the two large rectangles on either end.

Mary studied the lines, nibbling at the corner of her upper lip. "Yes. I can see that. What an excellent suggestion, Captain!"

"Wait. I'm not finished. If we build a wall across this end from here—" he hurried down to the far end of the line, placed the toe of his boot on the corner and drew another line in the dust to the corner of the kitchen wall "—to here, it will make this entire area in between these rooms and the kitchen into a comfortable sitting area, and large dining room, heated by one of the furnaces. That will free the main room on the boiler deck for the schoolroom and play area you want for the children. And here, in the center of this end wall, we can build a staircase that leads to the play area on the deck where the children's bedrooms are located, and place the door to go out onto the remaining portion of the main deck. A sort of porch." He came back and stood looking down at her. "What do you think?"

She could not speak. Her heart was too full. Her throat too tight. He had said *we*. Not once but several times. It was not a mistaken slip of his tongue. She lifted the hem of her gown, turned and walked to the bow of the boat to look down at the new lines he had drawn in the dust so he could not see the folly of her heart reflected in her eyes. "I think it is a *wonderful* plan, Captain. I should not have thought of anything like it."

She heard him come toward her and moved to the gangway. He held her elbow to help her down the ramp. She thought of Miss Stewart's soft roundness and longed to pull her thin arm out of his grip. "With your plan in mind, I am most eager to begin work. I shall start with the cleaning tomorrow."

"I am certain your brother knows of those who make their living renovating steamboats, Miss Randolph. But if you should need any advice as to who would perform best—"

She shook her head, followed his guidance around a pile of firewood, and continued walking beside him up the levee, acutely aware of the warmth where his hand still held her arm. "I do not have funds to hire the work done, Captain. At least, not yet."

The din and buzz of activity fell behind them. They crossed Front Street and, at last, he released his hold on her elbow. Disappointment warred with relief. They strolled up Market Street side by side, his long-legged strides making her hurry her steps. "But, as the children in jail cannot wait until I have the funds, I shall begin the work myself—in the morning, before the heat becomes oppressive."

His steps slowed. "Miss Randolph, that is not wise."

"But necessary."

He gripped her elbow again and drew her to a halt. She looked up at him.

"Forgive me." He released her. "But I do not believe you understand the risk involved. You should not go alone to the steamboat. There are—"

"Unsavory elements on the levee. Yes, I know, Captain. You told me of them that first day." She resumed walking. They turned the corner and strolled toward her gate. "And, as you also explained that first day, I realize it is your duty to be concerned over the safety of the citizens of St. Louis, but you need have no concern for me. I shall not go to the *Journey's End* alone. I shall have James escort me there when he goes to the office—and escort me home at dinnertime. And I will stay out of sight in the staterooms while I am working."

"Miss Randolph—"

"I shall take every precaution, Captain." She stepped through the gate he opened for her, turned and smiled up at him. She should invite him in—it was only right after all his trouble, but she could not do so. She wanted it too much. "Thank you for your excellent suggestions. I truly do appreciate your help, Captain. Good evening."

"All right it's settled then, Jackson. But you and Harmon do not get your money until the job is finished."

"Ah, Captain, that ain't right." The short, wiry man lounging on a cot in the cell hopped to his feet and came to the stand, holding on to the bars beside his friend. "Half now, half when the job is done."

Sam shook his head. "No. I'll pay for your meals at the Cock's Crow while you are renovating the *Journey's End*, but not one coin in your hand. I'll not have you drinking up the money—leaving Miss Randolph unprotected and the work undone."

Sam jiggled the keys in his hand. "And she is not to know I am paying you. You will offer to do the work for the privilege of sleeping on the boat. That will allow you to stay there all night and protect it from looters. Understood?" He jiggled the keys again.

The men looked down at the ring of keys, looked back at him and nodded.

"One more thing."

Their gazes sharpened.

"You eat your meals at different times. I want one of you on that boat at all times. And if either one of you gets drunk, I'll throw you back in jail and you will finish out this sentence, as well as serving a new one. Understood?"

"Yeah, we understand. Open the door."

"In the morning. That's when the deal starts."

Sam stepped down the dark hall and glanced at the children sleeping in the last four cells. He had managed to delay things so far, but the mayor had sent word that the children were to be taken to the courthouse tomorrow morning. Work had started on the additions to the building, and the children were to clear away unearthed stones.

Sam turned and headed back for his desk in the other room. It wasn't that clearing off stones was so hard. There were a lot of farm children who did much heavier work. But they did it because they were part of a family. And he had done much harder work himself when he was these children's ages. But he had been free. It had been his choice. And he had been paid for his labor. It was not right to make slaves out of these kids.

Sam scowled, stepped through the barred door, then plunked down in his desk chair and threw the key ring in the drawer. Turning that steamboat into an orphanage was a clever idea. Once he had gotten over his shock and started thinking about it, it made good sense. Renovating that boat would cost much less than buying or erecting a building of comparable size, and it could be ready quickly.

The big problem would be a plot of land to settle it on. He laced his fingers behind his head and tilted back on the chair's hind legs. That could be expensive. And, it appeared Mary Randolph dreamed beyond her means. Nothing wrong with that. He had done that all his life. And he had worked to make those dreams come true. Now...

He rose, stood again in the barred doorway and looked down the hall toward the children's cells. Now it seemed his dreams would have to wait a little longer—these children couldn't. Preparing this orphanage could get expensive, and Mary needed money now. There was no hurry for his showcase house. A year or so delay wouldn't matter. He had to wait on the property anyway.

And he had to convince the spunky Miss Mary Randolph to share it with him.

Mary stared out at the starry sky and reminded herself for the hundredth time since coming home to keep her head about her. To keep the wall in place around her heart. But the truth was, the captain had already breached that wall.

We. If we *build... If* we *move...* Her heart pounded. It did not matter how often she told herself that his only reason was to help the children. He had still said "we." He would be working with her.

How would she ever be able to hide her growing feelings for him, from him?

Chapter Eighteen

Sam fought back a smile. Mary was standing against the railing of the main deck of the *Journey's End* wearing a long white apron over her dress, a large handkerchief tied over her hair. A bucket of water sat at her feet, and she gripped a broom in her hands. But it was not her costume that made him want to grin. It was the wary, combative look in her eyes as she faced Harmon, perched on an upturned wooden barrel. What a woman! But that spunk and that broom wouldn't hold off anyone set to do her harm.

The smile died. Dealing with a woman as determined as Mary Randolph had its drawbacks when you didn't have the right to protect her. Sam frowned and trotted up the gangplank, Jackson at his heels. "Is there a problem, Miss Randolph? Jackson said you wanted to see me."

Her gaze shot to his and for a moment he read the relief, the trust in her eyes. It was so intense, it was almost as if she ran to him. His heart thudded. *God help me never to do anything that will destroy her trust in me again.*

"Yes, Captain, I do. It is good of you to come." Her

death grip on the broom relaxed. "These men want to help with the renovation of the boat in exchange for the privilege of sleeping on it. They said you would recommend them as good and honest workers."

Sam read the doubt in her eyes. He turned to the man beside him. "Run up against some hard times, Jackson?"

"*That's* the truth, Captain."

Harmon shook his head. "Yeah, me an' Jackson are havin' a *dry* time right now."

Sam shot him a warning look. "I do know these men to be good workers, Miss Randolph. They know how to get a boat back into shape, and they are quick about doing it. And it is more than a fair deal. Have you cleaning tools and supplies enough for them?"

Mary looked down at her bucket and broom, the pile of rags she had brought from home. "I have only these, but—"

He held up his hand and turned to Jackson. "You and Harmon go to Gardner's and get what you need for the cleaning. Tell Jim I'll stand good for it. And see you come straight back. I'll be waiting here with Miss Randolph."

He turned back. She was staring at him, her eyes wide. He fastened his gaze on hers and got lost in her eyes. Those brown eyes with tiny, honey-colored specks glowing with approval, warmth… He stepped closer. A deep-rose blush spread over her cheekbones. His heart kicked. She stepped back, groped behind her for the railing and lowered her eyelashes. They rested like an inky smudge on the crest of her cheekbones.

"Y-you are most kind to—" a quick little breath "—to offer to purchase the cleaning supplies, Captain." Hands rose to fuss with the handkerchief, lowered to grip and un-grip the railing. "But—" a quick glance up at him from under her lashes "—I do not know when I shall be able to—" a hand rose to pull at the knot of the handkerchief again "—to repay you." Soft, husky, *quavering* voice.

He made her nervous.

So she was not as cool toward him as she portrayed. The knowledge sent joy surging through him. His heart hammered. He wanted to whoop! To turn cartwheels. To show off for her like a ten-year-old. To take her in his arms and kiss her until—

"Capt'n Benton!"

Sam sucked in a breath, blew it out and turned. "What is it?"

"It's yer man, Buckles. He's got two mean drunks cornered at the Broken Barge, an' they done pulled knives. He told me t' see could I find you."

Sam braced his hand on the railing and leaped from the deck—"Stay here with Miss Randolph until Jackson comes back!"—and took off at a dead run.

Knives.

Mary shuddered, dipped her cloth in the bucket of vinegar water and scrubbed at the dirty corners of the small panes of glass. On tiptoe, she leaned her head against the window, trying to see through the dirt on the outside to the gangplank. Why did he not return? Of course, he did not say he would. And there was no reason he should. He did not know how she felt about him. How concerned she was about his welfare. Yet, there had been that moment when he had looked at her as if…as if…

"Cease that foolish dreaming this instant, Mary Randolph!" She glared at her dim, blurry reflection in the window. "You have far too much imagination. Captain

Benton is courting the beautiful Miss Stewart. Why would he have any interest in the likes of you? You are only placing yourself in danger of being hurt again. Do you never learn?"

She grabbed a cloth from her dwindling pile and swiped the window dry, studying it as if cleanliness were the most important thing in the world. It was difficult to tell if it was clean. She would have to do the windows again when the men had washed the outside. At least most of the grime was gone.

The rag twisted in her hands. She threw it back on the pile, sank down on the edge of the narrow bed and covered her face with her hands. What if he was hurt? Or…or worse. *Oh, please, God, do not let him be hurt. Please, do not let him be hurt.*

The worrisome thoughts nagged at her, knotted her stomach. She rose, picked up the bucket and the rags and moved on to the next stateroom. The men had said they would wash the walls and scrub the floors. All she should do was the windows. Thank goodness for the training to be a wife and run a household that she had received from her mother. She was not entirely unequal to the tasks she had taken upon herself.

She sighed, squeezed the extra vinegar water from the rag and swished it over the windowpanes in a first pass. She had to wash each window at least three times to get it clean. She had finished four. That left twenty more to do. On this deck.

"Mary?"

She started, then rushed to the stateroom door. "Here I am, James. Is it dinnertime so soon?"

"Yes." He frowned, looking over his shoulder toward the stairway. "Who are those men scrubbing down walls?"

"That is Jackson and Harmon." The vinegar water splashed against the bucket as she dropped in the rag she was using. She looked over her shoulder at the sound of James's footsteps. He was in the doorway. Grinning.

"What?"

"You look like Edda or Ivy. Only they are cleaner."

The words pierced the ache inside. The captain had seen her looking like a *maid*. She stuck out her tongue at James so he would not guess how his innocent teasing had hurt her, and took off the apron and handkerchief. "I will tell you all about the men on the way home." She smoothed her hands over her hair and walked with him to the stairway, forcing one foot to move in front of the other. She did not want to leave. How would she learn if the captain had been wounded? What if he needed care? Would Miss Stewart nurse him back to health?

"Mary?"

She looked up. They were already halfway up the levee.

"You were going to tell me about those men."

"Oh, yes. Of course." She shoved her anxieties away once more and smiled up at James. "The most amazing thing happened this morning…"

It was good to feel clean again. Mary picked up the green cording that matched the trim on her dress, wrapped it around the loose knot on the crown of her head and tied it in a bow at the back. There. All finished. And she had time to write a letter home before she began the children's schooling. It would help keep her mind occupied so she wouldn't worry about the captain.

She closed the dressing-room door and stepped to her desk, forcing herself to concentrate. There was so much she wanted to tell her parents. She would start with the events in church and—

"Miss Mary?"

Her heart stopped at the hail. For one wild moment she thought someone had brought her news of the captain. Perhaps Will had heard something. Her skirts billowed out as she turned and hurried to the top of the stairs. "Yes, Will. What is it?"

The boy charged halfway up the stairs. "Mrs. Lucas says, beggin' yer pardon for the short invitation, but would you please accompany her to the Ladies' Be— bene—"

"Benevolent?" She made the suggestion absently, still adjusting to the rapid change of subject.

A grin split his face. "Yeah, that's it. The Ladies' Benevolent Society meeting this afternoon. She said I was to tell you she wants to carry things in through the back door."

"Carry things in the back door?"

He shrugged his shoulders. "Yeah. That's what she said. I'm to take you, or your answer, to her."

She did not want to leave the house—in case. But she owed Mrs. Lucas so much… *Carry things in through—* Oh! What had Mrs. Lucas said that day? *But what won't go in a front door can be carried in the back.* Yes. That was it. But whatever could she mean? Mary sighed. This day was full of surprises. "All right, Will. Go to the kitchen and tell Ivy I will be leaving for the afternoon. I will be down as soon as I fetch my bonnet."

She hurried to the cupboard, found her green bonnet with the shirred brim and settled it on her head. *Carry things in the back door.* Well that certainly gave her something to think of besides the captain. She pulled the bonnet's ties into place and knotted them under her chin as she hurried downstairs.

"This here's the place. She said you was to go on in and ask fer her."

Mary swept her gaze over the stone house, grander than any she had thus far seen in St. Louis. "All right, Will. Thank you for bringing me. Now go straight home, please."

She smiled at his nod, opened the gate, walked up to the porch and knocked. The door opened.

"Yes?"

Mary took in the black dress, the white apron and cap. "I was told to meet Mrs. Lucas here for the Ladies' Benevolent Society meeting."

"Of course, miss. Right this way."

Mary stepped into the entrance hall and followed the maid to a room on her right. Muted women's voices flowed out into the hall.

"The meeting has already started. You can go in, miss."

Mary stepped through the door that the maid opened. Talk ceased. Heads turned her direction. She smiled, then froze—stared at Levinia Stewart... Levinia's mother... read their shock. Will had brought her to the wrong—

"Ah, there you are, Mary!"

Mrs. Lucas. She shifted her gaze. The elderly woman smiled and patted the empty space beside her on a linen-covered settee.

"Come sit beside me, dear. And don't bother to apologize for being a little tardy. I have already told the ladies it was my fault for issuing my invitation so late in the day. And the meeting has only begun."

The shock on several of the faces turned to anger. Heads swiveled back toward Mrs. Lucas. The elderly lady seemed not to notice. She merely smiled wider and patted the cushion again.

Mary lifted her chin. Everything in her wanted to leave, but she could not disappoint Mrs. Lucas no matter how uncomfortable she was. She pasted on a smile and made her way to the settee.

Mrs. Lucas beamed up at her. "My, you look lovely today, Mary. The green of your gown suits your vibrant coloring."

"Isobel, speaking as president of this organization, I would like an explanation, please."

The frost in the voice could have frozen the river. Mary glanced to identify the speaker. It was Mrs. Stewart. Her dander rose. It was one thing for the woman to freeze her out—it was quite another for her to be disrespectful to Mrs. Lucas.

"Why, I told you I had invited a guest with a worthy project for our society, Margaret."

What? Mary jerked her gaze back to Mrs. Lucas, and her shock dissolved into amusement. She had never seen anyone look so sweetly innocent. Clearly, Mrs. Lucas was not disturbed by the glares of outrage aimed at her.

"It is customary to discuss a proposed project with the officers of the society in advance of the meeting, Isobel. And you know it!"

"I do indeed, Margaret. But there simply wasn't time. You see, the idea came on me suddenly—while I was examining my heart in view of Sunday's sermon. You know, the way the pastor urged us all to do." Mrs. Lucas shed her beatific smile over everyone. "Anyway, helping Miss Randolph provide a home for orphaned children would be a very worthwhile project. And fully in keeping with the pastor's message. And I know it says in the Bible—though I cannot quote it exactly—that pure and undefiled religion has something to do with our treatment of the fatherless."

Mary scanned the faces of the ladies from beneath her lowered lashes. Some looked abashed, others—including Levinia—seemed as if they would choke on their anger. She looked at Mrs. Lucas in awe. The woman had placed them all in a position where they dare not protest her idea for fear of seeming to lack a Christian attitude.

"Now, as I said, my friend, Mary Randolph—" Mrs. Lucas reached over and patted her hand "—has a perfectly wonderful plan for providing a home for the orphans that presently roam our streets. Of course it is costly to provide for children. But with our help—"

"Mrs. Lucas, I believe this project is unnecessary." Mary watched as Levinia Stewart turned a dimpled smile on the elderly woman. The smile did not reach her eyes, which continued to glitter with anger. "Father has already put a plan in motion to rid our streets of those fil—fatherless children. And the city of St. Louis will bear the cost of housing them."

Mary stiffened. Mrs. Lucas squeezed her hand. She took a breath and sat back to let the elderly woman handle Levinia Stewart.

"You are young and without husband or child, Levinia. But, speaking as a mother, I do not consider a jail to be proper housing for a child. Especially one who has done no wrong save the misfortune of losing his or her parents to death. Nor do I believe it is right to force them to labor on city projects to earn their board of scanty meals and hard cots behind bars. And I am certain every mother here would agree with me. Now this is my idea…"

Mary shoved her toe against the porch floor and set the swing moving. Her head was still reeling. She longed to go for a brisk walk, but it was improper—and unsafe—for a young lady to do so in the evening without an escort.

She frowned and pushed with her toes again. Without James home to accompany her, she was confined to the porch and small yard.

Despite her restlessness, excitement bubbled through her. So much had happened today. Jackson and Harmon had offered to renovate the boat at no cost to her—for only the privilege of sleeping on it—which would keep it safe from vandals! And the captain had paid for the supplies they needed. And now—she shook her head in pure amazement—now the Ladies' Benevolent Society was going to provide all that was needed for the children's bedrooms! Mrs. Lucas had proposed the idea that each lady provide the accoutrements—window curtains, bedsheets, pillow and quilt or coverlet—for one stateroom and they had agreed! Why, once Mrs. Lucas had finished with them, some of the ladies were even eager and excited about the project.

Mary laughed and pushed the swing faster. The woman was a genius. Wait until the captain heard— Her laughter died. The swing slowed, the creaking of the chains a lonely sound in the twilight. If only she knew the captain was well, the day would be perfect. Oh, of course he was! He was probably this minute sitting on Miss Stewart's porch and—

"Good evening."

"Oh!" She jammed her toes against the floor, to stop the swing.

"Excuse me. I guess you did not hear me approach on the grass." The captain folded his arms on the porch railing and smiled up at her. "My patrol is over and I was on my way home when I heard you laughing. I couldn't resist coming over. Care to share what has made you so happy?"

She looked at the captain's blue eyes, his smiling lips, his strong arms. He was well. And he was here. She smiled and let the words come out, soft and full of joy. "A perfect day."

Chapter Nineteen

Mary glanced at the paper in her hand—fourth house on the right-hand side. This was the place. She nodded to James and squared her shoulders. They marched up the walk and knocked on the door—exchanged glances and stepped back as it was opened.

A gray-haired, plump woman peered out at them. "Yes?"

Mary smiled, waited for James to speak. "I should like to speak with Mr. Monroe, please. About the Spruce Street property he has for sale."

"Come in." The woman stepped aside. "Wait here, please." She disappeared into the dim interior.

Mary closed her eyes. *Please, Lord, this is the last name on the list the captain gave me. Please, let this man be willing to sell the land to us.*

A well-dressed, prosperous-looking man came striding into the hall. He looked them both over, addressing James. "You are interested in my Spruce Street property, young man?"

James smiled, held out his hand. "I am if you are Wilfred Monroe."

"I am." The man grasped James's hand. "And you are…?"

"I am James Randolph, Mr. Monroe. And this is my sister—"

"Randolph!" A scowl darkened the man's features. "I have heard about your sister. Making an *orphanage* out of a steamboat." He gave a disdainful snort. "A ridiculous idea. And I have been warned you are now coming around to decent people and trying to buy land from them to hold that disgrace." He pulled the door open. "You will get no land from me. No, nor from anyone I know, for I will tell them all of your scheme. You will devalue all the properties around your ridiculous steamboat orphanage. Good day to you!" He rattled the doorknob.

"And to you, sir." James took Mary's elbow and together they walked out the door. It slammed shut behind them.

"Is that the last of them?"

"Yes." Mary looked up at him, tears in her eyes, though from anger or defeat she could not say. "What are we to do, James? The *Journey's End* will soon be ready for the children, but we have no land to put it on. And none of these people will even talk to us."

"There is more property for sale than this small list, Mary." James smiled down at her. "The captain gave us a list of the best properties for our purpose. And the ones we might be able to afford. We shall simply have to expand our search, and extend ourselves more. I believe you should write Mother and Father of this problem. They are so proud of what you are doing for these children, I am sure Father will increase the amount he will pay for the land."

The thought cheered her. She smiled up at him. "Perhaps you are right. I shall write Mother and Father this evening." She sighed and glanced back at the house. "Sometimes it is very hard to maintain a Christian tongue."

He laughed. "I saw you swallowing your words. The truth is, I swallowed a few of my own." He sobered. "But I truly believe God has been blessing your efforts, and I am certain you will have your land when you need it."

"You are right, of course." She slanted a wry look at him. "I am new at trusting God, but I am learning. Thank you for coming with me today, James. I would not even have been received had I approached these people on my own."

"My pleasure, Mary. With all that has happened at the steamer line, I have had little time to help with your endeavors. But I am happy to do all I can. And now, my dear sister, you may help me in return."

"Oh? In what way? What do you wish?"

"Come with me to the office. Our new luxury steamboat is well under way and there are final decorating decisions to be made. I need your advice on carpet and paint and chandeliers."

"Goodness, Miss Mary!" Ivy stopped and shook her head. "I've been admiring the boat from afar, but it looks even better when you get near."

Mary laughed and swept her gaze over the *Journey's End*. The steamboat gleamed. The fresh white paint was so bright it hurt your eyes to look fully at it when the sun was high. The boat's name, which she had kept, deeming it so appropriate for the orphanage, was emblazoned on the side in the dark blue paint that also graced the window frames, the two tall stacks and the paddle wheel at the stern. The deck glistened. The windows shone. The outside of the boat was finished.

Her heart swelled. She was so proud of the steamboat orphanage, and so grateful to everyone who had helped make the dream come true. Her mother was right. God truly did work through His children. Why had she resisted that truth so long? She smiled at Ivy. "I agree. I cannot simply go aboard. Every time I come, I stop here by the gangplank to admire the steamer. And to remember how many people have helped along the way." She smiled at her cook. "You were the first, Ivy. You opened your heart and your home to help the children, and I am very grateful."

Mary shook her head. "I always scorned my mother's insistence that God watches over His children, and that the things that happen in our lives are not coincidences but God's blessings. Now I know that is true. The way the steamboat orphanage has come about in the face of the city fathers' opposition has proved that beyond any doubt. But there is more to be done. We need land." She looked down at the children fidgeting with impatience. "And you must all help by praying every day. Now, go ahead."

She laughed as the children rushed, sure-footed and fearless, up the bright red gangplank. But her heart ached for the children still in jail. *Almighty God, please, provide land so we may free those children.*

"Katy, please stay back from the rail. And, all of you, do not pester Jackson and Harmon while they are working!" She watched the children run inside chattering about their new home and glanced at Ivy. Her cook was gazing at the steamboat and seemed undisturbed by the children's remarks about their new home. Perhaps she hadn't heard them.

"Shall we go inside, Ivy? I cannot wait to show you around." She led the way up the gangplank and through the door in the new end wall. "The children's quarters on the boiler deck are all completed. But work continues here on the main deck. However, the kitchen is finished." She laughed at the sudden gleam in Ivy's eyes. "I will show it to you first. Come this way."

She swept her arm in an arc. "This large area will be the dining room. The tables and chairs are from the old dining room above. And here is a sitting room. Those rooms on either side will be for the headmistress—me—" she laughed and made a small curtsy "—and the cook. Who at present is unknown. And this is the kitchen." She led them through the archway, now boasting cupboards where the open crates had been, and stopped.

"Oh, my…" Ivy moved into the room, running her hand over the scrubbed-clean table.

Mary watched her and laughed. "Your reaction is very different than mine when I first saw this room." She looked around with a little thrill of pride. "It is much the same as it was, except now everything is repaired and clean and polished and in its proper place. And we have a new iron cookstove."

Ivy nodded, then began exploring the kitchen—opening the pantry doors and peering inside, moved on to the cupboard full of dishes, the dry sink with a new wide shelf above it, then turned and fastened her gaze on her. "Miss Mary, I want to be the cook. That's why I asked to come with you today and see the steamboat."

Mary stared, taken aback by the sudden pronouncement.

"I've given it lots of thought. I like helping these kids. But my place isn't any bigger than a mouse's squeak, and

I can't take in any more. But here, I could be doing for all of them."

"But—"

"And, it appears to me, Mister James will be marrying soon. His bride will want her own help and her own ways. And nothing makes me happier than baking up a batch of cookies and seeing those children's happy grins."

"Well..."

"Thank you, Miss Mary."

Mary lifted her hands in a gesture of surrender and laughed. "You are welcome, Ivy. But *you* get the honor of telling James!"

"Come in, Captain Benton. Have a seat." The mayor gestured to the chair at the end of the long table.

Sam removed his hat and moved toward the chair. Unease, that policeman's instinct that warned him of danger, rose. Something was in the wind. And it wasn't good. He could feel it. He took a quick scan of the aldermen seated around the table. They all looked tense but pleased. He gave a polite nod as a covering reason for his look and took his seat.

The mayor cleared his throat. "I have asked you to join this meeting, Captain, because I believe you are quite familiar with the person and the subject it concerns."

Sam's unease doubled. The mayor was seething under that polite mask he wore. Still, pleasure over what was to come lurked in the depth of his eyes, easy to read as an item in a newspaper. This was about Mary and the orphans. He placed his hat on his knee, leaned back in his chair and affected a guise of relaxed ease. No sense in giving the man the satisfaction of a response. He already looked too smug.

The mayor frowned. "I am, of course, speaking of Miss Randolph and this ludicrous steamboat orphanage she thinks she is creating."

Stay in control, Sam. He wants you angry. Defensive. He gave a short nod. "I know Miss Randolph. And I am familiar with the orphanage she *has* created out of a steamboat, yes." He couldn't resist the slight emphasis.

The mayor's eyes narrowed. "Oh, I know of all the renovation that has taken place, Captain. *And* that the Ladies' Benevolent Society has contributed generously to bring it about. Also that they intend to continue that philanthropy."

There was a general muttering and nodding of heads around the table.

Ah, so that was it. These men's pocketbooks were involved. No doubt Levinia—

"But all that has been accomplished is a useless, renovated steamboat, Captain. The orphans will stay in jail. And they will continue to work for their keep." The mayor looked straight at him and smiled. "And, of course, more will join them as you and your men continue to arrest them. You see no one can *live* on that piece of folly. Miss Randolph has no land to situate it on. Though it has come to my attention that she is trying to purchase land for that purpose." The mayor's eyes glittered. "I intend to see that she will *never* do so. *That* is what this meeting is about. And that, as an officer of the law, is the message you will convey to Miss Randolph when we adjourn."

Sam gripped the chair arms. It took all of his control to stay in his seat, to keep from rushing around the table to pummel the man more senseless than he already was. His jaw muscles twitched. His hands clenched and unclenched on the chair arms. The orphans did not deserve this. *Mary* did not deserve this. She was the most wonderful, the most beautiful, the most—

"And I assure you, Captain, that was *not* an idle threat."

The words shot out like bullets from a gun—fast and deadly.

Sam jerked his attention back to the mayor. The man grabbed the gavel by his hand and crashed it down on the table.

"*Gentlemen,* I am proposing a new law. From this day forth, there will be no steamboats or other river vessels permitted to be permanently situated or used as a residence on land in St. Louis. No matter what changes or renovations have been made to them! All in favor, acknowledge by saying aye."

One by one, clockwise around the table, each alderman spoke aye.

"Let the record show the new law was passed by unanimous vote." The mayor leaned back in his chair and smiled. "And that, Captain, puts an end to your Miss Randolph's steamboat orphanage."

Sam wanted to rip the smirking lips off the man's face. He took a breath, let it out slow and even. "*My* Miss Randolph?"

"Why, yes." The mayor's gaze bored into his. "Did I forget to mention I am also aware that you have been spending a great deal of time with the woman? Of course, that could change…"

So this was about Levinia, also. Spoiled Levinia who did not like to lose. Sam shoved back his chair and rose. "You are correct, Mr. Mayor. That could change." He smiled inwardly at the flash of victory in the mayor's eyes and drove home his killing thrust. "And I hope it does—to courtship and marriage."

He swept his glance over the men around the table, letting his contempt for their high-handed, unjust tactics show. "Good day to you all. I will deliver your message to Miss Randolph." He yanked his hat on his head, spun on his heel and strode from the room.

"Excuse me. Are you Miss Randolph?"

Mary turned at the soft query and looked over the pile of bedding in her arms at a young, thin woman with red hair and green eyes. "Yes, I'm Mary Randolph." She lowered her burden to a game table and smoothed the front of her skirt. "How may I help you?"

The young woman stepped forward from her position at the top of the stairs, her eyes rounding as she glanced around. "My. This is…this is…lovely."

"Thank you, Miss…"

"Oh. I am sorry." A blush swept over the pale skin, making the freckles stand out even more. "Please forgive my rudeness. I was not prepared for such a…a wonderful place." The blush deepened. "I am Jane Withers, and I—" She stopped and drew her shoulders back. "I have heard that you are making this steamboat into an orphanage. I wondered if, perhaps, you were looking for a teacher for the children who will live here?"

Mary smiled and shook her head. "I would very much like to have a teacher, Miss Withers. But at present, I will be teaching the children. I am afraid I do not have the funds to pay another."

"Oh." The young woman looked absolutely crestfallen. "I understand. Forgive me for interrupting your work, Miss Randolph." She turned to leave.

Mary scanned her clothes. The gown was neat and clean, but not of rich fabric or style. And the heels of the shoes peeking out from under the long gingham skirt were worn. "Miss Withers?"

The young woman turned back.

"Who told you about *Journey's End?*"

"A Captain Benton. He said he thought perhaps you would want a teacher when there are more children."

"I see." Mary's heart swelled. "I do not wish to pry, but…have you, perhaps, fallen on hard times?"

The shoulders firmed. "I have. Through no fault of my own. I was to marry and travel west with my new husband, and so journeyed here to St. Louis in the company of friends who were also going west. But when John saw me again, after two years apart, he decided I was too frail—not sickly, but *frail*—to be of much help to him on the trail or in settling on a new place. He chose another to be his bride."

Hurt flashed in Jane Withers's green eyes, but was quickly masked. The remembered pain and humiliation of being cast aside because of one's appearance spiraled through Mary.

"And so, Miss Randolph, I am here in St. Louis. I was a teacher back home in Pittsburgh, but I have been unable to find a position here. I have found employment as a seamstress." A wry smile touched her pink lips. "I am not very good at sewing."

Mary laughed. "And I am not very good at teaching, Miss Withers. Would you be interested in the position though I cannot pay much wage? Room and board aboard the *Journey's End* would be included, of course."

"Oh, I should be very interested, Miss Randolph!" The

young woman cast another glance around. "And where would the schoolroom be?"

"In the captain's and pilot's cabin above. There are tables and stools, and cabinets for supplies. It would be most helpful if you would make a list of needed supplies." Mary frowned. "I cannot say for certain when we shall be needing your teaching services. We are still looking for land to place the boat on. Will you be able to manage until then?"

"Yes, I will manage. Thank you so very much, Miss Randolph. I am most grateful for the opportunity to teach children again. But I have taken enough of your time. I shall make the list immediately. And should you need me for anything else…to help prepare the schoolroom or such…you have only to ask. Captain Benton knows where to reach me. I shall look forward to your summons to my duties as teacher aboard the *Journey's End.* Good day."

"Good day, Miss Withers." Mary watched the woman walk away knowing full well her heart had once again run away with her head. How would she manage a wage for a teacher? She could not ask her father for another increase in her allowance. He was already doing so much to help these orphans. And her personal monies were quickly dwindling. Well…she would simply have to find a way. And, with God's help, she would.

Mary smiled and turned to put the bedding, now lying on the table, into a cupboard. God's ways were indeed mysterious. Who ever would have thought stopping Ben from being jailed that day would lead to all that had happened? Or that helping the orphans would teach her of God's love for her. *And* teach her to trust Him. Though she was still learning to do that.

Her lips quirked. She put the last of the sheets on the

cupboard shelf and reached for the pillow slips. Was this another lesson? It seemed so. Her mother said there was always a blessing in God's teaching. And though the finances would be difficult, one more problem was solved. A definite blessing. She had been concerned about teaching so many children. It was limiting enough to teach four of them. Now she would be free to concentrate on all the other matters concerning the running of an orphanage.

Mary laughed and put the last of the bedding away. How happy her mother and father would be to know of the change God had wrought in her heart. It was as if she had been blind and could now see His blessings in every area of her life…save one. Her laughter died. She pushed away the sudden surge of self-pity. Perhaps one day God would see fit to bless her with a husband who loved her and children of her own. Until then, she would busy herself with the orphans. Her life was full with helping them.

Captain Benton's image burst upon her. The image that constantly hovered at the edge of her thoughts. She tried to shut it out, but it refused to go away. But now there was something else. Something gnawing at the fringe of her mind, wispy yet determined to be remembered.

She sank onto a chair by the game table and sat quietly waiting. Finally, her father's favorite saying floated into her mind. *Not even God can fill a hand or heart that is already full.* Was that what she was supposed to hear? Tears welled into her eyes. A sob broke from her throat. How could God bless her with a husband and children of her own when her heart was full of love for Samuel Benton? Captain Benton—a man who belonged to another.

Guilt smote her. She closed her eyes, forced words from her aching throat. "Forgive me, Lord, for coveting a man who belongs to another. I confess my love for Captain Benton to You, and I ask Your help in purging this love from my heart and opening it to only the love You have for me. Please help me to accept with joy whatever future You have chosen for me. Be it unto me according to Thy will. Amen."

She waited for a calmness, a peace to flow over her. But all she felt was the pain of her breaking heart.

Mary paused, nibbled at her upper lip. Wrote a bit more about James being serious about Rebecca Green, sent her love and signed her name. She put down the pen, stopped the ink well and stared off into the distance. Sarah was married and expecting her first child. James was in love, and would soon be married if she knew her little brother. And she— She would mail the letter in the morning.

Knuckles rapped against the front door. The sharp, staccato sound echoed throughout the house.

She pushed back her chair, then hurried down the stairs and opened the door a slit to peer out.

"Good evening, Miss Randolph. Might I have a word with you?"

A test of my sincerity so soon, Lord? Mary stared up at the captain, then nodded. "Of course, Captain. James is not home, but I will join you on the porch." She glanced at his face again in the lamplight, then stepped outside and closed the door. "Is something wrong?"

"A difficulty has arisen, yes." He smiled down at her and gestured toward the swing. "Why don't you have a seat and I will tell you about it."

She studied his face in the fading light and shook her head. "No, I prefer to stand." She moved to the railing and turned to face him. "I assume this is about the orphans?"

"Yes." He came to stand with her by the railing. "The mayor has learned you are turning the *Journey's End* into an orphanage. He also knows about the Ladies' Benevolent Society's ongoing efforts to help you."

Misgiving skittered along her nerves. "And what has that to do with the mayor? The city is not involved."

"True. But he has also learned of your efforts to purchase land to place the orphanage on."

She studied his face. He was very angry. Her misgiving blossomed into concern. "I do not follow you, Captain. How does that present a difficulty?" The small muscle along his jaw twitched. So did her fingers. She wanted to touch it—to calm him. He took a deep breath, and she knew he dreaded whatever he was about to say.

"The mayor is determined you will not be successful in your efforts. He called a meeting of the aldermen today and they passed a new law stating that no steamboat or other river craft can be permanently located or lived in on land in St. Louis."

The air rushed from her lungs. She stared at him, unable to speak, to even think. When she returned to awareness, she shook her head to rid herself of the numbness that had seized her. "I see." She lifted her hand and rubbed at the spot over her aching heart. Managed a small smile. "You are right, Captain. That is a…difficulty."

She turned toward the railing and stared at the orange, purple and pink twilight sky. "How shall I tell all of those who have trusted me? Who have given so generously of their time and talents and money to help make a home for these children? How can I tell them that it is over? That in spite of all they have done and given, the children will stay in—" Her voice broke. She forced a little laugh. "How shall I tell them, indeed? I cannot even say the word."

"You don't have to, Mar—Miss Randolph. All is not lost."

His deep voice flowed over her like a soothing balm. He was so kind. How could she ever have thought him heartless? She turned to look at him. "Please, Captain. Do not encourage me further in my foolishness. It is clear I am defeated. No one would sell me land. And now, even if I could buy land, it would do me no profit. You said the law states that no one is allowed to live on a steamboat on land."

"Exactly."

He grinned, that slow, breath-stealing grin, and leaned toward her. She looked at the excitement dancing in his blue eyes, caught her breath and waited.

"But there is no law against living aboard a steamboat on the *river*. And there never can be—unless they want to destroy St. Louis."

Mary stared up at Samuel Benton, memorizing the way he looked, the excitement and compassion burning in his eyes, the joy on his face. How had she ever thought him heartless and cruel? For one timeless, breathless moment, she allowed her love for him to swell her heart, to fill her soul, and then she tucked it away and gave him a polite smile. "Thank you, Captain. You have given me renewed hope. With your help, and the help of all the others, I will not fail those children."

Chapter Twenty

Mary pulled her lace-edged handkerchief from her pocket, dabbed the moisture from her brow, then put it back and adjusted the brim of her straw hat to shield her face from the sun. There was nothing she could do about the waves of heat shimmering off the cobblestones. At least she was almost there.

She shifted the basket she carried into her other hand and hurried across the street to stop beneath the shade of the large elm on the corner of the courthouse property. Lovely, wonderful shade!

Mary put the basket down, massaged her tired hand and searched for the children. They were spread in a line across the furrowed soil at the far end of the lot picking up stones and dropping them in the buckets they carried. Her heart ached for them. She had hoped they would not be put to work in this heat. Thankfully, Ivy had packed double the usual amount of cold mint tea.

Would the foreman let the children come now? Or would he make them work their way to her? She scanned the area, spotted him standing in the shade of the building talking with two of the workers. Of course he would be in the shade—he was the boss. A boss who resented her interrupting the children's work by bringing them something to eat and drink.

She looked back to the children, squinted her eyes against the sun's glare and frowned. Was Tommy staggering? She watched him a moment, lifted her skirts clear of her shoe tops and broke into a run, her gaze fastened on Tommy now down on his hands and knees with his head pressed against the earth. *Please, God, let him be all right.*

From the corner of her eye she saw the men in the shade look her way, then turn and look the direction she was running. She dropped to her knees beside the boy, now prostate on the ground.

She rolled him over, shaded his face with her body. "What is wrong, Tommy?" No answer, only a dull look in his eyes. Sweat sheeted off his forehead, soaked the hair at his temples, dripped to the ground. "Tommy?" *Dear God, let him be all right.*

The children clustered around, silent and staring.

Mary put her hand on his forehead. It was cool. How could that be in this heat? Footsteps thudded to a stop beside her. She looked up to see the foreman, the two workers behind him. Rage shook her. "This boy is ill. One of you men go for a doctor!"

One of the workers turned.

The boss grabbed his arm and halted him. He looked down at her. "There ain't no call to go fetching a doctor, miss. The boy's only had a mite too much sun. Some can't take the heat like others. He can rest a few minutes. He'll be all right."

"Rest a few—" Mary rose, lifted her chin and fastened her most aristocratic look on one of the workers. "You—

carry Tommy to the shade of the elm!" The man didn't even look at his boss. He stooped, picked up Tommy and started toward the tree.

"And you—" she pinned the other worker with another look "—go find Captain Benton and bring him back here immediately!" The man wheeled and hurried off.

"Now see here, miss—"

Mary spun to face the foreman. "And you, sir—*you* may come out of the shade and pick up your own stones." Her voice was low, quiet and cold as ice. She turned and held out her hands. "Come with me, children. There will be no more work for you today."

Sam opened the stable door and stepped out into the heat. Of all the days for Judge Simmons to order Seth Parker served with an eviction notice. It had to be over a hundred degrees. Good thing he had started for the Parker place early. He trotted across the lot, shoved open the door and stepped into the jail's dim interior. It felt good. The small windows and thick stone walls kept the place somewhat cool.

He tugged off his hat, threw it on a hook, then swiped his forearm across his moist forehead and looked over at Jenkins. "Parker's not happy. Made quite a fuss about that notice. But I got him calmed down some." He stretched and motioned the man out of his chair. "Thanks for holding down the fort. I'll take over now. You go get your dinner."

Jenkins grinned and pulled on his hat. "Y' don't have to tell me twice. I'm feeling kind of hollow." He strode to the door, looked back over his shoulder. "We got a new prisoner. The report is on the desk."

"Right. I'll look it over." Sam tipped back in his chair,

laced his hands across his abdomen and closed his eyes, letting the coolness seep into his overheated body. A nap would sure feel good right about now. But first he'd better read that report. He stretched out his hand and picked up the paper.

Mary Randolph!

The front chair legs crashed to the floor. Sam lunged to his feet, scanning the report while he snatched the key ring from the drawer. His lips twitched. By the time he reached her cell, he was chuckling. He unlocked the door, leaned his shoulder against the framing bars and grinned down at her. She was seated all prim and proper on the edge of the cot, looking very composed despite the dirt and grass stains on the skirt of her gown. "Good afternoon, Miss Randolph. What brings you here to enjoy our hospitality?"

Those brown eyes of hers flashed up at him. "Good afternoon, Captain. I am here because one of your policeman invited me."

"I see." His grin widened. She was not as unruffled as she pretended. Underneath all that poise, she was mad as a wet hen. "Would that be the one who found you at the courthouse ordering the laborers and foreman about, and refusing to allow the children to go back to work when they were told to do so?"

Another flash of those incredible eyes. "He did not *find* me. I sent one of the workers for you and he brought the other policeman in your stead. The rest of your statement is correct." She looked down and brushed at a spot of dirt on her skirt.

"And what did you hope to gain by such behavior?"

Her head lifted. "Medical treatment for Tommy. And a doctor's orders that the children were not to work in such heat. Which I accomplished." A look of pure satisfaction spread across her face.

His heart bucked. "And landed yourself in jail in the process."

She nodded, gave him a smug little smile. "Yes. And the children, also—where they are out of the sun."

Sam's heart thudded. He shook his head, gave her a mock stern look. "Miss Randolph, what am I to do with you?"

She slanted a look up at him from under her lashes and flashed him a cheeky grin. "Pay my bail?"

He had never wanted to kiss anyone so much in his life.

"In *jail*, Mary? You spent the afternoon in *jail!* I thought you were at the *Journey's End*." James lifted his hands and raked his fingers through his hair.

"I intended to be, James. But...well... I was waylaid as I explained." She smiled up at him. "You look exactly like Father when you do that."

He rounded on her. "Do not try to distract me, Mary. It will not work. What were you thinking of?"

Her chin lifted. "I was *thinking* of getting those children out of the sun before they all sickened...or worse." She tried another smile. "As you would have, had you been in my place."

James stopped pacing and looked down at her. "That is different! Forgive me, Mary, but you have got to stop being so—so bold! What would have happened to you if Captain Benton were not a friend?"

"He is. And he is also *present*, James." Heat climbed into her cheeks. She turned so the captain could not see. "Perhaps we could delay this discussion until later?"

James spun around, lifted his hands in surrender. "*You* talk to her, Captain. She will not listen to me." He stormed off the porch and strode up the road.

"Well, gracious! I am glad I did not tell him before we had supper. It would have quite ruined his meal. And ours. If it has not done so anyway." Mary turned from watching James to look up at the captain. He was half sitting on the railing, leaning back against the corner post with his long legs stretched out in front of him, looking at her. Her heart fluttered. She frowned and looked away. "I apologize for that unseemly display, Captain. James sometimes becomes protective of me. I wanted this to be a pleasant meal, to thank you for bailing me out of jail."

"No thanks were necessary, Miss Randolph. But it was a very pleasant supper. I enjoyed the company."

She could not sit there with him so close any longer. She rose and walked to the top of the steps. Light flickered across the southern sky. "James is very entertaining."

"I wasn't speaking only of James."

The soft words sent a delicious little shiver rippling through her. Foolish woman! She forced a laugh. "I suppose I am entertaining, too. At least, my escapades must seem so."

"I wasn't speaking only of entertainment, either."

She scowled. Why did he talk like that? So soft and deep. It was like...like dark, warm syrup. And it seemed fraught with meaning. Of course it was not. It only seemed that way to her feckless heart. *Help me, Lord.* She wiped her hands down the long skirt of her yellow cotton gown and stole a sidelong glance at him. He had not moved. It only felt as if he had drawn nearer. She wished he would go. Prayed he would stay. And was disgusted with herself for caring either way. He was another woman's beau.

Silence reigned.

She tried desperately to think of something clever or amusing to say, but all she could think of was him. How compassionate he was. How handsome and strong and kind and gentle and utterly special he was. Miss Stewart was a very fortunate woman.

A steamboat whistled. Another answered. A horse's hooves clopped against the cobblestones of Market Street.

"James is right, you know. I understand his concern over you."

The syrup again. Warm and sweet. She would probably dream about it tonight.

He moved, and every fiber of her being tensed, aware of each whisper of cloth as he rose—every tap of his boot heel against the wood porch floor as he came to stand beside her. Her lungs strained to fill. How foolish, foolish, *foolish* she was!

"You should be more careful of yourself. It will do the orphans no good should you come to harm."

The orphans. Yes. Of course. The orphans. She braced against the disappointment, swift and hurtful, that rose to dash the tiny bit of pleasure she had felt at the thought that he cared what happened to her. Why would he care? He belonged to another. She must keep reminding herself of that. Not that a man like Samuel Benton would be interested in her anyway.

Lightning glinted across the distant sky. Thunder rumbled. Perhaps it would cool off tonight. She brushed back her hair and nodded. "I know you and James are right, Captain. I am far too impulsive and bold for my own good. But…well… I had to help the children." She looked up. He was gazing down at her.

"I was not aware that you took food to the children every day."

She gave a tiny wave of her hand. "It is not much. Some biscuits and jam. A cold drink. Sometimes a pickle. They like pickles." Why did he not look away? She ran her hands down the sides of her long skirt again. Spoke to fill the silence. "It is to help strengthen them. And it gives them something to look forward to. I thought it would make their days a little better—for now, I mean. Until I can get them out of jail." She clamped her mouth shut to stop her chattering.

He nodded, but still his gaze held hers.

Heat crawled into her cheeks. "Is there something wrong, Captain? You are staring." She lifted a hand to her face. "Have I a smudge, or—"

"No. There is nothing wrong, Miss Randolph. Nothing at all." His eyes darkened. "You have very expressive eyes. The tiny honey-colored specks throughout the brown shine when you are happy and flash when you are angry. Your eyes glow with warmth when your emotions are touched."

The words flowed into her heart, settled there though the warmth she felt at them was unwelcome. She raised her chin. "I will thank you to not make such remarks to me, Captain. I find them inappropriate from a man who is courting another woman."

"My remarks stand as spoken, Miss Randolph. I am not courting another woman."

Disappointment flooded her. She had never known the captain to lie to her. "I *know* of Miss Stewart, Captain."

"What of her?" He leaned a shoulder against the post

beside him and looked straight into her eyes. "I have not seen Miss Stewart on a personal basis for some time. A fact you can easily verify to be true or false."

A rocky patch, Mrs. Lucas had said. Could it be there was a rift they had not mended? Would he be that relaxed if there was no substance or truth to his words? She *could* easily find out if what he said was true.

He was not lying. And she was too quick to believe all men were like Winston Blackstone. Remorse for her accusation brought an apology rising to her lips. "Please forgive me, Captain. I did not realize you were no longer courting Miss Stewart. I—I hope the loss of her companionship was not too painful for you."

He straightened to his full height and stepped close to her. "In truth, Miss Randolph, it was not. I discovered some time ago that Levinia Stewart is not the woman for me." He moved closer, locked his gaze on hers. "Would you like to know how I made that discovery?"

She nodded, held her breath.

"I looked into a pair of beautiful, honey-flecked brown eyes."

Chapter Twenty-One

Mary leaned forward, studied her reflection in the mirror and frowned. The captain could not have meant what she thought he had meant. It had *seemed* he said he… favored…*her* over Levinia Stewart.

She straightened and finished tying the ribbon encircling the thick fall of long hair at her nape. It was clear she had misunderstood. For such a thing was not possible. It was only her silly heart wanting its dream to come true.

Still…he was no longer courting Miss Stewart. Had Levinia perhaps refused his suit? She snorted. Now that was another ridiculous notion. And it would not explain his remarks about her eyes….

She stole another quick look in the mirror. No, they were still the same. Perhaps a little…dreamier. Oh, she was being utterly ridiculous!

She spun about, left the dressing room and walked to her bedroom window. The rain was falling in earnest now. It drummed on the roof, splatted against the window and sheeted down the small panes to splash against the sill and run down the brick walls of the house.

Sulfurous yellow streaked from the black sky to the

earth with a wicked snap. She flinched, listened to the thunder crack and grumble away and wished she could open the window to the welcome coolness of the outside air.

Outside.

She smiled, hurried to the cupboard and shrugged into her dressing gown and slippers. Light flickered throughout the room as she ran on tiptoe for the stairs.

"Ah-ha! I see we both have the same intention."

She jolted to a halt, looking up at James. "The porch?"

He nodded and stepped back to let her precede him down the stairs. She went down two steps, looked back over her shoulder and laughed. "I call dibs on the swing!"

"Oh, no. You will not pull that old trick on me." He leaped down the two steps.

Mary yelped, whirled, lifted the front of her nightgown and raced down the stairs, James's footsteps thundering behind her. She giggled and sprinted for the door, grabbing the knob.

Strong hands grasped her waist. Lifted her off her feet.

She squealed and pushed at his hands. "James, *no!*"

He gave an evil little laugh, set her down behind him, then opened the door and shot across the porch to plop down dead center in the swing.

Mary marched over, fisted her hands on her hips and stood in front of him so he could not swing. "Move over." She struggled to keep the laughter from her voice. "You have to share."

Lightning flashed and gleamed on the white teeth exposed by his grin. "Uh-uh. It was a race. I won."

"You cheated!"

"So did you."

She snorted.

They both burst out laughing.

James scooched over and patted the seat beside him.

"*Thank* you." Mary turned and smoothed her skirts forward to sit down, heard a creak and tensed to jump out of the way. She was too late. The forward edge of the swing caught her behind the knees and her legs buckled. She fell backward onto the slatted seat, bumped against the arm he held across the back to cushion her landing. She joined his laughter, waited for the right moment then pushed her toes against the porch floor in rhythm with his to keep the swing from wobbling.

He nudged her with his shoulder. "That felt like we were ten years old again."

"I know." She looked over at him and grinned. "We should do that more often. But not in front of the children."

The swing creaked. They pushed their toes against the floor in unison, maintaining the gentle to-and-fro motion. Rain beat against the shingles, sluiced off the roof and landed with a splash on the ground. Lightning sizzled from the sky, grounded with a sharp crack. She looked at him and they shared another grin. She jabbed him with her elbow. "You flinched."

"So did you."

Their laughter blended with the rumble of the thunder.

"The cool air feels good. Almost like back home."

She nodded, reached forward and pulled her dressing gown closed over her knees. Her nightgown was becoming damp from the rain spatters when they swung forward. "James?"

"Yes?"

"Are you in love with Rebecca?"

He leaned to his side, turned his head to look at her.

"That is quite a jump from 'you flinched—so did you.' Where did that question come from?"

She shrugged, rubbed at the sudden coolness where the warmth of his arm had been. "I was only wondering."

He relaxed back into their former shoulder-to-shoulder position. "Rebecca and I are in love with one another."

She felt his smile. "That makes it perfect." She looked up at him. "I am so happy for you, James. I want you to be happy always."

"Thank you, Mary. I want the same for you."

"I know." She looked down, fiddled with a button on her dressing gown. "How—I mean, *when* did you first know you loved Rebecca?" She glanced up, saw him smile into the distance.

"Remember that day we met her outside the church, when I helped her into her father's farm wagon? That was it. When she looked down at me and our gazes met—I knew."

I looked into a pair of beautiful, honey-flecked brown eyes. Her pulse skipped a beat. Could it possibly be that simple? Or was it only the longing of her heart? *Poor little Miss Mary. She'll have a hard time findin' herself a husband, bein' plain like she is.*

The swing wobbled. James glanced at her. "Sorry." She waited for the right moment and shoved her toes against the porch again. The swing evened out.

Veronica, my beloved, what man would not choose your petite, blond beauty and sweet nature over Mary's dark, angular plainness and bold, forthright ways? The memory still hurt…but not as much as it had. *I discovered some time ago that Levinia Stewart is not the woman for me. Would you like to know how I made that discov-*

ery? Her breath snagged. *I looked into a pair of beautiful, honey-flecked brown eyes.* What was she to believe?

"James? If you were not my brother—I mean, if you were another man. Would you think me…attractive?"

"No. I would think you beautiful."

"Truly? If you were another man?" She looked over at him. "Heart's promise truly?" She held her breath. You could not lie when you said "heart's promise."

"Heart's promise truly." He turned his head to look at her. "You have never been vain, Mary. Quite the opposite. So I know you are not simply questing after a compliment. Why are you asking?"

She shook her head. "No reason. I was only wondering. James, that day after church—when you were talking about how beautiful Rebecca was—I thought you were talking about Miss Stewart."

"Not likely."

"Do you not find her very beautiful?"

"I do not." He gave her a look as though she had lost her mind. "Men look at women differently than other women do. Not that we do not appreciate a beautiful face and form. But there is much more to beauty than dimples and curls, Mary. And the first time I looked into Miss Stewart's eyes, that day we met her and the captain on the portico at the courthouse, I knew how shallow and vapid her beauty was. The woman has no heart. When you look in Miss Stewart's eyes, all you see is Miss Stewart. There is nothing beautiful about a woman in love with herself. Does that answer your question?"

"Yes. I think I am beginning to understand. Thank you, James." *I discovered some time ago that Levinia Stewart is not the woman for me. Would you like to know how I made that discovery? I looked into a pair of beau-*

tiful, honey-flecked brown eyes. She sighed. Perhaps her heart had read too much into the captain's words. Most likely he had only meant that when he had compared her eyes with Miss Stewart's eyes, he had discovered Miss Stewart's vanity.

At least the captain did not consider her shallow or vain. That was something.

But how lovely it would be if she had not misunderstood him after all.

Had he said too much? Too little? Should he have stayed instead of walking away? No. He had said enough. Sam frowned and pulled off his boots. If he had stayed he would have asked Mary to marry him. And he could not do that. Not yet. He did not want to scare her away by saying too much too soon. Not that Mary frightened easily.

His lips twitched. He would have liked to have seen her ordering that foreman and those workers around. Standing there with those children gathered around her and defying the order that would have sent them back to work. He could imagine how her eyes had flashed, and how that little chin of hers had jutted into the air. She was a fighter. No doubt about that. But fighters sometimes got wounded. And above all he wanted Mary safe. Especially her heart. And the mayor was a formidable foe.

Light flickered throughout the room. Thunder clapped and boomed. The rain poured off the roof in a wide, shimmering waterfall. Sam walked to the window and tugged it open. Fresh, cool air flowed in. One good thing about this room—the storms came from the other direction. He could always open the window.

How did Mary feel about him? Would she welcome his suit? There were moments—like when she was perched on the cot in that cell and looked up at him—when he thought she might. Then the next minute she went all cool and prickly on him and he was unsure again.

Sam huffed, yanked off his shirt and tossed it over the back of the only chair in the room. That moment in the cell had been hard! He'd had to hold on to the bars of the cell to keep from charging over there and taking Mary in his arms. But he wanted it to be right, with everything proper and settled, before that happened. Because once he held her, he didn't intend to let go.

He turned at another flicker of lightning and walked back to the window. He loved her. Above and beyond anything he had ever known, thought, imagined or dreamed. And he'd give his life to have her love him, too. He might as well, because without her in it, his life would not be worth living.

He shook his head, leaned down and peeled off his socks. If he ever ran across Thomas, he was going to shake his hand. He'd arrest him first, but *then* he would shake his hand. If it hadn't been for Thomas's scheme of stealing the insurance money, he never would have looked into those steamboat mishaps. And if he hadn't been investigating them, he would not have met the Randolphs. Strange how that all worked out. It had sure saved him from making a costly mistake. He snorted. Costly was right! Levinia Stewart would most likely have gone through his money smooth as a canoe glides through water. But the real cost would have been all he would have lost. He never would have known love.

Sam tossed the socks at the foot of the chair and flopped down on the bed, staring up at the soot smudge on the ceiling and listening to the rain. It always made him think of a woman's tears. His mother's tears. But he didn't feel as if his mother was crying tonight. For some reason, it felt as if she was smiling. And Danny, too.

Poor Danny and Ma… Knots twisted in his stomach. He had a promise to keep to them. The old bitterness rose and twisted the knots tighter. He had heard James Randolph say that the Lord was blessing the orphans. That it was evident in the way things were working out in spite of the mayor and aldermen and other spiteful folks in St. Louis. Randolph said that God often worked His blessings through people—like him and Mrs. Lucas and the Ladies' Benevolent Society.

He couldn't go along with that. God wouldn't use a sinner like him. And while Mrs. Lucas had a good heart—she was lonely and helping these orphans gave her something to do. As for the Ladies' Benevolent Society, most of them seemed to want to help now, but they got into it because Mrs. Lucas shamed them into it. Still… things were working out. The orphans were being helped. Was Randolph right? Was it God?

Sam rose up on one elbow, pounded his pillow into shape and turned over onto his side. Mary had told him about the mayor's reaction to the pastor's sermon on God loving everyone equally and being no respecter of persons. But he didn't believe what the pastor said either. If it was true, why hadn't God sent someone to care for Danny and his ma and him?

His face tightened. He flopped onto his other side and stared at the plaster wall. One of those chips in the paint looked like a rooster…

Lightning flashed. Thunder rolled. Something flickered before him—like a picture against the wall. More of an impression really. Two women, each holding an umbrella and basket, standing outside a door with the lightning flashing behind them.

Sam rubbed his forehead, blinked and closed his eyes. There was something about those women...

Lightning flickered against his eyelids. Thunder crashed.

The images came again and memory broke through the walls of years of denial. More images flashed. The women standing outside their house, begging to be let in. His father drunk, shouting at them to go away, that Ruben Benton's family didn't need anybody's charity. His mother, sick in bed, holding Danny next to her. And him, huddled in the corner, crying and bleeding from the beating his father had given him for going to the church to ask for help.

Sam opened his eyes and stared at the wall. He had blamed God for not helping his mother and Danny and him. All these years he had blamed God for not answering his prayers, and for the beating he had received for turning to the church for help that never came. But help *had* come. God *had* sent someone to help them. And his father had sent them away. God didn't kill his mother and Danny. His father had.

Sam swallowed hard, all the hurt and sorrow and guilt swamping him as he faced the truth. He had known it when it happened. When he was only seven years old, he had known it was his father's fault that his mother and Danny had died. But no matter how terribly his father had treated them all—he was still his father. And he had not wanted his father to be guilty. So he had blamed God. And he had run away so he would not have to look at his father and remember.

And he hadn't.

Until now.

Sam scrubbed his hard, callused hand over his squeezed-shut eyes and cleared the lump from his throat. He was tired of harboring bitterness. It was time to be free of it.

He turned on his back, opened his eyes and stared up at the ceiling. "God, I was wrong to blame You for Ma and Danny dying. I ask You to forgive me. And I ask You to help me never to run from the truth again."

He listened to the rain, watched the lightning glint across the ceiling. And his dream house came to him, more clear than he had ever seen it. His showcase house sitting on the grassy knoll in all its splendor. And then it crumbled and disappeared. There was nothing left. Only the grassy knoll. And Mary. And behind her...

Sam smiled, snapped a salute toward the ceiling. "I hear You, God. I'll start out tomorrow."

Chapter Twenty-Two

Sam slipped his rifle into its scabbard, gave his bedroll a jiggle to be sure it was secure and led Attila out of the stables. The air was fresh and sweet after last night's rain. He took a deep breath of the invigorating coolness and scanned the sky. It was clear and blue, but the sun was already giving off shimmering waves of heat as it climbed. It was going to be another hot one.

He checked the knife at his belt, made sure his Colt Paterson was ready to hand and mounted. Too bad he could not have started earlier. But he had to get things set up so his men could cover his patrols and the jail while he was gone. And he had to wait till James Randolph was at his office. He tilted his felt hat forward so the wide brim would shade his eyes, gave Attila a pat on the neck and settled in the saddle. "All right, boy. Let's go."

He walked him out to Pine Street, reined left and urged him into an easy lope when they reached the road out of town. He scanned the area ahead, alert for any sign of trouble, but his thoughts traveled backward toward town, toward Mary. A smile touched his lips. It was a new, not unpleasant, sensation for him, missing someone.

* * *

Mary put the maps Miss Withers had requested on the highest shelf and aligned the edges. "Where did he go?"

James shrugged and looked around. "He only said to tell you he had something to take care of out of town. And that he did not know how long it would take him."

"Oh. I see." What of the children in jail? She knew the captain protected them as much as he was able. And what of the land she needed to purchase to have a permanent dock for the orphanage? Who would tell her where to locate it? And what of her? She smoothed her hands over her hair, then lowered them to dangle idle at her sides, aware of an empty feeling deep inside. How could she miss him already?

"I think this may be a mistake, Mary."

"What is a mistake?" She turned. James was standing at the huge wheel, his hands on the protruding pegs the pilot grasped to turn it, staring out the windows at the river. She smiled. In spite of his business garb, he looked like a little boy with a new toy.

"Putting the schoolroom up here." He swung his arm in a wide arc that encompassed the entire wheelhouse. "There are no walls up here, only windows. How are these young boys, and girls for that matter, to pay attention to their schoolwork?" He looked at her and grinned. "They will all be sailing the rivers and oceans playing 'pirates' in their minds."

She could not resist. "Is that what you are doing?"

He slewed his mouth to one side and squinted an eye at her. "Aaarrgh! Guilty, mate!"

Laughter bubbled up, burst out. She turned in a circle. The view *was* magnificent. "I fear you may be right, my dear brother. I believe some curtains forward of the worktables may be in order. Now get away from that wheel before I make you walk the plank. I am finished here and have work to do on the main deck." She started down the stairs.

He fell into step behind her. "You are a cruel and heartless captain, my dear sister."

"Headmistress, James." She smiled over her shoulder at him. "Headmistress of the Journey's End Orphanage... almost."

"Is that doubt I hear?"

"It is fear." She stopped in the play area of the main cabin on the boiler deck and faced him. "So many people have helped to make this orphanage possible, James. Look..." She walked to one of the bedrooms for the children and opened the door. There was a cream-colored quilted coverlet embroidered with trailing vines of small pink roses, and matching curtains at the window. A small, flower-patterned rug laid on the polished wood floor. "Mrs. Shields of the Ladies' Benevolent Society paid for this room. And she did the embroidery work herself. She said it gave her pleasure because she never had a daughter of her own."

Tears flooded her eyes. She spread her arms and spun in a circle. "All of these bedrooms are like that, James. And look at this playroom! A lovely new rug, and game tables and toys and—"

She stopped, clenched her hands and stared at him. It was too much. It was suddenly all too much. He rushed over and put his arms around her, tugged her close. She burrowed her head under his chin. "Oh, James. How can I tell all those lovely people the orphanage may come to naught because of that *mean-natured*—" she thumped his chest with her fisted hand *"—heartless—"* thump *"—cruel—"* thump *"—miserly mayor!"*

She lifted her head, looked at him through her streaming eyes. "I hope all of his mean acts toward those children are multiplied to him a thousand times!" She swiped at the tears on her cheeks. "And I am sorry if that is not a Christian attitude, and I disappoint you. But I cannot help it! I do not have any land. And no one will sell me any. And now the captain is gone and I do not know what to do!"

She burrowed her head back under his chin and sobbed out all the hurts she had held for so long.

"Shh, easy now, boy. Easy now." Sam drew Attila's head close to his chest and placed his hand over his muzzle. These Indians weren't of the friendly tribes from around the St. Louis area, and though it was likely safe, he would as soon not test that theory. It was too easy for a man to disappear in the unsettled lands of the frontier. Fortunate for him, he had heard them coming.

He scanned the area as best he could from behind the screen of vine-draped branches and frowned. The Indians were coming from the direction he was traveling and there was no telling how many more might be following in their path. Should he need to make a run for it, his best chance would be back across the river and into the woods on the other side.

He took another quick glance at the Indians, dropped his gaze to the path in front of them. Staring would draw their attention. The vines were thick and the air still. There was no breeze to betray his presence to them. Luck was with him today. Or maybe it was something more than luck. Maybe God had taken a hand. He'd give that some thought when he had time.

The Indians rode by, bare legs gripping their ponies, folded blankets for their saddles. Sam tensed, barely breathing as they passed, then thundered off down the trail.

He waited, straining to hear and identify every sound. A fish jumped. Birds flew over the water, the snap of their beaks as they caught their food on the fly loud in the silence. Squirrels ran along branches, jumped from tree to tree. The wilds returned to normal.

Sam released Attila's head, patted his neck. "Good boy." The horse pricked his ears at the whispered words, tossed his head. Sam led him out from under the tree branches and stepped into the saddle. He touched the handle of his knife, rested his hand on his Colt and let out his breath. "All right, boy, let's go find Charlie and Harry. But you warn me if any more Indian ponies come our way."

"All you kids, get back to work!"

Mary looked up at the foreman, but held her tongue. Captain Benton was not around to bail her out of jail. A band of worry clamped around her chest. Where was he? He had been gone four days. Was he all right? She managed a smile. "Goodbye, children. I shall see you tomorrow."

She watched the children hurry off to resume their work, then knelt on the grass to put the quart jars, tin cups and dirty, cloth napkins back in her basket. The unusual heat had ceased and there had been no more sickness among the children, but it still made her ache to look at them. Their thin arms bore bruises, their hands scratches and sores. They were all gaunt, with large eyes full of fear and distrust and pain. Most of them never smiled.

She longed to tell them to be brave, that they would soon have a new home, but, of course, she could not. She did not know if that would come to pass. She had tried, with James's help, to purchase land fronting the river for a permanent docking site, but no one would sell. It was always the same. The property owners would not speak with them once they found out their name. Now they had run out of prospects. And without the captain here—

"Tidying up after your daily charitable duty, Miss Randolph?"

Mary looked up. Levinia Stewart stood in front of her, beautiful in a gold linen gown. Her matching bonnet was a confection of shirred linen and lace rosettes.

But her expression was one of haughty condescension.

Mary's ire stirred. She rose, forcing Levinia to look up at her. And for once she took satisfaction in her height. "It is not a duty, Miss Stewart—it is a pleasure."

The blue eyes narrowed. "Oh, come, Miss Randolph— you may forget your pose as the virtuous woman. The captain is not around to see your performance."

She all but spat the words.

Mary took a breath, held it and counted. "My performance?"

Levinia's eyes narrowed farther. "Do not act the innocent with me, Miss Randolph. My father and I are aware of your little scheme. You forget his office is in the courthouse. He sees you through his window, playing the sweet maiden feeding and caring for the darling, hungry, little street children. It is disgusting!" She reached up and bounced a golden curl.

Mary looked away before she gave in to her desire to

reach over and yank it. "And what motive would I have for such playacting, Miss Stewart?"

"Why, to capture Captain Benton's affections, of course. A woman like you would need an excuse to gain his interest." The woman's eyes turned from hot to icy cold. "I do not know how you learned that Father has been grooming Samuel to be the future mayor of St. Louis, Miss Randolph, but that is not of importance."

Mary's mind raced. Captain Benton was to be *mayor?* He had said nothing—

"What *is* important is that you realize your little scheme with the orphans will not work. Captain Benton is also being groomed to be my husband. As his wife, I will continue my mother's role as the head of the women's organizations and charities of St. Louis. It is a position for which I am perfectly suited. Captain Benton realizes that. When the captain returns, I will let it be known to him that I have forgiven him for his small act of rebellion against Father and am willing to accept his suit again. I assure you, he will choose me over you and your pathetic street urchins."

Mary's heart lurched. *Was* it Levinia that had stopped the captain's courtship of her? Her stomach churned. Had he lied to her? What exactly had he said?

Levinia smiled. "You have failed, Miss Randolph. I do not know why you feel someone like you would be a fit wife for the future mayor of St. Louis, but Father has stopped you from opening that ridiculous steamboat orphanage, and that will end Captain Benton's little rebellion against Father's authority as well. I am planning a December wedding. There is nothing left for you here in St. Louis, Miss Randolph. I suggest you go home to wherever it is you came from. Good day."

"A moment, Miss Stewart." Mary waited until Levinia turned back to face her, drew herself up and looked straight into those blue eyes. "I know nothing of Captain Benton's plans of being the next mayor. Nor am I interested in the position of mayor's wife that you so crave. I am, however, very interested in the children who have no parents to love or care for them, and find no mercy in the hearts of those in authority. And I have *not* failed in my purpose to create a home for them. I *will* do so. You may take that message back to your father, Miss Stewart. Good day."

She turned her back and returned to her task. Not for anything would she let that woman see the doubts her words had raised—the uncertainty only Captain Benton could erase.

"I'm sorry to hear about Harry, Charlie. He was a good man." Sam looked down at his hands. Studied the dark brew in the tin cup he held. It was the most bitter coffee he had ever tasted. But it was nothing like the bitterness that had grabbed hold of his heart. How was he to ask Charlie to sell him the land Harry had prized? And he had thought God had directed him here for that purpose. He held back a snort, took another swallow of the bitterness instead. All that risk. All that way. For nothing.

"Harry thought high of you, too, Captain. He was always talkin' 'bout the chance y' took on us. Riskin' yer money so's we could come out lookin' fer the silver. Nobody else would listen t' us." The old miner stuck a fork in the meat in the frying pan and lifted it onto a tin plate. He added a scoop of beans and a biscuit, slid the plate across the table, then tossed a fork after it and turned to fill another. "Yessir, Harry thought high of y' all right."

And now Harry was dead. Crushed by a collapsed wall of a worthless mine he spent a lifetime searching for. And Mary's dream of an orphanage had died with him. Sam stared down at the plate, his stomach twisted in a knot so tight no food could get through it. Harry and Charlie had laid claim to that parcel of land on the Mississippi way back when they were young. Every time he saw them, Harry talked about living on that land when they were old. It had been their dream. But he had figured, for enough money, they would be willing to change their dream and sell him the property for his showcase house. Now, with Harry gone, that was unlikely.

"Bear meat's best et afore it gets cold, Captain. Mite gamy else."

Sam looked across the table at the old miner, nodded and picked up his fork. If he had to ask the man to part with the last link he had to his dead brother, the least he could do was eat the man's meat. He took his knife from the sheath at his belt and cut off a bite.

"Glad ya come out t' see how we was comin' along with the mine, Captain. Saves me makin' the trip back t' St. Louis." Charlie shoved back from the rough board table, then opened a trunk and rummaged through it. "This here's fer you." He shoved a folded piece of paper at him. "Harry said I was t' give it to ya should anything happen to him."

Sam put down his knife and fork and unfolded the paper. "This is a will." He hadn't even known Harry could read and write.

"Yep. He got that writ up all legal-like 'for we left town t' come out here."

Sam nodded, started reading. Read it again and looked

over at Charlie. "It says here Harry leaves the property on the Mississippi to me."

Charlie nodded, broke off a piece of biscuit and mopped up the meat juice on his plate. "Harry had high notions fer that land had he lived t' see 'em out. But he wanted you t' have it if anything happened t' him. Thought high of y' he did."

Sam slipped his rifle into the scabbard, checked his bedroll. "What are you going to do now, Charlie? Are you going to try and open the mine again?"

The old miner glanced at the rubble and shook his head. "Nah, it's a fittin' grave fer Harry. I'm fer the west country. Always did want t' see them high mountains I heard talk about. Now Harry's gone, I'm gonna do it."

Sam nodded and mounted. "Keep a sharp eye out for Indians. I ran into four of them on my way here."

The old man grinned. "If yer gonna go, an arrow's as good a way as any."

"I guess that's right." Sam returned the grin and leaned down to shake the hard hand. "If you ever come back St. Louis way, look me up. I'll be on Harry's land." *By God's grace and with His blessing.*

"He'd be right proud of that, Captain. Luck to y'."

"And to you, Charlie."

Sam reined Attila around and started down the trail, the will in his pocket, a smile in his heart and a new, strong confidence that God might have a plan for him after all.

Chapter Twenty-Three

"The steamboat is finished, Mrs. Lucas. It sits idle in a berth at the Mississippi and Missouri steamer line docks." Mary rose from the settee and walked over to look out the window. Behind her the floor clock ticked off the minutes.

"Everything is prepared for the orphans—the ones I know of. Even clothing." She looked over her shoulder at the elderly woman. "And Ivy has laid in stores enough for an army." She tried for a laugh—could not summon one. "And still I have no land—nowhere to dock the *Journey's End.*"

She turned and made her way back to the settee. "There are orphans in jail—and an empty orphanage. And I have run out of ideas for getting the two together. Without land, it is impossible."

Mrs. Lucas leaned forward and patted her hand. "Nothing is impossible with God, Mary. Trust Him. He will make a way."

"I know, Mrs. Lucas. And I believe His hand has been guiding all that has happened, that He has been blessing our efforts for the orphans' sakes. But now...well...even you have tried to help us purchase land, to no avail. And I— My faith is failing me."

The faded blue eyes studied her. "This is not like you, Mary. I have never seen you so discouraged. Is there something else troubling you?"

Doubts. Fears. A wounded heart that cannot quite trust, but refuses to forget. "I am tired. Perhaps that is my problem."

"Perhaps." Mrs. Lucas did not look convinced. Mary sighed and rose. "It is getting late. I have to go home. I have already stayed too long." She leaned down and kissed the woman's dry, wrinkled cheek. "Pleasant dreams, Mrs. Lucas."

"And you, Mary. Rest well."

That was not likely. Mary frowned and let herself out of the house—walked to the street. She could not remember the last time she had slept well. Yes, she did. It was the night before Miss Stewart had spoken to her. Since that day, in spite of her best efforts to keep believing her plan for the orphanage would succeed, doubt slipped in. And the captain... She did not know what to believe about the captain.

Mary pulled her long skirts to the side and stepped around a small pile of horse droppings as she turned onto Market Street. Had the captain hinted at an...interest... in her because Levinia had cast him aside? And, if so, now that Levinia wanted him back...

Her steps faltered. Mary steadied her pace and walked to the cottage. She must face facts. The captain would return to Levinia. There was no reason why he should not. Why would he, or any other man, choose her—with her bold, stubborn ways and her wild dreams—over a life of privilege and power with Levinia? Unless—her breath left her—unless Captain Benton had discovered who her father was. Justin Randolph was a far wealthier, far more influential man than the mayor. Perhaps—

No! Mary shoved open the gate, ran into the cottage and up the stairs. She removed her bonnet and gloves, put them in the cupboard and sank down onto the bed. She would not entertain such thoughts about Captain Benton—she would *not.* He had proven himself to be an honest and honorable man over and over again.

But Levinia is so beautiful. And you are plain. The hateful words whispered through her mind, insinuating themselves into her spirit. *There has to be a reason....*

The past crowded in on her, undermining the new confidence she had received from the belief that God loved her. God—not Samuel Benton. Mary closed her tearing eyes, struggling to hold on to her fledgling faith—her newfound belief that with God, all things were possible. But the hurt she felt pushed it beyond her grasp. She grabbed a pillow and hugged it tight against her aching heart. "Help me, Heavenly Father. Please help me. I don't know what to think—or who to believe. Please show me the truth. And help me to trust again."

Dawn was breaking. Sam rose, went to the window and looked at the pink and gold streaking the lighter gray of the sky over the river. He had ridden long and far yesterday. But he had never felt more rested and eager for a day to begin. *Please, Lord, bless my efforts today.* He grabbed his shaving gear and strode down the hall to the dressing room. He had a lot to do, though some of what he planned had already been accomplished. He had met James Randolph returning home from Rebecca Green's place last night when he had ridden into town, and they had worked things out between them.

Sam chuckled, looked in the cloudy mirror and ran his hand over the stubble on his chin. James Randolph was fast becoming his best friend. And soon, if things went as planned, he would be a lot more than that. Yes, sir, a *lot* more than that. He grinned, took out his razor strop and started honing the blade. He wanted a good, sharp edge. No chance of skipped whiskers today.

Mary shook out the long skirt of her gown and straightened the lace adorning the collar and the sleeves. She had to hurry. She had promised the children she would take them to the *Journey's End* today. They missed playing on the steamboat. But with the steamer now in a berth at the levee, it was inappropriate for them to stay for very long. And, truth be told, she could not bear to be on the boat. It saddened and infuriated her to see the bedrooms empty and the kitchen, dining room and schoolroom idle when there was such need. But her well was dry—she had been unable to come up with a solution.

Mary sighed, shook off the thoughts as she had shaken out her skirts and crossed to the dresser to search for a matching ribbon to hold her hair. She selected a narrow one of darker rose color, carried it to the mirror, wrapped it around the thick knot of hair at the crown of her head and tied it in a neat bow. Now for her gloves and bonnet, and she would be ready.

She started for the cupboard, paused at the writing desk, staring at the piece of paper resting there.

"Dear Mother and Father."

That is all she had written. There was nothing new to tell them. No good news to impart. But perhaps she would think of something cheering to write them about today. And James had good news to share with them. Rebecca had said yes to his proposal. Also, the new luxury steamboat he had commissioned was almost ready for her maiden voyage, though they had yet to choose her name. It was important to make the right choice.

She smiled and walked to the cupboard to fetch her bonnet and gloves. The *Right Choice...* That might do very nicely for the name. She would have to suggest it to James tonight.

A steamboat blew its whistle. She frowned and hurried toward the stairs. James was going to meet her at the dock. He said he had something to show her. If only it were a deed to a piece of land!

"Thank you, Judge. I appreciate your hurrying things along for me." Sam tucked the papers in his suit pocket and shook the judge's hand.

"Not at all, Captain Benton. I am pleased to help. That is a fine piece of land—some of the best acreage around. And I was not unaware of what has been happening lately. I think you are both prudent and wise to get the deed secured."

Sam nodded and put on his hat. "All legal and settled, sir. I am taking no risks."

He strode from the judge's office, his long legs making short work of the distance to the jail. The interior was cool and empty. He crossed to his desk and did the necessary paper work. When he finished, he shoved it in the drawer and rose. The papers in his pocket crackled. He grinned, patting it to make sure it was secure, and left the building.

The sun played hide-and-seek with white puffs of cloud. A soft breeze blew off the river. A beautiful day. Sam crossed Chestnut Street and cut across lots to Market Street, every step he took one of pure pleasure.

The children were working the land on the right side of the courthouse. Some were picking up stones. Some were carrying the buckets to dump in the wagon. Others were raking and leveling the soil. The sight hit him in his gut. He quickened his stride. "Children, come here to me."

They froze in place, stared at him, dread clear to read on their faces. They thought he was taking them back to the jail. "Come on. Leave your tools and come over here." He beckoned. They put down their buckets and rakes and started moving toward him, their steps slow. They preferred the hard work in the outdoors to sitting idle in their dark, dank cells.

"What is the meaning of this, Captain Benton? These kids work until suppertime."

Sam looked down into the foreman's scowling face and shook his head. "Not anymore. These children are no longer prisoners. They are free."

"We'll see about that!"

Sam turned.

One of the workers stepped out of the courthouse and pointed their way. A second—short, portly—figure emerged. The mayor bobbed down the steps, skirted the hole for the foundation of the new north wing and hastened across the broken soil toward them.

Sam could hear his labored breath before he reached them.

The children started backing away.

He looked down, read the wary looks on their faces and remembered the smell and taste of fear. When you were young and on your own, you developed an instinct about trouble. That highly developed instinct was one of the reasons he was a good policeman. "It's all right, stay by me." They obeyed. But he could sense their tension—their readiness to scatter.

The mayor puffed up to him, glared at the idle children and waved his hands. "Get back to work, all of you!"

Sam lifted his hand and stopped their movement. "The children stay with me, Mr. Mayor. They are no longer prisoners. I am taking them to the new home Miss Randolph has provided for them aboard the *Journey's End.*" He felt the children's reactions, knew they were hanging on his every word. "From now on, Mr. Mayor, you will have to hire laborers."

"Nonsense!" The mayor's eyes narrowed. "No one can live on that steamboat. She has no land—" He stopped. Stared at the folded paper Sam held. "What is that?"

Sam smiled. "That, Mr. Mayor, is the deed to the piece of property where the *Journey's End* will be permanently docked."

"Impossible!"

"Not with God, Mr. Mayor. Not with God."

The mayor snatched the deed from his hand, reading it.

"All legal—and settled in the city records, Mr. Mayor." How good it felt to speak those words. His only regret was that Mary was not here beside him.

The mayor's face turned purple. He crushed the deed in his fist and shook it in the air. "You are through in this city, Samuel Benton! I will see to it that you never get elected to any office, or position of importance, or—"

"That, too, is in God's hands, Mr. Mayor. And in the hands of the people of St. Louis. Now, I believe we are finished."

He looked down at the children who had crept steadily closer and smiled. "You all heard what I said to the mayor. Miss Randolph has prepared a home for you all—and that fulfills the requirement of the law. You are free. Now, follow me! I am taking you to her."

There was an explosion of shouts and laughter.

Sam grinned and started for the street with the children in a tight cluster around him.

"What have you to show me, James?" Mary tossed her bonnet on the table and smoothed her hands over her hair. The children had disappeared into the upper decks of the *Journey's End*.

"You will see in a moment, Mary. And then— Ah! There they are now. Come with me." He turned from the window, grasped her by the elbow and tugged her after him out the door. "Look!"

"What?" Mary turned to look the direction of his pointing finger and gasped. "What— How—" She lifted her hands to cup her chin, her fingers covering her mouth while her eyes filled with tears and her heart ricocheted around in her chest. She stared at the cluster of dirty, ragged, bone-skinny children marching toward her, Captain Benton in the lead. She had never seen a more beautiful sight. One of the figures broke free of the pack and ran up the gangplank to stand in front her. The rest halted where they stood.

"Miss Mary, the captain says you made this here boat a house for us. And we don't have to go to jail no more. Is that true?"

Mary swallowed hard, looked at the captain, saw him nod and looked back at the boy. "Yes, Tommy. It is true. This is your home now."

The boy turned, lifted his arm and whipped it forward. "It's true! It's true! We don't have to go to jail no more!"

There was a wild whoop. The children raced for the gangplank, ran up it and slid to a stop. They looked about, stared at the swings, at her, at James, uncertainty in their eyes. She got control of her emotions, smiled down at them. "Welcome home. I am so glad to see you all. Come, I will show you—" She stopped—looked down at James's restraining hand on her arm.

"No, Mary. Miss Withers and Ivy and I will show them around. There is someone waiting for you."

Mary turned, looked at the captain standing at the end of the bright red gangplank and her heart soared—then plummeted. It reached depths she had not known existed. He had stayed away so long. It must be because of Levinia. She brushed her hands down her skirt, pushed her feelings aside and started forward. She had to thank him. No matter how he had trifled with her heart, he had brought the children to her. Perhaps one day she would learn the truth.

She stopped in front of him and looked up. "I do not have words to thank you for what you have done for these children, Captain. But how did this happen? How is it that they are free to stay here, at last?"

A whistle blasted. Mary nearly jumped out of her skin. She spun toward the boat. Steam was pouring from its stacks. The paddle wheel at the stern was churning. And James, Ivy, Miss Withers and the children stood on the "porch" deck. They grinned and waved. She stared. "Where are they going?"

She whipped back around. "Stop them, Captain! They—"

"Will be fine, Miss Randolph. I give you my word."

He smiled. Her treacherous heart fluttered like a wild bird trapped in her chest.

"Now…if you will stop asking questions and come with me, I promise you will have all your answers soon."

He took her elbow and she could not refuse, though the words hovered on her lips. He led her to a chaise, handed her in and climbed beside her. The beat of the horse's hooves on the cobblestones matched the cadence of her heart when he looked at her and smiled.

Mary accepted the captain's hand down from the chaise, though it cost her a few lost heartbeats to do so. She moved a few steps away from him toward the top of a knoll and looked around while she gathered her frayed emotions. Trees of different varieties were scattered here and there over its surface and on the grassy fields at the bottom of its slope. She could hear the whisper of the river flowing by on the other side. "What is this place? And why have you brought me here?"

"More questions?" The captain smiled.

Mary looked away, lest she lose her train of thought. "Yes. And I believe you promised me answers, Captain Benton."

"So I did." He stepped toward her.

She backed up a step. "You can start by telling me where the *Journey's End* has taken the orphans." She gaped at him, struck by a sudden frightening thought. "Did—did they kidnap them? *Oh, my!* Whatever—"

"The children have not been kidnapped, Miss Randolph. I assure you, everything is perfectly legal. I am an officer of the law, after all. Or at least, I was. I believe I have been let go from my job."

"Let go! But—but—" She bit off the rude question. Made an effort to control her shock.

"But...why?"

Heat climbed into her cheeks. "I'm sorry, Captain. That is your personal business. I have no right to pry."

"Oh, but you do, Miss Randolph." He stepped closer. "You are the reason I lost my position."

"*I* am?" Understanding dawned. "The orphans."

The captain nodded. "The orphans, too. Certainly. But it was you personally who turned the mayor against me." His eyes held hers.

"I don't understand. What—"

"Levinia became jealous of you."

"*Jealous!* Of *me?*" Incredulity swept through her. "Whatever for?"

"Because you changed my dream."

She stared at him, bewildered. At a loss for how to respond. It was just as well. The look in his eyes had robbed her of the ability to speak. He looked away. Waved his hand through the air.

"This spot where we are standing is the place where I intended to build my showplace house."

"Your *showplace* house?"

He nodded. His face taut, his eyes shadowed. "My father was a drunk. Whatever money he earned, which was little enough, he spent on drink. There was seldom food in the house—and never enough of it. We lived in shanties and sheds with holes in the roofs and walls and with broken windowpanes."

He stared out into the distance, a faraway look in his eyes, and she knew he was seeing those hovels.

"I had a little brother... Danny." He shoved his hands in his pockets, hunched his shoulders. "He was a great kid—always smiling and laughing. Except when he was too hungry or sick." He stopped, took a deep breath.

He *was* a great kid. His brother had died. Her heart ached for him.

"Ma was sick, too. I tried to take care of them as best I knew how, but there wasn't anything to do for them. No food to give them the strength to get better." He glanced her way. "I stole some whenever I could find a way." He looked into the distance again. "There were no dry blankets to put on their bed that had not been wet through from the rain. So I prayed. I asked God to give us food to eat and a house with no holes in the roof so Danny and Ma would get well. That didn't happen, so I snuck out and went to a church and asked for help. Some ladies came. But my pa sent them away. Ma and Danny...died. Danny was four years old. I was seven."

He turned and looked at her. "I promised them before they died that I would be somebody someday. That I would be so rich and important nobody would ever sneer at me again. That's why I wanted a showplace house. Right here on this knoll where everyone would see and admire it."

He shrugged. "I ran away from my pa and I worked at everything I could find to do. I saved my money and invested it to make that dream come true. And Levinia Stewart was part of that dream, too. I was going to have a showplace house and a show-off wife. The mayor's daughter—my guarantee into St. Louis society."

Pain stabbed deep in her heart. She looked down and held herself quiet, waiting for him to finish.

"And then I met you."

The words were soft, deep, husky. She heard him walk to her. Stop inches away from her. She looked up.

"You ruined my dream, Mary Randolph. I looked into those beautiful brown eyes of yours and everything I thought I wanted simply crumbled away. God used you, Mary. He used you to show me what true beauty is. That is why Levinia is jealous. You know what I want now?"

She couldn't be hearing him right. It wasn't possible he found her more beautiful than Levinia.

She could not breathe—or speak. He placed his hands on her shoulders and turned her toward the river. There was a new dock jutting out into the water.

"I want this land used to fulfill your dream. It's perfect for that. There's a dock for the *Journey's End*. And fields to grow vegetable gardens and graze animals on. And plenty of room left over for the kids to run and play."

Something white fluttered at the corner of her eye. She turned. He was holding a piece of folded paper out to her. "It's yours, Mary. All legal and settled. I had the deed recorded this morning. And then I went to get the children and bring them to you. That's when the mayor told me he would see to it that I never held a public position again."

Tears streamed from her eyes. It was selfish of her. So selfish. But, oh, how she wished it wasn't all for the orphans. Oh, how she wished—

"Don't cry, Mary." He took hold of her upper arms, pulled her close. "There's one thing more I want."

The deep, hushed words flowed over her. She clutched the paper in her hand and made herself look up at him.

"If you agree, I would like to build a house here on the knoll. A home for you and me." He tipped his head down. His blue eyes dark and filled with tiny flames. "I love you, Mary Randolph. I've loved you since I first looked into your beautiful brown eyes. Will you marry me?"

The impossible had happened. Samuel Benton loved her. Mary nodded. Forced her soft answer from her constricted throat. "I will marry you with joy, Samuel Benton. I love you. Now and forever."

"Ah, Mary. My beautiful, beautiful Mary. My love." His arms slipped around her, tightened, his head lowered.

Her breath caught, hung suspended.

His mouth touched hers and her lips opened to the warmth like flower petals open to the sun. She went on tiptoe and slid her arms around his neck, answering his love.

A whistle blew.

On the river below the knoll, the orphans' boat steamed around a bend and nosed its way to the dock that was its *Journey's End.*

Epilogue

Mary took her father's offered arm and stepped to the doorway of the *Journey's End* dining room. Everyone assembled there turned and looked at her.

"She looks like a *princess!*"

Katy's voice, filled with awe, floated to her. Her eyes teared up.

"Uh-uh, she looks like a flower."

That was Ben. Her lips twitched in memory.

"No, she looks like a *bride*."

And that was Callie. Sensible, wonderful Callie.

Mary swept her gaze to the children grouped together with Miss Withers, Ivy and Edda on the left at the front of the room and smiled. Eighteen children beamed back at her. She glanced to the right, and there was Mrs. Lucas standing beside James and Rebecca—his bride of two days. And her sister Sarah holding her new baby boy, while Sarah's husband, Clayton, held their little girl, Nora. And her aunt Laina and uncle Thad, and her cousins William and Emma and Anne. And her mother—

"Ready, Mary?"

And Pastor Thornton. And Sam, who stood waiting

for her with that soft look of love in his eyes that was for her alone. She swallowed back a rush of tears and nodded. "Yes, Father, I am ready."

She smiled and walked toward her love.

Sam stood in the doorway of the main salon of the *Right Choice* and looked down at his bride. His heart thudded. Every time he saw Mary his love grew stronger. And to see her holding her baby nephew did queer things to his stomach. Mary looked up and their gazes met, held.

"All right, you two, stop looking like James and Rebecca!" Sarah laughed and reached for her new son. "Go kiss your husband, Mary, before he bursts or something."

"An excellent idea." Mary laughed and ran to him. He gave her a kiss with a promise attached, which she returned with an equal amount of fervor.

"Did I hear our names mentioned? Move over. Make way for my bride." James laughed, nudged Sam and Mary aside and started into the room with Rebecca beside him.

Mary nudged James right back. "You and Rebecca have been married a whole two days longer than we have. I am the bride here."

"Are not."

"Am, too."

"Children!" Elizabeth Randolph laughed and looked at her husband, Justin. "I despair of our children ever stopping their competitions!"

Justin laughed and lifted little Nora into his arms. "Pray God, you may be right, Elizabeth. Life would be dull without them. Though I do not know where their competitive spirits come from."

"Well, certainly not from me, dearheart!" Laina crinkled her nose at her brother, then smiled at her husband. "Tell them I am very mild of manner, Thad."

Thad grinned and dropped a kiss on the top her head. "And have the good Lord strike me dead?"

All the Randolphs hooted—Laina among them.

The whistle sounded. The paddle wheels churned up water as the *Right Choice*—the new luxury liner of the M and M steamer line—started downriver. Mary and Sam stood alone on the deck and waved to the children and her family on the shore. Their farewell was returned with enthusiasm.

The boat steamed around the bend on the way to St. Louis to pick up passengers for its maiden trip to New Orleans, and the children, running along the riverbank shouting and waving, were lost to sight.

A whole month alone together before they returned. Mary sighed with contentment, leaned back against Sam's broad chest and placed her hands over his hard-callused ones that joined the protective circle of his arms around her.

He bent down and placed his mouth by her ear. "Happy, Mrs. Benton?"

She glanced over her shoulder at him and smiled. "Very happy." Her smile widened into a cheeky grin. "Mother and Sarah both think you are devastatingly handsome!"

He raised his knee and knocked the back of hers. It buckled, and she pressed more closely against him. His arms tightened. She smiled up at him. "And Father thinks you are very intelligent and...um...intuitive about finances."

He gave her a mock scowl. "You should have told me your father was the owner of the M and M line."

She laughed, twisted around inside the circle of his arms, slid hers up around his neck and gave him a saucy look. "And have you marry me for my money?"

He grinned, that slow, breath-stealing grin that made her heart do all the foolish things a sensible heart would never do, and lowered his lips to hover over hers. "There would be no danger of that, Mrs. Benton. Not once I saw your beautiful, honey-flecked brown eyes."

* * * * *

Renee Ryan grew up in a Florida beach town where she learned to surf, sort of. With a degree from FSU, she explored career opportunities at a Florida theme park and a modeling agency and even taught high school economics. She currently lives with her husband in Nebraska, and many have mistaken their overweight cat for a small bear. You may contact Renee at reneeryan.com, on Facebook or on Twitter, @ReneeRyanBooks.

Visit the Author Profile page
at Harlequin.com for more titles.

HANNAH'S BEAU

Renee Ryan

Wherefore receive ye one another,
as Christ also received us to the glory of God.
—*Romans* 15:7

To my fabulous editor, Melissa Endlich.
Your suggestions, support and overall guidance
were invaluable in the process of writing this book.
Thank you for taking a chance on me.
You are, quite simply, the best!

Chapter One

The Grand Opera House, Chicago, Illinois, 1883

Shakespeare's delightful comedy *Twelfth Night* progressed toward its dramatic conclusion as planned. Lies were exposed with the perfect blend of surprise, satisfaction and charm. Truths unfolded at a precise, believable pace.

Usually, Hannah Southerland loved the challenge of translating every nuance and plot twist found on paper into a memorable performance onstage. But as tonight's final act drew to a close she found herself wondering if art didn't imitate life a bit too closely, at least in her case.

Mistaken identity? Twins separated by misfortune? A woman in disguise from her true nature?

Uncanny, really. Peculiar.

Eerie.

With nothing left to do but take her bows, Hannah stood poised in the shadows, watching the last moments of the play. The only sign of her growing unease came in the rhythmic tick-tick of her pulse and the slight shake of her hands. Otherwise, she held herself rock still, letting the sound of actors reciting their lines, and the rustle of patrons shifting in their seats, echo in her ears and pulse through her blood.

These moments, when fantasy blurred into reality, were why she'd first pursued the stage five years ago. She'd craved the escape. Needed it as much as breath itself. In the end, she had found a new home with a large family to love her as her own had never been able to do.

Unwanted memories slid into her mind, playing out as strangely real as the last moments of the play. She'd been so afraid that dark, wintry night when her father had banished her from his home. All because she had played a well-rehearsed role, one she would never take on again.

In the ensuing years since her exile, Hannah had discovered a more powerful force than fear. *Faith.*

Now, if only her twin sister could find the same peace in Christ that she had.

With that thought, Hannah leaned slightly forward, her eyes searching for the woman positioned off the opposite end of the stage. There she stood, a mirror image of Hannah, yet profoundly different. It was the look in her eyes that set Rachel apart from Hannah, the startling combination of purity and audacity that had turned the heads of many unsuspecting men.

Rachel's presence at the theater tonight evoked a myriad of emotions—happiness that Rachel had left her fiancé barely a month before the wedding for the sole purpose of reconnecting with her estranged sister. Disappointment that Hannah's father had chosen not to come with Rachel. Hannah had hoped that after five years the venerable Reverend Thomas Southerland could find it in his heart to forgive her.

As Hannah had forgiven Rachel.

If, during her sister's brief stay, Hannah could teach Rachel about true accountability, maybe, *maybe,* Hannah could move on with her life. Without the guilt. Without the burden.

Without the shame.

Her hands started to shake harder, threatening her outward calm. A deep, driving urge to run away washed through her. Instead of giving in to the cowardice, Hannah threaded her fingers together and clutched her palms tightly against one another. In this mood she could feel the edgy nerves of her fellow actors, the underlying desperation to deliver the perfect performance.

Unable to bear their emotions along with her own unsettled ones, she shifted her gaze toward the audience. Flickering light illuminated the theater, casting a golden glow over tonight's patrons.

Hannah squinted deep into the shadows until her gaze focused. Countless faces stared at the stage with the kind of rapt attention that widened the eyes and slackened the jaw.

As expensive and wealthy went, the affluent men and women viewing tonight's closing performance had no rivals. Except, perhaps, in London. And like those patrons of the British theater, they fully accepted the illusion of true love found in the midst of deception.

Hannah took a deep breath and turned her attention back to the stage.

At last, the actor playing the clown recited his final line and made his exit. A hushed pause filled the theater. Like waking from a lovely dream, eyes slowly blinked and then…

The applause thundered, passing through shadow, to light, to empty stage.

The curtain began its slow descent, but not before the audience played its own part in the production and surged to its feet. The sound of their approval rumbled past the velvet folds as the soft thud of the thick, heavy material landed on the stage floor.

Chaos instantly erupted behind the delicate veil between audience and actor.

"Places, everyone," yelled the director. He turned to Hannah and motioned her forward.

Hannah wove her way through the labyrinth of rushing humanity, gliding toward her spot in the center of the troupe. She pushed back an unexpected flash of trepidation—one she hadn't felt since that terrible night of her banishment—and moved with the liquid grace born from tedious hours of practice, practice, practice. Each step required concentration, control and commitment. The kind that set Hannah apart from her other, more talented contemporaries.

Once in place, Hannah allowed the soft buzz of excited chatter to drift around her as she waited for her fellow players to join her. She rubbed her tongue across her teeth, a nervous gesture left over from childhood, before turning her head to seek out her sister once more.

Rachel stood watching the commotion with the wide-eyed innocence that had led her to be termed the "good" twin. But as with the play just performed, the outward impression was pure illusion.

Hannah was suddenly jostled by the actor on her left, jerking her attention back to the drawn curtain. Her hair swung out with the swift gesture, curved under her chin, then settled.

With a flick of her wrist, Hannah shifted the ebony mass of curls behind her back. Thoughts of her sister were not so easily set aside. However, right now, Hannah needed to concentrate on the other, equally disturbing emotions warring inside her.

Lord, fill me with a humble heart.

How easy it would be to fall for the adoration displayed inside the deafening applause seeping through the velvet barrier. To believe the praise was for her alone. To give in to the temptation of accepting glory for a gift that was merely on loan to her from her heavenly Father.

Blessed are the poor in spirit, for theirs is the kingdom of heaven.

Hannah pressed her lips together. Her mentor, Patience O'Toole, had taught her how to focus on being a light in the dark world of theater—a modern-day Babylon that required the resolve of Daniel and the courage of Shadrach, Meshach and Abednego to keep selfish ambition at bay.

How she missed the grounding influence of Patience and her flamboyant husband, Reginald. The surrogate parents who, with the perfect blend of Christian grace and earthly truth, had helped boost Hannah's broken confidence and heal her battered heart.

With a shake of her head, Hannah forced her mind on the present and smiled at her astonishingly handsome co-star as he swept into view.

Golden, spectacular, larger than life, Tyler O'Toole—Patience and Reginald's youngest son—never missed an opportunity to make an entrance. Although likable and charming, Tyler had his own agenda in life. Three priorities ruled his actions. Amusement. Pleasure. And, lest she forget, merriment. Unlike the rest of his siblings, Tyler would always be a selfish boy at heart.

"You were breathtaking tonight, my dear." His voice

was as dramatic as the rest of him, a husky baritone that carried to the last row in any theater.

Prepared to offer her own congratulations, Hannah looked up at his chiseled, beautiful face. He was the brother she'd never had, the one member of the troupe—other than his mother and father—who had worked tirelessly with Hannah to perfect her stage presence. In spite of his many faults, and there were *many,* Hannah couldn't help but admire the man. Tyler O'Toole was a brilliant performer.

Tonight had been no exception.

But before she could compliment his performance, he reached for her hand, bent at the waist and dropped a kiss onto her knuckles. The gesture was pure Tyler Bartholomew O'Toole, sincerity wrapped inside an insincere, theatrical flourish.

He rose slowly, deliberately, and then sent her a suave, half smile that seemed to say, *But, truly, wasn't I equally brilliant?*

Hannah lifted a single eyebrow. "Tyler, you—" She broke off, realizing she'd already lost his wavering attention.

Against her better judgment, she followed his gaze with her own—across the stage, past the rest of the hurrying cast, straight to the spot where her twin sister stood a little off to one side.

Rachel stared back at Tyler, giving him the serene, artful smile that had brought several men to their knees. Standing separate from the cast and crew, with a single beam of light casting a soft glow around her, Rachel looked like a beautiful, mysterious siren calling to any man willing to fall for her fantasy.

Tyler's answering sigh came out pitiful, a tiny bit

miserable and yet, somehow...calculating. In the next moment he unleashed his own secret weapon, the careless wink that had been practiced and perfected over the years. And had left its own destructive wake along the way.

Hannah stared at the two in disbelief, a knot of anxiety tightening her stomach.

Different man. Same sister.

One perfect disaster in the making.

And somehow, some way, Hannah would be the one to bear the consequences. Just like last time. Just like *every* time.

She should have realized when she'd introduced the two yesterday she'd been putting an open flame to a haystack.

No. No, no, no. Hannah had spent too many years taking the blame for her twin sister's indiscretions, and too many months watching Tyler break women's hearts, to hold her tongue now. "Tyler, stay away from my sister. Neither of you has any idea what sort of trouble you're flirting with."

Her words came out flat, hard and—unfortunately for them all—fell on unhearing ears.

"Stay away from that gorgeous, stunning creature? You demand the impossible, Hannah darling," Tyler said. "Rachel's smiles slay me, and her voice is sweeter than any angel's."

Clearly oblivious to the tension growing between their two leads, the other actors continued scrambling into place.

"Don't, Tyler." Pressure built in Hannah's chest, stealing her breath and drying out her throat. "Just...*don't*."

"Why, my dear girl, you sound quite discouraging. One might start to think you disapprove."

A familiar, albeit unwanted, affection broke past Hannah's annoyance. Tyler had the kind of droll humor that reared at the most inappropriate of times and invariably took the sting out of an uncomfortable situation. It was hard to dislike a man who was as fully aware of his faults as his talents. Even if he used both to his full advantage whenever the occasion suited him.

Well, tonight, where too many lives might be harmed, Hannah could not—*would not*—allow a budding flirtation to turn into something more destructive. "Tyler, you must listen and take heed. She's—"

A groan from the rigging stopped Hannah in midsentence and had both Tyler and her turning toward the curtain to fulfill their final duty of the night.

Conversation among the rest of the cast halted, as well.

A few more seconds of rope grinding to metal and the curtain began to rise. The audience leaned forward, eager to get a better look at the actors. With every inch of the curtain's ascent, their palms pounded wildly together, again and again and again. Louder and louder and louder.

Hannah slid a glance at Tyler. With a sly grin lifting the corners of his lips, he reached out and twined his fingers through hers. Together they raised their joined hands in the air then bent into a well-rehearsed bow.

Rising first, Hannah shot a quick slash of teeth at Tyler, and then leaned forward again. They repeated the process until the applause died to a mere spattering.

As the curtain made its final descent on the Chicago production of Shakespeare's delicious comedy, Hannah feared a tragedy far worse than any fictional tale was already in the making.

With another warning perched on her lips, Hannah turned to Tyler, but she only caught the wild flourish of coattails as he spun in the direction where Rachel stood.

"Tyler, wait. She's—"

He dismissed her with a careless flick of his wrist.

Hannah lifted onto her toes to see past the other actors. "Rachel," she called out. "You can't. You're—"

But her sister shifted to her left, literally turning her deaf ear in Hannah's direction. It was an old trick of Rachel's, a hard kick aimed straight at Hannah's guilt, an open defiance that did not bode well for a reasonable end to the escalating situation.

Nevertheless, Hannah set out after Rachel and Tyler. The two quickly disappeared behind a side curtain. The backstage area was already filled with commotion, making it difficult for Hannah to see precisely which direction they had taken.

After several long minutes of searching, Hannah thought she saw two shadowy figures leave the building, but prayed her riotous imagination had taken over her logic.

There was one dreadful hope left.

Shifting direction, Hannah turned toward Tyler's dressing room. She'd only taken two steps when one of the crew materialized in her path. "Hannah, your sister told me to give you this after tonight's production."

He pressed a piece of paper against her palm, then turned back to assist the stage manager in breaking down the set.

Hannah squinted toward the backstage door then looked down at the small, folded parchment in her hand. A foreboding filled her, and a hard knot formed in the pit of her stomach.

She unfolded the note with trembling fingers. Her sister's looping script flowed through a single sentence.

Be happy for us.

"Oh, please, *please,* not again."

Chapter Two

~❦~

Denver, Colorado Three days later

Harsh, irregular breaths wafted through the tiny room. The acrid smell of death filled the air. Both occupants sat wrapped in their own state of despair, each struggling for answers to unbearable questions. One had lost her will to live. The other had come to bring a final, eternal hope.

With the burden of his mission weighing heavy on his heart, Reverend Horatio Beauregard O'Toole swallowed his own sense of helplessness and looked at the haggard woman battling for each breath. There was little left of the vibrant creature Beau had met when he was but a boy. The gifted lead actress who had inspired a generation of aspiring young girls was now a broken shell of her former greatness.

She had no more faith. No more purpose.

No more hope.

Beau could barely reconcile this beaten woman with the one who had played some of the greatest heroines onstage with such confidence and verve. Once her crowning glory, now her hair hung in blond, dirty strings. Her skin pulled taut across her thin face, while her eyes had sunk deep in their sockets. She was a mere apparition of the beautiful woman the public had adored with near obsession.

Beau dropped his chin to his chest and released a defeated sigh. No. He would not give up on the woman his mother had once called friend.

He lifted a skinny, limp hand into his, closed his fingers over the pale, graying skin. "Miss Jane, all is not lost."

She gave him a ragged, quivering sigh.

With his own answering sigh, he released her hand and brought a glass of water to her cracked lips. He lifted her shoulders with one hand and helped her navigate the glass with the other. "You may still survive if you turn from this life forever. We could leave for Colorado Springs this afternoon."

Jane took a slow, choking sip and then leaned back. "No." A slow, harsh breath wheezed out of her. "It's too late."

The words had barely slid off her tongue when she broke into a fit of coughs.

Beau pressed a white cloth against her mouth, afraid each cough wrenching through her fragile body would tear her flesh from the bone. After the bout ceased, Beau pulled back the cloth now filled with the red stain of blood.

Blood from her damaged lungs.

Another moment passed in utter silence.

Beau's heart pounded so hard with anguish for her, for what she'd become, he thought he might choke from it. Now that the stage was no longer a viable prospect, Jane

Goodwin had chosen to earn her money in the most hideous way imaginable. It hurt to see how far she'd fallen.

A shudder racked through him. If only she would accept God's grace and Beau's charity.

"Dear, sweet Beau." Jane turned her head and blinked her dazed, drugged eyes up at him. "My sins are too many to wash clean now. Why else would I be here?"

She waved her hand in a gesture that seemed to say, *Look where we are.*

The heartsick tone of her voice took him aback. Beau glanced around the tiny room decorated purposely for sin. In the bright light of day, beneath the expensive silk and satin, hung a shabbiness that spoke of the years of hard, ugly work that had acquired the worldly trappings. And yet the room had a sad, unkempt feel. Once brilliant, now forgotten.

Just like this woman.

Just like the rest who shared residence in this…house.

Too many for one man to help.

He closed his eyes, once again praying for wisdom. A small, still voice inside said, *One at a time, Beau. Start with this one.*

All right. Yes.

Beau asked God for the words to convince her to leave, but behind his confident demeanor he was soul-sick with the hollow feeling of defeat. "Miss Jane, please reconsider my offer. The sanatorium is only a day's train ride away."

He tried to capture her stare, but her gaze darted around, eventually locking on to his left shoulder. "I… No, it's impossible."

He reached out and cupped her hand in his, staring fiercely into her eyes. "All things are possible through Christ."

"Not for my kind." Her voice was uneven, shaky, the underlying disgust at herself no longer hidden behind false bravado.

She'd given up then, resigned herself to die thinking she'd turned so far away from God that she could never find her way back, had convinced herself she deserved this sort of hell on earth.

"God forgives all sins, even the seemingly unforgivable ones." He spoke with the conviction of his heart. "You need only to ask."

"You don't understand." Jane tugged her hand free, the sharp gesture at odds with her infirmity. She struggled to speak, her lips moving frantically while words seeped out in a soft wispy whoosh. "I have a daughter."

Beau studied Jane's vulnerable expression with mingled pity and horror. He hadn't known. Hadn't realized. But he should have. He'd seen it often enough. The unbearable chain of sin continuing from one generation to another. "She is here? Living in the brothel?"

"Megan is at Charity House. If I leave, if I don't work, I cannot continue to pay her board."

Charity House. Of course. Beau knew all about the special home where children born to women of ill repute were welcomed without question. Marc and Laney Dupree, the owners, never turned a child away. No matter the financial circumstances. Jane was worrying over something that would not be a problem, ever.

"But if you don't leave, you will make your daughter an orphan. How is that any better?"

Another fit of coughing was her only response.

Beau shut his eyes for a moment. He must not quit on Jane. He must not. God had called him to minister to the ones with no more dignity, no identity, no…hope.

He knew firsthand what it meant to be an outcast, never fitting in the world around him. Although he adored his family, without their passion for acting, the constant years of traveling from stage to stage had left him feeling alone and separate from the rest of his siblings. Even in seminary his modern ideas of preaching and evangelizing had never truly meshed with the more traditional views of his professors.

He had yet to find his place in the world. Thus, he traveled from mining camp to saloon to brothel, ministering to the outcasts of this world. Outcasts such as women like Jane.

But soon, if the vote went his way, he would have his own church in Greeley, Colorado. It would be a place where he could put down roots and begin a normal family with a traditional wife by his side. Her soft, compassionate nature would temper his overly bold, often impudent personality. He hadn't found *her* yet, but he would and then his days of traveling across the territory and ministering to the forgotten would come to an end.

Well, not completely.

All would be welcomed in his new congregation. No matter their past sins or current ones. His church would be a safe haven for the lost. For the—

The door flung open with a bang. In swept a whirlwind of angry female and bad attitude. "Beauregard O'Toole, you know your kind isn't welcome in this establishment. To think. A minister, here, in *my* brothel." Her voice was incredulous. "It's just plain bad for business."

Beau rose and turned to face the new occupant of the room. With her outrageously buxom figure, unnaturally blond hair and overly painted face, Mattie Silks looked far older than her reported twenty-nine years of age.

She took two steps into the room, and then relaxed into a pose that spoke as much of her profession as her vanity.

Notorious. Legendary. With her own unique flair for the dramatic. Even without formal training, she could hold her own against any stage actress Beau knew. His lips pulled into a wry grin. Clearly, the woman had missed her calling.

Nevertheless…

If there was one thing his childhood had taught him, it was how to appease a dramatic woman in a fit of theatrics.

"Now, Miss Silks." He gave the surly madam a smile so filled with O'Toole charm that even his rogue brother, Tyler, would envy the result. "I am only here to visit my mother's dear friend."

"No." She switched poses, thrusting out one hip and slamming her fist onto the other. "You are here to talk my best girls into leaving."

Perhaps. But if Beau didn't try, who would? The Bible had taught him to look past the outer wrapping of a person and see into their heart. Well, Beau had done that sort of looking in the past weeks he'd held vigil by Jane's bedside. Not a single "girl" in Mattie Silks's employ wanted to be in the notorious madam's…well, *employ*. Not even one.

But without a concrete alternative, most had no other means of supporting themselves.

Beau considered the situation to be an opportunity straight from heaven. There were only two things humans could accomplish on earth that they would not be able to do in heaven: sin and evangelize. Beau truly believed God had brought him to this den of iniquity to be a light of hope. To plant a seed that might bring the lost back to Him.

One ill-tempered madam wasn't going to run Beau off that easily. "I simply offer to listen, and give advice accordingly."

"You mean preach."

Love the sinner, hate the sin.

Even Mattie Silks deserved his best efforts. "Preach, give advice. Semantics, Miss Silks, nothing more."

She gave him a hard look. "Thanks to you, two of my girls have already quit."

Beau sighed. He'd hoped for more. Shaking away his feelings of powerlessness, he continued holding Mattie's stare. "Only two?"

Her lips twitched before she pointed at him with a gnarled finger that revealed her true age. "You are an arrogant man."

Beau couldn't deny that one. He was, after all, an O'Toole. His natural arrogance was a character flaw 'ne had to fight against daily. His professors at seminary had tried to break him because of it. His fellow students had shunned him. He'd been run out of countless churches. And even now, the Rocky Mountain Association of Churches still questioned his ability to shepherd the new congregation in Greeley. All because he was an arrogant son of...actors.

Beau dropped his gaze to Jane and watched her fight for each breath of air. "I won't leave my mother's friend in the midst of her distress." He brushed a hand across her brow. "There is no changing my mind, Miss Silks. I am determined."

Mattie's eyes flashed. "And if I say otherwise?"

Beau couldn't fault the woman for her territorial reaction. This wasn't the first time he'd walked into a brothel since leaving seminary, only to be unceremoniously tossed out when the madam in charge discovered who he was. Or rather *what* he was.

Nothing like experiencing a little shunning of his own to help him better relate to his unusual flock. "You'd deny one of your girls a moment of peace in her final hours of life? Are you so cruel?"

Her gaze wavered, just a bit, revealing that Mattie Silks might have a heart beneath the tough businesswoman veneer. "You think she's that ill?"

"*Dr. Bartlett* thinks she's that ill."

Mattie shifted from one foot to the other then peered slowly down at Jane, who had finally fallen into a labored sleep. For several long heartbeats the madam merely stared at the near-lifeless form dragging ragged breaths into its injured lungs.

"I saw her perform once. Years ago, here in Denver. Such a talent. Such a waste." She shook her head and sighed. "You may stay, Reverend O'Toole. But I'm warning you. Keep yourself hidden."

Beau blinked at the sudden capitulation. Mattie Silks, hardened madam, had gone from outraged employer to saddened friend in a heartbeat. Talk about dramatic range.

"I have no plans of leaving her side," he said.

"Then we understand one another. Stay away from my other girls. You *preach*—" she spat out the word "—and out you go."

Beau simply nodded.

Fanning herself with her hand, Mattie sighed again. "It's scandalous, really. A preacher taking up residence in a parlor house."

Beau gave her his best Sunday-school smile. "The Lord works in mysterious ways."

Three days of unsuccessful searching had brought Hannah to Denver, Colorado, feeling defeated and frustrated. Rachel and Tyler had completely vanished. The sheer gravity of their selfishness, the reality of the ensuing scandal, had nagged at Hannah during the entire journey from Chicago to Colorado.

Hannah lowered her head and sighed. Why would Rachel run off with Tyler when she was engaged to a man who had adored her since childhood? Why would her sister throw away the guaranteed devotion of a good, Christian man for the wavering affection of a fickle actor?

Well, this time Rachel would face the consequences of her actions. Hannah would make sure of it.

Of course, she had to find her sister first.

With Patience and Reginald O'Toole performing in London, and the rest of their acting brood in New York, Hannah had one potential ally left, a man who might be able to help her right this terrible wrong.

Exhausted from her travels, but resolved nonetheless, Hannah checked the return address on the letter, folded the paper at the well-worn creases and shoved it into the pocket of her coat. For several moments longer, she allowed her gaze to sweep up and down the street, taking note of the houses and rushing populace, before her attention came to rest on the building directly in front of her.

If houses had gender, this one was surely female. Elegant, whimsical, the two-story building was made of rose-colored stone. The bold lines of the roof and sharp angles were softened by rounded windows and sweeping vines. On closer inspection the house looked a bit neglected; the twisting wisteria covered a few sags and wrinkles that made the building look like a woman refusing to accept her age.

A swift kick of mountain air hit Hannah in the face. She pulled her coat more securely around her middle and shoved her hands into her pockets. As her gloved fingers brushed against the letter, a fresh wave of guilt threatened her earlier resolve. At first, she'd been reluctant to read the correspondence addressed to Tyler from his brother, but after that initial hesitation she'd been too desperate *not* to open the letter.

Unfortunately, all Hannah had gleaned was the deep affection one brother felt for the other, and Reverend O'Toole's last known address. Thus, here she stood outside one of the most notorious brothels in Colorado, shifting from foot to foot like a nervous schoolgirl and praying Reverend O'Toole was still here, ministering to his mother's friend.

Buck up, Hannah, she told herself. *God has protected you this far.* Even with the gravity of the situation weighing on her heart, it was hard to marshal the courage to walk across the street and pass through those heavy double doors.

But really, how did one go about entering such an establishment in the light of day?

She took a deep, soothing breath and prayed for the nerve needed to continue her quest. Contrary to the cold, stale air, the sun hung high in the middle of the sky, bleaching the street with a blinding white light.

Oh, please, Lord, he's my last hope now. Let him agree to help me.

If she found Rachel and dragged her home, would their father believe Hannah wasn't to blame, after she had carried the burden of Rachel's actions all these years? Ever since Hannah had refused to chase after Rachel when they'd fought over a neighbor boy, Hannah had faced the consequences of her selfishness. Rachel had lost her way in the woods that cold winter day. She'd caught a fever and ultimately had suffered permanent hearing loss in one ear. Out of guilt—the debilitating guilt of knowing she was to blame for Rachel's disability—Hannah had accepted responsibility for her sister's many transgressions.

The pattern had been set long ago, the roles so familiar, to the point where Rachel was now a master at using Hannah's guilt against her.

Tears pushed at the backs of Hannah's lids, bitter tears of frustration, of helplessness, of the sharp fear that she would once again bear the burden of shame because Rachel would not atone for her own sins.

Of course, no amount of feeling sorry for herself was going to bring her sister back. Squinting past the sunlight, Hannah was filled with the strangest notion that the answer to her heart's secret hope—one so personal she hadn't known it existed—was near. She took a step forward. And another one. On the third, she froze as the doors swung open and out walked the man she'd come to find.

Every rational thought receded at the sight of him. Why hadn't she prepared better for this first glimpse of the rebel preacher?

Hannah stared, riveted, as the tall, powerful figure stalked across the street. The bright daylight set off his sun-bronzed skin. His dark blond mane hung a little too long, artfully shaggy. She held her breath, enthralled by the bold, patrician face, the familiar square jaw and chiseled features that declared he was, indeed, an O'Toole.

So similar to Tyler, but even from this distance Hannah could see the lack of slyness in the eyes that defined his scoundrel brother. Oh, there was boldness there, confidence, too, but also…sadness.

Oddly attuned to him, this virtual stranger, Hannah could feel the barely controlled emotion in each step he took, as if he were about to burst from keeping some unknown pain inside too long. With his head tilted down and his eyes looking straight ahead, his face was a study in fierce sorrow.

She knew that feeling well. Had lived with it for years, ever since her mother had died and she'd taken on the burden of caring for her more fragile sister.

He turned his head and their stares connected. Locked.

Hannah couldn't move. Couldn't breathe. Everything Tyler O'Toole pretended to be was real in this man, his brother.

She quickly tore her gaze away from those haunted silver eyes and prayed for the bravery to approach him for his assistance. She had to remember why she'd taken a hiatus, why she'd come all this way to find this particular man.

"Reverend O'Toole?" Hannah called out. Her heart picked up speed, nearly stealing her breath, but she'd come too far to turn into a coward now. "May I have a word with you, please?"

He stopped and cocked his head. A strange expression crossed his face, a mixture of astonishment and wonder, much like a theatergoer suddenly surprised he'd enjoyed a moment in a play he hadn't been eager to attend.

He blinked, and the look was gone.

"Do I know you, miss?" His voice was the same smooth baritone of his brother, but held a softer, more compassionate timbre. A tone that reflected the patience needed to minister to the downtrodden, the people no one else would accept.

She brushed her fingers across his letter again, only now realizing how much she craved the tolerance and compassion she'd read in the scrawled words.

For the first time in the last three hideous days, Hannah understood her sister's motivation to run. But where Rachel was running away from her promises and commitments, Hannah wanted to run toward…something. Something kind. Something permanent and safe.

Is this what the woman at the well had felt, Jesus? This rush of hope that all would be different, perhaps bearable at last, after her encounter with You?

The thought left her feeling slightly off balance, but then she realized it didn't matter how she felt. This meeting wasn't about her. It was about ending a decade-old pattern of lies and deception.

Hannah squared her shoulders, tilted her chin up and silently vowed to put the past to rest at last.

Chapter Three

For an instant, maybe two, the grind of wagon wheels, bark of vendors and squeak of swinging doors tangled into one loud echo in Beau's ears. Sadness over Jane, coupled with a terrible sense of helplessness, made his steps unnaturally slow. He wanted to be alone to think through the awful situation, to determine what to do about Jane's daughter, but he knew he had to push aside the selfish feelings and focus.

"Miss," he repeated. "May I help you?"

He could barely look at her. Her refined beauty stood in stark contrast to the seedy backdrop of Market Street, making him want a reprieve from all the painful emotions of the last few weeks. If only for a moment.

Beau gave his head a hard shake and stepped in her direction. By the time he'd closed the distance between them, he'd drawn a few conclusions about the woman in the blue velvet coat.

Wounded, was his first thought. Fragile. Tragically beautiful. He'd always been drawn to the poignant and injured, as evidenced by his unusual ministry. But something about this woman, with her large, exotic eyes and heart-shaped lips, put him on his guard. He'd seen many like her living in hopeless desperation in Mattie's brothel. Who else in this town could afford the silk gloves and matching hat she wore to draw attention to herself?

The wind kicked up, whipping a strand of her pitch-black hair free from its pins. She shoved the lock back in place. There was such delicate grace and quiet dignity in that tiny gesture that Beau, exhausted from his efforts with Jane, felt something inside him snap.

On your guard, Beau. This one's trouble.

Beau couldn't shake the notion that no matter how young this woman was now, no matter how outwardly beautiful, she would end up just like Jane and the others in Mattie's employ.

I have set you an example that you should do as I have done for you. At the reminder from the Gospel of John, Beau knew he owed this woman his full attention and an open mind. Nevertheless, her mysterious allure somehow added to his earlier sense of defeat.

He swallowed. Blinked. Swallowed again.

"Reverend O'Toole, are you ill?"

At the warm pitch of her voice, his confusion vanished, and the sound of horse hooves hitting gravel separated once more from the shouts of vendors yelling over one another.

"No. Yes," he said. His stomach twisted at the hard note he heard in his own voice, and he struggled to soften his tone. "That is, no, I'm not ill. And, yes, I am Reverend O'Toole."

She sketched a small nod then glanced into his eyes again. He saw relief there. Determination. And something else. Fear? Desperation? "I've come from Chicago to find you."

Chicago? By herself? Without a chaperone? Beau could no longer hear the activity around him. He flicked his gaze behind her, searching the area to see if his suspicions were correct. Baffled, he shifted his eyes back to her face. "You came here alone?"

She clasped her hands in front of her, frowned, and then lifted her chin. "I'm on a desperate errand that could not wait to find an appropriate companion." She swallowed, locked her gaze to a spot on his shoulder. "I'm a friend of your parents'."

"Are my parents…" Beau's heart tightened and began to throb in his chest. A riot of emotions slashed through him—worry, fear, dread—too many to sort through. "Has something happened to them?"

Her eyes widened at his question. "No." She reached out to touch him and genuine kindness replaced her earlier agitation. "Indeed, they are quite well."

"Good." He gave her one solid nod. "Good." But his heart was still rattling in his chest. He took a slow, deep breath. "Then why are you searching for me?"

A shadow of some dark emotion tightened her features. Guilt? Shame? A mixture of both?

Beau felt something equally dark inside him come to life. He couldn't help but think of Jane again. The famous actress had once been beautiful, as well. She'd been a friend of his parents', too. And yet, that hadn't shielded her from making poor decisions.

"What made you travel so far, *alone?*" He knew his voice was too sharp, nothing like the way he spoke to Jane and the rest of the women in Mattie's brothel. But surely no errand was worth this delicate woman embarking on such a dangerous journey by herself.

"I must find your brother Tyler." Her eyes went turbu-

lent and she drew her lower lip between her teeth. "Before it is too late."

That wasn't the whole truth. Beau knew it with the same instincts that kept him from falling for every lie he heard from the less reputable in his flock.

But, still, it was only an instinct. And she'd said she was a friend of his parents'. Calling on the patience he'd used with Jane, Beau commanded this woman's gaze with his. He saw a deep pain there, much like the look in the eyes of the women he'd met in Mattie's parlor house.

Despite knowing she couldn't possibly be one of them, not with her obvious connections to his parents, why could he not stop comparing them? Was it the way she dressed with the sort of expensive, flamboyant clothing that captured his attention?

"Please. You must help me find Tyler," she said. "It is a matter of grave importance."

Moved by the distress in her eyes, the somber tone in her voice, his breath turned cold in his lungs and ugly possibilities assaulted him. He touched her sleeve. But her arm seemed very fragile, too fragile for handling, and he let go gently. "Tell me what sort of trouble my brother has put you in? Miss…"

"Southerland. Hannah Southerland. But I think you've misunderstood me. That is—" she sighed and folded her hands in front of her "—*I* am not in trouble. It's my sister."

Southerland? Beau knew that name well. But the odds were too great that there could be a connection between this woman and the imposing reverend. Thomas Southerland was many things, including a respected member of the Rocky Mountain Association of Churches. He was also a man who openly questioned Beau's dedication to

Christ because of Beau's penchant for ministering to hard drinkers, gamblers, prostitutes and the like. Although the age of the two would make a father/daughter relationship possible, Beau could not imagine a situation where the man would allow his own girl to travel alone.

Besides, this woman was too delicate to be related to the stern, hard-faced reverend. Except…there was something about Miss Southerland that was familiar to him. A look, a fierce determination, perhaps?

"Miss Southerland, my mind has been occupied all morning with pressing concerns of my own. I'm afraid I'm not following you."

Her answering sigh was filled with impatience—at him—at herself—at them both? "I'm not making myself clear."

She blew out a miserable breath, and he realized her cheeks were growing red from the frigid air.

Where were his manners? Had he been so long out of polite society he'd forgotten the basics?

"Let's find another place to talk. Out of the wind and cold," he offered.

She nodded, but in the next instant she was jostled by a passing man. Beau reached out to steady her, quickly releasing her when she cast an odd look at his hand on her arm.

"I am staying at the Palace Hotel, several blocks in that direction." She pointed behind her. "There is a respectable restaurant on the ground floor."

"The Palace Hotel it is."

Beau fell into step beside her. A dull drumming started at the base of his skull. His brother, her sister…

The news couldn't be good. But he held his tongue as they crossed the street and continued forward. Two

blocks later, as they entered Denver's business district, the seedier buildings of Market Street morphed into more respectable brick and granite structures.

Beau quickly noted how Miss Southerland drew sidelong looks and murmurs from some of the men they passed along the five-block trek. Did she not see their interested stares? The speculation in their eyes? Hoping to shield her from the predators, Beau shifted her slightly behind him as they walked.

Best not to take any chances.

Once they turned onto 16th Street, the Palace Hotel loomed large and impressive before them. The nine-story building was one of a kind in the West, viewed as the best in town for both its elegance and service. Built exclusively from red granite and sandstone, the hotel was fashionable, eye-catching and well-dressed. Beau hadn't seen so handsome a building since he'd left New York seven years ago to pursue his education.

Upon entering the large structure, Beau took note of the opulent decor of rich fabrics and expensive mahogany paneling as they crossed the marbled lobby.

In no mood to sit through the ordering of food and subsequent false pleasantries as they waited to be served, he stopped walking. "Perhaps we should conduct our business here." He indicated two chairs in the corner of the room.

They would be out of the common traffic area but still visible enough to be considered decent. Potted plants in priceless urns lined the perimeter of the room. Several were grouped around the two chairs he'd pointed out and created an alcove of sorts.

Once she was settled, Beau began the conversation with complete honesty. "Miss Southerland. I must confess my imagination has been running wild. Tell me what has happened."

She placed her hands gently in her lap. Once again, Beau was struck by her refined movements. There was nothing hard about this woman, which was at odds with her boldness in coming in search of him.

"I don't know quite where to start," she said in a very low, very quiet voice. What sort of woman could look so fragile and yet travel hundreds of miles alone? She had a strange blend of polished confidence and naiveté about her that didn't mesh with his first impression of a woman seeking attention.

His interest was stirred, but his plan for the future did not include a beautiful woman who drew attention to herself by merely existing.

With that thought, Beau shut down any personal feelings and looked deep into her eyes again. He saw a vulnerability that she tried to cloak as tightly as she'd cinched the velvet coat around her tiny waist.

The woman stirred his compassion. Yes, that was it. His compassion.

Nothing more.

"Perhaps you should start at the beginning?" he said in a gentle tone.

"Yes. Of course. The beginning." She nodded, sat up straighter and squared her shoulders. "I suppose I should first tell you how I know your brother."

He offered an encouraging smile.

"Until three days ago, I was on tour with the same company as Tyler."

Beau's heart sank at her words. She was an actress, just like Jane. Although in light of her connection to his parents he should have expected this. A cold, unreasonable anger began to stir inside him, outdistanced by a sense of dread. He held his odd fury in check. Barely. He had no doubt that audiences adored this woman—how could they not?—but he also knew the public had once adored Jane, as well.

A fresh image of the broken woman he'd left in Mattie's brothel shot through his mind. No longer able to fill theaters with her talent and youth, she'd turned to a life of prostitution.

And now this woman, this *actress* sitting before him, with her youth and beauty and painful vulnerability, could easily end up in the same predicament as Jane.

Alone. Dying. Destitute.

The temper he rarely acknowledged swirled up so fast, so unexpectedly, his throat ached from having to swallow back the emotion.

Lord, show mercy to this woman. Guide her path.

"Go on," he said in a remarkably calm voice.

She ran her tongue across her teeth and nodded. The words spilled out of her in a rush, her voice halting and emotionless as she told the story of Tyler running off with her sister.

With each detail Beau gripped his chair harder and harder, trying to ignore the shock and anger that rose within him as the sordid events unfolded before him. Amazingly, Beau remained silent throughout Hannah's incredible tale.

As she came to the end of her story, she tapped her fingers quickly against her thigh in a rapid staccato. "I pray I'm not too late. The last time anyone saw them was three days ago."

Needing a moment to process all the information,

Beau punched out an angry breath and batted away a fern leaf dangling close to his head.

Too many thoughts collided inside his brain, making it pound from trying to sort through the particulars. Tyler had often been thoughtless, but he had never gone so far before. This time, Beau's rash, selfish brother had done the unthinkable. And now a young woman's reputation was all but ruined.

The pain their parents would feel when they discovered Tyler's indiscretion would destroy them. Patience and Reginald O'Toole were good, honest, moral people. They had created a brood of four boys and one girl. Each member of his beautiful family, other than Beau, had made a life for themselves in the theater in some form or another. All had continued to honor God as their parents had taught them. Except, apparently, Tyler.

"There's more." Hannah's words broke through Beau's thoughts and jerked his attention back to her.

The pattern on her dress blurred before him, and Beau found he had to lower his gaze to her shaking hands to gain control over his own emotions. "Go on."

"Rachel isn't free to run off like this. She's engaged to be married. Her fiancé is my father's protégé, of sorts. Although each will handle my sister's recklessness differently, neither will take this news well. My father, especially, is not a man prone to forgiving selfish acts of any kind."

Beau gave his head a hard shake, but dread consumed him. He breathed in the scent of expensive perfume and fresh soil from the potted plants. One thought stood out over the rest.

He had to ask the question. Had to know. "Is your

father Thomas Southerland? *Reverend* Thomas Southerland?"

Her mouth dropped open. "You have heard of him?"

"I met him when I was in seminary." And to say they
hadn't seen eye to eye was a gross understatement.

Worse, the good reverend now held Beau's future in
his hands. His voice was strong among the other members
of the Association. With a few well-chosen words, Reverend Southerland could decide Beau's future in Greeley,
Colorado. Although the man didn't trust Beau's modern
views, he had been coming around.

What would the reverend think when he found out
what Beau's brother had done, with the man's own daughter no less?

Beau couldn't let it matter. *Trust in Him at all times,
O people; pour out your hearts to Him.*

The Scripture gave him hope, and he lowered his head
to pray. *Lord, tell me what to do. Give me wisdom to—*

Hannah's voice broke through his prayer. "If you've
met my father, then you understand why I must find Rachel. If I can get to her before she…before they… Well,
the point is—" Hannah closed her eyes and swallowed,
looking as though she had to gather her courage for the
rest. "Rachel must accept the consequences of her actions."

Beau sensed there was more to the story, a personal
element Miss Southerland wasn't going to reveal to him
just yet.

It would be wise to focus on the particulars. "Why do
you think they've come west?"

"They were last seen boarding a train headed this
way." Her words came out steady, suspiciously controlled.

"With your mother and father in London and the rest of your siblings in New York, you are my only hope."

He opened his mouth to speak but clamped it shut as a couple strolled by, their heads bent toward one another in an intimate gesture that spoke of familiarity. Partners. Beau ignored the odd spasm in his throat at the sight and said, "How did you know where to find me?"

She gave him a sheepish grin and pulled a letter from her coat pocket that had his handwriting on it. "I apologize, but I read your latest letter to your brother. I was desperate. I had hoped to find out…something." She lifted her shoulders in a helpless gesture.

Before he could comment, she added, "Rachel's fiancé will be devastated at the news of her disappearance with Tyler. But, as you can imagine, it is my father who will find the whole scandalous affair unacceptable. He warned Rachel to stay away from me. I'm afraid he'll blame me for this."

Beau had a terrible, gut-jerking sensation at her words. "Does your father not approve of you? Of your career?"

She looked away from him, but not before he saw the same sad, vulnerable light in her eyes that he'd witnessed earlier. "No. He does not."

"Well, then. That's one thing your father and I would agree on."

Her face drained of color, the pale skin standing out in bold contrast to the dark slash of her eyebrows. "What… What did you say?"

Beau moved his shoulder, a gesture that communicated his own frustration. "Don't you realize what can happen to you?"

"To…*me?*" Her angry gaze slammed into him like a punch.

All right, yes. He knew he was speaking too boldly, but he had to make his point now that he'd begun. "Jane Goodwin, one of the premiere actresses of her day, and once a dear friend of my mother's, is dying of a terminal illness in a brothel."

Beau ignored the shock in her eyes and pressed on. "Is that the legacy you want?"

Chapter Four

Hannah sat motionless under Reverend O'Toole's grim stare. Who did this preacher think he was to judge her, to heap her in guilt for a lifestyle someone else had chosen?

"You can't possibly believe every actress turns to…" She wound her hands tightly together in her lap. "Prostitution."

"Most do. Especially those without family support."

At his toneless response, bitter disappointment built inside her. In all things that mattered, Beauregard O'Toole was just like her father. Quick to judge. Unwilling to see past the exterior of a person to the heart that lay underneath.

"The point is this," he continued, his voice flat and emotionless and nothing like the rich baritone of earlier. "Once your looks are gone, there will be few options left to you."

My looks? Few options? The gall of the man!

He'd judged her before knowing all the facts. Her future plans were solid *and* well thought-out. The real estate in which she'd invested had already made her five times the money she'd earned on the stage. In a few years, she could retire a wealthy woman, free to offer her time and money to abandoned women and children in need.

She steeled herself as she'd done in her father's presence and ignored the hollow, shaking feeling of loneliness that took hold of her. "How can you talk like this? What about your mother and sister? They are actresses as well."

"They have family who love them, who accept them and will provide for them no matter what." He leaned forward and rested his elbows on his knees. "Can you say the same, Miss Southerland?"

She gave him a noncommittal sniff and focused her gaze on the plant behind him. As she absently counted the leaves, instant fear tripped along her spine. How could she face her father with this defeat? She'd failed to protect Rachel, again. And Thomas Southerland would never forgive her for it. Never.

But Hannah couldn't turn back now. She would not continue accepting blame for Rachel's bad choices. The time had come for Hannah to confront her father armed with the facts.

It would be up to him to decide if she spoke the truth.

Hannah fixed her gaze on Reverend O'Toole. She would confront her father with or without this man's help, with or without Rachel by her side. Hannah *would* break the cycle of sin in her life at last.

She had three weeks before Rachel's wedding. Three weeks to redeem them both. Three short weeks.

Yet here she sat with a man who saw her in the same ugly spotlight as her father did. Beauregard O'Toole had let her down, to be sure, but Hannah would not hold a grudge against the man. The fault lay mostly with her. She'd been a fool to build him up in her mind. She had wrongfully put her hope in him, a mere man, and not the Lord.

That was one mistake she would never make again.

Disappointed with them both, Hannah stood.

The reverend unfolded his large frame and rose, as well.

"I was mistaken in asking for your help," she said. "I thank you for your time."

"Wait." He took a step to his right, effectively barring her exit. Although he stood close enough for her to smell the scent of lime on him, a deceptive calmness filled the moment.

But when he still didn't speak or move aside, Hannah's heartbeat picked up speed. Surely, he wasn't trying to trap her, to use his size to intimidate her?

Just as real panic began gnawing at her, he took a step back. She started to push around him, but he stopped her with a gentle touch to her arm.

"Don't leave," he said, surprising her with his mild tone. "I fear we've become sidetracked from the real issue here. Please, sit back down and we will discuss the next move together."

Hannah was tired. She was frustrated. But she was also out of options. With a reluctant sigh, she lowered herself back into the chair she'd occupied earlier.

Reverend O'Toole settled in his seat, as well. "You were right to come to me, Miss Southerland." He cleared his throat. "I have contacts all over the territory, in areas most wouldn't dream of going."

Hannah closed her eyes and pressed her fingertips to the bridge of her nose. Was he offering his help after all?

Did she still want his assistance knowing he'd already judged her and found her wanting? Should she risk the humiliation of spending hours, perhaps days, with a man who considered her one step away from prostitution?

She lowered her hands and slowly opened her eyes. "I don't believe I want your help." Her tone came out a little too spiteful, a little too high-pitched, and she regretted her rash words as soon as they left her mouth.

Where else could she go? Who else would assist a woman traveling alone, one who knew nothing of the surrounding territory? Certainly, no one with honorable intentions.

Feeling incredibly vulnerable, Hannah flattened a palm against her stomach. The twisting inside warned her she had little time left. But then she remembered what Patience O'Toole had always told her. "If you're unsure what to do, allow God to take the lead."

How do I do that, Lord?

As the silence between them continued, Reverend O'Toole rubbed a hand across his mouth and nodded as though he'd come to an important conclusion. "When we first met, outside the... That is, when we met on Market Street, I was on a special errand for Jane Goodwin, one I am afraid cannot be neglected much longer."

His odd change of subject took Hannah aback. Was this his way of dismissing her? Unexpected panic threaded through her. "I don't see how that is relevant to—"

"I want you to accompany me to Charity House. If after our errand you decide you want to continue your search for your sister, you won't go alone. I won't allow it."

"You won't *allow* it?"

His arrogance stunned her into silence.

She opened her mouth to speak. Closed it. Opened it

again. But still no words came forth. Her fingers brushed across the letter folded neatly in her pocket. Was the compassionate man she'd found on the pages a complete fabrication?

As though reading her mind, regret flashed in Reverend O'Toole's eyes and his expression softened. "Forgive me, Miss Southerland, I spoke abruptly. What I meant to say is that this concerns my brother as well as your sister. I have a responsibility as much as you do to see matters restored."

Of course he had a stake in the outcome of this debacle. And yet…why did she sense his offer of assistance was more personal than he was admitting? He claimed he knew her father. Was there more of a connection than he was letting on?

A slow breath escaped from her lungs and she pressed farther back into her chair. What was keeping her from trusting Reverend O'Toole? Why couldn't she simply accept his assistance and proceed to the next step in finding Rachel?

All right, yes. She admitted that she'd come here hoping to find something special in this man, the admired son of her beloved mentor and friend. She'd hoped to find something more in him than she'd found in other men, something she hadn't been able to define.

But, *again,* Hannah reminded herself this wasn't about her. With nowhere else to turn, she needed Reverend O'Toole's help. She would trust God to take care of the rest.

The plans of the Lord stand firm forever, the purposes of His heart through all generations.

Yes. She would trust the Lord to guide her path.

"Thank you for your offer, Reverend O'Toole. I would

very much like to accompany you on your errand." She pulled herself to her feet. "Please, direct the way."

Beau followed Miss Southerland's lead and stood, as well. But as his gaze captured her closed-lipped expression, something dark in him shifted and realigned itself. What had previously been anger and frustration now gave way to guilt.

Feeling like a fiend, he knotted his hand into a fist at his side, sucked in a harsh breath and then relaxed his fingers. Because of his own arrogance, Miss Southerland was wary of him.

Understandable, under the circumstances.

"Follow me," he said, accepting that he would get very little warmth from her now.

He'd unfairly judged Miss Southerland because of the hours he'd spent with Jane Goodwin. Setting aside his own prejudice now, he studied the woman walking beside him with fresh eyes. Her clothes were elegant and fashionable, her carriage graceful and refined. She was everything clean, unblemished...pure. No one in their right mind would mistake this woman for a prostitute.

Except, of course, a preacher too caught up in his own grief and frustration to see the truth standing before him.

Beau was reminded of a verse from the book of James. *The tongue is also a fire, a world of evil among the parts of the body.*

He'd spoken from the bias of his own circumstances, not with the compassion of a minister. What sort of preacher did that make him?

Lord, forgive me my bold, outspoken words. Help me to make amends to this woman properly in a way that will bring You glory and her peace.

The moment they exited the hotel, cool mountain air slapped him in the face and shimmied under his collar. Beau immediately steered Miss Southerland back inside. "Wait in here, out of the wind, while I find us suitable transportation."

As he turned to go, he shot a quick glance at her over his shoulder. She stood gazing at him with a quiet, clear-eyed look that held far too much worry in it.

A muscle locked in his jaw, and he let out another quick hiss of air. Why hadn't he focused on easing her concern for her sister, instead of allowing his own worries to influence his behavior?

Returning to the curbside, Beau blew into his cupped palms and silently reviewed the harsh words he'd used with Miss Southerland.

His delivery had been insensitive, to be sure, but he didn't believe he'd been wrong in warning the actress of the life she could find herself leading if she didn't take care. She might be pure and innocent. Today. But she was only a few bad choices away from becoming another Jane. And then men would flock to her for all the wrong reasons.

Everything in Beau rebelled at the notion. The responding growl that came from his throat sounded almost primitive.

Men could become blind idiots, often treacherous, around the sort of devastating beauty Miss Southerland possessed. Although she believed otherwise, she wasn't safe traveling by herself in this part of the country.

Beau shouldn't have left her alone in the hotel.

Far too impatient to wait for a carriage to pass by, Beau informed the doorman of his transportation needs and went inside to retrieve Miss Southerland.

She stood along the edge of the lobby, hidden slightly in the shadows. As before on Market Street, he found himself no longer able to walk, to breathe, to...*move*. He simply stared at her like an idiot. The impact of her beauty hit Beau like a punch thrown straight to his heart.

Separate from the other patrons, Miss Southerland looked incredibly sad. And with her arms crossed over her waist, her eyes blinking rapidly to stave off tears, she captured the image of a tragic heroine. Beau had the sudden urge to wrap her in his arms, to protect her against the ugliness he knew was in the world.

If Miss Southerland's sister was half as beautiful and delicate as she was herself, it was no wonder Tyler had snatched her up and run away as fast as he could. Tyler was selfish, to be sure, but the man wasn't stupid.

No. That line of thinking was senseless and dangerous.

Beau could not start feeling compassion for his brother or the heinous act the man had committed. A stop at Charity House would restore his own priorities and remind Beau of the dangers both Miss Southerland and her sister faced if either ended up alone in this harsh land.

Lord, not that. Use me as Your instrument to prevent such a tragedy.

With his mission in mind, he forced his feet to move. "Ready?" he asked.

She nodded, the wary expression in her eyes cutting him straight to the bone.

Had he betrayed this woman's trust before he'd earned it?

Perhaps the damage wasn't permanent. Through Christ all things were possible. Yes. *Yes.* All was not lost.

His steps were lighter as he led her through the hotel's front door. Once outside, a burning cigar stump arced in the air and landed near Miss Southerland's feet with a thud. Beau took her elbow and circled her in a wide berth to avoid the glowing ember. Still holding her arm, he offered his other hand to assist her into the waiting carriage the doorman had summoned for them.

She looked at his outstretched palm as though she didn't want any further physical contact with him. He waited as a myriad of emotions ignited in her eyes. Finally, she relented with a soft sigh and placed her hand in his.

Palm pressed to palm, Beau liked how her warmth passed through her gloves and straight into him. With an odd sense of reluctance, he released her, gave the driver the address of their destination and climbed into the carriage, as well.

He settled on the bench opposite her. In the ensuing silence, he took the opportunity to study his surroundings. The blue upholstery had seen better days. It was faded in places, frayed at the edges and missing several buttons. The air hung thick and heavy, carrying a musty, unpleasant odor.

At least the wooden floor was clean.

Once the carriage began moving, Beau could no longer remain silent. "I apologize for the harsh tone I used earlier. I have no excuse. My mind was on other concerns, but that doesn't mean I had the right to judge you so quickly."

She waved her hand in dismissal. "It's forgotten." But her guarded eyes and distant tone told him otherwise.

Accepting momentary defeat, Beau shifted the conversation to the reason Miss Southerland had sought his assistance in the first place. "Charity House has a school connected to it. The headmistress's husband is a U.S. Marshal."

"Do you think this man will help us?" she asked, her voice filled with a weariness Beau had missed until now.

Stunned at his own lack of insight, Beau took note of the purple circles under her eyes, the lines of fatigue surrounding her mouth. "When did you say Tyler and your sister left Chicago?"

She blinked at him, but kept her lips tightly clamped together.

He softened his tone and touched her gloved hand. "How long ago, Miss Southerland?"

"Three days," she said, pushing out of his reach.

"How much sleep have you had since then?"

Sighing, she turned her head to look out the carriage window. "I've had enough."

"Miss Southerland—"

"I'm fine. Truly." She returned her gaze to his. "Tell me about this U.S. Marshal you mentioned."

Beau let her switch the topic—for now—and called to mind the last time he had been in Denver. Trey Scott had helped him find a miner who'd run out on his wife and five children. Clearly an advocate for abandoned women and their families, the lawman had been ruthless in his search.

"He's a good man," Beau said with sincerity. "He'll do all he can to locate your sister, or, barring that, he'll find someone who can."

"Thank you."

Relief glittered in her eyes. Still, she sat with her shoulders stiff and unmoving.

Time, he told himself. In time she would learn to trust him, perhaps even forgive him.

Uncomfortable on the bench that was far too small for his large frame, Beau shifted and rearranged his legs. "While we have a moment, I should tell you about Charity House so as to avoid any confusion once we arrive."

She nodded slowly, her eyes searching his as though she wasn't sure why his voice had changed but had decided to hold on to her curiosity while he explained himself.

What sort of woman had that kind of controlled patience?

"Charity House," he began, "is an orphanage—"

"Orphanage?" Her eyes lit up, and she tilted her head forward. "How many children are housed there?"

"Forty."

"So many." She relaxed her head against the cushions and blinked up at the ceiling. Her eyes took on a faraway expression, as though she was calculating what forty orphans would look like.

"I should warn you," he said, pulling at a loose thread in the upholstery. "When I say orphanage, I don't mean it in the strictest sense."

She cocked her head at him. "I don't understand."

He tugged on the string, the gesture releasing three more strands. "It's a baby farm."

She lifted a shoulder and shook her head in obvious confusion.

Releasing the thread entwined in his fingers, he boldly pressed on. "A baby farm is a home for prostitutes' illegitimate children."

Her eyes widened. "I've never heard of such a thing."

"The children aren't accepted in other, more traditional homes because of their mothers' profession. They can't live in the brothels, so Marc and Laney Dupree take them in without question." Beau kept his voice even, but the passion he felt for the orphanage sounded in his tone despite his efforts. "If not for Charity House, most of the children would have nowhere else to go. The cycle of sin and crime would continue in their lives."

"How—" Tears filled her eyes, skimming along her dark lashes like tiny ice crystals. They disappeared with a single swipe of her wrist. *"Marvelous."*

Beau hadn't expected such a positive, heartfelt response from her.

Why not? he wondered. Why had he expected her to show immediate prejudice?

Because you were so quick to judge, yourself. You saw her from your own failings, not hers.

"Yes." Beau swallowed. "It is marvelous."

They shared a small smile between them, but then her forehead scrunched into a scowl, effectively dousing the moment with a dose of reality. "Didn't you say you were going there on an errand for Jane Goodwin?"

"Yes, to pay the board for her daughter."

Surprising him once again, Miss Southerland looked at him with glowing respect, as though he'd transformed into something good and noble right before her eyes. "How very kind of you."

Unnerved by the change in her, he rolled his shoulders. "It's what I do."

"I know."

She really smiled at him then. It was nothing more than an attractive lifting of the corners of her mouth that revealed straight, white teeth, but the gesture carried a spectacular wallop.

Beau had thought her beautiful before, but now...

He had to cough to release the breath lodged in his throat.

He should start anew with this woman, here and now. He should find a way to earn back her trust, in degrees if not all at once. He should do a lot of things that involved words and a healthy dose of groveling on his part.

Instead, he repositioned his weight on the bench and released his own grin.

Her smile widened in response. And for the first time in years, a sense of utter peace settled over him.

Words, Beau decided, were highly overrated.

Chapter Five

Hannah sank back against the seat cushion and studied the pastor from beneath her lowered lashes. His eyes crinkled at the edges when he smiled. She hadn't expected that. Although she should have.

There was something familiar about this man's masculine good looks, a charming vibrancy that was one hundred percent O'Toole. And yet the tilt of his head, the slash of his cheekbones, the bewildering sorrow in his eyes were all profoundly his own.

Hannah released a slow sigh. After the last three days, she should be immune to any man with the last name O'Toole. She certainly didn't want to be attracted to the one sitting across from her. Anger and distrust were much more manageable emotions, certainly easier to define.

But he'd thrown her off balance with his passionate description of Charity House and the home's special mission.

The carriage bumped, jostling her forward then back again. Another bump. Another jostle, and Hannah had to place her palms on either side of her to prevent an unfortunate incident—oh, say, like diving headfirst to the floor.

As she struggled, Reverend O'Toole's smile dipped into a frown. "Can I assist you?"

She made a noncommittal sound in her throat.

He lifted a hand toward her.

"No." She glided smoothly out of his reach. "I'm steady now."

"We're nearly there," he said in a soft, understanding voice.

Oh. Perfect. *Now* his tone and manner held the compassion she'd hoped to find in him earlier.

At the genuine show of concern in his gaze, she had to work to catch her breath. His silver eyes held such depth, such consideration. He was worried. *About her.* Which made him infinitely more likable.

The cad.

The carriage suddenly felt too small, too confining.

Hannah reached for her collar. Cleared her throat. Forced a smile. Cleared her throat again. "It's hot in here."

His teeth flashed white, and the crinkles deepened around his eyes. "It is."

Careful, Hannah, she warned herself. *He's far too charming when he smiles.*

She had to keep her mind on the task she'd set before her. *Not* on the beautiful gray eyes of a rebel preacher who unfairly judged her one moment and showed genuine contrition the next.

A surge of impatience had her tapping her fingers against the seat cushion. Time was running out. The longer Rachel and Tyler remained hidden, the harder it would be to uncover their location.

Hannah reached up and fiddled with the top button

of her coat again. As much as she wanted to rush to the next town, she had to trust this small interruption in her search was part of God's plan. Just as Jesus had stopped unexpectedly to heal the bleeding woman on his way to save Jarius's daughter, this detour had to mean something important, something significant Hannah didn't yet understand.

Hadn't good already come from this slight change in plans? An introduction to a U.S. Marshal was imminent. Certainly, seeking the expertise of a trained lawman was better than chasing around the territory with no real direction.

Not to mention, they were headed to an orphanage for abandoned children. *Go where God leads...*

The carriage slowed and stopped with a shudder, jarring her out of her thoughts.

"We're here," he said unnecessarily.

Hannah craned her neck to look out the window, but the reverend's shuffling of legs and arms captured her attention before she could focus on the scenery. He was so tall. She hadn't realized how confining the carriage must have been for him.

Rearranging his position one last time, he stooped forward and exited the carriage. Hannah clutched the seat tighter as the bench tilted from the sudden shift of weight.

Continuing the role of gentleman, the reverend reached back into the cabin to offer his assistance once again. Hannah stared at the outstretched palm, unsure whether to accept his help a second time or not. Even through her gloves, something strange had happened when their hands met.

Her reaction worried her, of course, but not enough to be rude. Bracing for the jolt, she slowly placed her

hand in his. The expected tingle started in her fingertips and moved swiftly up her arm. In an effort to be
free of the disturbing sensation, she scrambled out of the
carriage and nearly pushed the wall of man and muscle
away from her.

He looked at her strangely, dropped his gaze to his
now-empty hand and sighed.

With a theatrical flourish reminiscent of his brother,
he motioned to the home standing behind him. "I give
you Charity House," he said, adding a shallow bow and
a flick of his wrist to emphasize his point.

Hannah blinked at the massive structure. "*This* is an
orphanage?"

"Spectacular, isn't it?"

She blinked again.

Despite the grubby clouds that rapidly swallowed the
pristine sky above, the house, with its clinging vines,
stylish brick and soft angles, captured her imagination
and made her think of fairy tales…rescued damsels in
distress…happily ever afters…

"It's quite lovely," she said at last.

Unable to say anything more, she craned her neck and
looked to her left and then to her right. It was evident
that they stood in the middle of an exclusive neighbor-
hood. Modern gas lamps sat atop poles at every street
corner. Large, brick homes similar to Charity House in
their grandeur marched shoulder to shoulder in elegant
formation along the lane.

Caught between surprise and puzzlement, Hannah
slid a glance at the man looming large and silent beside
her. He stood patiently, his hands linked behind his back.

She turned her attention back to the orphanage. The

sheer glamour of the home—or rather *mansion*—took her breath away.

Dragging cold air into her lungs, she said, "I've never seen an orphanage quite like this."

And she'd seen plenty in the last few years. The buildings were usually sterile and functional, never as inviting as this one was.

She focused on the sound of laughter and good-natured shrieks coming from somewhere in the near distance. The joyful noise of children hard at play made her ache with an unexpected sense of homesickness. It was an odd sensation that was part confusion, part longing, and she felt her shoulders stiffen in response.

"Marc and Laney have spared no expense," the reverend said. "Each child in his or her own way has suffered a great deal in their short lives. At Charity House they receive a little beauty in their previously barren worlds."

Hannah noted the manicured lawn scattered with blooming autumn plants. "It's wonderful."

"It is."

A sudden thought occurred to her. "The neighbors don't mind living this close to an orphanage?"

"Most tolerate it."

It was an acceptable answer, but something dark flashed in his eyes and made her press the issue. "What about the others?"

"As you can imagine, some don't approve. They file complaints occasionally, but don't worry." His voice took on a convicted edge. "The Lord's hand is on Charity House. The orphanage is here to stay."

"Praise God."

He gave her a heartening smile. "Couldn't have said it better myself."

"Is the inside as grand?" she asked.

"You'll find out soon enough. Here come Marc and Laney now." He tipped his head toward the front door.

Hannah turned her attention back to the house in time to see a young couple negotiating the front steps together. Both were as beautiful as their home.

The dark-haired, clean-shaven man was dressed in what Hannah would have thought more appropriate for a successful banker. He wore a gold and black brocade vest and a matching tie, while a shiny watch fob hooked to a middle button dangled toward a small pocket. The entire ensemble looked both expensive and elegant.

The woman was dressed more casually, in a simple blue dress with a white lace collar. Her mahogany hair was pulled into a fashionable bun and she walked with an inherent grace any actress would envy.

The couple held hands, as though they were newly married, madly in love, or both. Other than Patience and Reginald O'Toole, Hannah had never seen two people so finely attuned with one another.

A gnawing ache twisted in Hannah's stomach. Would she ever find that sort of connection with a man? Or was she destined to be alone, to serve other abandoned women and children without the benefit of a husband by her side?

Only God knew for sure.

As they drew closer, Hannah studied their faces. Compassion and strength of character were evident in their smiles and sparkling eyes. Eventually, the couple separated and the woman pushed slightly ahead.

"Pastor Beau, what a pleasant surprise." Beaming, she gripped both of the reverend's hands and squeezed. "We didn't expect you until Sunday."

He lifted one of her hands to his lips then released her. "The pleasure is mine."

"Beau." The man slapped him on the back in a friendly gesture. "It's always good to see you, no matter the day of the week."

"Marc and Laney Dupree, I would like to introduce Hannah Southerland." He turned and gestured to her. "She's a friend of my…parents'."

Marc nodded at her. The accompanying smile was so genuine and guileless Hannah found herself smiling back.

Laney, however, clearly wanted none of the distant politeness required of first meetings. She boldly yanked Hannah into a tight hug. "Any friend of our favorite pastor is certainly welcome in our home."

At the genuine warmth in Laney's words and the open acceptance in her embrace, Hannah's stomach curled inside itself. Feeling more than a little desperate, she clung to the other woman with a fierceness she hadn't known she possessed. Fear, frustration and terrifying hope braided together in a ball of awkward longing. Hannah hadn't realized how alone she'd felt these last three days as she'd searched for Rachel and Tyler with no leads, no help and no advice.

As though sensing her mood, Laney patted her on the back and whispered in a voice only Hannah could hear, "You're safe with us."

Unable to respond, Hannah simply gripped the other woman tighter.

"Tell me, Beau," Marc asked from behind her. "What brings you to our home, on a Wednesday no less?"

Feeling awkward, foolish even, Hannah stepped quickly out of Laney's embrace. She was too emotional to speak, not that the question had been directed at her. But still…

She gave the reverend a pleading look.

His questioning gaze was so serious, so concerned, she lost the tiny thread of her control and tears pricked the backs of her eyelids. It took everything in her not to reach up and wipe at her lashes.

He touched her arm. "Are you all right?"

She nodded her head, a little too quickly, a little too intensely.

His eyes softened. He squeezed her hand a moment, and then turned back to Marc. "I have a delivery from one of Mattie's girls. Miss Southerland was kind enough to accompany me."

"I'm glad," Marc said with a kind look directed at her.

"And while we're here," the reverend continued, "we thought you might have an idea where your brother-in-law is today."

Marc and Laney shared a look. "You're searching for Trey?" they asked in unison.

Beau nodded, but didn't divulge any of the particulars.

"Well, you're in luck. He's actually here today," Laney said. "Last I saw, he was out back playing baseball with some of the older children."

Marc looked like he was going to add to the explanation, but he was interrupted by a high-pitched squeal of delight. "Pastor Beau! Pastor Beau!"

All four adults turned toward the gleeful sound. A little girl about seven years old skipped down the steps. Her sky-blue eyes sparkled with delight. Her broad smile showed off a missing front tooth, while two long black braids bounced from side to side with each step she took.

The adorable little girl was filthy from braids to bare

feet and, quite frankly, the happiest child Hannah had ever seen.

Skidding to a halt mere inches short of running into the pastor, she asked, "Are you here to play with us today?"

Unfazed by the near collision, *Pastor Beau* stooped to her level and plucked at one of the messy braids. "Hello to you, too, Miss Molly Taylor Scott. What sort of game are you playing?"

Rocking back and forth on her heels, Molly performed a perfect little-girl swish with her shoulders. "Baseball, of course. My daddy's pitching right now."

Grinning, the reverend rose and placed his palm on her head in a gesture that spoke of genuine affection.

Man and child continued smiling at each other as though they shared some humorous secret.

Charmed by them both, Hannah just stood watching the two interact.

"Her daddy is the man you're looking for," Laney whispered.

Surprised at the news, she turned to Laney. "Molly isn't one of the orphans?"

"Not anymore."

Their voices must have carried, because Molly noticed Hannah then. With the typical attention span of a child, she deserted the pastor and bounced over to Hannah. "You're very pretty."

Completely captivated by the precocious child, Hannah lowered to her knees. "You are, too."

Lifting her nose higher in the air, the little girl slapped her own shoulder. "My name's Molly."

"I'm Hannah."

"Oh." Big blue eyes widened. "Like Samuel's mama."

More surprises, Hannah thought. "You've heard of her?"

"Well, of course." Molly let out a sound of impatience. "Pastor Beau told us about her last Sunday. She's the one that prayed for a baby."

"That's right. I was named after her."

Molly jammed two tiny fists on her hips and narrowed her eyes in pitch-perfect seven-year-old concentration. "You don't look like anybody's mama to me. You're too fancy."

"I'm not anybody's mother. Yet." Hannah smiled at the child, even as something a little sad quivered through her. "But one day I hope to be a lot of somebodies' mother."

Molly giggled. "Me, too. Someday."

Hannah joined in the child's laughter, feeling the tension ease out of her with the gesture.

Just then, a clap of thunder sounded in the distance.

Molly looked to the heavens, scrunched her face into a frown and marched back to Pastor Beau. "Well?" Her fists returned to her hips and her foot started tapping on the ground. "Are you playing or not?"

"Molly, honey," Marc said in a practical voice. "I think you're going to get rained on very shortly."

The little girl's face fell. "But—"

"Not to worry." Hannah rose to her feet and tapped Molly on the shoulder to get her attention. "I know several games we can play inside."

Molly's eyes lit up. "You do?"

Hannah nodded, then looked at the approaching clouds. The breeze had grown still, and the sharp, pungent odor of rain pulsated in the air. "I'll teach one of them to you later."

"That sounds nice."

But clearly, Molly Taylor Scott was made of very stern stuff. She wasn't relenting without a fight. "Come on, Pastor Beau." She grabbed his hand and tugged. "Before it rains."

Beau lifted an eyebrow at Hannah as though seeking her permission. He looked so sweet standing there with the child's hand gripped gently in his.

He'll make a great father.

Now where did that thought come from?

"Go on," she said, more than a little touched by the picture the two made. "We can talk to her father after the game."

"I'll make sure of it."

"I know." Her heart punched two solid thumps against her ribs. "Thank you for that."

Opening his mouth to speak, the pastor shifted his weight toward Hannah, but Molly tugged on him again. "Let's go."

"I think I'll join you," Marc said. Pausing a moment, he angled his head toward Hannah. "It was nice to meet you, Miss Southerland."

"You, too, Mr. Dupree."

As Marc followed behind the other two, Laney let out a loud sigh. "Five years of marriage, and I never get tired of looking at that man."

"Sounds like love to me."

"That it is."

The other woman's face glowed as she spoke, and Hannah felt her earlier sense of yearning grow more powerful. Home. Safety. Permanence. Until now, Hannah hadn't realized how much she craved all three. The years of traveling from stage to stage were obviously taking their toll. Hopefully one day she would find her own place in the world.

"You're very fortunate to have found such love," Hannah said on a soft whisper choked with emotion.

"You have no idea. I'll tell you the story someday." She tilted her face toward the incoming clouds. "For now, let's head inside. I'm sure some new drama is unfolding as we speak. Children." Laney gave her an ironic grin. "I do so love their unpredictable ways."

"Bless their impertinent souls," Hannah said with a wink.

Laney burst out laughing. "My sentiments exactly." Fastening their arms together, Laney steered them both toward the front steps. "Whatever your story is, Miss Hannah Southerland, I've decided to like you."

Hannah smiled in mingled surprise and pleasure at the unexpected announcement. "Well, glory, because I've decided to like you right back."

Chapter Six

An hour later, Beau watched as dark, ominous clouds devoured the last patch of blue sky. Consecutive cracks of thunder traveled along the back end of a powerful wind. The earthy scent of rain filled the air. All of nature stood poised for the watery attack, while seventeen children and three grown men—Beau included—pretended nothing was amiss.

Another succession of thunder rumbled closer, the sound reverberating through the backyard ball game.

And still the contest continued. For three more seconds. Two. One…

The rain let loose.

Fat drops of icy water pummeled man and child alike. Feet pounded. Shouts lifted in the air. Childish giggles and adult commands wrapped inside one another. Orders to get out of the mud and into the house were barked in a masculine, authoritative tone. A flash of lightning highlighted the urgency.

When the bedlam continued, the order came again. "Everybody inside the house," Marc shouted. This time his tone brooked no argument.

A chorus of groans and complaints rose up.

"Now."

One by one the children scrambled onto the back porch. Bringing up the rear, Beau hoisted one of the smaller boys into his arms and dashed up the stairs. By the time he commandeered the last step, he had to shuffle his way through a maze of arms and legs vying for space, as well.

Marc made quick work of gathering equipment in one pile and wet shoes in another before herding the motley group inside.

From his vantage point, Beau watched the giggling horde poke and pull and elbow one another en route to the house. The children managed to arouse his amusement and sympathy all at the same time. There was a reserved nature to their movements, something sad and self-preserving that kept the boys and girls from fully engaging in the fun. It was as if they were holding back a part of themselves.

Understandable. Given their histories.

There was a lot of God's work to do at Charity House. The orphanage could use a full-time minister on staff. But it wouldn't be Beau. Even if he didn't have his own plans for the future, he was already committed to the church in Greeley. Of course, that didn't mean he couldn't help Marc and Laney find a preacher who would fit in with the ministry already started here at the orphanage.

Despite his efforts to mentally organize a list of potential candidates, his mind shifted to another, more urgent subject. Beau owed it to Miss Southerland to get down to the business of finding her sister.

Shaking water out of his hair, he waited until the last of the children banged inside the house behind Marc.

Only then did he pull Trey aside. "I need a word with you, Marshal."

Eyes never leaving Beau's face, the lawman removed his hat and set it on a nearby rocking chair. "Trouble again?"

A cold ball of dread settled heavily in Beau's belly. "You have no idea."

Hitching his hip against the porch railing, Trey rubbed his jaw. The day-old stubble and grim twist of his lips made the man look as fierce as his reputation. With the nickname Beelzebub's Cousin, it was no wonder Trey Scott was known as a ruthless lawman who hunted criminals with a vengeance.

However, when Beau looked into Trey's eyes, he saw past the U.S. Marshal and found the loyalty and integrity that had won the heart of Charity House's schoolteacher, Katherine Taylor, and her little sister, Molly.

"Another runaway husband?" Trey asked.

"Not precisely." Beau shook his head. "This time, it's personal."

To his credit, Trey's expression never changed. "I see. Tell me what I can do for you."

The wind chose that moment to kick harder, pelting razor-sharp needles of rain straight into Beau's eyes. He shifted slightly and set his shoulders against the storm. "I need you to help me find my brother."

Frowning, Trey stared up at the ceiling. He stood in that contemplative pose so long that Beau looked up, as well. But then Trey shoved away from the railing and lowered his gaze back to Beau's. "Let's finish this conversation in Marc's study."

Beau nodded. "That'll be fine."

As he followed the marshal through the back of the

house, Beau had to fight the urge to rush his steps. Even the homey scent of baking bread couldn't pacify his impatience. Now that the initial shock of the situation was wearing off and the possible repercussions were settling in, he wanted Tyler found. Immediately.

As they strode through the house, the only sound in the hallway came from their heels pounding against the wood floor like hammers to nails. An uneasy feeling darted toward the surface before Beau tamped it down. So much time had passed. Tyler and Miss Southerland's sister could be anywhere by now.

Lord, Beau prayed, *I'm overwhelmed by this task You've brought before me. Please, give me strength, wisdom and clarity, so I may guide Miss Southerland in this search.*

At the end of the hallway, they rounded the corner and came across Marc, who was exiting a room on their left.

"We'd like to borrow your study awhile," Trey asked in explanation of their presence.

Marc looked from one man to the other, and then nodded. "Take your time."

Remembering his original mission, Beau reached into his pocket and pulled out an envelope with Marc's name scrawled on the outside. "This is from Jane. For Megan's care."

"Set it on my desk," Marc said, but then his gaze turned serious. "How is Jane?"

Beau's chest pinched tight as he called to mind the unnatural pallor of the former actress's skin and the lack of fight in her eyes. "Time's running out for her."

Marc released a resigned sigh. "I'll prepare Megan."

"At some point I'd like to speak with her, as well."

"I think that's a good idea." Marc turned to go. "Let me know if you need anything."

Trey answered for them both. "Will do."

While Marc disappeared in the opposite direction, Beau followed Trey into the empty office. Once inside, Beau's mind circled back to Miss Southerland. He wondered how she was faring. She'd looked so fragile earlier, practically dropping from exhaustion.

Yet she hadn't complained once. He told himself he appreciated that rare quality in her, but it wasn't true. If only she would lean on him, just a little. But that would require trust. Something Beau had destroyed with an ill-timed, harshly worded snap judgment.

"Have a seat." Trey waved his hand toward a matching pair of leather, wingback chairs facing a large mahogany desk.

Beau lowered himself into the one on his right and looked around. The dark furniture, with its bold, masculine lines, lacked all sign of feminine frills. A fire snapped in the hearth, giving the room a pleasant, smoky odor. One day Beau hoped to have a similar room, a place where he could write his sermons and conduct the business of his ministry.

A private refuge all his own. No women allowed.

It wasn't that Beau didn't like women. On the contrary. They fascinated him, intrigued him. He liked the way they took such care with their hair and clothing, liked how they found joy in silly things like a new bit of lace. But as a child he'd been unable to get away from the flounce and feminine scents that were commonplace backstage.

Even now, as an adult, his ministry brought him to

places like Mattie's, places that held many of the same female sounds and smells of the theater.

At least the women in the theater kept their dignity when they conducted the business of their trade.

Beau thought of Jane then. He needed to return to her bedside as soon as possible. Perhaps he could still convince her to move into the sanatorium. Perhaps there was still time to save her. Perhaps...

Thunder rumbled overhead. The rain made a hard hissing sound as it scraped against the windows in the back of the room.

Undaunted by the commotion building outside, Trey settled into the chair behind the desk and pulled out a sheet of paper from the top drawer. "Let's start with the basics. Tell me about your brother."

Where to begin?

In an attempt to gather his thoughts, Beau rose from his chair and walked over to the hearth. The fire cracked and popped, radiating a strong blast of heat. Rubbing his hands together, Beau cast a sideways glance at Trey. How did he go about revealing his dark family secret, one he had only learned of a few hours ago? For all intents and purposes, the man was a stranger to Beau.

And yet, without revealing the full truth of the matter, the marshal wouldn't be able to help him. "Did you see the woman that came outside to watch part of the game with Laney?" Beau began.

Trey's face went carefully blank. "Couldn't avoid noticing her. Nor could most of the older boys." He chuckled softly. "Thought I was going to have to scrape a few of their chins off the ground so we could continue the game."

Smiling at the reminder, Beau rolled his shoulders

and dug his toe into the stone hearth at his feet. There was no denying the fact that Miss Southerland turned heads, stopped baseball games in midinning and literally dropped the jaws of men and boys alike.

Of course, it wasn't the boys that bothered Beau. It was the men. What lengths would the less reputable go to in order to win Miss Southerland's affection?

A dozen of the uglier possibilities came to mind, and a hot surge of uneasiness made Beau's breath back up in his lungs. Unwilling to explore the new emotion too deeply, he tapped an angry rhythm against his thigh.

"Is she a friend of yours?" Trey asked at last.

"No." Beau assumed a neutral expression and turned to face the other man head-on. "I met her this afternoon for the first time. She's with the same acting company as my brother."

A single eyebrow shot up. "Would that be the same brother you want me to locate?"

"Yes. Unfortunately, the situation is complicated. The short version is that after a two-day acquaintance, Miss Southerland's sister and my brother ran off together." Beau gnashed his teeth. "The girl in question is engaged to be married to another man. Her father, not to mention her unsuspecting fiancé, will find the situation unacceptable, perhaps even unforgivable. Miss Southerland wishes to locate her sister before anyone discovers she's missing."

As he retold the story, Beau realized the situation was indeed as dire as Miss Southerland had indicated. What could have induced Tyler to do something so devious, so selfish?

Love, perhaps? Hardly. Love was patient. Love was

kind. It was *not* self-seeking. No. What Tyler had done wasn't about love. It was about Tyler.

"Am I to assume you want me to uncover the location of the fugitives?"

"Precisely."

Beau went on to explain how Miss Southerland knew the two had come west. He then laid out the rest of the details in order of importance, ending with a description of Tyler—a younger, slicker version of Beau—and Rachel—an identical replica of Miss Southerland.

When Beau finished, Trey set the pen down. "I'll start making inquiries at once."

"We have less than a month before Rachel's scheduled wedding. I can't stress enough how desperate Miss Southerland is to find her sister." *That was certainly an understatement.* "She won't wait long for trickles of information."

Trey pressed his lips into a flat line. "Nor can she go off without any clear direction."

"Understood." For a few painful seconds, the churning in Beau's stomach became unbearable.

He didn't envy the poor soul who had to tell Miss Southerland to sit tight and wait for concrete news about her sister. And since *he* was that poor soul, Beau had a mind to throttle his baby brother the moment he found him. Maybe then they would talk.

Or…maybe not.

Hannah finished drying her hands just as the sun peeked through a seam in the clouds. The rain had stopped, but if the black sky hovering above the distant mountains was any indication, the storm wasn't over yet.

Setting the rag down, she pivoted to study her handiwork of the last hour. Five loaves of bread sat in a straight row atop the counter, waiting their turn for baking. It had been years since Hannah had dug her hands into dough. The sensation had felt nice, soothing. *Distracting.*

Mrs. Smythe, the housekeeper and resident cook, beamed at her. "Such lovely work, Miss Southerland." She motioned to the rising loaves. "Simply wonderful."

A swift jolt of pleasure shot through Hannah at the compliment. "Thank you. I enjoyed helping."

As if she'd timed her cue to perfection, Laney glided into the room and immediately honed in on Hannah's efforts. "You've been busy."

"Can't stand idle hands." Hannah waggled her fingers to punctuate her statement.

"I see that."

"What's our status with the children?" Mrs. Smythe asked.

With her face scrunched in concentration, Laney ticked off the specifics on her fingers. "The older children are getting cleaned up after their latest adventure in the mud. Trey and the pastor are shut in behind closed doors in Marc's office."

She shot a questioning look at Hannah but didn't wait for an answer. Lifting a third finger, she continued with her inventory. "Katherine and Mavis are deep into bath time with the little ones. And Marc is coordinating the rest. That means we have approximately twenty minutes before mayhem erupts again."

Mrs. Smythe blew out a satisfied sigh and shuffled toward a side door in the corner of the kitchen. "Well, then, I think I'll take a few moments to put my feet up before I start supper."

"Sounds good. And you." Laney pointed a finger at

Hannah. "Why don't you rest, as well? You look exhausted."

Without waiting for a response, Laney placed a hand on her shoulder and gently guided Hannah into a nearby chair.

Officially too exhausted to fight, Hannah relaxed into the wooden seat. "I *have* been traveling for three days now." She shook her head at the declaration. "I can't believe it's been that long since I left Chicago."

Three days. And every moment spent at Charity House was time lost on the trail. Her entire body trembled with impatience. But what could she do? Hannah squeezed her eyes shut and sighed. There was no point in rushing off. Yet.

Just thinking about the vast number of places Rachel and Tyler could have gone made Hannah want to cry. More than a little heartsick, she felt the beginnings of a headache build behind her eyes.

Laney touched her arm. Hannah opened her eyes and looked into a gaze filled with genuine sympathy.

"Want to talk about it?" Laney asked.

Breathing slowly, Hannah seriously considered the offer. There was something about Laney that made Hannah want to confide in her. And then she remembered the verses from Ecclesiastes. *Two are better than one, because they have a good return for their work...*

Perhaps it would help to have another person on her side.

Laney pulled two mugs out of a cabinet and began pouring coffee. "I find it often helps to confide in a third party, someone objective."

Hannah nodded.

Oh, Lord, give me the courage to be honest with this kind woman. Help me to trust her with the truth.

"First, you should know that I'm an actress," Hannah said, waiting for the condemnation she often received at such a declaration. When none came, she let out a sigh of relief and continued. "I travel in a Shakespearean company with Pastor Beau's brother Tyler."

Laney set one of the cups in front of Hannah and brought the other to her lips. Curiosity sparked in her eyes, but she simply said, "Go on."

"A few days ago my twin sister came to Chicago to watch me perform. We'd become estranged over the years, and I'd prayed her visit would end the bitterness between us."

Her hope had been overwhelming, daunting even, but Rachel had quickly demonstrated that Hannah had built her dreams of reconciliation on shifting sand.

"I can tell by your sadness that she disappointed you." Laney looked at her with soft, understanding eyes.

"After a two-day acquaintance, Rachel ran off with Tyler. They haven't been heard from since."

"Oh my." Laney's eyes widened. "That certainly puts you in a bad situation, especially since I'm assuming she met the man through you."

How had Laney assessed the situation so accurately? Was her guilt that transparent?

"You're correct, I did introduce the two. And now I'm afraid my father may never forgive me for it."

Laney placed her hand over Hannah's. "I'm so sorry."

"I have to bring Rachel home." A rush of emotion threatened to overwhelm her. Hannah rose and started pacing. "The sooner the better, because she is to be married in a month."

"Do you have any idea where they went?"

"No. I only know that they were seen boarding a train headed west."

"Then you'll have to let Trey do the hunting for a while."

"I can't just sit here and do nothing." Hannah pounded her fists against her thighs. "I feel so…so…helpless."

"Of course you do." Laney pulled Hannah into her arms. "But you can't go blindly chasing after them, either. You have good men on your side. Have a little faith."

Faith. Trust. Both came at such a high price. Could she let herself become that vulnerable? Should she take the risk? Did she dare not?

Leaning into the other woman, Hannah shut her eyes and let the tension drain out of her. "You're right, of course."

"I usually am."

Hannah smiled at the lack of guile in the high-and-mighty statement.

"So, it's settled. Until you get more information, you'll just have to keep yourself busy." Laney patted her on the back and released her. "Would you consider moving in here until you get some direction? I could use the extra hands, and I'm thinking you could use the diversion."

Surprised at the instant desire to accept Laney's offer, Hannah forced her mind to focus, to concentrate on the particulars. No matter how appealing she found the prospect of living at Charity House for a while, she didn't want to make any more hasty decisions. "Can I think about it?"

"Absolutely. For now, let's get you—"

Laney's words were interrupted by the pastor's entrance. "Miss Southerland, could I have a private word with you?"

Hannah spun around. Her breath caught in her throat at the sight of Pastor Beau standing in the doorway. His broad shoulders filled every available space. No man had the right to look that tall, that masculine and that in charge when she was so worn-out.

Worse, he looked so much like Tyler that Hannah had to lower her gaze in order to contain the sudden spasm of anger that shot through her. Taking a few slow breaths, she swallowed back her irrational temper and lifted her gaze once again. This time, she saw the sadness, the fierce sorrow he so carefully masked.

He's lonely was her first thought. But that was impossible. Wasn't it?

Laney cleared her throat and stepped toward the doorway. "I'll just leave you two alone."

And that seemed the most frightening prospect yet. At least with Laney in the room, Hannah had an ally.

Unfortunately, her new friend—the turncoat—deserted her without a backward glance.

Chapter Seven

The moment Laney disappeared down the hallway, the temperature in the kitchen dropped several degrees. As easy as it would be to hold on to her resentment, Hannah decided the time for anger and blame had passed. Now she needed to focus on the next step in the search for Rachel and Tyler.

"What did the marshal have to say?" she asked in what she hoped was a mild tone.

"He's agreed to help us. He'll begin making inquiries immediately." The obvious relief in his eyes was evident in his gaze.

"Good. Good." Her own sense of relief coated her voice. "How long do you think it will take for us to hear something?"

"Hard to say. A day, a week." His gaze slid to hers, dark, serious and apologetic now. "Perhaps longer."

A gasp flew from her lips, and her heart pounded hard against her ribs. "Longer than a week? But we don't have that much time."

"I know."

"There has to be something we can do." She slammed

her fists against her thighs and circled the room again. "I can't stand this feeling of helplessness."

The reverend's patient gaze followed her movements, but he remained in his spot near the door. "It's hard, I know. We'll have to pray we get news soon."

She nodded. Prayer, yes. Always good.

"In the meantime, I have a favor to ask of you."

Slowing her pace, she glanced at him from over her shoulder. "And what would that be?"

"I'd like you to accept Laney's offer to move in here."

The question stopped her in midstride. "You heard that part of our conversation?"

"I did." He gave her an uncomfortable smile. "Your voices carried as I was making my way down the hallway to find you."

That seemed possible. Nevertheless, why would he want her to stay at the orphanage instead of the hotel? Unless he thought she needed a babysitter. She narrowed her eyes at him. "Are you afraid I'll set out on my own?"

"I can't say the thought didn't cross my mind." He raised his hand to keep her from speaking over him. "But the real reason is that I don't wish for you to be alone in a cold hotel room, fretting over something you can't do anything about."

"Are you saying you're worried about me?" Her pulse picked up speed at the notion.

"That's what I'm saying."

Hannah simply stared at him. What was she supposed to do with that startling declaration? And more to the point, what was she supposed to do with the jolt of pleasure spreading through her at the prospect that this man was actually concerned about her. Her! A virtual stranger. A woman whose own father had banished her from his home without a moment's remorse.

Hannah wasn't usually prone to self-doubt, not lately, anyway. But something about this man, something in the way he threw her off balance with a simple declaration of concern, made her question whether or not she'd truly dealt with the lasting repercussions of her banishment.

That last thought made her bristle.

"I'll tell you what I told Laney," she said, keeping a careful lid on her conflicting emotions. "I'll think about it."

He crossed his arms over his chest and leaned his weight against the doorjamb, looking as though he had all the time in the world. "I'll wait."

Hannah frowned at him. "You want me to make my decision *now?*"

"Within the next few minutes will do." He wound his wrist in the air between them. "Carry on with your thinking and pacing and whatever else you need to do to settle this in your mind."

Her mouth dropped open. "Has anybody ever mentioned your phenomenal arrogance?"

His eyes filled with amusement. "At least a dozen people, half of those just today."

A charming man was bad enough, but a charming O'Toole, Hannah decided, was downright dangerous. "So few?"

He put his unreadable pastor face on and continued to lean against the doorway. He wound his wrist in the air between them again. "Continue considering Laney's offer."

"You're not going to budge from that position until I say yes, are you?"

"Stubbornness is another one of my finer qualities."

"What about smugness, haughtiness and overconfidence?"

His eyes crinkled around the edges. "Those, too."

"You win," she said with a soft, feminine snarl that belied her growing amusement at his absurd attitude. "I'll check out of the hotel. But just so we're clear, I'd already decided to make the move *before* you asked it of me."

"Of course."

"Your suggestion carried no weight, none at all."

"Whatever you say."

"Did I mention you have an arrogant streak?"

A slow grin spread across his lips. "I seem to remember something along those lines."

"I stand by my assessment."

"I expected as much."

"Are you going to continue staring at me with that pompous smile on your lips?"

"There's a large possibility."

She sighed. Why, why, why did he have to be so utterly appealing when she so desperately wanted to hold on to her initial distrust of the man? There was just no winning when it came to combating an O'Toole. "Can we call a truce?"

It was her only hope of maintaining a portion of the control.

"Thought you'd never ask." He shoved from the doorway and covered her hand with both of his. "To new beginnings."

His tone was sincere. His gaze was genuine. His grip was gentle. So why did she feel the battle had only just begun?

Because anointed pastor or not, the frustrating man was still an O'Toole through and through.

Several hours later, Hannah was officially a resident of Charity House. Ever the gentleman, Reverend O'Toole had left to care for Jane only after ensuring Hannah had everything she needed. For a moment, just before he'd turned to go, his eyes had held such grief, such painful sorrow, that Hannah had wanted to reach out and comfort him. But when she'd stepped toward him, his eyes had gone glassy and unreadable.

Sighing, Hannah now slipped out the back door for the express purpose of capturing a moment alone with her thoughts. The simple pleasure of the solitude made her smile.

Even curtained in shadows, the mountains stood like sentinels. There was a chill in the air tonight, made raw by the drizzling rain. Rubbing her arms for warmth, Hannah drew in a deep breath. The scent of stirred-up mud and pine reminded her of home.

Her *former* home, she corrected. She didn't have a home anymore.

Hannah shut her eyes and sighed again. Behind her, she could hear the chatter of the children as they filed into the dining room for their evening meal.

Tuning out the voices, Hannah allowed her thoughts to run to Pastor Beau and their odd encounters throughout the day. She recognized the curling in her stomach as confusion. In the matter of a few hours, he'd frustrated her, angered her and then had the nerve to make her laugh.

Oh, he'd woefully misjudged her—at first—but Hannah truly believed he felt remorse over his mistake.

Pressing her palms to the porch railing, she leaned into the night and sniffed the clean air. As her mind cleared and she traced the morning's events, Hannah realized that she had met the reverend mere seconds after he'd left the bedside of a lowly prostitute who had once been the premiere actress of her day. A woman who had called Patience O'Toole friend, as Hannah did now.

Given those facts, it was no wonder the man had judged her as he had. And if she was going to be completely honest in her thinking, she'd admit he'd had a point. It was no secret that many actresses ended up like Jane. How was Pastor Beau to know that Hannah had a plan for her future?

Her mind settled at last, Hannah pushed away from the railing and nodded to herself.

She would forgive and forget. And, of course, trust.

If Rachel and Tyler were meant to be found, they would be found. In the end, it all boiled down to who was in control.

Oh, Lord, Hannah prayed. *I surrender this seemingly impossible task into Your hands. Please bring us news of Rachel and Tyler soon. In the meantime, I pray You protect them both and keep them safe. Let them—*

A loud bang of the screen door cut into her prayer. Hannah jumped at the sound and spun quickly around. "Oh."

Two years of traveling with odd-looking characters prevented her mouth from gaping open. But, truly, standing before her was the strangest apparition Hannah had encountered in quite a while.

"You must be that pretty actress the pastor brought over from town," said a hard, raspy voice of uncertain gender.

The woman—and yes, it was a grown woman, Hannah assured herself—was very small, rail thin and stood eye to eye with Hannah's chin. She wore a bright red dress over a pair of what looked like—Hannah narrowed her eyes—men's denim pants? Her hair was white as snow and shot out in wild waves from every direction. Her age was indeterminate, anywhere from fifty to a hundred.

Hannah estimated closer to a hundred.

If she was casting a play, this woman would be perfect for the role of the nurse in *Romeo and Juliet.*

Realizing she was gaping after all, Hannah shook her head and said, "Yes, I'm Hannah Southerland. You must be Mavis."

The answering grin revealed an uneven row of teeth with a few gaps thrown in for added character. "That I am. Marc and Laney adopted me a few months back."

Playing along, Hannah asked, "How are you settling in? Are you getting along with the other children?"

Mavis let out a cackle that would have been better suited for a character in *Macbeth*—oh, say, one leaning over a cauldron. And Hannah meant that in the best possible way. "So, tell me, Mavis, what do you do around here?"

"What don't I do? I'm the official bath mistress, naptime general and all-around helping hand to forty-some-odd orphans." She shot a line of spit through the gap between her front teeth. "Give or take a toddler or two."

"I'm pleased to hear it."

Leaning forward, Mavis looked to her left, then to her right and back to her left again. "Are we alone?" she asked in a perfect imitation of a stage whisper.

Hannah looked to her left, then to her right and back to her left again. "It appears so."

Mavis released a slow, happy sigh. "What. A. Day." She parked her nonexistent behind on a rocking chair and started rifling through one of the pockets on her dress.

Enjoying herself immensely, Hannah sat, as well.

"Them little ones hate their bath time. Don't mean to complain myself, but that U.S. Marshal's gonna get an earful from his wife. He's been telling the kids that playtime is more important than a 'stinkin' bath'—his words, not mine."

Hannah kept a straight face. Barely. "That can't be helpful."

"There's mutiny afoot." Mavis pointed a scrawny finger at Hannah. "You mark my words, that marshal's gonna get his. His deputy, too, if it were up to me."

Annoyance hiked Mavis's chin up a notch or two, but she continued digging in her pocket.

"Not to sound contentious myself," Hannah said. "But I always thought children hating baths was pretty universal."

"Yeah, well, it certainly helps to have someone to blame." The spark of amusement in the older woman's eyes told its own story.

But just to be sure.

"Marshal Scott isn't a troublemaker by nature, is he?"

"No sirree, I love that boy, even if he tells them younguns to run for their very lives when it's bath time."

Hannah shared a grin with her new friend. Obviously, Mavis adored the man.

"Aha, there you are." Mavis pulled out a leather pouch from her pocket. Fingers working quickly, she dumped a generous amount of brown tobacco onto a thin piece of paper and began rolling.

Hannah blinked. "What are you doing?"

"Making myself a paper cigarette," she said without bothering to look up from her task. "You want one?"

Hannah shook her head. "I don't smoke."

Mavis wiggled her eyebrows at her. "Don't know what you're missing."

"I'll take the risk."

"You know, Miss Hannah," Mavis said, her eyes focused once more on her work. "I used to tread the old boards in my day."

This information should have shocked Hannah, but as she further studied the older woman, she saw the flair in her movements, the tendency toward the dramatic in the flourish she used to roll the tobacco. "How long were you on the stage?"

Seconds ticked by before Mavis answered. "Well, I can't really say I was an actress for long. At least not in the traditional sense. Oh, I've played some role or another all my life, but I weren't no good onstage."

Hannah doubted that. With her personality alone the woman would have fit in perfectly with any acting troupe, past or present.

"I ended up finding employment in the age-old profession," Mavis said, her eyes dark with emotion.

"Age-old profession?"

"You know." She released one side of the paper and gave a vague gesture with her hand. "Like that girl in the Bible that done saved those Jewish spies in Jericho, the one that ended up in Jesus' lineage."

Hannah thought a moment. "You mean Rahab?" *The prostitute?*

"That's the one."

Mavis struck a match off the bottom of her shoe, lit the cigarette with a long inhale and then took her time exhaling. "Glad to be done with that nasty work. I like it here better. Who knew I'd love helping with them kids in there?"

Hannah reached out and squeezed Mavis's hand. "Children have a way of doing that." And if working at Charity House kept this woman from living a life of sin, what a heaven-sent blessing. As Pastor Beau had said, God's hand was truly on Charity House.

"Maybe in my small way I can prevent these kids from going down my same road." Her eyes turned sad, almost haunted. "Maybe I can atone for my—"

"Mavis Elizabeth Tierney," came a high-pitched, angry female voice from just inside the house. "You drop that death stick right now."

Mavis heaved a dramatic sigh. "Here comes the spoil-sport now," she whispered behind her cupped hand.

Out walked a very angry, stiff-backed woman. The screen door shut behind her with a bang. Even with her face scrunched into a scowl, the woman was extraordinary. And with her dark hair and blue, blue eyes, she reminded Hannah of a grown-up version of the little girl, Molly.

This must be Katherine, the marshal's wife, Hannah thought.

"Hand it over, Mavis." She thrust her hand out between them. "I mean it."

Mavis treated the woman to a withering glare, which had no effect whatsoever.

The stalemate continued a few more seconds.

"You're just not tolerant no more, Katherine Scott. Not since you got in the motherly way." Mavis looked pointedly at the woman's rounded belly.

Reminiscent of Molly's mannerisms, Katherine parked

fists to hips and narrowed her eyes. "Dr. Shane said you can't keep smoking those and continue living." Her frown deepened. "I, for one, won't stand by and watch you kill yourself."

Mavis rose, muttering the whole way up. With exaggerated slowness, she took a mutinous drag of the cigarette and then blew out a long, thin stream of smoke.

Katherine snorted in disgust.

Mavis grinned fiercely, but then heaved another big sigh and handed over the incriminating cigarette.

"Thank you," Katherine said, her shoulders still stiff and unmoving.

"Humph." With a dramatic flick of her wrist, Mavis whipped her hair over her shoulder and marched back into the house without another word.

Staring at the screen door, Katherine took several deep breaths before throwing the cigarette to the porch floor. She folded her arms across her chest and dug the toe of her shoe over the burning ember. "Honestly. That woman tries my soul."

Unsure what to say, Hannah rose.

It was Katherine's turn to sigh before clearing her expression. "You must be Hannah."

"And you're Marshal Scott's wife."

"I am." Katherine blinked rapidly, clearly fighting to gain control over her emotions. "I'm sorry you got caught in the middle of that."

"No, I'm sorry." Hannah swallowed back a surge of guilt. "I didn't realize she was under doctor's orders. I would have tried to stop her."

Katherine peered at her with troubled eyes. "You didn't know. But if you ever see her smoking again, I'd appreciate it if you would discourage her."

"You have my word."

A look of exasperation crossed the other woman's face. "Honestly, she's worse than the children."

"And just as lovable."

Their stares connected, a ripple of feminine understanding passing between them.

Katherine let out a soft laugh. "She is at that. It's why I'm so hard on her." She took another steadying breath. "Actually, I came in search of you. Supper is nearly over. Laney sent me to tell you she'd like to discuss the indoor games you mentioned earlier."

Hannah nodded. "I'd be delighted."

As she followed Katherine back inside the house, Hannah realized the moments she'd spent with Mavis were the first in days she hadn't worried about her sister. In fact, she hadn't thought of Rachel once.

Hannah didn't know whether to be glad for it or incredibly sad, but either way Mavis Tierney had been a colorful diversion.

Chapter Eight

The scent of death cloaked the tiny room like a thick, heavy blanket. The raw odor gripped Beau's throat and squeezed it shut. A soft moan of misery drifted out of Jane Goodwin as she lay limp on her bed.

Dejected, Beau crossed to the back corner of the room and gave the young doctor who had arrived hours before plenty of space to work.

The time has come, Beau thought in frustrated agony.

At the realization that he hadn't been able to save this lost lamb, a strong sense of helplessness pulled sweat onto his brow. Lowering chin to chest, he prayed that the Lord would give him the right words to bring reassurance to the dying woman.

An eerie silence fell over the room, broken only by Jane's ragged breathing and the doctor's soft murmurs of comfort. Out of respect for Jane, Beau cleared his face of any expression.

But it hurt deep in his soul to watch the poor woman struggle for air. Her breathing was different tonight, more labored. For about an hour now, she would suck in a breath, pause, and then wheeze out hard before pausing again. Just as Beau would give up hope for her next breath, the pattern would begin all over again.

The death rattle.

He'd heard it before, and his own breathing rasped in his lungs.

"Is she in as much pain as it appears?" he asked.

Working with efficient hands, Shane Bartlett lifted Jane's wrist and checked her pulse again. "No more than expected."

Beau offered up a prayer of thanksgiving for the competent young doctor. Shane was the only physician in town who would dare to step into a brothel—in an official capacity, that was.

Straightening, the other man clicked his black bag shut and let out a slow stream of air. His brown hair stuck out at the ends, looking as though he'd run his hands through it far too many times and now the thick mane was on permanent revolt.

"Doctor?"

Shane turned sad, tired eyes to Beau. The empty, resigned expression said it all.

Jane Goodwin's journey here on earth had come to an end. All that remained was her final curtain call.

Breaking eye contact, Beau lowered his head. *Heavenly Father, I pray You bring Miss Jane some peace in her final moments. Most of all, I pray for her salvation.*

Opening his eyes, Beau connected his gaze with the doctor's once more. "Is there anything I can do? Any thoughts on how I can make her more comfortable?"

Shane shook his head. "You've done all you can." He reached down and dragged his thumb across Jane's furrowed brow. "I'm sorry, Reverend. There are some things we humans can't control. It's simply her time."

"I understand." And yet, Beau's heart clenched at the news. For a moment, he stared at the pale, limp figure lying on the bed. The lines of fatigue around her eyes and the odd angle of her mouth were clear indicators of how ill she truly was.

Jane moaned, twisting and kicking until she'd wrenched one arm free of the covers.

"Beau?" Her frail hand lifted a mere inch off the bed.

Beau rushed to her side, knelt down and wrapped his fingers gently around hers. "I'm right here."

She rattled through several more breaths before her eyes blinked open and focused on him. He was surprised at how clear her gaze looked, clearer than he'd seen in weeks.

A relieved sigh lurched through him.

"My daughter, Megan, is she…" Her words trailed off, turning into a soft moaning in between quick pants. Apparently, her body couldn't keep up with her will.

Beau looked at Shane for direction. The other man nodded for him to proceed.

"Megan is happy and safe at Charity House." Beau lifted her hand and gently squeezed. "She will always have a home there."

A smile spread across Jane's lips, and she struggled to lift her head. Her gasping increased until Shane moved in behind her to support her shoulders. Thanks to his assistance, her breathing eased a bit.

"Lie back, Miss Jane," Shane urged. "You must reserve your energy."

Once he had her settled again, Shane nodded at Beau to continue.

"I gave Marc the envelope," Beau said. "You truly have nothing to worry about."

She shut her eyes and relaxed back against the pillow. "Tha... Thank you."

Her breathing grew strangely calm then, as though she'd been waiting to hear about her daughter before she could finally give up the unbearable fight.

It was time.

But the most important work was yet to be done. *Oh, Lord, God, please open her heart to You.*

"Miss Jane, you have a Savior ready to welcome you home," Beau began. "A place where you will receive a new body, where you will be free of pain."

Out of the corner of his eye, Beau noticed Mattie slipping into the room and shutting the door quickly behind her. The moment her gaze dropped to Jane, her lips parted in shock. She staggered back, flattened against the wall behind her and stared wide-eyed at Beau.

But Beau had more pressing matters to attend to.

Giving Mattie a quick nod of acknowledgment, he opened his Bible and began to read from Matthew 11. "Come to me, all you who are weary and burdened, and I will give you rest. Take my yoke upon you and learn from me, for I am gentle and humble in heart, and you will find rest for your souls. For my yoke is easy and my burden light."

A lump formed in his throat, and his voice shook.

Beau lowered his head and continued to pray softly over Jane. Her eyes fluttered shut and her breathing calmed, the gasps of air coming shorter and more softly. The violence slowly slipped out of her, replaced by a sense of tranquillity.

With very little struggle now, she took a shallow breath. Paused. Took another breath. Paused again, continuing the pattern until there were simply no more breaths left.

A surreal silence spread through the room.

Beau shut his eyes in a moment of devastating grief. A muscle locked in his jaw while a lone tear escaped from his right eye.

"Is she…?" Mattie whispered.

"Yes," Shane said.

Beau looked over at the madam. Tears ran unbridled down her cheeks. Never had he seen such a vulnerable look of anguish on the woman's face.

Catching his gaze on her, Mattie hardened her expression and quickly escaped from the room without a word or a glance behind her.

Another moment passed before Shane moved forward and lifted Jane's flaccid wrist. He felt around and then moved his fingers to her neck. "She is at peace at last."

Beau nodded, sucked in a lungful of the room's hot, putrid air and blew out a sad sigh. Miss Jane had been young by most standards, not yet forty. Such a waste of a promising life.

"I'll leave you now and start making arrangements for removing her body," Shane said.

Unable to tear his gaze from the now-peaceful face of his mother's former friend, Beau simply nodded. "Thank you, Shane."

The other man gripped Beau's shoulder then dropped his hand. "You did your best."

"I'm not sure it was enough."

"Only God knows a person's heart, but she and I spoke on the matter of her salvation before you arrived." Shane angled his head to stare at Jane. "She made her peace with her Savior."

Beau knew he should feel relief at the doctor's words. But lying before him—in the slack repose of death—was the personification of the uglier side of the acting profession.

A burning throb of anger knotted in his chest, stiffening the muscles throughout his body.

While Shane gathered his things and left the room, Beau gently pulled the blanket up to Jane's chin.

Silent and brooding, he stared at her without really seeing her anymore.

How many women died in equal desolation and solitude every day? How many lived in condemnation, without experiencing Christ's love in their lives? How many lived without family or friends to care for them when times turned hard?

Far too many was the only answer that came to him.

If only he could stop the vicious cycle.

But the task was too large for one man. Overwhelmed with the magnitude of such a burden, Beau lifted his gaze toward heaven. *I can't do it, Lord.*

A memory from the last time he sat at Jane's bedside lurched forward in his mind, and Beau recalled what the still, small voice had said to him. "One at a time, Beau."

Beau thought of Miss Southerland then, and his confusion instantly cleared into a single purpose. *Yes, Lord, one at a time.*

He would start with her.

Fighting sleep a little while longer, Hannah sat at the dining room table with Laney. Laney had an inkwell on her right, a pen in her hand and a sheet of paper spread before her.

They were alone in their task.

With everyone else either in bed or back in their own home, the house had a nice, relaxed silence about it. As tired as she was, Hannah felt a strong sense of peace wash over her. Charity House was no mere institution. It was a home that had welcomed Hannah as though she'd belonged here all her life.

She had visited many orphanages, but had never been inside one so filled with love and compassion. And to think most of the children were born under unholy circumstances. In her mind, that made Charity House that much more special.

Hannah's unclear idea of a future ministry had taken form in this tiny world within the harsher world surrounding it. She was both humbled and inspired by all the possibilities before her.

Feeling lighthearted and energized, Hannah turned to her new friend and smiled. "We have our two spies, the king and Joshua. Now we need to pick our Rahab. It should be one of the older girls." Hannah tapped her fingers on the table. "Any suggestions?"

"Megan." Laney's eyes turned sad, haunted even, but very, very determined. "It *has* to be Megan."

"Jane Goodwin's daughter?"

"With Jane dying soon, it will do Megan some good, or at least take her mind off her mother's illness."

Hannah felt the jolt of understanding all the way down to the soles of her feet. Her own mother had died around this same time of year. The memory shifted, materialized and then cleared just as quickly, leaving a sharp pain of loss whipping through her.

Hannah shuddered.

Death was an inevitable part of life. But for a young girl to lose her mother—well, that was something no child of any age should have to experience, especially not alone.

Unlike Hannah, Megan was not alone. And Hannah would do her part to help the girl through this tragedy.

"Yes," Hannah said once she had her own emotions under control. "Megan will be perfect in the role of Rahab."

Smiling, Laney rubbed a finger over her temple and bobbed her head up and down. "I love the idea of putting on a play from the Bible. You said you do this all over the country?"

"If I'm in a city long enough. I've found it's an effective way to teach the children about the Bible." She lifted a shoulder. "We could read the story to them, give them a short lesson and then ask them questions. But when they physically participate in the telling of the story, they remember it better."

Setting her elbow on the table, Laney rested her chin in her cupped palm and let her gaze drift over Hannah's shoulder. "I can't believe we never thought of this before. The story of Rahab is the perfect choice."

Normally, Hannah wouldn't start with such a powerful story, one filled with intrigue and an unconventional heroine. But if there was ever a group of children that needed to learn about God's glory and how He often chose flawed individuals to carry out His plan it was the Charity House orphans.

"I'm looking forward to putting it all together," Hannah said.

"What will the others do, the ones who aren't given a part in the play?"

Hannah gave Laney a heartening smile. This had always been a concern, but Hannah had long since found

a way to include all the children. "Everyone will participate. Either in a small role or behind the scenes making
the sets or getting together the costumes."

Clearly unwilling to let the matter go without concrete assurances, Laney lifted a perfectly arched eyebrow.
"And the ones who want the parts that other children
have?"

"Understudies." Hannah raised a hand before Laney
could interrupt. The orphanage had a large number of
children in residence. There was only one way to ensure
every child that wanted to be in the play got a chance.
"We'll make sure some of the adults can't make the first
production, whereby we'll have to put on a second show
with the understudies in their roles."

Laney leaned back in her chair, her eyes brimming
with satisfaction. "You've thought of everything."

Uncomfortable under the praise, Hannah repositioned
herself in her chair. "Well, these things never go without a hitch, but we'll do our best to minimize the worst
of them."

Laney slapped her palms on the table and pushed out
of her chair. "That's good enough for me." She stretched
her arms over her head. "I'll leave the particulars to you.
I'm going in search of my husband."

The obvious affection Hannah saw in Laney's eyes
made Hannah's heart lurch against her ribs. "Sleep well."

"I always do." She reached across the table and
squeezed Hannah's hand. "Do you have everything you
need for tonight?"

Hannah nodded, tears pricking at the backs of her
eyes. "You've been very kind. I owe you."

"Don't think I won't collect."

"I hope you will."

Laughing, Laney waved a hand over her head and left the room.

As she watched the other woman leave, a sense of belonging crept through Hannah. It was a feeling she hadn't experienced since her mother died twelve years ago. How was it she had a twin sister, a woman that should have been her best friend, her confidant and ally, and yet she felt closer to Laney Dupree after a half-day's acquaintance?

Guilt tapped a painful melody across her nerves.

Hannah had spent a lifetime failing her sister in one capacity or another, especially when there was a man involved. First had been the boy they'd fought over as children—a fight that had ultimately resulted in Rachel's hearing loss. Then there had been the married school-teacher who had been Rachel's secret tryst and the reason for Hannah's banishment. Their father had never questioned Rachel's claim that Hannah had been the one dallying with Mr. Beamer. He'd thrown Hannah out of his home without hesitation.

Now, Tyler stood between the sisters.

Why hadn't Hannah seen the pattern before?

Well, no matter—she was through letting a man come between them. Whether Rachel agreed at first or not, Hannah was going to push all men aside and forge a true bond with her only sister.

A passing flirtation with a man would carry no more weight. It was time to put family loyalty and the love of sisters ahead of a man.

And now that Hannah had made up her mind, Tyler O'Toole didn't stand a chance.

Chapter Nine

Early the next morning, Beau strode across the grounds of the Arapahoe County Courthouse with a clipped, impatient pace. Marshal Scott had requested an urgent meeting at his office before the start of the day. Beau could only hope the lawman had good news.

Cold, dark clouds drifted overhead, casting a gray, depressing light over the morning sky. The manicured lawn and geometric angles of the sidewalks did nothing to soften the imposing architecture of the three-story courthouse. Made from solid stone and marble, the building brought to mind stability. The obvious statement being that no matter how corrupt any one individual became, the courthouse itself would remain steadfast and true.

Still locked inside his grief over Jane, Beau was too weighed down with sadness to notice the rest of his surroundings as he strode across the grounds.

As he continued toward the front steps, his mind shifted to Jane's daughter. Megan would have to be told about her mother. It would not be an easy conversation.

Oh, Lord, You promise to be with us always, to the

very end of the age. I pray you are with Megan today and always.

A roll of thunder rippled loud and menacing in the near distance. Beau darted up the marble steps and shoved inside the building. At the same moment the heavy brass door shuddered closed, another clap of thunder shook the air.

Beau circled his gaze around the wood-paneled lobby. Men and women of all ages milled about. With a resolute frown pulling his eyebrows lower, he searched the sea of faces and wondered how he would find Marshal Scott. Thankfully, his search was short-lived. On the other side of the cavernous room, Beau caught sight of Trey in deep conversation with a younger man. Both were dressed in solid black with a tin star pinned to their chests.

Picking up speed, Beau crossed in their direction. "Marshal Scott," he called out.

Trey lifted his head. "Ah, Reverend O'Toole, we were just discussing your…case." He gestured to the other man. "This is my deputy, Logan Mitchell."

Beau nodded at the other man. Blond, lanky and with an open, honest expression in his eyes, Deputy Mitchell looked more like an inexperienced ranch hand than a lawman. But Beau had heard the rumors. A year ago, the young deputy had saved Trey's life during a gunfight in Mattie's brothel, of all places.

"Do you have news of my brother?" Beau asked.

Before answering, Trey looked around the lobby, his gaze landing on a few people slowing their pace as they passed by. "Let's continue this discussion in the privacy of my office."

Beau fell into step behind the other two men as they wound their way through a labyrinth of marbled floors and paneled hallways. Taking a deep lungful of air, Beau breathed in the scent of important business, a spicy blend of leather, wood and tobacco.

Along the way, several men stopped their conversations to look at Marshal Scott. A unique mixture of awe and fear filled their eyes.

Rounding a final corner, Trey directed Beau across the threshold of a tiny room that contained one wooden chair, one functional desk and a thick layer of dust.

"I take it you don't use this office very often," Beau said, flashing a conspiratorial smile.

With one quick slash of his hand, Trey dismissed the small space. "Now that I have my own home, I complete most of my paperwork there."

Beau didn't blame the marshal for avoiding this austere room. The man had a beautiful wife, a lovable daughter and a baby on the way. It was no wonder he spent every free moment he could with his family.

Beau's own dreams of the future slid unexpectedly into focus. The images came so abruptly, so unyieldingly, he had to gulp for air. Perhaps grief and the subsequent reminder of his own mortality increased his sense of urgency, but Beau wanted what Trey Scott and Marc Dupree had. He wanted a wife, a houseful of children and a home filled with Christ's joy.

"Have a seat." Trey motioned to the lone chair in the room.

Trudging forward with heavy feet, Beau took note of the thick grime on the indicated chair. "I'll stand."

Trey gave him a wry smile. "Probably for the best," he said as he reached a hand toward Logan.

The deputy presented a small stack of papers Beau hadn't noticed him carrying before now.

Trey adjusted the pile in his grip. "I'll get straight to the point. We've received several telegraphs in response to our inquiries about your brother." He riffled through the papers, paused, riffled some more. "Two came in from the Springs area, one from San Francisco, another from Laramie and, finally, one from our office in Cheyenne."

Cheyenne?

At the mention of the booming frontier town, memories of lost hope and a failed relationship threatened to materialize in Beau's mind. One he had purposely worked to forget. Squaring his shoulders, Beau shoved the reminder aside. If the Lord meant for him to return to Cheyenne after that last disastrous trip, then Beau would go out of obedience. Even if he didn't relish the opportunity.

Heavenly Father, please, not that. Not *Cheyenne.*

Head still bent over the telegraphs, Trey continued. "Several actors have arrived in San Francisco this week, but none that meet the description of your brother."

A relieved sigh passed through Beau. Tyler and Rachel hadn't made it to the coast. Yet. At least not together. But if they'd separated and Rachel was traveling alone...

No, Beau didn't want to think about the ugly possibilities of such a disaster.

"Two female dancers showed up in Colorado Springs three days ago, but both are much older than Miss Southerland's sister."

Beau grimaced. "That leaves Laramie and Cheyenne."

"No arrivals in Laramie to date. However, Cheyenne is a different story." Placing the bottom piece of paper on top of the stack, Trey slanted a quick look at Beau. "A famous Shakespearean actor arrived just under a week ago. The man was accompanied by a beautiful young woman. The descriptions of the two match your brother and Miss Southerland's sister."

The jolt of disappointment took Beau by surprise. There had been a small part of him—the part where blood and family loyalty resided—that had hoped Miss Southerland had been wrong about his brother.

Now there could be no doubt. But to have his younger brother land in Cheyenne of all places.

Beau's breath tightened in his lungs, and he fought the urge to clench his hand into a fist.

Oh, Lord, I know Your plan is bigger than my understanding. I pray for Your guidance and Your steadfast courage to face her again.

"Are they still in Cheyenne?" he asked.

Trey's gaze cut to Logan, and he nodded at the younger man.

Taking over the conversation, Logan reached to the pile of papers and sorted through the stack until he came to one in particular. "According to Marshal Montgomery, their room at a local hotel is paid through the end of the month," Logan said.

"*Room?* As in singular?"

Logan fixed his gaze on the wall behind Beau's left shoulder. "One room. Two guests. Registered as—" he looked back at the telegraph in his hand "—a Mr. and Mrs. Duke Orsino."

Mr. and Mrs. Duke Orsino?

Annoyance, quick and hot, shot through Beau. Leave it to Tyler to pick an alias from the popular Shakespearean play *Twelfth Night,* where the main characters were twins separated by misfortune. It was as if his brother was hiding in plain sight and daring Beau to come after him.

Well, the gauntlet had been thrown.

And Beau had no problem accepting the arrogant challenge.

"I need to give Miss Southerland the news," he said. "I suspect she will want to leave right away."

But this time she would not travel alone.

Once Beau had assisted Megan through the initial stages of her grief, he would make arrangements for his and Miss Southerland's journey to Cheyenne.

They would, of course, need a chaperone. And perhaps a guide. Or at least a written introduction to the marshal in Cheyenne.

With his mind organizing, calculating, Beau paced toward the lone, dingy window at the back of the room. Seeing none of the scenery beyond, he continued thinking through the particulars.

Trey's voice interrupted Beau's mental list-making. "Ordinarily I would offer to accompany you on the journey. But I'm in the middle of an important trial, and I can't leave my wife now that she's carrying our child." His voice sounded slightly troubled yet very, very resolved.

Beau turned to look at Trey. Unasked questions hung in the room between them. Maintaining eye contact with the other man, Beau waited.

"I realize Miss Southerland will have questions," Trey said in a toneless voice. "But I won't be able to go to Charity House with you this morning." He opened a watch linked to a fob on his vest. "Today's proceedings begin in less than an hour."

Logan shifted into view. "I'll go in your stead, Marshal."

Beau looked from one man to the other. The two appeared to be communicating without words, an important message passing between them.

When neither man broke the silence, Beau said, "Thank you, Deputy Mitchell. I would appreciate your assistance."

Remaining silent, Logan unbuckled his gun belt and handed it to Trey, who then circled the desk and locked the weapons inside the bottom drawer.

Confused, Beau asked, "Why are you leaving your guns behind?"

Logan lifted a shoulder. "We never wear our weapons around the children at Charity House."

Even with all the conflicting thoughts scrambling for attention in Beau's head, one point drew into focus. The men and women of Charity House were beyond compare.

Hannah touched Megan's shoulder. The teenager turned a questioning look to her. An old soul. Wise beyond her years. Those had been Hannah's first thoughts when Laney had introduced her to the seventeen-year-old this morning. And they still held now. With thick, wheat-colored hair, green, intelligent eyes and clear, flawless skin, Jane Goodwin's daughter was nothing so benign as pretty. Nothing so ordinary as beautiful.

She was spectacular.

"Did I do something wrong?" Megan asked when Hannah didn't speak. Her eyes filled with worry, and she drew her bottom lip between her teeth.

"No, no," Hannah assured her. "You're wonderful. All I need is for you to turn slightly to the left when you say that last line and place your chin a little higher in the air. Remember, Rahab is a courageous woman, one who is instrumental in the Israelites' victory. She has no doubt Yahweh is the one, true God."

"But she's a prostitute." Megan shifted from one foot to the other, her brows slammed together in a frown. "Why do you speak about her with such, I don't know... reverence?"

Activity around them stopped and all eyes—all twelve curious pairs—turned and waited for Hannah's response to the question. Knowing who their mothers were and what sort of life they'd chosen to lead, she knew her response would be important. Perhaps life-changing for these children.

Before speaking, Hannah offered up a quick prayer. *Oh, Lord, please fill me with the right words.*

"That's the best part of the story," she began in a light tone. "At least in terms of seeing God's glory shine over man's."

"Huh?" one of the boys asked.

Hannah took a deep breath. She wanted to keep her explanation simple, yet profound. "If God had chosen a perfect woman to carry out His plan that day, then how could we know the Lord was in control all along?"

All twelve sets of eyes widened.

"How would we know to trust in God and not mere people? Understand?"

A few heads angled in confusion, while others bobbed up and down in agreement.

"You see—"

"What Miss Southerland is trying to say," a familiar voice said from behind her, "is that by using Rahab as His instrument for rescuing the Israelites, God showed us that even the most unexpected people have a place in the Lord's plan and, ultimately, His heart."

Catching a wisp of limes and pine that was uncomfortably appealing, Hannah spun around and faced the reverend head-on. "Exactly," she said, holding his gaze.

Leaning against the open doorway, he loomed large and masculine as always, but something in his off-kilter stance made her stop and study him more closely.

Hannah gasped at the unconscionable grief rimming his golden gaze. And for a split second, his wounded, grief-stricken eyes simply stared back at her.

Hannah gasped again. Glory. *Glory.*

Like many women, she was drawn to people who needed her. And she was *always* at her best when one of those people actually asked for her help.

Beauregard O'Toole, although he didn't know it yet, needed her. Of course, the question still remained.

What was she going to do about it?

Chapter Ten

Beau tried to think brotherly thoughts. But once again the impact of Miss Southerland's appeal overpowered his efforts. For one shocking moment, his future had a face. Panic surged so violently at the notion that he had to lean against the doorjamb to catch his balance.

Mentally, he forced himself to step back, to evaluate. To…*think*. Running a hand down his face, he organized his thoughts as best he could. One ultimate truth came into focus. Miss Southerland would never make a suitable wife for a preacher in a small, conservative community.

She was too flamboyant, too alluring, too…*conspicuous*. And with his own reputation already controversial enough, Beau needed an unassuming woman by his side.

Hannah Southerland was *not* that woman.

Yet, as she continued to stare at him with that sweet, understanding expression, Beau was struck by a wave of tenderness, and he had trouble remembering exactly why she could never fit into his life.

She was a friend of his parents', after all. No doubt, his mother loved her. The two women were cut from the same mold, all the way down to their clear understanding of Scripture and outer beauty.

But Beau was a preacher in search of a conventional wife. She would definitely need to be plain, traditional, and would reflect the sense of stability so many of his superiors questioned in him.

A tug on Beau's leg jerked him out of his disturbing thoughts. "Hey, Pastor Beau, are you here to help us with the play?"

Happy for the distraction, Beau angled his head to look at little Molly Scott grinning up at him. "Play?" Her words didn't quite register. "What play?"

"The one Miss Hannah is helping us put on. It's about Rahab. I get to be a merchant. Bobby and Mitch—" she pointed to the boys behind her "—are the spies."

"I…see." Which, of course, he didn't. Not fully.

Beau shook his head in confusion.

Molly scooted to her left, leaned forward and waved frantically. "Hi, Deputy Mitchell. Are you here to help us, too?"

Caught in his own confusion, Beau had completely forgotten about the young deputy. Shuffling to his right, Beau moved out of the doorway and allowed Logan to step forward.

"Hey, kitten," the other man said as he plucked at one of her braids. "Help with what?"

"The play," a soft, feminine voice announced from the interior of the room.

Lifting his gaze, Logan instantly straightened and stood gaping at a pretty girl of about seventeen.

The young beauty seemed equally enthralled with the deputy. There was something familiar about her. But before Beau could make the connection in his mind, Miss Southerland cleared her throat.

"We're putting on a play about the Israelites' defeat of Jericho," she said.

She extended her hand to Logan, smiling as though she had a private joke all her own when he completely ignored her.

Shoving her hand forward again, she wiggled her fingers. "I'm Hannah Southerland, and you are…"

"I…uh… I'm…" Logan blinked, blinked again, shook his head and very, very slowly turned his attention to Miss Southerland. "Deputy U.S. Marshal Logan Mitchell, Miss…uh… South-land?"

His voice held the absent note of someone merely going through the motions of the introduction. Beau held back a grin as Logan ignored her outstretched hand and returned his attention to the girl.

The little beauty fluttered her lashes in a gesture surprisingly without guile.

Logan swallowed, audibly sighed.

The battle was won and lost in that moment. And Logan Mitchell was a goner.

Grinning at the smitten pair, Miss Southerland made an exaggerated effort of looking from Logan to the girl and then over to Beau. With an ironic tilt of her chin, she fluttered her lashes in an gesture identical to Megan's.

The humor was there in her eyes, but Beau found himself feeling as stunned as the young deputy looked.

Molly tugged on his hand again. "So, are you joining us or not?"

Beau forced his mind back to the conversation. He wasn't usually so daft. "You're turning Bible stories into plays. I think that's…" Beau paused, searching for the right word. "Brilliant."

Clearly pleased with his approval, Miss Southerland sent him a quick, lovely smile.

Sensing he was a goner himself, Beau felt his stomach lurch.

"Everyone gets a chance to help," she continued with her explanation. "Either as actors or set designers or costume mistresses." Her eyes went serious as she offered her hand to the young girl still trapped inside Logan's gaze. "And Megan here is going to play our heroine, Rahab."

Megan. Beau's mind focused to pinpoint clarity. Of course the girl looked familiar. She was Jane Goodwin's daughter. And now that he looked, now that he *really looked,* the resemblance was uncanny.

His pulse thundered loudly in his head, and for a moment he was transported back in time to when the magnificent Jane Goodwin was in her prime. The hope that the generational cycle of sin would be broken in this younger, fresher version came abrupt and violent.

And he was here to break her heart.

But not yet. He couldn't do it just yet.

Beau shifted his gaze to Miss Southerland. "I need a private word with you."

Logan's brows knitted together, but before he could speak, Beau said, "I won't need you for this conversation, Deputy, but I ask that you stick around in case I need you to fill in details I might have forgotten."

Logan nodded. "Of course." He turned his attention back to Megan. "Would you care to take a walk with me?" he asked.

His softly uttered words were in direct conflict with the intense expression in his gaze.

Looking both mystified and pleased, Megan's eyes widened. "Do you suppose it would be all right, Miss Southerland?"

"Of course, but take Molly with you. And stay close to the house." She paused to give Logan a meaningful look. "I'm sure you understand my meaning, Deputy."

"Yes, ma'am," Logan said, his face a study of obedience and propriety. "I certainly do."

In spite of the other man's promise, Beau could feel the anticipation in Logan as he offered his hand to Megan. But as the young adults left, with Molly chattering away by their side, Beau couldn't help but smile in relief. Miss Southerland had known exactly what she was about when she'd sent the pair off with Molly, who was, unbeknownst to the child, doubling as a very attentive chaperone.

Well, well, well. The unconventional, flamboyant actress had a conservative streak.

And as he nursed the surprising thought, Beau was beginning to suspect he had no idea who Hannah Southerland truly was under all that fluff and lace. The woman confused him, to be sure. The sensation was a lot like standing in quicksand.

Hannah waited until Megan, Molly and Deputy Mitchell left the house before breaking eye contact with the pastor. She didn't especially like the intense look the man had been giving her since he'd arrived, studying her as though he was trying to see past her exterior and straight into her heart. She should feel glad, happy that at last he was trying to see her for who she was, not what she looked like on the outside.

But what if he looked deep enough to see beyond her good intentions, deep down to her core, where she feared there was nothing of worth?

If her own father could see past her facade and find something repulsive, how could this stranger not? If her own father found her wanting, wouldn't this fellow preacher do so, as well? Because of her bold attitude and outspoken nature, Thomas Southerland had chosen to believe there was only sin below the colorful exterior. He'd chosen to believe Hannah was the bad daughter, and Rachel the good.

He'd never doubted, never sought facts or details. And he certainly never questioned the validity of Rachel's stories, which had been filled with holes the size of the Royal Gorge.

Was there something lacking in Hannah that brought on his unfavorable judgment? Would Beauregard O'Toole see it, too, if he looked deeply enough?

No. She'd promised herself she wouldn't allow this minister, a mere man, to have such power over her. And thus she would *not*.

Annoyed with herself, she took a deep breath and focused on the two boys she'd chosen to play the Israelite spies. "Bobby and Mitch, while I'm talking with Pastor Beau, you two go with Mary to work on some ideas for costumes." She turned in a circle, taking in the other children in one quick glance. "The rest of you start thinking about what you want the sets to look like."

With a smoothness that blanketed her nerves, she cocked her head and directed the pastor to follow her outside. Head held high, she didn't dare speak until they were completely alone.

Under her lashes, though, she threw a quick glance at

the pastor as he shut the door behind them and made his way along the side of the porch. Her heart did one long, slow dip against her ribs at what she saw. His guard had slipped. Much like the first time she'd met him, he held his shoulders stiff. And his eyes glittered with pain.

He looked so lonely, she thought, so hopeless.

And then she knew. He had bad news.

Oh, Lord, give me the courage to hear what he's come to tell me.

She leaned against the railing and waited for him to speak. But when he lowered his head and shoved his hands into his pockets, she touched his arm. "Has something happened to Jane?"

It was the only thing that made sense, given his sorrow.

His head shot up. "How did you know?"

She rubbed his arm in the same way she would when she was trying to soothe a young child. "It's in your eyes." She dropped her hand. "Tell me what's happened."

"Jane Goodwin lost the fight. She died early this morning."

Hannah's stomach lurched. His tone was so flat, so unemotional.

"I'm sorry," she said, knowing how inadequate her words sounded. "Was it a peaceful death?"

"Yes." His gaze burned with anguish as he placed his hands on the railing in front of him and breathed in. "Megan will have to be told. Soon."

Tears sprang to Hannah's eyes. "The news will devastate her. Oh, Beau." She placed her hand over his, only partly conscious of the fact that she had used his first name. "What will you say?"

Releasing another slow breath, he turned his palm to

mold it against hers. "I have to trust the Holy Spirit will give me the words."

Hannah stared down at their joined hands, stunned at how soothed she felt by the contact. The sensation didn't last long. Sorrow rose up and tightened in her throat. Her heart wept for this godly man, for what he had to do. But most of all, her heart wept for Megan and her loss. "I want to be with you when you tell her."

"I think that's a good idea."

He pulled his hand free of hers then. The loss of the warmth of his fingers hit her like a physical blow. She felt her eyes sting and a hot fist of guilt grabbed at her stomach. How could she be thinking about this man, and what he was beginning to mean to her, when Megan was the one she should be worrying about?

She could because she saw how hard this was for Beau, the part of pastoring that no man could train enough for.

"I'll need to tell Laney and Marc, as well," he said.

"We'll tell them together, and we'll tell them first. That will give Megan some time with the deputy."

She turned to go back inside the house, but he stopped her with a hand to her shoulder. "Hannah."

She lifted her gaze to meet his.

"I have news of your sister, as well," he said.

The softly spoken words should have staggered her. But she felt nothing. Waiting for the expected relief to come, she stared at him. Resignation was the only emotion she could muster.

There was no more putting off the inevitable. Hannah would go after Rachel. It was time to end this contention between them, to settle the real issue underlying their estrangement. To move on with their lives, separate or together.

But then a frightening thought occurred to her. "Is she…safe?"

The fact that she hadn't worried about her sister's safety until now shamed her.

"Perfectly safe." He gave her a wry look and slipped his hands back into his pockets. "They're in Wyoming and will be there long enough for us to travel to them."

Surprised at the confidence in his voice, Hannah lifted her eyebrows. "How do you know they'll still be there?"

"Their hotel *room* is paid through the end of the month."

She heard his emphasis on the singular, and yet couldn't find it in her to be scandalized by the information. This was all so familiar. So typical. So much like the night of her own banishment five years ago.

"You don't seem surprised," he remarked.

Her heart stuttered. "I'm not."

Clearly sensing there was more to her answer, he leaned back against the railing. "Do you want to tell me why?"

"No." The word came out too harsh, too firm, and she wanted to mean it. *Desperately.*

Despite their rocky start, Hannah sensed Beauregard O'Toole would understand if she burdened him with the truth of that night. Torn between bravery and uncertainty, she lifted her hands, let out a weary sigh and gave in to cowardice.

"Now isn't the time," she said. "We must first focus on Megan."

"Of course."

His voice was kind, but his eyes told her that he badly wanted to push for more information. The fact that he restrained himself showed another layer of his patient nature.

And in that moment, she knew she would trust him with the facts of that horrific night. Just not quite yet.

Chapter Eleven

The mood in Marc's study was one of somber acceptance, as though the people gathered around Jane's
daughter were used to hearing the devastating news of
death. Head bent low, Megan sat in a mahogany arm-
chair with her hands clasped tightly together in her lap.

Beau grimaced. The girl looked terribly young, terribly small. At least she didn't have to bear this burden
alone. Marc and Laney stood in front of her chair, their
faces drawn in identical expressions of concern. Miss
Southerland held vigil next to them while Logan Mitchell leaned over Megan's lowered head.

The young deputy murmured soothing, unintelligible
words to her. Beau wasn't sure she was fully listening to
him, but every once in a while she would nod her head
at something he said.

Logan had surprised Beau by refusing to leave Megan's side when Marc had asked her to join them in his
study.

It was as if Logan had known.

Perhaps Megan had, as well, which explained why
she'd all but begged the young deputy to accompany her.

Eventually, Logan's words trailed off. He rose and exchanged a resigned glance with Beau.

"I'm sorry, Megan," Beau said. "Dr. Shane did all he could."

She lifted her chin to look at him. Her large, round eyes were drowning in sorrow, but they were bone-dry. "I'm sure he did."

Her shoulders stooped forward and down went her head again.

Making a sound of distress in her throat, Laney pressed forward. "Oh, Megan, don't worry. Your mother is at peace with the Lord now."

Megan sighed. "Do you really think so?" she asked the room in general, her voice a study in doubt.

Biting her bottom lip, Laney shot Beau a silent appeal. He had trained for situations such these, and yet he never felt adequate when the time came to ease another's suffering. Death was always worse for the ones left behind. Beau stared at Megan's pale profile and prayed.

Lord, Lord, give me the words to ease her pain.

Beau slid a glance to Hannah. She nodded in encouragement, as though she understood how hard this was for him. In that moment a verse from the gospel of John came to mind and Beau moved into the young girl's line of vision.

"Megan," he began, "Jesus warned that we will have troubles in this world. But He also told us to take heart. Christ has overcome death. Death is not the end. It is only the beginning. Your mother has a new body and a pain-free existence now."

Beau stepped closer, but Logan moved more quickly, barring further approach with his entire body. Narrowed, wolflike eyes warned Beau to keep his distance. Beau tensed. If the lawman's concern wasn't so palpable *and* genuine, Beau would have answered the challenge. The kid was obviously confused in the face of Megan's grief, making him forget Beau was a minister here to *help*. So, instead of joining in Logan's ridiculous contest of wills, Beau nodded in acquiescence and took a step back.

"In spite of your mother's...profession," Beau continued from where he stood, "she knew who her Lord was and what He did for her on the Cross."

As Megan held his stare, confusion flitted across her gaze. Her shoulders jerked, but still she searched Beau's face.

He waited for her to look her fill.

At last, she caught her lip between her teeth and lowered her head to stare at her clasped hands again.

Before he could reach to her, Miss Southerland rushed ahead of him, nearly sideswiping Logan as she knelt in front of the girl.

"Megan, listen to me." She took the girl's hands in hers and pulled them close to her heart. "Your mother was a brilliant actress in her day. I will remember her fondly, as will many others."

"You knew my mother?" Megan's voice squeaked with the dry, raspy sound of grief not yet released.

Lowering their hands, Miss Southerland offered Megan a kind smile. "The first time I saw her perform was when I was about your age. I'd never seen such talent, such *presence,* on or off the stage. The audience adored her. *I* adored her."

"Was she very beautiful?" The eagerness and raw vulnerability in the young woman's expression pierced Beau's heart. Clearly, Megan wanted to hear that her mother had once been more than the broken wretch she'd become in her last days of life.

Brushing a wisp of hair off the girl's forehead, Miss Southerland's smile brightened. "She was stunning, nearly as beautiful as you."

Megan's cheeks turned bright red. "Tell me more."

"I'm not ashamed to say your mother is the reason I'm an actress now. I had the privilege of meeting her backstage that night. She was very kind. She told me I could do anything I set my mind to. Years later, when I had to make a life for myself out of nothing—"

She broke off, looked past Megan with a glazed expression in her eyes, but then she shook her head and continued. "That is…when I had to make a change in my life, I remembered how glorious Jane Goodwin had been, and I wanted to be just like her. I was proud to have known her."

Miss Southerland rose then and opened her arms to Megan. Sucking in a huge gulp of air, Megan leaped into the offered embrace and collapsed into choking, heart-wrenching sobs.

Logan shuddered at the unbearable sound of Megan's grief, his face a study in masculine panic. Yet he found the courage to place his hand on the young girl's back and rub gently.

Megan sobbed louder. Logan's face crumbled.

Sighing, Laney gently pushed the poor man aside, gave all the men in the room a meaningful look and then cocked her head toward the door.

Beau took the hint.

"Megan, we'll leave you alone with Laney and Miss Southerland for now," he said. "Come on, boys. Let's give the women a chance to speak privately."

To Beau's surprise, especially after Logan had been so uncomfortable in the face of Megan's grief, the young deputy moved his chin in a sharp gesture of denial. "I'm staying."

"You can come back later," Marc said in an unrelenting tone. "For now, come with us."

Catching Beau's eye, Marc made a motion with his hand toward Logan. Beau moved to the other side of the deputy. In unison, they gripped Logan's arms and tugged.

Logan shrugged them off with ease.

Clearly at the end of his patience, Marc lurched forward, eyes gleaming, and caught Logan by the arm again. Beau moved in, as well. Together, they calmly escorted Logan out of the room. Sensing more distance was needed than a closed door, Beau silently directed Marc to keep pulling.

Once in the hallway, Logan complained and threatened and generally spoke ill of both men along the way.

They passed through the kitchen and down the porch steps without incident. However, the moment they hit the backyard, the deputy broke free. Swinging wildly, he attacked.

Beau ducked to his left.

Marc swiveled to his right.

The deputy stumbled forward, righted himself and shot forward again. "How dare you take me away from her like that? She needs me."

Anger made the young man's movements awkward.

Of one accord, Beau and Marc shifted again. This time, when Logan struck, each man gripped a shoulder. With momentum on their side, they swiftly pinned the young deputy against the side of the house.

Spitting and muttering under his breath, Logan's muscles bunched, relaxed, bunched again.

Neither Marc nor Beau loosened their grip.

Logan fought harder.

"Calm yourself," Marc said. "You can't do anything to help her right now. And if you try to touch her again, even in the guise of helping her mourn, I'll do more than dodge your punches. I'll throw a few of my own."

"It's not like that." Logan fairly spit out the words.

Beau and Marc shared a knowing look.

"It's *always* like that," Beau said for them both.

Struggling under their grip, Logan's lip curled into a snarl. "I was just… She and I were… That is, she looked so…*lost*."

"She's too young for you," Marc snapped.

Logan looked shocked, then seriously offended. "She's seventeen."

"And you're twenty-two." To drive home his point, Marc shoved Logan harder against the house, lifting him several inches higher on his side. "In my book, that's too many years separating you."

Breathing hard, Logan's expression turned mutinous. "You're eight years older than Laney."

Beau tried not to smile. The deputy made a valid point.

"Granted," Marc said in a surprisingly reasonable tone. "But at seventeen Megan is still too young for you. Or any man, for that matter. And if I see you sniffing around her again I'll make sure you know exactly what I mean."

"I get it." Logan scowled. "But, just so *you* understand. There'll come a day when you will no longer have a say. And I'll be there. You can't keep us apart forever."

"Can't I?"

Logan struggled in response. Working together, Beau and Marc tightened their hold and slammed him back against the house.

"This isn't over," Logan snarled.

Marc grinned. "It is from where I'm standing."

"Yeah, well, you're standing too close."

As the verbal warfare heated up, Beau's patience drained out of him. "That's enough. Both of you." Beau dragged Marc off the deputy and placed a hand on each man's chest to keep them a good distance apart. "Now is not the time for this argument."

Completely ignoring him, both men glared at one another.

"Think of Megan," Beau said.

Both men slid a quick glance at him, but then resumed glaring and snarling at each other.

"Marc."

"What?"

"Go tell Mrs. Smythe to make Megan some tea." When Marc just stood there, Beau turned to the other man. "Logan, come with me back to the courthouse. We have to make arrangements for our journey to Cheyenne."

"Our journey?" Logan turned his head to Beau. Lines of confusion encircled his mouth. *"What* journey?"

Beau tamped down another wave of impatience and spoke as calmly as possible. "Miss Southerland and I will need help with the law in Cheyenne. Since Marshal Scott is in the middle of a trial, you're our man."

Logan continued to gape at him. "You can't decide that on your own."

"I just did."

"But—"

"It's settled. You know our case, the players and the

various details. But most of all, you know the law in Cheyenne."

Grinning now, Marc nodded his head enthusiastically. "Certainly makes sense to me. And, while you're at it, feel free to stay as long as you like. You—"

"Marc." Beau cut off the other man before he said— or did—something they would all regret. "Miss Southerland cannot travel alone with two men. Do you have any suggestions of a suitable chaperone to accompany her?"

"Let's see." Marc rubbed his jaw between his thumb and forefinger. After a thoughtful pause, his expression turned downright gleeful and he smiled. Or rather, bared his teeth. "Mavis."

"Mavis Tierney?" Logan gasped the name, his eyes round with shock and horror. "That old woman hates me."

Marc folded his arms across his chest. "You don't say."

"You have a mean streak, Dupree," Logan ground out. "Bordering on cruel."

"That I do." Marc looked entirely too pleased with himself as he shoved his nose an inch short of Logan's. "You'd be wise not to forget it."

"How could I? You won't let me."

And so the verbal sparring began anew.

This time, Beau just shook his head at the pair. At least they weren't throwing punches. Yet. And with the way his day was going so far, Beau considered that quite a victory.

Quite a victory indeed.

Chapter Twelve

The mournful sound of the train's whistle rent the air, while the burning scent of coal wafted on a steady stream of smoke. Wrinkling her nose against the unpleasant odor, Hannah made her way to the steps leading into her designated compartment. She left the rest of her party arguing over the appropriate number of bags needed for a three-day journey.

Well, Logan Mitchell and Mavis argued. The reverend mediated.

Shaking her head at them all, Hannah switched her *one* very small satchel to her left hand and boarded the train. After taking a short inventory of available seats, she chose one at the back of the railway car.

As she worked her way through the crowd, she breathed in the rich aroma of pipe tobacco, women's perfume and lemon-seed oil. The interior of the compartment had an expensive, stylish feel to it. Red velvet upholstery covered rich, dark mahogany seats. Large, rectangular windows were framed with intricate crown molding. The carpeted flooring and brass fixtures completed the pretty picture.

But as beautiful as the compartment was, Hannah's heart wasn't in admiring the decor. For many reasons, she hadn't wanted to leave Charity House this morning. She'd found a kindred spirit in Laney Dupree. And thanks to her time with the orphans, her dream of serving abandoned women and children had morphed into something far more tangible than "someday."

Although she'd promised to return and produce the play about Rahab, the entire group of children had been unusually quiet at her departure.

Sighing, Hannah smoothed out a wrinkle on her skirt and thought of one girl in particular. Megan.

Poor, dejected Megan.

Hannah had felt an especially strong bond with Jane Goodwin's daughter. It was yet another glaring reminder of how lacking the relationship with her own sister had grown through the years. Well, this time, when Hannah stood face-to-face with Rachel, she would not let the same old patterns of behavior control their encounter.

Oh, Lord. Her eyes fluttered shut. *I pray for the courage to face my sister in truth. Give me the courage to end the lies between us.*

Sighing again, Hannah opened her eyes in time to catch sight of her chaperone waddling down the aisle. Or, rather, she suspected the moving bundle was her chaperone. The wild white hair peeking over three large carpet bags certainly indicated her assumption was correct.

Hannah immediately rose to help her new friend. "Let me take those for you."

"Don't touch." Mavis teetered to her left, then quickly righted herself. "I'm perfectly balanced."

Hannah raised her palms in the air and stepped back. With a loud plunk, all three bags hit the floor. Drowning in satchels up to her knees, Mavis shot her a triumphant look. "There. You see."

Hannah made a noncommittal sound in her throat.

Kicking and muttering and kicking some more, Mavis broke free from the luggage carnage and dropped into the seat next to Hannah.

Mavis's outrageous outfit brought a smile to Hannah's lips. The older woman had chosen a purple tunic to wear over her men's denim pants today. She'd topped off the shocking ensemble with clashing red gloves and a floppy hat that had real flowers pressed along the edges. Real. Dead. Flowers. The pungent odor was astonishing. Astonishingly *awful*.

Hannah covered her nose and coughed delicately. Although there should have been generous room for both women on the two-passenger seat, Mavis squirmed and burrowed like a prairie dog fighting to get out of a windstorm. She huffed and kicked and hoisted until she eventually situated two of the bags on her left and the largest on her right—which happened to be the side where Hannah sat.

Hannah's left shoulder was pressed so tightly against the window that her breath fogged up the glass. If she could, she'd move to the empty seats facing them. But those were reserved for Logan Mitchell and Pastor Beau.

Grimacing, Hannah wiped away the condensation on the window and turned her head to study the loot Mavis had deemed appropriate for the short journey. No wonder the deputy had given her such a hard time.

"What do you have in there?" Hannah asked, more amused than miffed.

"Only the necessities, dearie." Mavis patted the bag she'd positioned on her lap. "Only the necessities."

Hannah didn't know any one person with that many necessities. "Such as?"

"Oh, this and that." She puckered her lips and started whistling a cheerful tune.

Mavis was certainly happy. A little too happy, especially after her heated argument with Logan Mitchell on the platform.

Hannah narrowed her eyes. "This and that wouldn't include tobacco, now, would it? Because I promised Laney and Katherine you wouldn't smoke while in my care."

"*Your* care?" Mavis snorted at her. "I'm the chaperone of you, missy, not the other way around."

Hannah had her doubts. In fact, she knew exactly how sneaky Mavis could be when in need of a smoke. Hannah and Katherine had caught her three separate times with a homemade cigarette in her hand. Hannah made a mental note to keep a close watch on Miss Mavis Tierney. Age indeterminate. Sneakiness a definite.

As people began filing into the compartment, Hannah lifted her gaze in time to catch the rest of their party entering the railcar. Moving with masculine grace, the reverend came into view first. His shoulders were set. His jaw tight. His expression unreadable. Something, or someone, had obviously upset him.

Hannah suspected that certain someone was Deputy Mitchell, especially since the young man lagged a good three feet behind the reverend, dragging his feet and looking like one of the orphans after a good scolding.

The moment the reverend stopped beside Mavis, he lifted an ironic eyebrow at the booty jacketing every available piece of space on their seat and laps.

Hannah shrugged her shoulders in a helpless gesture. Shaking his head, the reverend tossed a book on the seat across from her and moved to allow a passenger to pass him on the other side of the aisle. "I need to speak to the conductor."

But before he left, Hannah thought she heard him whisper to Logan, "Behave."

"Yeah. Yeah." Frowning, Logan plopped into the seat across from Mavis. He glared at the older woman, looking as though he was daring her to say something that would require a nasty response from him.

"Good morning, Deputy Mitchell," Mavis said in a singsong voice that brought to mind pure sugar. Dripping molasses.

Logan's gaze settled on the duffel bags, and his lips curled into a sneer. "What did you pack in there, old woman, your entire wardrobe?"

Leave it to Mavis to notice the offensive name and nothing else.

"Hey! You call me old woman again—" she shook her finger at him "—and I'll tan your hide."

"I'd like to see you try."

Mavis started to rise. Hannah stopped her with an arm across the bag cradled in her lap.

"What is it with you two?" she asked. "You've been at each other since we left Charity House. One might start to think you both just turned four years old."

As if to prove her right, Mavis snorted. Logan responded in kind. And then both crossed their arms over their chests and began to pout. Well, Mavis pouted. Logan sulked. If Hannah didn't know how worried both were about Megan, she'd say more. Instead, she left them to their silence.

But when Logan stretched his legs in front of him, and

Mavis kicked his foot in response, Hannah rose. "Oh, honestly, switch seats with me, Mavis."

"I think that's a grand idea," Beau said, returning to their happy little group just as Mavis started to argue over the suggestion.

Clamping her mouth shut, the older woman glowered.

Beau regarded her with a patient, albeit unbending, expression.

"Fine," Mavis huffed. "I'll move."

After a round of dodging bags and Mavis rearranging positions—four times—and Logan's refusal to move his feet—all four times—they eventually exchanged seats.

Just to be contrary, the moment Hannah sat across from Logan he gave Mavis an innocent smile and then made a grand show of moving his feet back to his side of the compartment.

Hannah had no idea what had caused such animosity between the two, but she was losing her patience with them both.

"This certainly promises to be an interesting trip," she said with a perfect mixture of sarcasm and distress.

"It does at that." To punctuate his remark, Beau performed an exaggerated wink in her direction.

The gesture had O'Toole written all over it, but there was a special flair in Beau's delivery that set him apart from the rest of his siblings—one in particular came to mind.

"We won't arrive in Cheyenne until tomorrow morning," Beau said to the group in general, but his eyes never left Hannah's.

Her heart did a soft flip in her chest then meandered into a rhythmic tap, tap against her ribs. Slow. Steady. Agonizing.

"The dining car isn't due to open for several more hours," he continued. "I suggest we try to get some sleep before then."

"Right." Logan shot a pointed glare at each of Mavis's three satchels. "I'm confident that'll happen with all this room at our feet."

Normally, Hannah would have been amused by the deputy's sarcastic quip, but her mind chose that moment to focus on the life-altering nature of this journey. Soon, her business with Rachel would be complete.

And then what?

Pain, hope, dread, fury—all four slammed into her, blinding her, making her dizzy and warning her that once she faced Rachel, *none* of them would go on as before. Not Hannah. Not Rachel. Not Tyler. Not even Beau.

The thought left her trembling.

As dusk settled over the land, Beau looked out the window and smiled in satisfaction. God's handiwork was evident everywhere—in the steep incline of crumbling rock and the glorious pine trees that peppered the mighty slopes.

Beau wasn't surprised he was moved by the obvious manifestation of God's majesty. He was surprised by the depth of his reaction.

He'd been ministering in Colorado for years now, and he never grew tired of the rugged territory. He felt at home here, as he'd never felt in London, Paris or New York. He wanted to spend the rest of his life serving the people bold enough to settle this harsh part of the world. He wanted—

A loud snort followed by an equally loud moan jolted

him out of his thoughts. He turned toward the noise.
Smiled.

Mavis Tierney, bless her ornery soul, had set into snoring with remarkable gusto. The woman was well past her prime but she had a passion for living—and, apparently, sleeping—that most people half her age would never achieve.

Logan had long since left for the dining car, leaving Beau alone on his side of their tiny area. He stretched his arms overhead, careful not to disturb either woman across from him.

While Mavis slept, Hannah sat quietly reading her Bible. With her head bent over the book, she was oblivious to his scrutiny. He took his time watching her, trying to pinpoint precisely when he'd stopped considering her an adversary and more a partner in this fiasco he liked to call "Not My Brother's Keeper."

Today, she wore a soft pink dress with darker rose adornments. In the dull light of dusk, she looked feminine, fragile. She made a man want to protect her.

Beau felt a sudden, overwhelming urge to grind his teeth together. He could not allow himself to fall for Hannah Southerland. He ignored the whisper in his mind that said, *Too late*.

He gave his head a brief shake and swallowed, suddenly feeling as though he was choking. The woman represented everything he didn't—*couldn't*—want in a wife. Not that she'd applied for the position. But Beau couldn't get the notion out of his mind that she was the one he'd been waiting for God to bring to him.

Which was absurd.

Surely, God had led Hannah Southerland into his life merely to help prevent a tragedy in their respective families and for no other reason. Especially when Beau needed a less conspicuous woman to help minimize his own penchant for the outrageous. His preaching spoke of a radical acceptance of sinners. Not radical by Jesus' standards, but certainly radical by the Association's standards.

The West was still untamed. He'd learned the hard way that the people settling in the frontier towns wanted safety. They wanted comfort in rules. He would win their trust first. Only then would he challenge them to look beyond the law—to the compassion Jesus required in all His followers. He would never win the necessary respect with a flamboyant woman like Hannah Southerland by his side.

Look past the exterior, Beau. Look to her heart. She accepts the unacceptable.

The thought brought him up short. Was he once again judging her unfairly? Hadn't she stepped into Charity House and won over the adults and children alike?

And who said she even wanted to consider becoming his wife?

Confusion made his head spin. Frustration pulled sweat onto his brow. Regardless of how he felt about her, at first or now, he should have told her about his association with her father long before now.

As though she sensed his eyes on her, Miss Southerland looked up from her Bible.

"Miss Southerland, may I call you Hannah?"

She leaned back, cocked her head and then smiled. "I suppose it makes sense at this point in our acquaintance."

"I have something to tell you," he said, pushing slightly forward in his seat. Now that he'd made up his mind to confess the truth, he wanted this business done.

She simply stared at him, unblinking.

He stared back for only a split second. "Your father holds my future in his hands."

She stared at him some more.

He continued to hold her gaze, his pulse raging loudly in his ears and his shoulders tightening in a spot just below his neck. "Well, not completely," he corrected. "But he could."

"Go on." She eyed him with the same wary look in her eyes she'd had at their first meeting.

However tight his shoulders were now, he continued to gaze at her directly. "I have been given the opportunity to plant a new church in Greeley, Colorado. The Rocky Mountain Association of Churches is sponsoring my efforts."

Her eyes widened. "My father was the chairman of the Association."

"Still is."

"I see." She looked flustered and irritated and completely disappointed in him.

A little finger of panic curled in his chest. "You misunderstand. I'm not on this journey to please your father. I'm here because it's the right thing to do. Your sister must be found and brought back home."

It was the surprise in her eyes, surrounded by a note of genuine concern and understanding, that gave him hope she believed him.

"What if Rachel refuses to return with us and my father blames you for your part? Could he take away your church?"

Tension the size of a railroad tie roped around his chest like an iron band. But at this point Beau owed her the complete truth. "Yes."

Dread leaped into her eyes. "Then you can't—"

"Yes, I can." He reached out and touched her hand. "Like I said before, going after your sister is the right thing to do."

"Oh, Beau. I'm so sorry."

Still holding his gaze, she turned her wrist until their palms met. He instinctively twined his fingers through hers.

For a moment, sitting like that, with a simple holding of hands, they were a unit.

"Don't be sorry for me, Hannah. The risk is mine to take. To be quite frank, my brother owes all of us an explanation. It is my duty to make sure he gives us one that will satisfy all the injured parties."

A look storming with emotion settled into her eyes. Now that they'd come this far, he had a choice to make. He could leave the conversation alone, stop where they were and let everyone settle down. Or he could press the conversation in another, equally volatile direction and be finished with the secrets between them.

Beau chose the harder of two routes. "Tell me about the night you were sent from your father's home," he blurted out.

Counting the seconds until she spoke, Beau waited for her to respond. When he made it to ten and she still kept silent, he feared she might ignore his bold request. But she surprised him by pulling her hand free and shutting her Bible with a smooth snap. "You're sure you want to hear this now?"

Beau recognized the bleakness in her eyes, the desire to avoid the conversation. He touched her hand gently. "I do."

She paused, blinked slowly and then nodded. "I suppose it started when my mother died. Rachel and I were only ten years old at the time. On her deathbed, Mama made me promise to take care of Rachel because she was small for her age, and fragile, much weaker than I ever was."

Beau couldn't imagine a more fragile woman than Hannah. With a sudden flash of insight, he wondered if her parents had mistaken her inner strength for physical strength. "And so you did as your mother requested."

She studied her hands a moment. "At first it was just picking up her chores when Rachel was too ill or too tired to complete them herself."

Beau shook his head at the notion. She couldn't be serious. His eyes lingered on her face a moment, and he saw that she was indeed serious.

She cleared her throat. "What started as small chores here and there turned into far more the night Rachel ran off after she and I had a fight over a boy." Her eyes became haunted. "It was a stupid argument, and I refused to go after her. Rachel lost her way that night. When she was eventually found the next morning, she had caught a bad cold and suffered permanent hearing loss in one ear."

"You blame yourself." A lump, hot and thick, stuck in Beau's throat at the realization.

She dropped her gaze to her hands again. "I should have gone after her."

"It wasn't your fault she ran off and got lost."

"Wasn't it?" she whispered.

Troubled by the stark guilt he heard in her voice, Beau opened his mouth to speak, but she talked over him. "I tried to make it up to her. And so I began taking the blame for bigger transgressions."

He didn't want to ask. How could he *not* ask? "Such as?"

"I don't know." She shrugged. "If Rachel broke a valuable item, I told our father I did it. If she said something mean to make a kid cry, I confessed I said it."

Beau could see the hurt Hannah was trying to hide. It was in the slump in her shoulders, in the shake of her voice. "How could he not know it wasn't always you? No child is all good or all bad. Surely your father could see the truth."

"My father has always thought the worst of me." The calm resignation in her voice startled him. "I was different from every other kid, more colorful, more dramatic. It was easy enough to assume I was bad. A rose is still a rose by any other name." She snorted. "Or in my case, a thorn is still a thorn by any other name."

He wanted to deny her words, but Beau understood those particular dynamics all too well. By preaching in "dens of iniquity," by associating with sinners, he was suspect among the more pious ministers of the Association. By answering God's calling for his life in the way he felt most productive, he'd been labeled a rebel.

But there was a difference between Hannah and him. He was guilty of everything they claimed. She was not. "Those weren't your sins to bear," he said softly.

Her head shot up, and her eyes speared daggers at him. "You think I don't know that? That I haven't scolded myself over and over and over in the past five years? But what else was I supposed to do? I promised Mama. If it wasn't for me, if I had gone after her, Rachel would still be able to hear in both ears."

Beau recognized the conflicting emotions on her face. Guilt. Sorrow. Despair. Anger.

"Hannah, listen to me." He lowered his voice and allowed the compassion he felt for her situation to flow into his tone. "By taking the blame for your sister's actions, you played your own role in her ultimate selfishness."

She bowed her head. "I know that. It can't continue. No more will I accept responsibility for her actions." Her gaze held his, determination blazed in her eyes. *"No more."*

"Good. *Good.*" He tilted his head and studied her mutinous expression. "But none of this explains why your father banished you from his home."

She broke eye contact and looked out the window, gulped in a deep breath as though she was gathering her courage to finish her story.

Beau waited in silence, giving her the time she needed.

"As you can imagine, the pattern had been set. By the time we were eighteen, Rachel was a master of manipulation. She had a secret tryst with the young, newly hired schoolteacher in town."

He'd heard of worse. He'd *seen* worse in some of the mining camps. And yet, her words startled him. In an attempt to erase all expression from his gaze, Beau rubbed his hand across his face. "That couldn't have ended well."

"He was married."

An odd combination of shock and fury left him speechless. He blinked, noticed how the moonlight streamed through the window and cast her in a pale, eerie glow.

"There's more."

Too many secrets. Too many shadows. Too much pain. "I can't imagine anything worse than adultery."

She gave a short, bitter laugh. "During the entire liaison, Rachel pretended to be me."

He should have guessed, should have been emotionally prepared. But his temper snapped anyway. Rage, hot and uncontrollable, bubbled just below the surface.

Beau suddenly wanted to hit something. He swallowed back the emotion. Swallowed again. But still the urge to unleash his anger held him in a death grip. Alarmed at his violent reaction, he turned to scowl out the window.

"I could never understand Mr. Beamer's strange, inappropriate looks," she said. "Or the way he tried to touch me when no one was looking. I never understood, that is, until the night the truth of the affair came out. The town instantly assumed it was me. *He* thought it was me. He'd been given no reason to believe otherwise."

Beau had to force his words out slowly and carefully in order to contain his temper. "And your sister let you take the blame."

"Yes."

"She never spoke up?"

Hannah crossed her arms in front of her in a protective gesture and looked at him with her own anger and grief warring in her eyes. "No."

For once in his life, whether in the role of pastor or friend, he didn't know what to say.

"I thought I'd forgiven her. And when she came to visit me in Chicago, I thought all would be different between us. After all, she was set to marry Will, a boy who has adored her since they could walk."

A muscle locked in his jaw. "Then she ran off with Tyler."

The sound that came from her throat was a rumble of pain and humiliation.

"Hannah—"

"I want her to pay, Beau. And I want it to hurt her. I—"

She gasped and her hand flew to her mouth. Hot color flooded her face. Tears welled in her eyes.

Beau's heart responded immediately, even as his head told him to remember where they were. He struggled to keep from pulling her into his arms. It wouldn't be right. It wouldn't be proper. Nevertheless, he had to let her know there wasn't something inherently wrong with her for thinking such ugly thoughts.

He hunkered down in front of her and grabbed her hands in his. "Hannah, it's only natural to feel anger at your sister over this."

She was shaking her head before he finished speaking. "No. Holding a grudge is a sin."

"Yes. But once you confess that sin, you must try to accept God's forgiveness and let go of the guilt. Don't allow this to turn into shame."

Her chin trembled. "What if it's too late?"

"It's never too late with Christ."

She stared at him, searching his face.

Beau held her stare. He'd never met a woman quite like Hannah Southerland. Even in her anguished state, she recognized that her bitterness was wrong. And because she knew it was wrong, she agonized over it.

In that moment, he realized his own enormous mistake. At the start of their acquaintance he'd judged her because of her outward appearance. He hadn't looked deep enough to see her real beauty, the beauty inside. That made him no better than the men and women who judged him.

It wasn't Hannah's character in question. It was his. And now the truth hung heavy in the air between them.

She wasn't unworthy of him. *Beau* was unworthy of her.

Chapter Thirteen

Hannah slept.

Mavis slept.

Beau, however, did not.

He had too much to consider, too much to organize in his mind. Now that he'd begun to get a good sense of who Hannah Southerland really was, on the inside, he only wanted to know more.

The woman was clearly the worst thing that had ever happened to him. For all intents and purposes, she was everything he shouldn't want in his life. Everything he *couldn't* want. Yet he did want her in his life. And now that he knew her better, *knew himself better,* there was no way he would be able to walk away from her. Not without leaving a part of himself behind.

Merely sitting in the same compartment with her felt too confining, too constricting, too...personal.

There was no question he had to fight this secret attraction. No matter how kind, compassionate and merciful of heart, she wasn't the right woman for a man starting a church in the conservative Rocky Mountain Association, even if her own father led the largest congregation in the organization.

And it wasn't for his sake, it was for hers. She wasn't conventional enough. The people in Greeley could easily ostracize her, judge her, perhaps even look down on her merely for her profession on the stage. Beau could never put Hannah in that vile situation. She was too full of life, too full of joy to suffer a moment of that kind of prejudice. Prejudice that he himself had held.

Surely these feelings he had for her would pass. They *had* to pass, for both their sakes. Then he could resume his search for a nice docile wife. Until that time, Beau would simply keep his distance from the appealing actress.

Starting now.

His jaw tight and teeth clenched, he rose and went in search of Logan in the dining car.

The young lawman sat at a table in a back corner, looking woefully out of place among the fine white linens, sterling silver utensils and crystal water goblets. He had a full plate in front of him, heaped with all sorts of rare delicacies. But instead of eating, he stared unblinking at the untouched food.

"Are you planning to eat any of that?" Beau asked.

"At some point," Logan said, keeping his head bent over his plate. With his fork, he drew a series of invisible geometric shapes on the tablecloth, repeating the same pattern over and over and over again.

Beau lowered himself into the seat opposite the deputy. "Want to talk about it?"

"No."

"Want me to leave you to your brooding?"

Logan snapped his head up and give Beau one long,

frustrated stare. "I'm not brooding, I'm just..." His voice trailed off.

"Thinking?" Beau supplied.

"Something like that."

Knowing precisely what was troubling the young man, Beau went straight for the crux of the matter. "Megan will be there when you get back."

Logan gave a nod, which might have been acknowledgment. "I hated leaving her," he said as he shoved the plate of untouched food away from him. "She was so... quiet."

"Her mother just died."

"Yeah, well, I wish I could have helped her with—" He broke off and shrugged. "I don't know. I wish I could have done something."

In spite of the seriousness of the situation, one side of Beau's mouth kicked up. "You'd risk Marc's wrath?"

Logan's face tightened into an angry knot. "He doesn't scare me."

"He should. Marc takes his guardianship very seriously," Beau pointed out in the smooth, patient tone that marked his occupation far more than the words themselves did.

"Yeah, yeah. I've faced down worse. One overdressed dandy isn't going to put me off from something I know is meant to be." The words came out strong, but Logan's gaze showed hesitation. "What does he have against me, anyway?"

"Try to understand. It's not personal, Logan. In his mind, Marc is protecting Megan, as any good guardian would."

Logan made a noncommittal sound in his throat, but

the uncertain look in his eyes was enough to make Beau lean forward and speak in earnest.

"You're both young. There's plenty of time to be together. You just have to believe it will all work out in the end."

"In other words—" Logan blew out a disgusted snort and sneered "—trust in God's plan. Is that what you're saying, preacher man?"

"Yes." Resting his weight on his elbows, Beau commanded the young man's gaze with a hard one of his own. "That's what I'm saying."

"I'm supposed to do nothing? Just wait for everything to work out?"

Logan's expression was mutinous, frustrated. And very, very angry. Beau registered all three, and then noted the panic underneath the emotions.

"Faith," he said, choosing his words carefully. "*Real* faith requires patience."

"I thought the Bible said God helps those who help themselves?"

How many times had Beau heard that blatant misquoting of Scripture? "That's not precisely what the Bible says."

"No?"

"No. Have faith. Fear not. Trust God. Those are clear commands set out in the Bible. But for a man to forge ahead with his own purpose motivating his actions, and then to tell God to bless the outcome, well, that's not Biblical. It's dangerous. And selfish. And more often than not leads to destruction."

Logan opened his mouth to argue, his eyes continuing to blaze with confusion and a good dose of youthful rebellion. Beau held the other man's stare, knowing they'd come to a moment of truth for the deputy. At last, Logan clamped his lips into a hard, thin line and nodded. "You'd know better than me."

Ignoring the belligerent tone, Beau pressed on. "If you and Megan are meant to be together, you will be together."

And in that moment, Beau knew he should listen to his own advice, especially where Hannah Southerland was concerned.

Have faith. Fear not. Trust God.

It was time Beau started walking his talk.

"Even if we don't understand the 'why' behind our circumstances," he said, "we can always trust that God works them out for our own good."

"Words, Reverend O'Toole, fancy words filled with nothing but rhetoric."

"Not just words," Beau said in a firm, unrelenting voice. *"Truth."*

"Well, here's some truth for you." Logan nailed Beau with a hard warning in his glare. The look revealed the seasoned lawman inside the boyish face. "If I lose Megan, someone will pay."

Gauging Logan's frustration, Beau ignored the threat and switched the conversation to a less volatile topic. "Since we're on the subject, what's all the animosity between you and Mavis?"

Logan shoved at his hair and made a face. "We aren't talking about Mavis."

"We are now."

"I say we don't."

"I say we do."

Logan's scowl deepened. "The woman hates me."

"Want to tell me why?"

Logan lifted a shoulder. "I don't know, maybe because I call her *old woman.*" Frowning, he slapped his palms on the table and pressed his weight forward. "But I don't mean any disrespect. She just takes it wrong."

Beau stared at the other man for a full ten seconds. The deputy couldn't possibly be that dense. Trey Scott would never hire a stupid man to cover his back. "Let me see if I heard you correctly. *You* call Mavis *old woman,* and yet *she* takes it wrong."

Logan sat back. His mild blue eyes flickered with a faraway expression. "I used to call my grandmother *old woman.* She fancied the nickname. And unlike a certain woman in our impromptu search party, Granny had a sense of humor."

Beau nodded in understanding. Every family, even his own, had its set of codes and pet names and forms of speech that outsiders never quite understood, and often considered odd.

Given that fundamental truth, Logan hadn't meant any disrespect when he'd called Mavis *old woman.* He'd been giving her a compliment. Of sorts.

Breaking the silence, Logan sighed. "Granny kind of looked like Mavis. Well, not really. *Nobody* looks quite like Mavis. But there's something about the old woman that reminds me of Granny. It's in the way her face scrunches up when she's mad. And how she gets all ornery when you cross her. I kind of like the old bird. There, I said it. Happy now?"

"Have you ever told Mavis how you feel?" Beau asked. "Tried to apologize for the misunderstanding?"

"Are you insane?"

Beau smiled at Logan's horrified expression. "Do I look or sound insane?"

"If I so much as hinted at an apology, Mavis would never let me live it down."

"Would that be a bad thing?"

Logan looked like one of the Charity House orphans, full of belligerence and bad attitude. "I'd rather face Armageddon."

Pride, Beau thought. It got a man every time.

Hannah unfolded her legs, maneuvered past the pile of luggage on the floor and tumbled into the empty aisle beyond. Righting herself with as much dignity as possible, she lifted her arms overhead and released a jaw-cracking yawn. Every muscle ached from hours of inactivity. But that would soon come to an end. According to the conductor, they were due to arrive in Cheyenne within the hour.

Instead of feeling joy that they were another step closer to Rachel, Hannah found herself dreading the confrontation all over again. The revelation of her own unresolved bitterness toward her sister was still too fresh, too strong, in her mind. How could she face her sister with so much anger still in her heart? How could she prevent herself from saying something they would all regret?

Perhaps with Beau by her side, everything would go smoothly.

Beau. *Ah, Beau.*

Just thinking how far they'd come since their disastrous introduction brought a smile to her lips.

There was no denying that the rebel preacher had disappointed her at their first meeting, proving he was nothing like the compassionate minister she'd dreamed of encountering when she'd read his letter to his brother. And yet, in the ensuing days, his behavior had been above reproach. He'd been accepting of the children of Charity House, an advocate for Jane, an instrument of hope for Megan and a rock for Hannah.

The truth was irrefutable. Hannah was starting to care for Beauregard O'Toole. In the way a woman cared for a man.

But what did that mean for her, for him, for the future? For—

Mavis snorted.

Grateful for the interruption, Hannah turned toward the sound. As she stared at her chaperone, a jolt of affection hitched Hannah's breath. Mavis Tierney was quite a character. The woman snored louder than the train wheels churned. She squirmed and burrowed like a rodent. Most of the time, she chose to be surly, mean, and spoke her mind without thinking of the consequences.

And yet, Hannah adored her.

Mavis mumbled, snorted again but continued to clutch the smallest of her three satchels against her. Hannah bit back a smile. The older woman seemed overly attached to that canvas bag. In the realm of obsession. A fixation. A...

"Now hold on just a moment," Hannah whispered to herself.

Using the soft steps earned from years of ballet training, Hannah edged closer to Mavis and narrowed her eyes at the woman's white-knuckled grip.

Understanding dawned.

"You little sneak."

With slow, measured moves, Hannah wrapped her fingers around the handle of the bag. Inch by careful inch, she tugged. To no avail. Mavis's death grip was a force all its own, which only dug Hannah's suspicions deeper.

Another yank, a quick snatch, and Hannah freed the bag from Mavis's hold.

The woman didn't stir.

"Thank you, Lord, for sound sleepers."

Gliding through the railcar on her toes, Hannah moved to an isolated corner and turned her back to the rest of the occupants. Relatively alone, she rummaged through the contents of the satchel until she found what she was looking for.

"I knew it."

She poked her hand into the bag, quickly palmed the objects in question and turned back around. Only to come face-to-face with an engaging preacher.

"Oh," she said.

He smiled.

"I… Oh!"

He smiled some more. "You said that already."

"I… I…" Her heart stopped beating altogether, held a full five seconds, gave a slow pitch and then picked up speed. "You gave me a fright."

"I'm sorry."

He didn't look sorry in the least.

But he did look handsome. Confident. Charming.

Glory. When Beauregard O'Toole produced that particular smile, he had all the charisma and style of his rogue brother. With none of the cunning.

Hannah wondered if Beau knew how engaging he was, in that masculine sort of way that made a woman want to rest in his strength. She wondered if he knew his charm was utterly irresistible. She wondered if he knew his smile was a powerful weapon, one that should never be misused.

She wondered if he knew she was getting very adept at wondering.

"Stealing from a helpless old woman?" he asked.

Caught in the act, Hannah grasped the tobacco pouch tighter in her fist. Then slowly, very, very slowly, she nodded.

"I'm shocked at you, Miss Southerland." His eyes crinkled at the edges.

Hannah caught his playful mood—at last—and returned his smile with one of her own. "I am what I am."

A single eyebrow arched toward his hairline. "Have you no shame, my dear?"

"Absolutely—" her smile widened "—*none.*"

He leaned in closer and lowered his voice to a conspiratorial whisper, creating a world all their own in the crowded railway car. "Can I get in on this brazen robbery of yours?"

"Only if you promise to dispose of…" She made a grand gesture of peering around him and then lifting her palm a bit higher. "The contraband."

"I'd consider it my personal duty."

Hannah's stomach performed a stunning flip, and then another, refusing to settle for even a moment. She didn't quite know what to do with Reverend O'Toole in this lighthearted mood.

She decided to take his lead and respond with a bit of comedy of her own. "You are a man after my own heart."

Unfortunately, her words escaped from her mouth in a far more serious tone than she'd intended. Mortified, she clamped her lips shut and waited.

She'd never been tongue-tied before. After all, she was Hannah Southerland. Esteemed actress in her own right. A woman who made a living donning roles and speaking words the greatest playwrights had penned. Yet this man, the son of one of her most valued and trusted friends, not only stole her breath, he stole the words right out of her mouth.

He must have noticed the change in her, because his eyes widened and then narrowed just enough to indicate his confusion. "Am I, Hannah?" he asked in an equally serious tone. "Am I a man after your own heart?"

Hard as she tried, she couldn't force her lips to form around a response. She had no idea how to answer such a question when her own emotions were in such turmoil. "I... I don't..." She swallowed. "I don't know."

"Then I have a bit of work to do," he said. The solemn glint in his eyes told her he wasn't teasing.

In that moment, she knew that she was in over her head with this man.

Nevertheless, she was an actress, a well-trained one at that.

Pretending they were still talking about the tobacco she'd confiscated, she jiggled the pouch in front of him and said, "You do indeed."

His gray eyes swept across her face, measuring, gauging.

She remained in character, standing mute under his scrutiny with a playful glint in her eyes.

Still, he made no move to retrieve the tobacco. Just when the moment became uncomfortable, his smile relaxed. "Then I'd better get rid of that before our girl awakens."

"Right," Hannah said, thinking she was in the clear. But then he plucked the pouch from her palm, and his fingers brushed against hers. The instant warmth and comfort that braided through her should have surprised her. Especially after all they'd been through. Instead, she felt a sense of rightness.

A sense of homecoming.

The emotion scared her spitless and her pulse fluttered in response.

"Give me a five-minute head start, then go wake our little sneak." His tone was very businesslike now, the minister firmly back in place.

Hannah knew she should be grateful for the return of Reverend O'Toole. Yet she couldn't stop a sigh from slipping past her lips as he pivoted on his heel and left her to stare after his retreating back.

In her years on the stage, she'd met the most captivating, charismatic men of the world. She'd socialized with heads of state and crown princes. She'd had offers, some honorable, others dishonorable. And yet none had inspired her to consider anything more than friendship. Not one.

But now, when she needed to concentrate on her sister and then go forth with her own future plans, a rebel preacher with no place to call home had not only turned her head, he had captured her heart.

She placed a hand to her throat and breathed in slowly.

Hannah didn't know what to do with all the emotions rushing through her. She needed discernment to guide her. She needed prayer, a lot of prayer. Because, when it came to her future, one thing was certain: Horatio Beauregard O'Toole had become an unexpected complication.

Chapter Fourteen

Beau knew Cheyenne well. Originally a rowdy home for railroad personnel, the Wyoming town had once boasted at least seventeen saloons providing three to five burlesque shows a night. But now, thanks to the completed railroad and the rise of cattle barons, the residents enjoyed a social life on par with larger cities back East.

Despite the limited population, the cultural advances and stylish set alone would entice Tyler to stay awhile.

Or so Beau surmised.

With the shocking turn of events of the last week, he couldn't pretend to know what had been in Tyler's mind when he'd run off with Rachel Southerland. Thus, Beau led his tiny group away from the railroad station in silence, while his mind worked overtime.

He wondered if Tyler would be performing in the new opera house, or the reputable playhouse, or if he'd dare subject himself to playing in one of the seedier saloons left over from the rowdy days. The information from the town marshal hadn't been clear on the matter.

And at this point, speculation was useless.

As Beau directed his party around a corner and onto

17th Street, he took a moment to study the familiar surroundings. Not much had changed in the year since his last visit. Clean, stylish, rich—those were the words that came to mind when he looked around. The sidewalks were free of debris. Even the tracks left by wagon wheels in the street were in straight, neat rows. All in all, the fashionable buildings outdid one another. But none were as grand as the large structure on their left. The famous Cheyenne Club.

"That's some building," he heard Mavis whisper in awe.

"It is," Beau agreed.

He'd been inside a number of times. Much like the gentlemen's clubs of London, the clientele was the wealthiest and most influential of the community. Constructed mostly of red brick and sturdy wood, the building made its own unique statement of style and impeccable social standing. A wide veranda and seven chimney stacks surrounded the outside perimeter of the first and second floors, respectively. On the main floor alone, there were two large dining rooms, four billiards rooms and three card rooms.

The club was top-notch, a spectacle to the eye, palate and senses. If Beau was a betting man, he'd have said Tyler was already a member.

The wind suddenly kicked up, bringing a chill to the air and the scent of cold. A sly hint that winter was on its way. Beau remembered how the weather bit hard and left casualties in this harsh northern land.

During his stay, Beau had helped the community grieve a mining accident where the snow had played a nasty role. It had been a grim time for many, but not always so for Beau. Amelia Jane Nelson had caught his attention, and his admiration. Beau had thought himself in love. Yet the memory of that feeling was drowsy and uncertain now. Try as he might, he couldn't recall her face in his mind.

Lord, why can't I remember her? Help me. Help me to sort this out and move on if that is what You want for me.

In the next moment, Beau sensed he wasn't supposed to remember Amelia or the painful blow she'd dealt him with her rejection. Which made little sense. Thus, he forced his mind to drift back in time.

Daughter to a local cattle baron, Amelia had been kind, godly and well-spoken. Although not a great beauty, her behavior and manners had always been impeccable— unassuming and proper. In Beau's estimation, she'd represented the perfect choice for a minister's wife. He'd nurtured hopes that she might become his wife and move to Greeley with him.

She'd dashed those plans with her appalled refusal of his proposal, for equally appalling reasons. He was a son of an actor, after all, a man who ate with sinners. Amelia didn't want to be the woman to make him a better man, mostly because she thought the task would be impossible.

A sense of lingering dread came with the memory, making his stomach churn.

Would he see her again? Would the pain of her rejection still burn, especially now that she was married to a man who'd attended seminary with Beau? Had Beau's pride been hurt, or his heart?

Hannah chose that moment to laugh at something Mavis said to her. Beau angled his head in time to watch the two link arms. Pulling Mavis closer, Hannah pointed at one of the buildings on their right and then another.

Mavis giggled and beamed at her new friend, clearly smitten with the beautiful young actress.

Hannah had that way about her, Beau realized as he watched her steer Mavis to the inside corner of the wooden sidewalk. She made the people around her feel special, as though they mattered more to her than anyone else. She was gracious, captivating, a fairy-tale princess come to life.

And watching her now, he was finally able to pinpoint what made her special.

Hannah Southerland accepted people. All people. She liked them, too, genuinely liked them. And they gravitated to her because of it.

It was no wonder Mavis cherished her.

Of course, the older woman hadn't discovered her missing tobacco yet, nor Hannah's role in the confiscation. There would surely be a bit of drama between the two at that point.

Then again…

Hannah would probably know exactly what to do and say to soothe the older woman's temper.

You're hooked, Beau.

Which he already knew. The question, of course, was what he planned to do about this unexpected turn of events. One woman had already spurned him because of his bad blood and unconventional ministry. He could never subject Hannah to that sort of prejudice. But what if she was the one for him?

Lord, I'm losing perspective.

Needing a moment to organize his thoughts, Beau looked to the western sky. Puffs of cotton white drifted against the clear blue backdrop. Much like his life, the fluid clouds glided in random, unpredictable directions, colliding with one another and then bouncing aimlessly in a new direction.

"I'm gonna head over to the jail," Logan declared when they stopped in front of their destination.

The two-story hotel, with its clapboard front and unassuming entrance, wasn't grand by any stretch of the imagination, but it was respectable. And, like the rest of the town, clean.

When Beau didn't respond, Logan turned to address him directly. "I'll find out what I can about the fugitives while you get the women settled in their room."

Beau's gut clenched. Of course. This was not a time to be thinking about his past or his future. There was work yet to do in the present. "I'll speak with the hotel manager while you're gone. We'll meet in the restaurant on the ground floor in an hour."

Logan nodded, then shot a quick glance to the women. "I'll see you in a little while, Miss Southerland."

Hannah touched his arm. "Thank you, Deputy Mitchell. Thank you for accompanying us on this search."

The deputy's eyes stared into Hannah's—a little too long for Beau's way of thinking—but, eventually, Logan tipped his hat and said, "It's been my pleasure, ma'am."

Mavis snorted and then shot her nose into the air.

Logan sighed. His blue eyes flickered with annoyance, but he kept his tone mild. "Good day to you, too, Miss Tierney."

Without waiting for a response, he crammed his hat farther on his head and took off in the opposite direction.

Mavis stared after the young man with her jaw slack.

"Close your mouth, Mavis," Hannah said with a soft smile playing at the edges of her lips.

"Miss Tierney?" she said, still gaping after Logan. "Did that boy just call me *Miss Tierney?*"

Beau and Hannah shared an amused look. Snared in her gaze, Beau's heart hammered hard against his rib cage. He had a surprising urge, one that stunned him with its strength, to grab Hannah's hand and bring it to his lips.

Of course, now wasn't the right time or place for such an intimacy.

"That's what I heard him say," he said, turning his attention back to Mavis.

"I heard it, too," Hannah agreed, her voice a breathy whisper.

Was she as affected by Beau as he was by her?

"Humph." Mavis's lips pulled past a tight flash of crooked teeth. "We'll just see about that, now, won't we?"

She pivoted on her heel and started marching in the direction Logan had taken. Hannah's hand shot out and grabbed Mavis by the sleeve before the older woman took two full steps.

"You can give him a piece of your mind when he gets back," she said.

Mavis glared after the young deputy, but acquiesced without further physical resistance. However, she did mutter several epithets about young men who had the nerve to call her names. Some of the terms, if Beau heard her correctly, would have blistered the wallpaper off Charity House's parlor room.

Miss Mavis Tierney was certainly an interesting woman.

Two hours later, Hannah had made her own observations about her appointed chaperone. None of them were pretty.

"You cannot go to the theater dressed like that," Hannah said, dropping her gaze over the bold-colored, East Indian tunic that stopped midthigh on Mavis's scrawny *bare* legs.

The dress, and Hannah used that term loosely, was downright shocking.

"I can and I will."

Honestly, it was like trying to reason with a two-year-old. Yes, the term *theater* was stretching things a bit. In truth, Tyler's play wasn't in the new opera house or the playhouse Beau had told them about. Instead, Tyler had chosen to produce, direct and star in an untitled play in the back of a saloon on a makeshift stage.

Well, no matter where the play was performed, Hannah would not allow Mavis to step foot outside their room dressed so inappropriately, both for the weather as well as for propriety's sake.

"You'll catch your death," Hannah said in answer, thinking she deserved a medal for diplomacy when what she really wanted to say would have offended the poor dear.

Mavis crossed her spindly arms over her bird-thin chest. "It's September."

"I don't care what month it is, we're in Wyoming. The temperature has already dropped several degrees in the last hour. You need more clothes on your body." Hannah picked up the pair of men's denim pants the older woman had worn on the train. "At least put these on."

"I ain't wearing no man pants to the theater."

Right. That made sense. Since Mavis wore man pants everywhere else.

Hannah pawed through the pile of clothes strewn on top of Mavis's bed. She didn't have time to argue with the stubborn woman. Thanks to Deputy Mitchell's investigations, and Beau's persistence with the hotel manager, they'd discovered that Tyler and Rachel were most definitely in Cheyenne *and* staying in the same hotel as they were.

Unfortunately, the renegades had left for the saloon-turned-theater before the information had been conveyed and verified.

Perhaps that had been for the best. Hannah had needed the time to prepare. To pray. To ask God for the courage and wisdom to carry out the most important confrontation of her life.

Eventually she found what she was looking for. "Then wear this."

Hannah tossed the skirt to the other woman, then watched in frustration as the garment fluttered to the floor untouched.

"Put it on, Mavis, or I won't let you come with me."

Mavis stomped her foot. "No."

Hannah prayed for patience, a prayer that was becoming dangerously close to rote whenever she was in the older woman's company for longer than a few minutes.

"Why are you being so ornery?" she asked.

"If you'd give me back my tobacco, I'd do whatever you asked of me."

"Are you blackmailing me, Miss Tierney?"

"Absolutely."

Hannah shook her finger in her friend's face. "You are bad. Very, very bad."

"You don't let me have a smoke, then I don't wear no pants *or* no skirt. That's my deal. Take it or leave it."

Hannah sighed. "Right then. It's settled." Picking up her handbag, she added, "I don't expect I'll be back until late tonight. But I'll bring you something to eat when I do."

Mavis's face went dead white, the only sign of her shock. But she recovered quickly. "Sarcasm does not become you, missy."

"Who said I was being sarcastic?"

"You can't do this to me. I'm going. And that's the end of it." She puffed out her bird chest. "And before I go you're going to give me back my tobacco."

With one quick slash of her hand, Hannah dismissed the order. "No."

"No, I can't go? Or no I can't have my tobacco?"

"No to both."

As if time had slowed, both women took two very determined steps toward one another. Their gazes locked and held.

Mavis scrunched her face into a frown.

Hannah did the same.

Mavis jammed her hands on her hips.

Hannah did the same.

Frozen to the spot, Hannah waited, held firm, gauged her adversary and waited some more.

Five minutes later Hannah was close to losing the patience she'd prayed so hard for earlier.

Thankfully, Mavis cracked first. "I just want one—"

"No."

"But—"

"No."

Mavis stomped her foot again. "You can't—"

"Oh, but I can."

Mavis cocked her head and studied Hannah for a long moment. "You ain't gonna budge, are you?"

"Not an inch."

"This stubborn side of you is not going to win many hearts."

Hannah gave her a quick, unrepentant grin. "Perhaps not, but I will win this argument."

With a snort, Mavis snatched up the skirt at her feet. "Fine. I'll wear this one."

"Wise decision." From the pile on the bed, Hannah plucked a light wool jacket and held it between her thumb and forefinger. "Add this to your ensemble and we'll call you stage-ready."

Frowning, Mavis yanked the jacket out of Hannah's hands and jammed her arms into the sleeves. "You can be downright mean when you want to, Hannah Southerland."

"So I've been told."

"You remind me a little too much of..." A smile slipped onto the corner of Mavis's lips. "Me."

"It's why you love me," Hannah said. Dragging Mavis into a tight hug, she kissed the top of her head as she would a child's. "And why I love you."

"Humph," Mavis said between suspicious-sounding sniffs. Was the woman crying?

Hannah released Mavis and touched the lone tear running down a weathered cheek. "Oh, Mavis."

Not to be outdone, Mavis lifted onto her toes and kissed Hannah smack on the forehead. "Take that."

"Well," Hannah said through watery eyes of her own.

Mavis just smiled at her, but then got that crafty look in her gaze that meant pure trouble. "Now that we're friends again, you wouldn't reconsider giving me back my toba—"

"No. Absolutely not."

Before Mavis could start the argument all over again,

Hannah wrapped her own shawl around her shoulders and trod to the door leading into the hallway. As she passed the nightstand, she caught sight of the flyer that the deputy had brought to her less than an hour before.

Compelled, Hannah picked up the parchment and studied the drawing of her former friend turned traitor. At the sight of Tyler's smiling face, Hannah sank her teeth into her bottom lip.

The drawing was a near-perfect rendition of the man, all the way down to the jaunty angle of his head and the cocky half smile that had become as much his trademark as his outrageous talent had.

Mavis rested her chin on Hannah's shoulder and peered at the sketch along with her. "That boy sure does look like our Pastor Beau."

Hannah bit down harder on her lip, then took a slow breath. "No. Not at all." She traced her finger across Tyler's jaw. "Beau has a stronger chin, with just a hint of a cleft in the middle." She moved her finger upward. "And his eyebrows are more winged. His eyes more pale silver than green."

"Poor Hannah," Mavis said, snatching the flyer from her fingers and setting it back on the nightstand. "You got it bad for the preacher."

Why deny the truth, when it was so glaring, so obvious? "You have no idea."

The admission didn't bring much comfort, though. Instead, Hannah felt a sense of dread run across her spine, as though she was about to lose her solid, predictable future. The one she'd worked so hard to chart and organize ever since her father had banished her.

Did God have a bigger plan for her life, one that didn't include worldly security?

And if so, did she have enough faith? Enough to obey His design for her life, even if it went against her own plans?

She shook her head at the frightening prospect.

"Come on, Mavis. Let's go witness one of the most famous Shakespearean actors of our day perform on a stage set up in the back of a rowdy saloon."

Mavis let out a loud cackle. "Can't think of anything more absurd than that."

Hannah's sentiments exactly.

Chapter Fifteen

Beau had made his share of mistakes in life. But he didn't usually make them on such a colossal scale. A raucous saloon, even one turned into a temporary theater, was no place for a decent woman of good, moral, Christian upbringing like Hannah Southerland.

But they were here now. Close to the end of their journey. And he doubted Hannah would be willing to put off the confrontation with her sister any longer.

At least Logan had thought ahead and ordered box seating for their party of four. The deputy might be young, but he was smart. And Beau was glad the lawman had agreed to accompany them tonight.

With as little spectacle as possible, Beau escorted Hannah and Mavis toward the back stairwell leading to their private box. The steps were old, and creaky, but out of sight from most of the other patrons. Nevertheless, Beau had insisted Logan bring up the rear, sufficiently shielding the women against interested stares.

At the top of the landing, he waved his party into the curtained booth. Following closely behind Logan, Beau took a quick look around while the others settled into their seats.

His stomach dropped at the sight before him.

It was much worse than he'd anticipated, and he'd expected ghastly. The box's walls were adorned with the same red velvet as the cushioned chairs and balcony railing. In the center of the room sat a plate of fresh fruit and an empty silver bucket that would have chilled a bottle of champagne if they'd been any other group. Obviously, the management had attempted to create an illusion of upper-class elegance.

But it was only an illusion.

Even if he ignored the smell of stale whiskey and unwashed bodies, there wasn't much to hide the fact that the Bird Cage was nothing more than a saloon with chairs lined up in front of an empty stage.

There was no orchestra, just a bass drum set up next to an ancient piano. An equally ancient gentleman sorted through a pile of sheet music. But for now, the only melody came from the bawdy jokes yelled out across the general seating area. Every few seconds, the shouts were interrupted by the high-pitched ping, ping, ping of tobacco hitting spittoons.

As if determined to turn the experience into a Wild West cliché, a fight broke out over an empty seat. Beau couldn't tell which of the cowboys won the ridiculous match. Within moments, they both ended up passed out on the floor.

Speaking his thoughts for him, Hannah muttered, "What on earth was Tyler thinking?"

Beau took his seat next to her and said, "That's just it, my dear Hannah. He's *not* thinking."

Just then a bottle came sailing their way. Palm to nape, Beau forced Hannah's head forward and ducked, as well.

"Lovely," he mumbled. "First-rate."

Hannah didn't respond. She just raised her head and stared at the stage. Her sudden gasp had Beau following her gaze to an easel and placard. Squinting, he could just make out the words through the veil of cigar smoke. *Faust. A Tale of Damnation.*

"Love-ly," he muttered again.

At the precise stroke of ten, a man sauntered toward the oversize drum and began beating a rhythmic cadence. After a round of hooting and shouting, a dark-hooded figure glided onto the stage. A hush came over the crowd.

The drumming ceased.

The mysterious character continued to stand in silence.

A gun fired, its bullet hitting the ceiling and spraying plaster over the audience. Hannah jumped in her seat. "Oh!"

Beau reached out and took her hand.

She braided her fingers through his and held on tight. "What is this?" she whispered.

"I have no idea."

Using the thrill of suspense, the dark figure stretched its arms slowly overhead.

The audience leaned forward, paused and held its collective breath. The apparition reached down and, with a flick of a wrist, whipped off the cloak.

The crowd went wild.

A loud gasp escaped Hannah.

Logan muttered under his breath.

Mavis looked to Hannah, back to the stage, then to Hannah again. "It's…it's you."

Speechless with shock, Beau blinked at the woman standing in the center of the stage. Her eyes gleamed with impish delight as she accepted the bawdy roars as her due. Beau shifted in his seat, fighting the urge to mutter an expletive. Dressed in a red silk gown in the latest Parisian fashion, the woman *was* Hannah. Only... somehow...less.

Taking command of her audience, Rachel Southerland stretched out her arms again and the noise died down to a smattering of whistles and howls.

The man at the piano poised his fingers over the keys, then started banging out a happy melody.

Rachel sashayed across the stage, humming along to the tune. Her movements weren't elegant or even practiced, but rather coarse. Suggestive. Beau was ashamed for her. And disgusted with his brother. Tyler should have taught her better.

There was acting. And there was what Rachel Southerland was doing on that stage.

Even as anger gnawed at his shock, an ache clutched at his chest. Tyler *knew* better. But did Rachel?

Raise up a child in the way that he should go...

The Scripture said it all. Reverend Southerland had done Rachel a disservice by shutting his eyes to the truth all these years. By allowing Hannah to take the blame for her sister's transgressions, without once questioning the veracity of her stories, he'd failed both daughters. Rachel most of all.

Jesus had said a man's enemies would be members of his own household, but surely the cycle could yet be broken.

Lord, may redemption be at hand. May You shine Your

light into this darkness and bring healing to both women, bring peace to their family.

Flicking her hair over her shoulder, Rachel began to speak. "I present to you a story as old as time. A sad tale full of sin and ultimate damnation."

The male-dominated crowd went wild again, laughing and calling out promises to take a trip to hell as long as she joined them in the journey.

She stuck out her hip and parked her fist there. "Let this be a warning to you all."

Hannah buried her face in her hands—the safest place for her eyes in Beau's estimation. Unfortunately, she raised her head in time to catch Tyler's entrance.

Always the showman first, actor second, Tyler strolled toward Rachel with confidence and purpose in his steps. His slow, deliberate pace made him look almost predatory while the crafty light in his eyes made Beau bristle.

Whatever Tyler was about to do, it was not going to be proper.

With a bold wink to the audience, Tyler roped an arm around Rachel's waist and drew her slowly—very, very, *very* slowly—into his arms.

He dipped her low. Lower still. Then...

He kissed her. Right on the mouth.

The endearment had nothing to do with love, but possession. Ownership. Beau's gut twisted with a fresh surge of disgust.

"Oh, oh!" Hannah shook her head violently, as though she couldn't believe what she was witnessing.

Unfortunately, Beau wasn't quite so shocked. He'd seen worse in the brothels. He knew sin was rampant in the world, knew evil lurked in every man to some extent. Hence the need for a Savior.

But Beau hadn't expected to see such wickedness displayed so blatantly in a member of his own family. He found himself harboring a strong desire to wrap his fingers around his brother's throat and squeeze.

Humiliated for them all, Beau touched Hannah's arm in a show of sympathy. Even Mavis made a clicking noise with her tongue. And as the kiss turned into two, Logan pretended grave interest in his thumbnail.

Hannah jumped to her feet.

Beau followed suit.

Wild-eyed, she clutched at her throat. In a haphazard fashion, her gaze bounced off the far wall, to the stage and back to the wall again. "I can't watch any more of this."

Beau eased her around to face him. He placed a finger under her chin and pressed gently until her eyes met his. "Hannah, listen to me." He kept his tone low, but he could feel his own temper licking at the edges of his calm. He gulped. "It's all right. We'll wait outside. Together."

Hannah opened her mouth, shut it and then nodded. "Yes, yes. Thank you."

"I'll stay a bit longer, myself." Mavis snorted in dismay. "I ain't so easily shocked as you two. And someone had better find out what those two naughty children are up to."

Beau turned a questioning stare to Logan.

The deputy's expression was as bleak as Beau's mood. "What do you want me to do, Reverend? Just ask."

"Keep an eye on Mavis for me," Beau said. "Take her back to the hotel if we don't reappear shortly."

Neither Mavis nor Logan argued, which would have taken Beau by surprise if he'd been in a more lucid state.

Laying his palm on the small of Hannah's back, he

led her into the empty hallway. Once they were alone, Hannah spun around. Beau reached to her, hoping to give her comfort, but she shrank back and collapsed against the wall.

Gasping for air, she closed her eyes on a shudder.

Beau shifted his body so that he shielded her from the view of any wandering patron. Guilt gnawed at him.

Lord, what have I done? Why did I bring her here? She shouldn't have witnessed that unseemliness.

"Hannah, I'm sorry. I shouldn't have—"

"I knew it was going to be bad," she choked out, wringing her hands together and blinking rapidly. "But I never thought..." She let her words trail off and gazed up at him.

The shock and helplessness in her eyes made him want to wrap her in his arms and protect her from the bad in the world. Even if that corruption was in her own family. And his.

Speechless with frustration, Beau drew in a sharp breath. Heart pounding, head reeling, one powerful thought arose.

There was going to be a reckoning tonight. And Tyler had better come bearing answers.

"It's all my fault," she said through clenched teeth. "All of it."

"Hannah," Beau began, but she cut him off with a finger to his lips.

"No. Let me say this." She dropped her hand. "If I hadn't always accepted the guilt for her transgressions, Rachel wouldn't think she could get away with such... such behavior."

Her words were so close to his earlier thoughts that Beau couldn't deny their veracity. Whether Thomas

Southerland had believed her or not, Hannah had told untruths. She might have been motivated by her promise to her mother. Perhaps guilt had played a role, as well, but in the end she had chosen to claim acts she hadn't committed herself.

That had been wrong.

At least she was here now, in this ugly world where she didn't belong, accepting her share of the responsibility and attempting to break the destructive cycle at last.

He admired her courage, and would support her to the end. At this point, his loyalty belonged to Hannah alone.

Using a gentle touch, he brushed a strand of hair off her forehead. "This is your day, Hannah. You have the opportunity to undo the dangerous pattern once and for all."

"I know." Hannah sighed, then lifted her chin at a determined angle. "That's why I've traveled so far. It ends here. Tonight."

Beau doubted this would end clean and neat, nothing between families was ever that simple—especially when something as complicated as an estrangement was involved.

But Hannah was right about one thing. The end was near.

And once the performance was over, Beau would demand answers from his brother. Tyler's explanations had better be worthy of them all.

Hannah had never wanted to punch another human being. Never. She wasn't prone to violence. But Tyler O'Toole was asking for a fist right in the middle of his nose.

Needing a moment to calm her distress, she let her gaze rest on Beau. He leaned against the wall on the other side of the room. His expression was unreadable, but she could see his tension in the rigid angle of his shoulders and the thin line of his lips. She could tell it cost him to remain silent. But he'd promised to let her handle this initial confrontation. So far, he'd held to that promise.

Hannah had never met a man with that much patience and strength of character. His presence alone brought her the courage to finish having her say.

Rising to her full height, she broke eye contact with Beau and ran her gaze across the jars of face paint to the dirty tissues strewn about the dressing table. The tools of her trade looked ugly in this cold, dank room. Mere items used to create deception, rather than entertainment.

If the saloon-turned-theater had seemed sordid from the box seating, this dressing room was far worse. The furniture was faded and threadbare. The scent of mold, stale cigars and rotting wool cloaked the damp interior.

Hannah couldn't understand why Tyler would choose to perform in such squalor, such filth. Not when he could have top billing at the most prestigious theaters in the world.

And to subject a woman he reportedly loved to this dark existence? Something didn't add up.

"I don't understand why you chose to stay here, when you could have escaped to New York. Or Europe. Or even San Francisco." She tasted the bitterness on her tongue, heard it in her voice and accepted it as her right.

Unwilling to see the seriousness of the situation, Tyler let out a jolly laugh and placed Rachel in the crook of his arm. Side by side, they made a ridiculously beautiful pair. Her dark to his light. And yet, something about the way they stood together was...ugly. Sordid.

Bile rose in Hannah's throat.

"Soon, Hannah darling," Tyler said, completely unaware of her growing dismay. "We will make our move in a few weeks. For now, this is our secret adventure."

Tyler smiled down at Rachel then, the look far too intimate for public viewing. Hannah's stomach rolled over itself, and again she sensed that she was missing something important.

As though hearing her thoughts, Tyler abruptly released Rachel and took Hannah's hands in his. She desperately wanted to pull free of his grip, but she refused to allow him to see her distress. Nevertheless, she found she couldn't look at him, couldn't force her eyes off the lapel of his jacket.

He'd once been a good friend, a surrogate brother of sorts and the son of her most trusted mentor. Their shared history alone had to be worth something. "What am I missing, Tyler? What aren't you telling me?"

"Hannah, darling, don't you understand?" Tyler gave her the kind of smile adults spared unruly children. "We are anonymous here. Free to do whatever we wish. No rules. Just Rachel and me. *Together.*"

Shocked at the lewd implications of his words, Hannah snatched her hands free. Men like Tyler were so predictable. She'd hoped for more from him.

He'd proven less.

"You mean share a room while remaining unwed," she said, then placed her gaze deliberately on Rachel. "How could you do this again? Didn't you learn anything from your disastrous affair with Mr. Beamer?"

There, she'd said it out loud. Perhaps now they could get to the heart of the matter.

Owl-eyed, Rachel's expression turned blank, placid

even. And she completely ignored the question. "Can't you just be happy for me this *one* time?"

Happy? How could Rachel be so indifferent to all the people she was hurting by embarking on this indecent liaison with Tyler? How could she be so selfish?

Hannah opened her mouth to speak, but Tyler spoke over her.

"Happy doesn't begin to describe my feelings when I am with you, my darling," he said, pulling Rachel into an embrace more suitable for a brothel. "Blissful. Ecstatic. Delirious. Those are much better adjectives."

Rachel touched his cheek, ran her finger along his jaw.

Tyler kissed her on the nose.

Hannah averted her eyes.

Their bold, public intimacy was disconcerting, something that shouldn't be shared with anyone but each other.

With a loud hiss, Beau pushed abruptly from the wall. "Tyler! Enough. You can't—"

"No." Hannah stopped Beau's approach with a hard shake of her head. "Let me finish this. Please. You'll get your turn. For now, this is still *my* fight."

His face constricted with barely controlled emotion. And with that hard look in his eyes, Hannah expected him to deny her request, but he gave her one sharp nod and stepped back.

"Rachel," she said through her teeth. "You *cannot* share a room with a man you aren't married to. It's a sin."

Rachel snuggled up against Tyler and rolled her eyes to heaven. "You are such a prude, Hannah. Father never did understand how different we are, and that he had us mixed up from the start."

And here it was. The moment of truth. The reason Hannah had traveled all these miles. She struggled to hold on to her temper, but angry heat flushed into her cheeks. "Father never knew because *you* never told him."

Rachel cast a dark look in her direction. "Did you?"

Hannah staggered back as if slapped. "I... You..."

"Did you?" Rachel said.

"No," Hannah whispered, her heart dipping in her chest at the ugly realization of her own guilt.

Oh, Lord, forgive me. Forgive me. *All this time, all these years, I've blamed Rachel for not speaking up. And resented her for it. But I never spoke up, either.*

"No," she repeated. "I didn't say a word."

"Then mind your own business now."

Hannah's heart beat wildly at the prospect of her impending defeat. She'd traveled all this way, and once again a man was proving more important to Rachel than her own sister. "You can't hide like this forever."

"I know that," Rachel snapped.

"Good. Because I'm performing the marriage ceremony," Beau said, pushing from the wall. "This very night." His words were clipped, controlled and very, very angry.

Shocked at his forcefulness, Hannah swung around to stare at him. She drew slightly back at the intensity of emotion on his face. She'd never seen him that implacable, that righteously disgusted. And yet, his unbridled anger made him seem more vulnerable to her. Even as his eyes blazed with resolve, she knew he was ashamed and hurting.

Hannah understood his pain. Tyler had wounded him as only one sibling could hurt another. Deep at the core.

Clearing his expression, Beau stepped between Tyler and Rachel, sufficiently separating them with a hard shove at Tyler's chest.

Tyler stumbled back, caught his balance and then took a menacing step forward.

"Stop right there." Beau squared his shoulders. "Neither of you will leave this room until you are wed."

"Is that so, *brother?*" Tyler spat, the first chink in his perfectly polished armor sounding in the sour tone of his voice.

"It will be done," Beau reiterated.

The two men stared into each other's eyes. The anger between them was palpable. Hannah feared they would come to blows any moment. With each beat of her heart, the standoff turned more intense, more angry and bitter, becoming a ruthless clash between brothers as old as Cain and Abel.

Eventually, Tyler lowered his head and sighed in defeat. "As you wish."

Beau placed his hand on Tyler's arm. "It's the right thing to do."

"I know."

Recovering quickly, Tyler placed a careless grin on his lips. With a challenge in his eyes, he held Beau's stare as he tugged Rachel into his arms once again.

"Rachel Southerland, will you marry me?" he asked, still glaring at Beau as he spoke. Eventually, he dropped his gaze to Rachel and cocked his head at a jaunty angle. "Will you be my wife, in name now as well as in deed? Will you——"

Beau cleared his throat, cutting off the rest of whatever improper request Tyler had been about to ask of her.

Hannah whispered a silent prayer of thanks that at least one O'Toole sibling was a gentleman.

Giggling, Rachel trailed a finger down Tyler's cheek. "I suppose it wouldn't hurt to make it official."

Hannah gasped. The realization of what marriage between the two would mean was finally sinking in. "Wait. What about Will? What about Father?"

Rachel flicked a speck of dust off Tyler's shoulder. "What about them?"

"You must tell them of your marriage to Tyler. They deserve to hear it from you."

"Me? No." She slid Hannah a bitter glare from under her lashes. "You tell them. Save the day like always. It's what you live for."

At Rachel's feral glance, Hannah's lips parted in shock. She'd never seen such revulsion in her sister's eyes before. "You must tell them yourself," Hannah insisted, but her voice shook at the realization she was losing the fight.

In response, Rachel twisted on her heels, lifted her chin in the air and turned her deaf ear toward Hannah.

With that one gesture the battle was complete.

Rachel had made up her mind. There would be no reasoning with her now. She had literally shut Hannah out.

Hannah shouldn't have been surprised. She shouldn't feel this devastating sense of defeat, this...*hurt*.

This was their pattern, after all. She had been naive to think anything would change between Rachel and her.

Hannah slowly set her hands on Rachel's shoulders and turned her sister to face her directly. "Write one letter to Father and another to your fiancé. I'll deliver them personally," she said with little expression in her voice. She turned to Beau. "It's the only way now."

He gave her an understanding nod.

Perhaps this had been part of God's plan for Hannah all along. *Thou shalt not bear false witness against thy neighbor.*

Hannah had lied all her life. But now she would make restitution. She would confess her sin to the one person she'd offended most. Her father.

"You won't face Reverend Southerland alone," Beau declared, closing his hand over hers in perfect understanding of the situation. "I won't allow it."

Even in her devastated state, Hannah felt a smile tug at her lips. For once, this man's arrogance brought her comfort. And a unique sense of safety. Beauregard O'Toole was a good man. By accepting his generous offer, she would make her own bold statement. Would he understand?

"I would consider myself fortunate, fortunate indeed, to have you stand by my side," she said.

Rachel snorted, ruining the moment. "Hannah? You? Traveling alone with a man? I'm shocked."

Hannah's entire body wanted to tremble again, but she would not give in to her anger now. "*I* have a chaperone."

Rachel rolled her gaze to the ceiling, looking as though Hannah's sense of propriety was anything but. "Of course you do."

Beau touched her arm. Needing his strength, she turned to him. His eyes crinkled at the edges, and he gave her hand an encouraging squeeze. "It'll be over soon. I promise."

Perhaps this wasn't the ending Hannah had hoped for when she'd set out in search of Rachel and Tyler. But a sense of peace filled her at the prospect of her imminent confession.

This was the right course of action. The web of lies would be broken at last.

Chapter Sixteen

An hour later, Beau completed the marriage ceremony with very little pomp. "I now pronounce you husband and wife."

He didn't bother telling Tyler to kiss the bride. The two had certainly done enough of that prior to the exchange of vows. Regardless of how uncomfortable it made Hannah or Beau—or anyone else, for that matter.

In truth, Beau had never met two more selfish people in his life. He didn't think either was inherently evil, just unaware of the pain they were causing others as they pursued their own ends. They were like children, entitled children who hadn't been told "no" enough. Or, rather, hadn't suffered the consequences of "no" enough.

Watching them now, with their heads bent toward one another, Beau didn't doubt they would be happy together—their love was easy enough to see—but now others would be hurt.

Hannah most of all.

Beau glanced over at her. She stood rigid, her shoulders stiff. She looked more fragile than the first time they'd met, more wounded. His heart weighed heavy in his chest because he knew there was nothing he could do for her now. Informing the venerable Thomas Southerland that his favorite daughter had run off and married an actor would not be an easy task.

Beau gulped back his rising concern, but only succeeded in wedging the lump of dread deeper in his chest. He walked over to Hannah and asked, "How are you faring?"

She lifted a shoulder, sighed. Her eyes held all the pain he knew she must be feeling. He'd seen the look of betrayal often enough to realize he was staring at it now.

That enigmatic blend of melancholy and defeat mocked him. He was a minister with no tools to erase her sorrow. He had a fierce, primitive need to rush her out of the room and fight off anyone who so much as looked at her oddly.

"What will I tell him?" she asked in a shaky breath. "And Will. Oh, poor Will."

Beau took her hand and threaded her fingers through his. He remembered her advice back at Charity House when he'd worried in a similar manner over Megan. "The Holy Spirit will give you the right words at the right time."

She turned large, round eyes toward him. Clearly, his words hadn't settled her nerves. Well, there was one worry he could remove. "I promise you this, Hannah, you aren't alone anymore. I will share this burden with you."

He knew he was pledging more than a solid presence during a hard conversation. By standing with her, by confronting Reverend Southerland, he would be jeopardizing his future with the Rocky Mountain Association. And yet, he didn't care as much as he should.

Hannah needed him. That was all that mattered at the moment.

There would be time to sort through what that meant to his future and his future ministry. He had to trust that God would provide, as the Heavenly Father always did.

"Oh, Beau." Tears wiggled along her eyelashes. She looked both relieved and bemused by his declaration. "Are you certain?"

His answer came without hesitation. "Yes."

"What if my father—"

"It doesn't matter." And he meant his words.

The risk to his future *didn't* matter anymore. He'd done the right thing by marrying Tyler and Rachel. Even if Reverend Southerland considered Beau the most culpable party for having officiated at the ceremony.

He had no regrets. "Hannah, fear not, we're in this together now."

She smiled then. And, oh, what a smile. It was the one that grabbed at his heart and twisted.

"You aren't going to relent on this, are you?" she asked.

"I treated you abominably the first time we met." He lifted her hand to his lips, forced himself not to linger. "Think of this as my way of saying I'm sorry."

"You don't owe me—"

"Yes, I do." He dropped her hand. "I cannot be swayed in my decision. You are stuck with me now."

Her smile turned watery, and Beau's heart dipped in his chest. He would have said more, but Hannah's twin shoved him out of the way with a nudge of her hip.

Eyes gleaming with female satisfaction, Rachel kissed Hannah on the cheek. "Be happy for me."

Hannah blinked, a contradictory look of pain and hope

flashing in her gaze. Beau understood the conflicting emotions all too well. As angry as he felt toward Tyler, the man was still his brother.

Of course, that didn't mean he wouldn't confront him. Alone. Now was as good a time as any. Before leaving the two to their conversation, Beau whispered in Hannah's ear that he would be close by.

She offered him a sweet smile and then turned her attention back to her sister. Beau motioned to Tyler to meet him on the other side of the room.

Tyler joined him and boomed out a laugh. "I'd say we're both fortunate in our choice of women. What say you, brother?"

Beau stiffened, fearing where this conversation was leading. He would not allow Tyler to sully his feelings for Hannah. They were private and pure and not up for discussion with his brother. "Say nothing more, Tyler."

Unaware of Beau's growing frustration, Tyler slapped him on the back. "There's something about those Southerland women, eh?"

Beau tensed like a tightened coil. "Don't."

"Perfect matches. Rachel and me." Tyler wiggled his eyebrows. "You and Hannah."

Tyler often surprised Beau with his perception. But there were times—times such as this one—when his brother used his unexpected insight to rile Beau. Beau, however, would not give him the satisfaction of taking the bait. And he certainly wouldn't discuss his feelings for Hannah with a man who had no sense of decency when it came to relations between men and women. "What you did was wrong, Tyler. Fornication is a sin. Worse, Rachel was engaged."

"Please, Beau." He blew out an exasperated breath. "If she wasn't married, she was fair game."

Shocked at his brother's callousness, Beau stared at Tyler with new eyes. Throughout their childhood, things had come easy for Tyler. His charm had been present from the start. And he'd learned to use the O'Toole good looks to full advantage. Never had Tyler been reined in. Well, certainly not enough. The youngest of five siblings, he'd been doted on by everyone. Beau included.

Was this egocentricity and self-centeredness the by-product of that indulgence?

"Tyler, this time what you've done has hurt people." Beau looked at Hannah and took note of her tenuous expression as she spoke softly with her sister. His heart ached for her.

As always, Tyler homed in on the wrong portion of Beau's argument. "*This* time? Are you saying I'm irresponsible by nature?"

"Yes, I am." Beau raised his hands to ward off Tyler's arguments. "Don't misunderstand. I love you. I always will. But life has been too easy for you."

Tyler narrowed his eyes to tiny slits. "And you hold it against me, is that it?"

"No."

Tyler continued to study him. "Yes, you do." He snorted. "But you're wrong."

Beau lifted his eyebrows but didn't respond. Tyler was being sarcastic, at any rate. It was part of his makeup, as much a part of him as the practiced smile and theatrical gestures.

"I wasn't born with natural acting talent like you, Beau. I've spent my life honing and practicing. While you—" Tyler pointed an accusing finger at him "—were born with the most natural talent of us all. Did you choose to pursue it? No. You went into the ministry."

Tyler's expression was a perfect mask of outrage, but there was a great deal more going on behind those eyes. Mostly resentment. And jealousy.

Beau held the odd stare for a long moment. "I chose to follow God's calling for my life," he said with conviction. "How is that wrong?"

"It's not, but you hold your family's profession against us every time you fail."

Beau had no intention of leaving that foul statement alone. "Now there you *are* wrong."

"Am I?" Tyler crossed his arms over his chest and gave Beau a haughty look. "What about when you got kicked out of the church in Laramie? *You* said it was because of us, because of the scandalous nature of your family's profession. Scotts Bluff, the same excuse. Kearney, again, the same. You were chased out of those churches, *according to you,* because of your family."

An ache squeezed around Beau's heart. "It's true."

"No."

Beau's head snapped up at the hostility in that one word.

Tyler leaned closer until his nose was an inch from touching Beau's. His pale green eyes were hard and unrelenting. "You were run out of those churches because of you. Not me, or our parents, or our family. You!"

A fleeting shadow of uneasiness passed through Beau, only to be replaced by white-hot fury. "You weren't there," he said. "You don't know."

"I know you." Tyler growled, and a flush came over his face. "Take a good look into your own heart, Beauregard. Take a look at that dream of yours to have a traditional church and see where it comes from."

Beau looked into Tyler's face and knew the man's pride was hurt. That explained the attack. Didn't it? "Tyler, I—"

"You're the selfish one here. Not me. I've never pretended to be anything other than what I am, a hardworking actor who loves the stage and all the trappings that come from my success. You, on the other hand, have never been honest with yourself."

Beau clenched his hand into a tight fist. A muscle jerked in his jaw. He tried to hide his anger behind a wall of superiority. "This isn't about me. And you know it. You are the one who ran off with a woman already engaged, the daughter of the one man who could take away everything I've worked for."

"Aha!" Tyler snapped his fingers and smirked. "I knew it."

Beau glared at him.

"You're worried about losing your new church." The sound that came from Tyler's throat was a growl of distaste. "Where's your faith, Beau? Maybe you should listen to God for a change, instead of telling Him to bless your own plan for your future."

Beau's sense of outrage swelled. "Now you're a pastor, too? You stand there and tell me how hard you've worked. Well, so have I. I want this church in Greeley. It's a traditional church with a stable lifestyle attached."

"And then you'll get a boring, staid, unassuming wife who will bear you perfectly behaved children." Tyler sneered.

"What's wrong with wanting those things?" Beau

asked. "What's wrong with not wanting to travel across continents, with wanting to live a settled life?"

His anger clearly spent, Tyler leaned against the nearby wall and gave Beau a pitying look. "Nothing is wrong with that. Nothing at all. In truth, it's a good goal, maybe even a noble one. But you're missing who *you* are in the scenario. You're a rebel, Beau."

"I am a man of God."

Tyler's lips twisted in sympathy. "Can I give you some advice?"

It was Beau's turn to sneer. "Can I stop you?"

"You'll die a slow death in that little church in the meadow, the one you seem to think you want."

Sweat broke out on Beau's skin. Panic crawled up his spine. "You're wrong."

"Beau. There are people who need you, just as you are, in all of your unconventional, eat-with-sinners glory."

"You don't know me or what I want," Beau said in frustrated anger.

"Ah, but you see, my dear brother, the problem isn't whether I know you. It's whether you know yourself."

Beau felt the blood draining from his face. He opened his mouth to speak, but Tyler slapped him on the back and dislodged the breath right out of him. "But I digress. Are we going to continue arguing, or are you going to congratulate me on my good fortune?"

Beau swallowed back a load of arguments and forced a smile onto his lips. Tyler was wrong. He was wrong about everything. His brother would never truly understand him, as *he* would probably never understand Tyler.

There was no reason to argue any further. "If you are as happy as you seem——"

"I am."

"Then congratulations. May you have a satisfying marriage filled with few regrets and many healthy years together."

Tyler laughed. "Count on it, because, dear brother, I plan to work harder at this than I have at anything else in my life."

Beau sighed. *Lord, may that be true.* "Then I give you my blessing."

Just by looking at Beau's intense expression, Hannah caught the seriousness of the brothers' conversation. Whatever they were discussing, she doubted it included joyful tidings.

She completely understood. Rachel hadn't stopped extolling Tyler's many virtues since she'd nudged Beau aside.

Hannah had quit paying attention some time ago.

Turning back to Rachel, she decided to stop pretending to listen and got straight to the point. "What were you thinking?" she demanded.

"What?" Rachel stopped in midsentence. "When?"

"You weren't going to let Will or Father know of your change of heart, were you?"

Rachel crossed her arms over her chest in a defensive, angry gesture. "They'd have figured it out when I didn't come home."

Hannah sighed at the antagonism in her sister's voice. "When did you get so callous, Rachel?"

"Isn't it a burden always making the right decisions?"

"Don't be snide. It's beneath us both."

Rachel snorted in disgust. "What do you know? All my life I've never had the chance of doing the right thing."

"Nobody told you to lie or cheat or have an affair with a married man," Hannah said, refusing to allow her sister to throw the full blame at her feet. "And when the deeds were found out, you never accepted the blame."

"You never gave me a chance. You always had to step into my business."

Hannah's teeth clenched. Her heart filled with frustration and regret. There was probably pity and disdain there, as well, but she chose not to sort through the rest.

It seemed unnatural for Rachel to blame Hannah like this, unreal even. Except it was real. It was very real. At least to Rachel.

Out of fairness to her sister, Hannah forced her mind to the past and thought over all the incidents and many transgressions throughout the years.

No, Hannah's memory was clear. Rachel had willingly committed the acts in the first place. When caught, she hadn't stepped forward. Not once.

Did you give her the chance?

Hannah didn't know for certain. However, there was one incident that ran firm in her mind, the one time when Rachel hadn't tried to step forward. The night of Hannah's banishment.

"Even if what you say is true, what about your affair with Mr. Beamer? That night, I waited for you to come forward. You never did."

"I know." Rachel's face contorted with annoyance but not remorse. "I miscalculated that one. I never thought Father would disown you. And once he had, I knew he wouldn't believe the truth."

Hannah stared at her sister. "How could he? By pretending to be me throughout the affair, you made it impossible for *anyone* to believe the truth. That was very badly done of you, Rachel."

"Perhaps." And yet, *still,* she didn't ask for forgiveness.

"Why didn't you at least warn me?" Hannah asked.

"Because I thought you would take it badly, or worse, lecture me." She blessed her with an ironic smile. "Good thing I was wrong."

Hannah ignored the sarcasm. "You could have confessed all this in Chicago."

"I met Tyler," Rachel said, as though that explained her lapse. As though finding her one true love erased her from any further blame.

Hannah stared at her in disbelief. Surely, she didn't think resolution came that easily. "Rachel—"

"Don't look at me like that, with that self-righteous snarl on your face. You played your own role, Hannah. If you hadn't set the precedents, I wouldn't have pulled it off."

"Maybe." All right. Yes. Hannah *had* played her role. She couldn't pretend otherwise. Regardless of the fact that Rachel had taken advantage of the situation, Hannah owed her sister an apology. "I'm sorry."

Rachel said nothing.

And in that moment, Hannah finally saw the truth for what it was. Rachel would never ask for forgiveness. Hannah could either love her as she was, flaws and all, or carry the burden of her own bitterness in her heart forever.

Hannah chose freedom.

She chose to give forgiveness where forgiveness wasn't earned. As her Lord and Savior had done for her.

It wasn't easy, and she would probably lapse, but

wasn't that the point? Wasn't the path Christ asked His followers to walk a narrow one?

Lord, please fill me with Your forgiveness. I can't do it on my own power. It's too big for me.

"It's over, Rachel. I hold no ill will toward you." She wanted to mean her words. Perhaps one day she would. "I pray you and Tyler have a lifetime of happiness together."

Relief washed across Rachel's face, and she yanked Hannah into a hard, bone-rattling embrace. "Thank you, Hannah. Thank you."

Hannah knew it was as close to an apology as she would get from her sister. It was enough. It had to be enough.

Beau and Tyler joined them just as Hannah pulled out of the hug.

Ever the gentleman, Beau took Rachel's hand and kissed the knuckles with a theatrical O'Toole flair that had amusement beaming in Tyler's eyes.

"Be happy, my new sister," Beau said to Rachel.

"I already am," Rachel said.

Tyler bent at the waist before Hannah. "Thank you, my good friend, for bringing the love of my life to me."

At the genuine note of joy on Tyler's face, Hannah's heart softened toward the rogue. "It's the least I could do. After all, you taught me the finer points of my craft when I knew nothing."

He wrapped her hands in his and squeezed. "You deserve the best in life. And I think you know what I mean."

He slid a sly glance in his brother's direction, but, thankfully, Beau wasn't looking at him. He was looking at Hannah. Looking at her with his pastor face on, steady and unwavering, unrelenting strength in the set of his jaw.

Her heart thumped one strong, powerful knock against

her ribs. The truth had been there from the start. God's hand in the process all along. All this time she'd thought this journey had been about her past. She'd been wrong.

Beauregard O'Toole was the man of her dreams. The man of her heart. The man of her future. He just didn't know it yet. But with God's help, and a little nudge from Hannah, he would.

Tyler lowered his voice to a stage whisper. "Don't let him blow it. He's just foolish enough to ruin it for you both."

"Don't worry, Tyler. I have a plan."

Well, not precisely. But Hannah had every intention of making sure Beau came around very soon. Very soon indeed.

Chapter Seventeen

The next morning, the sun shone brighter, the sky blazed bluer. Hannah's mood, however, failed to navigate the atmosphere quite so well. Unable to calm her sporadic thoughts, she'd spent a sleepless night sorting through all the mistakes she'd made with Rachel over the years.

By dawn, she'd been completely worn out. Thus, it was with leaden feet that she followed the others to the local church for Sunday meeting. Wanting to file away every detail in her mind of the town where her life had taken a dramatic turn, she scanned the streets and buildings. But she found her eyes focusing on the townspeople instead.

They seemed as unfriendly as she herself felt. They stared. Unashamedly. Their eyes filled with open curiosity tempered with…disdain?

Hannah shook the ugly thought aside and continued watching them watch her.

Their strange attitudes notwithstanding, what struck Hannah as most odd was their homogeneous nature. The men were dressed identically in clean black suits of understated fashion. The woman wore nondescript dresses in pale, lifeless colors, buttoned tightly to their necks. Their bonnets were tied snugly around their chins.

On the surface, they were typical churchgoers. Yet there was something different about them, a definite note of scorn in their stares that put Hannah on edge.

Surely she was seeing disdain where there wasn't any. She was simply feeling vulnerable after her encounter with Rachel and Tyler from the night before. Yes, that must be it.

Then again…

She took a quick survey of her companions. They certainly stood out. Hannah was considerably overdressed in her favorite blue silk dress. While Mavis was underdressed in her men's pants worn under a homemade dress. *Burlap,* no less.

And then there were the two men. Logan wore a suit identical to most of the men in the city, but his cowboy hat, tin star and pair of six-shooters set him apart. Beau, smooth, slick and neat in his brown suit and gold brocade vest, could pass for a man of distinction in any large city.

Hannah couldn't help but notice how he caught the eye of every woman that passed by.

Most probably focused on his physical beauty. Hannah, however, saw his reliability. His strength of character. And his… All right, yes, his outward appeal, as well.

Just looking at him now, her throat went dry, turning her speechless. Following the others a full step behind, she silently mulled over how she would approach her father after all these years.

As much as she wanted to blame Rachel for putting her in such an unpleasant predicament, Hannah also knew it was long past time she confronted Thomas Southerland with the truth.

The truth shall set you free…

Yes, in truth there was power. The power of Christ.

Shooting a quick glance over his shoulder, Beau slowed his pace until he came alongside her.

Logan took the lead without question.

Beau didn't speak right away, and so they walked in companionable silence side by side for several minutes.

A cloud crossed over the sun, deadening the light at the precise moment he broke the hush between them. "I have something to tell you before we get to the church."

At his serious tone, her heart stumbled. "You do?"

As they drew closer to the church, people nodded at Beau. He smiled and nodded back. A few times he responded with a personal greeting.

Waiting until they were alone again, Hannah asked, "Did you give a sermon here before? Is that what you wanted to tell me?"

Beau stopped walking.

She stopped, as well.

A grimness passed over his features. For the first time in their acquaintance, Beauregard O'Toole looked unsure of himself. "You could say that."

There was an odd note to his voice, and an apology in his eyes. Hannah had to work hard to keep her throat from slamming shut. "You don't have to join us this morning," she offered. "If you—"

"I wouldn't miss this opportunity to worship. But I wanted you to know there might be a woman here, a woman from my past."

She concentrated on his voice, on his words, anything but the implication of what his declaration meant.

"I asked her to marry me."

Hannah's heart took a tumble at the news.

"She said no."

The muscles in Hannah's stomach quivered out of control. Oh, but she was glad. Glad, glad, glad the woman had turned him down. But her joy came from purely selfish reasons. So she made herself respond, made herself speak with sincerity. "I'm sorry, Beau."

He cast a look to the darkening sky, frowned, then gave a short laugh. "I'm not."

Although his tone was mild, he held his shoulders tense and unmoving. No matter what he claimed, the woman's rejection had hurt him.

"I just wanted you to know," he said, lowering his gaze back to hers.

"Why?" she asked. "Why are you telling me this now?"

He planted considerable O'Toole charm in his expression. "Because I wanted you to know about my past. All of it."

He kept his eyes on hers as he spoke—*directly* on hers. And then his gaze filled with a quiet intensity that sent a promise of the future dancing along her skin.

"I don't want any secrets between us," he said.

She laid her hand on his arm. "Thank you for telling me."

Before she could comment any further, Logan stopped short of joining the queue entering the church and stepped slightly back from the crowd.

"Are you two joining us?" he called out.

"Of course." Beau took Hannah's arm and steered her forward.

"Please, go ahead Miss Southerland," Logan said. "You too, Miss Tierney." He offered a smile that encompassed both women.

Mavis hesitated.

Logan held his smile.

Mavis cocked her head at him.

"Ma'am." He winked at her, and then removed his hat. "Ladies first."

At last, she smiled. Sort of. Perhaps it was a baring of teeth; one could never be sure with Mavis.

Before climbing the steps, Hannah slid a final glance toward Beau. His face was a cool mask of indifference, but she could feel that he was wound tighter than before. Wondering at the cause, she followed his gaze to the top of the stairs.

At the threshold of the church stood a young man and woman greeting each person as they walked in.

Looking respectable, yet somehow hard, the man wore a black suit, black tie and crisp, white shirt. His dark hair was cut meticulously close to his head. And his eyes held a severe, hawklike expression.

Hannah ignored the little flutter of uneasiness in her stomach and turned her attention to the woman standing next to the serious man in black.

She looked irritable, and not at all welcoming. Her dark blond hair was pulled into a tight bun, and her face held a pinched expression. She was thin, also perfectly groomed, and yet the most uninviting woman Hannah had ever seen.

They couldn't be the pastor and his wife. And yet, who else would they be?

The young woman's gaze widened as she caught sight of Beau. Her eyes held just a hint of joy at the sight of him but then just as quickly flashed with anger before becoming a blank slate.

Taking an audible breath of air, Beau moved in front of Logan and led their group up the steps himself.

"Why, Reverend O'Toole, we didn't expect you to grace our humble little church with your presence again so soon." The woman's voice came out colder than Hannah would have expected of someone standing outside a church.

Nonetheless, Beau smiled at her. "Amelia, you are looking well."

Amelia fiddled with one of the buttons at the neck of her dress.

Was this the woman Beau had once wanted to marry? The woman who had turned him down?

Beau shifted to look at the stern-looking gentleman and offered his hand. "Jim, that is, Reverend Smith, I understand congratulations are in order."

"Amelia and I were married two months ago." There was a flash of derision in Reverend Smith's eyes as he pumped Beau's hand. Behind the contempt was a challenge, as if he were saying, *Ha, the better man won after all.*

"I bet you could build a mighty large snowman in that bedroom," Mavis whispered through her teeth.

Hannah shushed her.

Taking notice, Amelia's gaze shifted to Hannah. Her eyes turned flat and her nose went up. "And who is this?" she asked.

Beau boldly took Hannah's hand and gently drew her forward to join him. "This is Miss Hannah Southerland. She is a dear friend of my family's." Still holding her hand, he gave Hannah a smile that spread warmth all the way through her. "And of mine."

Amelia didn't seem impressed. In fact, her eyes bulged and then narrowed. "A family friend, you say?"

"Yes," Beau said, with a flick of iron in his tone. "She tours with the same acting company as my brother."

"I see."

Hannah had a strong urge to slap the smirk off Amelia's face. But she held back. She had experienced this sort of petty reaction before, especially once her profession was revealed. She wasn't here to start an argument. And after the turmoil of the past week, she just wanted to forget about herself and focus on praising the Lord.

Obviously finished with Hannah, Amelia's eyes searched the rest of their group. The moment her gaze landed on Mavis, she gasped, blinked hard and then whispered to her husband in a furious manner.

Hannah's heart dropped to her toes when she heard the words "prostitute" and "how dare he bring that person here."

Mouth thin, Reverend Smith stuck out his chest. "Reverend O'Toole," he said in a haughty tone that carried halfway down the block. "You cannot bring that woman in here." He pointed directly at Mavis.

Hannah tugged her hand free of Beau's and rushed to Mavis, shifting her slightly behind her. "Mavis is a remarkable woman and I'm honored to call her friend," she said.

Amelia lifted her chin higher still. "I know for a fact that *woman* worked in the brothel at Laramie. I did charity work there once. One doesn't forget a woman like that."

Reverend Smith clicked his tongue in disapproval. "That makes her a—"

"Don't say another word, Jim," Beau warned. There

was a quick flash of rage on his face, and almost as quickly it was banked.

His control was impressive.

Just then, a bell tolled the top of the hour. People continued to rush past them as they made their way inside the building. Most looked at their unhappy little group, but none stopped to speak to them.

"Service is starting. We must get inside, Amelia," Reverend Smith said, pivoting on his heel.

Amelia followed suit.

"Not so fast," Beau said. "You would deny us access into the Lord's house on a mere impression from years ago?"

Reverend Smith spun back around. His unsmiling face looked harsh under the bright morning sun. "That woman is a sinner, O'Toole. And thus is not welcome in my church."

"*Your* church? Jesus came to call sinners into His church, Jim, not the righteous," Beau said, his eyes hard. Clearly, he wasn't bothering to hide his anger from them now.

Reverend Smith's gaze was just as unrelenting. "You know we have a covenant. Sinners who have failed to repent publicly are not allowed inside our church. It's how we protect our congregation from evil."

Hannah actually saw the pulse jump in Beau's throat. "How do you know she hasn't repented?" he asked.

"I…*know.*"

"You can see into another's heart?" Beau asked, stepping in front of both Mavis and Hannah and easing them behind him. "And here I thought only God could do that."

Amelia snorted. "We all know what she is. Just look at her. It's obvious she's a harlot."

Beau lowered his voice to a dangerous whisper. "She is a child of God."

Hannah had never seen Beau so angry. She reached out and touched his forearm. "I think it's time we left."

Beau's gaze still burned, but he covered her hand with his and leaned slightly toward her.

Wide-eyed, Amelia blinked at Hannah's hand on Beau's arm, clearly shocked at the public intimacy.

Hannah quickly dropped her hand. The woman could easily spew poison over the innocent gesture. Beau deserved better. "I don't much care for your brand of Christianity," Hannah blurted out.

"Nor I," Beau agreed.

Amelia gurgled in indignation.

"You cannot bring that woman in my church," the pastor boomed. His face a study in scorn.

At the unconcealed insult, Logan joined in Mavis's defense. "I don't care if you are a minister. Nobody talks to Miss Tierney like that. *Nobody.*"

He pushed all three of their party aside and stood toe-to-toe with the pastor, prepared to do bodily harm to the man.

Beau nudged Logan back. "Let me handle this, Deputy." He looked at Hannah. "Take Mavis back to the hotel. I'll rejoin you in the lobby and escort you to the depot before our train leaves."

Nodding, Hannah pulled gently on Mavis's arm. Mavis turned to look at her then. Devastation wavered in the other woman's eyes.

Hannah blinked back tears of her own. "Let's go, sweetie," she said.

Mavis shook her head. "We leave together." She

twined her other arm with Logan's. "Isn't that right, boy?"

"That's right, Miss Tierney."

"You may call me old woman, if you like."

Logan leaned over and kissed Mavis on the cheek. "I'd be honored."

Amelia snorted at the show of affection between the two.

Beau's eyes narrowed coldly. "I don't know how you both got so hard of heart. You've read the same Bible as I have. If we are to follow Christ's example, that means we should bring up a person's past only so that we may point to the future with love, not condemnation."

Tossing his shoulders back, Reverend Smith glared. "You dare lecture me?"

Beau sighed, and although his eyes still blazed with anger he lowered his voice. "You're right. It's not my place." He turned on his heel and looked at the rest of their group. "Let's go."

Hannah, still linked with Mavis, waited for Beau to pass them and then lead their group down the street. He walked at a clipped, angry pace. Compelled, she released Mavis's arm and trotted to catch up with him.

"I only have one thing to say to you," she said.

He looked at her. Fury, anger and sadness shimmered in his gaze. She had a sudden urge to hug away his pain.

Instead, she said, "Amelia didn't deserve you."

His expression didn't change, but his eyes softened with an emotion she couldn't quite define. "Thank you," he said.

And with those two simple words, her future turned a little clearer.

* * *

Beau wasn't a man who liked being wrong. It went against his nature. Yet, he had been wrong on so many points.

Tyler, of all people, had been right.

For years, Beau had thought he'd wanted what Jim and Amelia had. But he'd forgotten about the Rocky Mountain Association's required covenant for all its member churches. The covenant stated that known sinners were not allowed inside the building without having publicly confessed their sins in front of the congregation the week before.

Although the covenant was designed to prevent its members from living in unapologetic sin, it also made it impossible for a pastor to shepherd those in his flock still questioning their salvation. Certainly, none of the people Beau had ministered to in the last five years would be allowed to enter his church in Greeley.

He would not be allowed to minister to women like Jane Goodwin on their deathbed, for fear their sin would rub off on others. There were so many other restrictions, as well.

Too many.

Tyler had claimed that Beau would die a slow death in a church like Jim's.

Tyler had been spot-on with his assessment.

But Beau didn't want to keep traveling forever. There had to be a way to reconcile his dream of a stable church home with his unique calling to the lost.

There is, Beau. Look deeper in your heart. The answer is there.

Still confused, Beau shook his head. He knew God guided his life. Nothing happened to him by chance. Perhaps this upcoming journey to Reverend Southerland's home would reveal the answers he sought. Perhaps this bump in the road had been part of God's plan all along. Perhaps Beau needed to listen to God more, and talk less.

On more matters than starting his own church.

As he sat on a bench outside the train station, Beau watched Hannah's gentle treatment of Mavis. The older woman was still sad and hurt over Amelia's abominable treatment of her. No wonder. Amelia had claimed to see inside Mavis's heart.

Beau had done the same with Hannah.

The dangerous combination of impulse, pride and temper had colored his initial judgment of her. He was no better than the very people he criticized.

"Don't let that nasty young woman get to you," Hannah said, her soft voice cutting across his thoughts. "She was *wrong* to say those things about you."

"She spoke the truth." Mavis's eyes filled with tears of shame. The kind of shame the enemy used to keep God's children separated from Him. "I am a former prostitute with sins a mile long that can never be taken back."

Beau moved closer, prepared to boldly speak of God's love, but Hannah continued. "No, Mavis. Your sins are in the past. You're a godly woman now."

A lone tear rolled down Mavis's cheek.

Hannah gripped one of the older woman's hands.

"What I did is the worst sin of them all," Mavis said.

Beau had heard a similar argument from Jane. No longer able to keep silent, he said, "There's no hierarchy of sin in God's eyes. Sin is sin. But God can *and* does forgive all. You just have to ask for His forgiveness."

Beau took Mavis's other hand and nodded for Hannah to continue.

She gave him a grateful smile. "You are a beautiful, kindhearted woman, my friend. The children of Charity House love you. And we all know children are excellent judges of character."

Mavis gave them both a watery smile. "Don't forget small animals. I have a way with them small animals, too."

Hannah laughed. "There you go."

"You're a good girl, Hannah Southerland."

"Yes," Beau agreed. "Yes, she is."

He shared a look with Hannah before he released Mavis's hand and the two women hugged. He couldn't believe he'd once considered Amelia his ideal image of a wife, while he'd considered this beautiful, softhearted actress inappropriate in all ways.

Forgive me, Lord.

Boot heels clicked in rapid succession along the platform. "Sorry I'm late. I got detained at the jail." Logan deposited the last of the luggage on the platform. "I've received an urgent telegraph from Marshal Scott. I have to pick up a prisoner in Laramie and escort him back to Denver for trial. I've already hired a horse for my journey."

The way Logan refused to make eye contact with him alerted Beau that trouble brewed.

Taking Logan by the arm, he led the young deputy out of earshot of the women. "Did you truly get a telegraph from Marshal Scott?"

Clearly offended, Logan glared at him. But instead of responding, he yanked a piece of paper from the inner pocket of his jacket and shoved it under Beau's nose.

"That's not what I meant." Beau lowered the man's hand by applying pressure to his wrist. "Are you using this as an excuse to go back to that church and defend Mavis before you head out of town?"

Logan made a noncommittal grunt that could have meant either yes or no.

Beau pressed for an answer. "I want a firm response out of you."

Logan's gaze darted all around, bounced off Mavis then back to the platform. "Maybe."

"Don't do it, Logan. Violence won't solve anything."

"It couldn't hurt to try."

Beau blew out a slow breath. "You know that's not true. You're not thinking rationally. Now, give me your word you won't do something stupid. Stupid, as in defending Mavis's honor with a fist to Reverend Smith's face."

"And here I thought that oily pastor needed a little rearranging of those pretty, girlish features."

"I'm picking up the sarcasm."

"Gee, truly?"

Beau felt a line of annoyance carve its way into his forehead. "I want your word you're finished with Smith."

Logan scowled. "You're as relentless as Marc Dupree. Especially when you know a well-placed right hook would give you just as much satisfaction as it would me."

Beau looked away, just for a moment, so Logan wouldn't see his amusement and consider it silent agreement. "I won't condone violence."

"Fine." Logan gave him a frustrated sigh. "I won't go back to the church before I head out of town."

"And?"

"And." Logan grinned in a wolfish, arrogant pull of lips over teeth. "I won't hit the pastor so hard in his nose it'll mess up his pretty face forever."

Beau rubbed a hand down his face. "Can I trust you're a man of your word?"

Logan snorted at him. "I said I wouldn't go back, and I won't. But, you gotta admit, it's certainly a tempting idea—"

"Logan."

Logan held up his hand. "You have my word."

Beau finally allowed the smile tugging at his lips free rein. "That's enough for me."

"Can I go tell Mavis and Miss Southerland goodbye now, or do you need to yell at me some more?"

Beau waved him off with a flick of his wrist. "Go on. Say your farewells."

Logan swung around, stopped and looked back over his shoulder. "For the record, you handled that pastor and his wife real well. You're a far better man than I am."

Beau had his doubts. Serious doubts. After all, now that Logan had given him the idea, he wasn't sure he wouldn't head back to the church himself and—how did the lawman put it?—rearrange Reverend Smith's pretty face.

Apparently, Beau needed to work on a few of his anger issues. But at the moment, he had other matters on his mind. Matters concerning his future.

Tyler had planted a seed. So had Marc Dupree.

Jim and Amelia, unbeknownst to them, had watered them both.

Now, with the Lord's help, Beau needed to figure out the particulars.

Chapter Eighteen

The train ride to Colorado Springs had gone far too quickly, Hannah thought as she stood on the platform of the train depot just outside town. Five years. Five full years had passed since she'd left home. Nothing had changed.

Everything had changed.

She had changed.

The early-morning air slapped her in the nose and stung her throat. Pike's Peak, purple in color under the soft dawn light, rose high above the land, lifting its mighty face past the clouds as if to say *I'm larger than the earth can handle.*

The welcoming smell of fresh pine filled her nostrils.

She had returned.

But was she home?

Time would tell.

One thing was certain: Hannah had matured in the last five years. She was twenty-six years old, a fully grown woman with a large amount of money saved. Would it make a difference? Would she be strong enough to face her father as the confident woman she'd become? Or would she fall back into old patterns and turn into the surly, arrogant, young girl with a boulder-size chip on her shoulder?

Reviewing the past with an adult perspective, she now understood her father's disapproval of her. She'd been a willful child. Hard to handle. But, in her defense, she'd been missing her mother. And with her father choosing to favor Rachel, Hannah had felt abandoned.

Well, she was here now. Prepared to the reveal the truth and ask for her father's forgiveness.

The rest would be up to him.

Glancing around, she wondered why he wasn't at the depot. She'd sent a telegraph ahead to warn him of her impending arrival. That small courtesy had been Beau's suggestion, one Hannah had initially fought. She'd relented because she'd known he'd been right.

As usual.

She looked over at him standing next to Mavis, who was guarding their baggage as though she expected some miscreant to steal their valuables. Hannah could only smile at the silly, adorable picture the old woman made sitting perched on top of the pile of bags. Laced up in Hannah's fancy boots, Mavis's feet dangled near the ground without quite reaching the wooden platform.

Hannah's heart clenched. Mavis was a grown woman, nearing the end of her life, with a childlike joy for living. Hannah loved the old dear as if she'd been her own grandmother.

Beau shifted his stance, drawing Hannah's attention back to him. She worried for him, more than she probably should. He'd been quiet on the journey from Wyoming to Colorado. Was he mourning the loss of Amelia?

Why did that thought steal her breath?

He turned slightly to consider the mountains. She took the opportunity to study him. She cataloged his handsome features, one by one, starting with the aristocratic sweep of his nose that was so much like his mother's. And the strong jawline that came straight from his father and proclaimed his O'Toole heritage.

Her heart stumbled at the sight of all that masculine strength of character. For a brief moment she couldn't gulp in enough air. She couldn't think. It was just a moment, but her world tilted, her head grew light and she knew. Oh, she knew.

She loved him.

She loved Beauregard O'Toole.

But instead of bringing fear, she felt an inner peace she'd never known before. And then a soft voice whispered from deep within her. *Everything will work for the best for both of you, together.*

The thought brought some comfort. But they had a long way to go to become a "both of you, together." For one, Beau wasn't on board with the "both of you, together" part. But he would be. And she would be.

And, together, they would be—

A hard clearing of a throat jolted her out of her thoughts. "The prodigal daughter returns."

Hannah froze.

With panic clawing at her throat, she pivoted around to stare at the man who had banished her from his home five years ago.

There was no mistaking this was her father. The harsh features and unyielding expression in his eyes were the same as always.

He still judged her.

After all these years.

Why, Lord? Why?

Numb from too many emotions surging through her blood, she blinked up at him.

He looked older. Thinner. More haggard.

And so very, very sad. She'd never noticed that sadness before. It made him seem more approachable. Yet all the more distant.

"Hello, Father."

He didn't acknowledge her greeting, merely cast his gaze around the platform. "Where is your sister?"

"She—"

"What's happened? What have you done to her? What—"

"Reverend Southerland?" Beau cut him off in midsentence.

Hannah didn't know where Beau had come from. Or when he had joined them. She hadn't realized he could move so quickly and without any sound.

Then again, she couldn't hear anything over the pounding of her pulse rushing in her ears.

"Reverend O'Toole." Her father's gaze collided with Beau's and his eyes sharpened to thin slits. "What, may I ask, are you doing here?"

"I am escorting your daughter, sir."

Beau held the other man's gaze, but he didn't explain any further.

Why not? Hannah wondered.

Her father's chin rose a mere fraction of an inch, but it was enough to indicate his genuine displeasure. His brow scrunched into a disapproving frown. Hannah was familiar with the look. She'd been on the receiving end far too often.

"You traveled with Hannah?"

Beau nodded, but still he kept silent on the particulars. "Alone?"

Beau lifted a shoulder.

In that moment, Hannah realized this was some sort of standoff between the two men, a masculine battle of wills she didn't understand.

"You're not helping matters," she whispered to Beau. "Tell him the rest."

Beau kept his gaze locked with her father's.

"Beau, please."

He didn't budge. Not one single inch.

Nor did her father.

Hannah sniffed her impatience at them both.

Did they have to be such...men?

"Father," she said. "Reverend O'Toole was good enough to accompany *both* Mavis and me on our journey."

Her father's quick eyebrow flick was the only measure of his surprise. "And who might this Mavis be?"

Hannah resisted the urge to tug on her collar and straighten her skirt. She ran her tongue across her teeth and pointed to Mavis, who chose that moment to adjust her chamois strap and shoot out a stream of spit between her front teeth.

Sensing inspection, she looked up and gave them her trademark gap-toothed grin. The gesture was pure Mavis Tierney, with a bit of an imp thrown in for good measure.

"Ah." Reverend Southerland dismissed Mavis with a grunt and returned his attention to Beau. "I would have expected you to be in Greeley by now, working with the committee on the plans for the new church building."

Beau's shoulders relaxed. With a hard blink, he wiped

his features of all expression. "I was called to Denver on a personal matter, sir. A family friend was in need."

"That's where I met Reverend Southerland," Hannah said. "In Denver."

She wanted to say more, but she was jostled by someone walking by, reminding her they weren't alone on the platform.

When she stumbled, Beau rushed to her aid. He steadied her with one hand on her back and the other on her arm.

Her father frowned at them both, but Beau didn't release her until she found her balance.

"Where is your sister, Hannah?" His gaze traveled across the platform, then darted back to her. "What have you done with her?"

"That's why we're here," she said. "To tell you of Rachel's…fate."

Shock and worry traced a hard line along his forehead. "Is she hurt? Ill?"

His concern was so familiar, so painfully genuine, that it broke Hannah's heart. Her father had never, *never,* worried about her like that. "She is well."

"I don't understand."

Hannah sighed. "I know. And that's my fault. I—"

"So you haven't changed."

At the disappointment she heard in her father's tone, her stomach knotted. She wanted to toss Rachel's letters at him and run. But Hannah wasn't that impetuous, angry little girl anymore. She was a woman, a mature woman of independent means. God had brought her to this point in her life to end the lies of the past.

She would not cower now.

"No, Father, in that you're wrong. I *have* changed."

She lifted her head and stared Thomas Southerland in the eyes. "In more ways than one."

But whether the change was for good or evil was all a matter of perspective.

Beau could not stand the pain on Hannah's face any longer. But he had to show respect to her father, for her sake. Starting an argument now would only hurt her more. He'd already made matters worse with that silent battle of wills of a few moments ago. Yet how could he show respect when all he wanted to do was slam his fist into the other man's nose?

Didn't Thomas Southerland see how much pain he was causing his daughter? It was one thing to threaten Beau with his future in Greeley. That was man-to-man. But what sort of parent had such little regard for his own child as to treat her so coldly and with such lack of affection?

"Reverend Southerland," Beau said, clearing his throat of the resentment he heard in his own tone. "I think we should find another, less populated spot to speak further. I assure you, we will explain everything." Beau didn't add that the explanation would not be to the reverend's satisfaction.

As though yanked out of a trance, Reverend Southerland shook his head and began moving toward Mavis and the baggage.

Mavis stood, winked and then offered her hand. "I'm Mavis. And I say any father of Hannah's is a friend of mine."

He gave a noncommittal grunt and completely ignored her outstretched hand.

She sighed, rolled her eyes to heaven and stepped aside

so he could lift the largest of the pieces of luggage off the top of the pile.

Beau followed his lead and began hoisting bags, as well.

They were a silent group as they left the train depot and loaded their belongings into the reverend's smart carriage. It wasn't until they were in the heart of town and stopping in front of a hotel that Beau realized the good reverend was not going to open his home to any of them.

As healing old wounds went, it was a vile start. For Hannah's sake, Beau hoped this obvious slight was merely a temporary show of distrust on the reverend's part and not the start of worse things to come.

Chapter Nineteen

"I respectfully disagree, Reverend Southerland," Beau said, lowering his voice so the other diners in the hotel restaurant wouldn't hear the angry edge in his tone. He was glad Hannah was still up in her room, changing into fresh clothing. She didn't need to hear this conversation. "You don't know either of your daughters very well."

"Might I remind you exactly who you are talking to?" The older man leaned forward. He kept his voice equally low, but his anger was just as evident as Beau's. "I have the power to pull the Rocky Mountain Association's support from your new church. One word in the right ear is all it would take."

Beau acknowledged the threat with a low growl. He held back from open defiance. Giving in to his temper now would be nothing more than a dangerous indulgence, so he forced a bland expression on his face. "Nevertheless, you have misjudged both women."

With predatory slowness, Reverend Southerland sat back, rested his elbows on the arms of his chair and then steepled his fingers under his chin. "You dare judge me?"

Beau blew out a tense breath that scalded his throat.

He wanted to give his anger free rein, wanted to let it spread, but that would only hurt Hannah in the end. So he rubbed a hand down his face and relaxed his shoulders. "I'm only speaking the truth as I see it."

"Ah, truth." The reverend spoke with a perfect mix of challenge and scorn. "You sit there, with your youthful arrogance and bold words of truth, yet who are you to speak of such matters? You, who spends his time in brothels, mining camps and saloons. You once came to me and said you wanted out of that life, yet I wonder. Do you enjoy living amongst sinners, Reverend O'Toole?"

Beau bristled. How many times had Beau heard this same accusation from men who should know better?

Jesus himself had lived and eaten among tax collectors and sinners. Beau was only trying to model his life after his Lord and Savior. "Sinners are in need of the love of Christ as well as the righteous, perhaps more."

The older man's cold, black eyes swept over him. Hesitation flickered over his harsh features, softening them for a tense moment. He looked as if he fought an internal battle. And lost. "What you say is true enough, to a certain extent. But our association has a strict doctrine that must be obeyed. Without exception, members are to be excluded from the church for the sins of intoxication, disorderly conduct and living in adultery, to name only a few."

Beau felt the other man's annoyance. And wondered at it. Yet he couldn't stop himself from defending the Jane Goodwins, the Megans and even the Matties of the world. "The covenant also states that exclusion can be rescinded if the sinner appears at the next church service, confesses and asks for forgiveness."

"Which they never do."

The clear sign of defeat in the other man's eyes took Beau by surprise. Determined to have his say, he placed his palms on the table and pressed forward. "What of those excluded? Do we just let them live damned forever? What of the parable of the lost sheep?"

"A pretty ideal, O'Toole, but in my experience most are happy in their sin."

Beau should have been outraged at the observations, but he saw the genuine disappointment in other man's eyes, the lost hope that the world could never be different. Sadly, Reverend Southerland had given up and taken the easier path of excluding those who needed him most.

Beau couldn't let such a tragedy pass without comment. "Perhaps it's time for a change in how the Association ministers to the lost," he ventured.

Reverend Southerland's expression instantly closed. "Young people put too much emphasis on change."

In that moment, Beau's confusion disappeared. Right then. Right there. The answer he'd been seeking had been there, waiting for him, in Isaiah 1:17. *Learn to do right! Seek justice, encourage the oppressed. Defend the cause of the fatherless...*

Yes. Beau would go where God was leading him, right to the spot where the Heavenly Father was already working.

"It's time for a *real* change," Beau whispered aloud.

A snort was the reverend's immediate response. "When young people say *change* what they mean is rebellion. Take my Hannah, for example." The lack of grief and defeat in his eyes was as unexpected as it was unbearable.

Beau shifted in his seat. "You're wrong, Reverend Southerland. Hannah doesn't need to change. She is the most kindhearted, Christian woman I have had the pleasure of knowing."

"She is an actress." And with those four simple words, the angry, closed-minded pastor returned.

"She is so much more." A sense of urgency swam through Beau's mind, thundered in his chest. "Yes, she is an actress, but one who follows the same Almighty God you introduced her to when she was a child."

A tiny spark of hope lit in Reverend Southerland's eyes, right before it was doused with a bold slash of skepticism. "You know this about her? How?"

Beau took a deep breath and began regaling Reverend Southerland with every glorious detail of the daughter he never knew, starting with her work at Charity House.

At precisely an hour after arriving in Colorado Springs, Hannah went in search of her father and Beau. She'd left Mavis with strict orders to stay in their hotel room and consequently out of trouble.

Mavis had responded with the same saucy wink she'd tossed at Hannah's father on the train platform. But then she'd given Hannah her word and a swift, bone-rattling hug of encouragement.

Mavis had become a genuine friend.

The thought gave Hannah comfort as she made her way across the lobby. With nerves fluttering in her stomach, she barely took note of the expensive decor, hardly eyed the rose-patterned wallpaper.

The only sound she heard over the beat of her heart was her heels clicking along the marble-tiled floor. Click, click, click. Like a clock marking time.

This would be the hardest meeting in her life, far harder than that first night backstage of the theater. Unpleasant memories assailed her. She let them come. Desperate, alone and full of shame from her father's words of condemnation, she'd joined a traveling troupe headed to New York the very night of her banishment.

Instead of punishing her for her sins, God had protected her on that initial journey toward independence. Her outer beauty had opened the door to an immediate position in the troupe. Once in New York, God had led her straight into the loving world of Patience and Reginald O'Toole.

Thank you, Lord.

As prayers went, it was one of her shortest. As passionate intent went, it was one of her most fervent.

Click. Click. Click.

Her heels hammered against the marble, echoing through the cavernous lobby. Each step took Hannah closer to her father and one final confrontation. This time, however, she would face him as an adult. She would tell him about Rachel, hand over the two letters and then confess her own sins. No matter his reaction, Hannah would be free.

It is for freedom that Christ has set us free.

This was it, then. Her chance to stand firm.

A quick burst of fear stole her breath. The resulting pain was repulsive, like sharp, needle-thin icicles stabbing in her chest.

Lord Jesus, please fill me with Your courage.

Drawing in a tight breath, she stuffed her gloved hands in the pocket of her skirt. Her fingers connected with Rachel's letters, and the air hitched in her throat again.

Almost there.

Pasting a smile on her lips, Hannah negotiated the final corner then circled her gaze around the dining room.

At the height of the noon-hour rush, most of the tables were full. She continued searching for her father.

There he was, in the back left corner. Sitting at a table with Beau.

Her smile slipped.

From their body language, she could tell that they were in a heated discussion. Even from this distance she could see that they each kept their voices in check.

However, both had an identical look of intensity in their eyes. Both leaned forward, neither backing down from the other's heated words.

They were so similar. Why hadn't she noticed that before? Why hadn't she acknowledged the parallel?

She waited for the rush of antagonism from the sudden insight. It never came. And then she knew. She wasn't angry at her father, had never been so.

She was hurt. She was sad. And yet, she was…hopeful.

Oh, Lord, do I need his approval that badly? Am I that weak?

Maybe she was. Maybe when it came to her father, she *was* that weak.

Shattered. Everything in her felt like it was shattering into tiny pieces.

Is this what it feels like to have a heart break, Lord? I love my father and I need his love in return, but he doesn't *love me. Not enough.*

As if sensing her presence, Beau glanced up and quickly rose from his seat to gesture for her to come closer. As she wove a path between the tables, the drone of the other diners drummed in her ears. Her head grew dizzy from the effort to focus on Beau. Only Beau.

So much strength there.

With each step she took, her pulse slowed, while everyone around her seemed to speak and move at a quickened pace.

At last she drew alongside the table, and her father finally rose, as well.

Beau touched her arm and smiled at her. The support in his gaze made her want to smile in return, but she couldn't make her trembling lips obey.

For courage, she retrieved Rachel's letters and clutched them in her fist.

Still smiling, Beau held out his chair for her then dropped his head close to her ear. "Remember, you aren't alone. I'm with you. God is with you." He straightened and then spoke loud enough for her father's ears. "I'll leave you two to speak privately."

Her hand shot out and gripped his arm. "No, please stay."

Gently pulling her hand free, he pressed on her shoulder until she sat down in the empty chair. "It will be all right, Hannah. Your father is willing to listen to the truth now."

"I—"

"I'll be across the room if you need me." He leaned forward and kissed her on the cheek.

Her father's gasp alerted Hannah to his opinion of Beau's public display. She refused to cringe.

"I'll wait for you," Beau said. His eyes told her he meant more than merely waiting for the end of this conversation.

Did he return her feelings, then? Was there a chance for them to be together?

Her father cleared his throat. In a single sweep, Beau lifted his hand off her shoulder and walked away.

Needing a moment to gather her courage, she watched him go.

"That young man certainly thinks highly of you. If half of what he said is true, I've misjudged you."

Unsure what he meant, Hannah turned her attention back to her father. "I... I'm sorry, what did you say?"

Watching her with a speculative look in his eyes, he lifted a glass of water to his lips, sipped slowly, then set the glass back on the table. "I see it's mutual."

"It is?" Her stomach twisted in a frightening mix of hope and dread. "What is?"

And what an odd conversation to have with her father after so many years had passed.

"You both wear your hearts in your eyes." His tone was not unkind. Rather, it was a bit wistful, as was the expression in his gaze.

"It's the same way I used to look at your mother."

There was sadness in his words. An emotion she knew all too well. The mention of her mother brought back so many memories. Too many to sort through all at once. "I still miss her," Hannah said.

Her father merely nodded. Took another sip of his water.

Couldn't he say more? Couldn't he make this easier for them both? Hannah balled her hands into fists, the sound of crumpling paper reminding her why he couldn't give her the benefit of the doubt.

Rachel stood between them.

"I have a letter for you from my sister." Her voice broke. She couldn't stop it, didn't even try.

The expression in his eyes turned unreadable as he stretched out his palm.

She handed him the two letters. "The top one is for you. The other is for Will."

His mouth thinned as he examined the folded pages in his hand. The waiter chose that moment to ask for Hannah's order. "I'm not eating," she said. "Thank you, though."

Clearly baffled, his eyes shifted to her father. He dismissed the young man with a flick of his wrist. "We'll let you know if we need anything else."

"Very well, sir."

By the time the waiter scurried off, her father was bent over Rachel's letter. His gaze ran furiously across the page. His abrupt gasp was the most emotion Hannah had seen him display in her entire life. There was such fury in the sound. Such anger. And pain. So. Much. Pain.

At last, he folded the letter with agonizing slowness and said, "To run off with an *actor*." His voice cracked. "I don't understand why she would do such a thing."

Hannah crossed her arms around her waist and tried to hug away the cold. "I'm sorry, Father," she whispered. "But it's true."

He looked at her with tears in his eyes. At the obvious sign of his vulnerability, a fist of ice clutched around her heart and squeezed. She didn't know what to say in the face of such raw emotion. He'd always been a rock. A stone-faced rock.

"It makes no sense," he said. "This is so unlike her."

With awkward movements, Hannah reached out and touched his hand but he flinched away from her.

Shaking his head, he blinked away the tears and then narrowed his eyes. "Did you have something to do with this?"

Determined to be truthful, Hannah sat back and folded

all emotion deep inside her and nodded. "I introduced them."

"That's not what I meant. Did you talk her into marrying him?"

"No." She forced herself to sit still under his penetrating stare. "I *insisted*."

"And Reverend O'Toole? Am I to assume he performed the ceremony?"

"Yes." She held up her hand before he could speak over her. "Rachel ran off with Tyler. Beau married them once they were found. Those are the facts, but not the entire truth. For that, let me start at the beginning."

And she did. At the very beginning, at the scene of her mother's deathbed. She explained about her promise to care for Rachel, and all the subsequent lies Hannah had told to protect her sister ever since.

As she spoke, her father never once interrupted, but he looked at her with devastated eyes. When she got to the part about the affair with Mr. Beamer, another, equally horrified change came over him. And his eyes widened with alarm. "Weeks later, she tried to tell me *she* had the affair, not you."

The muscles in Hannah's stomach shook. Perhaps Rachel had tried to explain. But it had been too little, too late. "You didn't believe her, did you?"

He shut his eyes and released a shudder. "Of course not."

"No, why would you?" For a moment, a tiny one, everything seemed to slow down while Hannah's thinking sped up. A tiny trickle of apprehension slid between her shoulder blades as one thought surfaced. In her own way, Hannah had been as guilty as Rachel.

"Can you forgive me, Father?"

"But you said you didn't commit any of the…sins." The merciless look in his eyes would have made a brave woman quiver. Hannah was not a brave woman.

Nevertheless, she had come this far. "No. I've sinned, as well. In my own way. I bore false witness," she whispered. "All these years, I allowed you to believe one lie after another. Thinking I owed it to Mama, I played my role."

And all these years she'd thought of herself as the victim, the tragic heroine in the story of her life. But the reality was nothing so glamorous. How could she not have seen her own ugly role? How could she have lied to herself?

"I was ready to believe the stories. I never questioned them. Not once. I wanted to believe you were the bad sister." His eyes turned haunted. "For that, I owe you my own apology."

Hannah held her breath. A little crack in her heart opened, begging him to fill it with fatherly love. "Father? Are you saying you believe me now?"

"You were so close to your mother. She relied on you because you were strong, like her. You are so much like her." He shook his head, blinked. "Even now, I see her in you, in the way you hold your head high, in the way you look me straight in the eyes." He released a shaky sigh, his sorrow stripping away the hard exterior. "When she died, I saw too much of her in you. Perhaps I resented you for that."

In spite of the pain and anger she'd harbored all these years, a portion of her own resentment washed away with his confession. "Perhaps you were grieving in your own way."

"That was no excuse." For once, the hard tone of judgment was centered on himself.

Hannah reached out and gripped his hand. This time he didn't pull away. But even through her glove, his fingers were ice-cold. "We were both wrong," she said.

"Yes, we were."

The ragged shake of his breath was identical to hers. But then his gaze fell to the other letter, and he abruptly released her hand to grip it in his fist. "Will," he whispered. "This will devastate him."

With a sinking heart, Hannah lowered her gaze to her lap. Her hands were shaking. She couldn't deny that his obvious devotion to Will Turner hurt. "I know you love Will like the son you never had."

"I must be the one to tell him." He motioned to the waiter and took care of the bill in a frenzy of orders and money tossed to the table.

Watching her father's agitated movements, Hannah tried not to feel abandoned. "Of course." She allowed herself a tight smile. "You should go to him at once."

He rose. "Yes."

Hannah stood, as well, and caught sight of Beau heading quickly toward them.

Her father shut his eyes a moment and took a deep breath. "Hannah, we have much yet to discuss, but I fear Will must be told of Rachel's marriage. Would you and your friends do me the honor of coming to my home for supper this evening?"

Beau arrived before she could respond. It was a comfort to have him standing next to her. Like an anchor in turbulent seas.

His gaze searched hers, a question raising his eyebrows. "Is everything all right here?" he asked.

"Yes, everything is fine," Hannah said to him. Then she turned to her father. "Thank you for the invitation. We would be pleased to dine with you this evening."

He nodded. "Be at my home promptly at six-thirty."

His tone was gruff, demanding, and, as always, he refused to accept any argument on the matter.

What had she expected? A complete change in the course of a single conversation?

"We'll be there on time."

No, Hannah would make sure they arrived a full five minutes ahead of schedule. Just to be safe. Just to be respectable. Just to be…contrary. A smile tugged at her lips.

Apparently, a single conversation hadn't completely changed her, either.

Chapter Twenty

Beau took Hannah's hand as he led her down Monument Street. With a brief smile, he tightened his grip and pulled her a little closer. The smell of pine was strong in the air tonight. Crickets clicked out their evening song. The city gas lamps provided a golden glow at their feet, making the world seem a little softer, a little more welcoming.

With each step away from her childhood home, Beau could feel the tension leaving Hannah. They'd had a pleasant enough evening with her father, all things considered, but Beau had sensed the conflicting emotions rushing through her. By the end of the meal, she'd been trembling with nerves and bravely hiding that fact behind a serene smile and gracious manners.

Her acting abilities were good. But not that good. No one, not even his glorious mother, was *that* good.

Consequently, Beau's protective instincts had reared, and he'd invited her for this walk. Right now he wanted a moment alone with her, to enjoy her company and discuss anything other than her sister, his brother and painful childhood memories.

"Hannah, I—"

"Beau, I—"

They laughed together, their voices uniting in flawless harmony. A surge of satisfaction filled him. Tonight,
everything felt right. "You first," he said.

She paused, turned to look him in the eyes. The big
silver moon cast its pale light across her face, making her
look ethereal and fragile. A storybook heroine come to
life. A surge of affection jammed the breath in his throat.
Beau would not risk losing the gift that stood right in
front of him by focusing on what he didn't yet have and
certainly couldn't control.

No matter where his ministry took him in the future,
no matter where he settled, he wanted to spend a lifetime comforting and protecting this woman. If she would
have him.

"I just wanted to thank you," she said, her eyes burning with silent gratitude. "I don't know what you said to
my father at the hotel, but by the time I sat down he was
willing to listen to me, actually listen. More so than he's
done since my mother passed away."

Beau lifted her hand to his lips, forgetting everything
but how soft her skin felt against his palm. "I merely
told him you are the most amazing woman of my acquaintance and that he'd regret losing an opportunity
to know you."

"Oh, Beau." Tears spiked along her lashes.

Like most men, Beau was helpless around feminine
tears. But Hannah's slaughtered him. The reflex to hold
her came so fast, so powerful, he had to shut his eyes and
pray for strength. He silently counted his heartbeats—
one, two, three—until he had control over his baser im-
pulses.

"Hannah, my beautiful Hannah, I can't tell you how

sorry I am for the way I treated you at our first meeting." He pressed a finger to her lips to prevent her from interrupting him. "I know you've already forgiven me," he began. "I know we've moved beyond this, but I still feel the need to make it up to you."

"You already have." She smiled at him, that soft lifting of lips that punched him straight in the heart. "You came here with me, knowing my father could take away your new church."

"That no longer matters." He was startled by the surge of peace that came with the declaration. "I've been fooling myself for so many years, chasing a dream I only *thought* I wanted. Tyler was the first to help me see the truth."

"Of all people." But her eyes told him she didn't doubt that his brother had helped him. That was part of Hannah's appeal—her ability to see the good in others, even when no one else could.

It was why he loved her. And, oh yes, he loved her. With all his heart.

And that was why he had to confess all. "I thought if I could settle in a nice church in the meadow, I could win the good people's support. Their approval. And then, once I'd earned their trust, I would open the doors to others, the outcasts."

"Oh, Beau, don't you know how courageous you are?" She patted his cheek.

Such pretty eyes. Such softness.

His stomach did a quick pitch.

When had this woman's approval become so important to him? Far more important than a shaky dream surrounding an elusive brick and mortar building.

"I've always thought I was too stubborn, too arrogant,

to be a good preacher," he said. "I thought if I could find a calm, sedate wife, she would help smooth my rough edges and take the flamboyant son of an actor out of me."

Her gaze softened with understanding. "You would die in a life like that."

Home. Family. Permanence. Those were the things he'd always wanted. Still did. He hadn't realized God would give them to him in an unexpected way. But God had made him wait for his perfect match. In the process, Beau had learned patience. And now, he understood that the best things in life were worth a little delay now and then.

"All this time, I thought I had to prove I was a man of God by fitting into the usual image of what that looks like."

"Oh, Beau." She sighed. "You serve so many just as you are—the kind of people who would never learn of God's mercy if you didn't teach them." She cupped his cheek. There was acceptance in her gaze, a quiet understanding that eased his concerns. Hannah Southerland drew feelings out of him no one else ever had.

It was a heady sensation. One he rather enjoyed. And hoped to continue enjoying the rest of his life.

"Did I ever tell you how proud your parents are of you?" she asked. "They speak of you with such love. It would break their hearts if they thought you were unhappy because of them."

A quick flash of guilt kicked in his gut. He tried to talk and coughed out air instead. Gulping, he tried again. "All this time, I've thought of my childhood as a curse. But now I see that the constant travel and inconsistencies, all my dealings with crazy characters on and off the stage, were equipping me to do the work God had planned specifically for my life."

"You've found out who you are."

"Yes."

"I'm happy for you, Beau."

Her gentle tone affected him far more than her words. "There's only one thing missing." The hope in her eyes gave him the courage to continue. "Hannah, I want you to be... No." He stopped himself.

What was he thinking?

After what Tyler and Rachel had done, he couldn't let impulse drive his actions. Hannah deserved better.

Their future demanded more.

He looked over his shoulder, back toward her father's house. The lights were still blazing. There was time yet tonight. If he hurried.

"I want to do this right," he said and touched her cheek. With gentle fingers, he pushed her hair aside and studied her face. "No mistakes. No selfish acts. I must speak with your father first."

Her eyebrows slammed together, and she tilted her head at a confused angle. "Now? You need to speak to my father at this hour?"

His mouth curved at the sign of her bafflement, and he dropped his hand. "I don't want to wait until morning." Surely, she understood what he meant. Surely, she understood why he had to ask her father for her hand in marriage before he asked her. Tyler and Rachel had made propriety all the more necessary.

She took a shaky breath. "But why tonight? I don't understand the rush."

"Because I have to..." Fearing time was running out, he stabbed a glance toward her father's house. Urgency sent his blood screaming through his veins. "We have to go quickly, before he retires for the evening."

He spun on his heel and made his way back toward the house at a hurried pace.

"Beau, wait."

She trotted after him.

He slowed his gait to accommodate hers.

"Have you gone mad?" she asked when she caught up.

With a quick flash of teeth, he grinned down at her. "Mad? No. In fact, I'm the sanest I've ever been."

Hannah couldn't imagine what was taking so long. Her father and Beau had been holed up in the church's office for well over an hour. What could they possibly be discussing that couldn't have waited until morning?

Beau had been so agitated earlier.

Weariness swamped her suddenly, made her want to collapse in a puddle of shivers. If only she had someone to help her sort out the confusing facts. But for all intents and purposes, she was alone with her worry.

Mavis had long since abandoned the vigil and had fallen asleep in a chair in the far corner of the parlor, snoring and muttering in her sleep.

Hannah didn't have the heart to wake the older woman.

When she looked over at her chaperone-turned-friend, a flutter of affection shifted in her stomach. Mavis was a part of her family now. Would Beau be a part of it, as well?

A rush of excitement surged through her at the thought.

Beau had mentioned he wanted to do things right. With Tyler and Rachel running off the way they had, she could understand that desire. But surely Beau wouldn't ask her father for her hand without speaking with her first. He couldn't be that dense, that heavy-handed. That…male.

Please, Lord, let me be wrong about this.

But when another handful of minutes passed by, and the door remained firmly shut, Hannah's fears increased.

She paced.

She worried.

She paced some more.

Looking around the parlor, she took more than a cursory inventory of the room this time. Nothing had changed in the last five years of her absence. The room was still clean. Neat. Unpretentious. Much like her father.

And yet, it had her mother's stamp on it, as well, left over from all these years. The rose and peony wallpaper had been hung on Hannah's seventh birthday. The memory of the day when her mother had allowed her to help pick out the pattern still burned in Hannah's mind. But just as quickly, it skipped away.

Hannah sighed and continued her inspection.

Although the pattern was unique, the brocade upholstery on the furniture matched the colors on the walls seamlessly. The sturdy mahogany chairs and tables, brushed golden from the firelight, brought to mind permanence. Stability. Reminding her of—

The door to the office swung open, and Hannah jumped.

As both men approached, Hannah desperately tried to calm her nerves. She looked from Beau to her father and back to Beau again.

Although they were smiling, there was something in their expressions, something a little too arrogant and a little too masculine, that sent trepidation hovering at the back of her throat.

Beau's eyes danced with an unreadable look as he took her hands in his. She hated that he was so inscrutable all of a sudden. Something deep inside her, something inherently female, warned her that the ensuing conversation was not going to go well. "Beau? What is it? What's happened?"

His expression transformed, and he gave her the lazy O'Toole smile that should have warmed her heart. Dread settled hot in her chest instead.

"As soon as I can make the arrangements, we'll break ground on my new church."

Hannah's stomach pitched at the news.

No, Lord, please no. Not this.

She stole a glance at her father, who was watching them with an air of satisfaction.

Oh, Lord, no.

Beau had settled. In spite of what he'd said earlier tonight, he'd settled for a life that would eventually suck his passion for the Lord dry. And yet, his eyes gleamed with joy. She tried to be happy for him, tried to understand. "I... That's wonderful."

But it wasn't wonderful. It was awful.

She loved Beauregard O'Toole, and silently wept over the mistake he was making. Her heart broke a little and she selfishly mourned the loss of her own dream.

Because, no matter what words came out of his mouth next, that new church of his would not include her. Beau might be able to settle. She, however, could not.

"And now, Hannah, your future will be safe, as well," her father said.

Switching her attention to him, Hannah pulled free of Beau's grip. "*My* future?"

She tried to sound haughty, but her voice held a hollow edge even to her own ears. Her world had just turned crooked and off balance, and she had no idea how to set it right again.

Clearly unaware of her disappointment, Beau continued smiling. "What your father is trying to say is that you don't have to worry about your future ever again. You'll never be scared and alone." The look in his eyes was possessive.

And broke her heart a little more.

"But I'm not alone now." She glanced toward her loyal chaperone, who was stretching and blinking herself awake. "I have Mavis."

Mavis smiled at her. "That's right, dearie." She pounded her birdlike chest with a fist, then released a round of harsh coughs. "You'll always have me," she declared once she had herself under control again.

Beau touched Hannah's arm, and she turned to look at him again. "That's not what I meant. With me, you'll never end up like Jane."

Of course she wouldn't end up like Jane. She'd already taken care of that herself. But the inflexible look in Beau's eyes hiked her chin a little higher, and the first threads of despair roped through her blood. Beau looked as though he'd just given her the greatest gift in life—male protection.

Her heart pounded thick with fear.

It wasn't that she didn't want his protection. She didn't *need* it. Why didn't he understand that essential truth? After everything they'd been through, Beau didn't know her. He didn't know her at all.

Her father cleared his throat and gave her the smile he usually reserved for Rachel. In fact, he looked like the happy patriarch presiding over his brood. "And best of all, you're going to be a minister's wife."

"That's right," Beau said. "We're getting married."

She opened her mouth, closed it and then said, "Who's getting married?"

But she knew what he meant. How could he believe all was settled when he hadn't even asked her the question?

As though she hadn't spoken, her father added, "Of course you have my blessing." He turned to Beau. "I think you will make my daughter a fine husband."

Mavis gasped. Loudly. Then she snorted. *Then* she mumbled something that sounded like "idiot men."

At least one other person in the room understood.

Beau couldn't be doing this to her. He respected her too much not to properly ask for her hand in marriage.

Too stunned to do much more than stare at them both, Hannah responded with a growl in her throat, a furious shake of her head and a narrowing of her eyes.

Still, the idiot men forged ahead.

"Your father will perform the ceremony, of course."

She gawked at him, terrified of how easy it would be to break down and cry. But the vicious stirrings of pride began weaving through her, and she promised herself she would never cry in front of Beauregard O'Toole. *Never.*

As though sensing her mood at last, Beau's shoulders stiffened in alarm. "Hannah?"

She tried to speak, she could even feel her jaw working, but discernible words eluded her. Finally, she said, "Let me see if I have this straight. We're getting married." She pointed to her and Beau. "And he's performing the ceremony." She pointed to her father.

She held the pause, praying, wishing, hoping either

Beau or her father would redeem themselves at any moment.

Which, of course, they didn't. They both stared at her, eyes blinking in identical displays of confusion.

The ticking of the mantel clock mocked her. Tick, tick, tick went the pendulum. No, no, no went her heart. Wrapping her dignity around her like a shield of armor, she set her chin and held to her silence.

When Beau scrunched his forehead, indicating he was deep in thought, Hannah prayed for a miracle.

Mavis came up next to her and clutched her hand. Hannah held on for dear life. Tears pricked in her eyes. The tears were more from loss of pride than pain, or so she told herself, and that made controlling them so much harder.

In slow, clipped tones that would have sent a sane man running for cover, Hannah broke the silence. "And you two have planned all of this so I won't end up like Jane."

Beau's eyes narrowed, and she saw the exact moment when understanding dawned. His face instantly fell and he raked a shaky hand through his hair. "Hannah, I didn't mean——"

"Oh, but you did." Seething anger replaced the hurt. His apology had come too late. The damage had been done. "I thought you said you were sorry for the way you treated me at our first meeting. But I see you truly believe that I will fall into a life of sin without you guarding me against that terrible fate."

Oh, but this time, *this* time, he'd hurt her deep at the core—where she trusted most.

"I *am* sorry. You are a kind, compassionate, Christian woman. You are——"

"A woman who will end up like Jane if left to her own devices?"

Obviously stunned by her vehemence, he blinked. Then blinked again.

Didn't he understand? "There is no shame in what I am, in what I do. I am a successful *actress,*" she shouted. "Do you hear me? An actress."

Mavis snorted. "*I* certainly heard you." She clutched Hannah's hand tighter. "And I don't blame you for being angry. Not one bit." She glared at Beau with disappointment in her eyes. "You should know better, boy."

"You stay out of this," Reverend Southerland said.

"*You* stay out of this, as well." Hannah jabbed a finger in his direction. "This isn't about you, either."

Her father lifted himself to his full height. "You are my daughter. And that makes this my business. I've turned my back on you for five years. I was wrong to abandon you. You could have been hurt—" he shuddered "—or worse. I can't allow you to walk out of this house unprotected again."

"Oh, Father."

His eyes looked so somber, so full of pain and regret. "Beauregard can protect you as I never did," he said.

Hannah stared at her father in awe. Wisps of childhood memories flitted across her mind. But tonight, she didn't see the unforgiving preacher who'd condemned her for her sins. No, tonight, she saw the grieving widower unprepared to care for two young daughters. One too wild for him to handle, the other too weak and needy. She saw a man who had escaped in the safety of the rules and rituals of his religion.

He hadn't been a bad man. Just a hurting one.

He'd done the best he could. And now, in his own, arrogant way, he was trying to make up for his mistake.

She took a deep breath. And forgave.

"Father, I understand your concern."

She stopped, shook her head, suddenly very tired, and frightened, and confused. But then, she did something she never thought she'd do in this lifetime. She rushed to her father and hugged her arms around his waist.

He stood rigid at first. With awkward movements, he finally returned her embrace. "I'm so sorry, Hannah." His voice hitched with emotion.

"Me, too. But, Father, you don't have to worry about me. I have money. Lots of it. And I own property. And stocks and bonds, too."

She swung around to glare at Beau, pinpointing all of her turbulent emotions into one seething spark of anger. "When your mother took me in, do you think she only taught me about acting?"

"I—"

"No." She cut him off. "Patience taught me how to save and invest and manage my money properly, once I started making more than I knew what to do with."

"I don't understand." There was such male confusion in his eyes that Hannah almost felt sorry for him. *Almost.*

His arrogance had cut her too deeply to stifle her pride now.

"I am a wealthy woman in my own right, Beau. So, you see, I don't need you."

Oh, but she lied. She lied, lied, lied. She did need him, needed him like air. But stubborn pride, that evil, evil character flaw that ran deep and wide within her, wouldn't let her take back her words.

His face collapsed and he reached out his hand to her.

All facades were gone. He wore no mask. And no O'Toole charm softened his features. All that was left was raw exposure. "But, Hannah, I need you."

She lowered her head, unable to bear the pain in his eyes. Her pride wouldn't release her enough to give him the words he wanted. "Maybe you do need me," she whispered. "But not enough to ask me to marry you."

"I did."

"No." She sighed. "You *told* me."

When he stared back at her and didn't declare his love for her right away, Hannah knew she'd lost him. No, she thought, she couldn't lose something she'd never had.

He might think he needed her. But it wasn't her he needed. It was some ideal woman who would smooth his rough edges.

"Come on, Mavis," she said, her tone flat. "Let's go."

Beau found his voice then. "That's it?" he asked, a hard steel of anger edging his words. "That's how this ends? You just walk out on me? Don't you want to know the particulars of my new church?"

"No." She turned her back on him, felt his hand hover near her shoulder but then drop without making contact. She desperately wanted to swing around to face him, but she was too proud to let him see the helplessness in her eyes. "It would break my heart."

Chapter Twenty-One

The Grand Opera House, Chicago, Illinois
Six weeks later

Shakespeare's *Hamlet* progressed toward its dramatic conclusion. Crimes were exposed with the perfect blend of shock and retribution. Schemes and false loyalties were revealed at a precise, well-rehearsed pace.

Unfortunately, Hannah no longer found joy translating every nuance found on paper into a memorable performance onstage. The irony of playing Ophelia, an obedient young woman dependent on men to tell her how to behave, brought back poignant memories of her last meeting with Beau.

If only that night had been a dress rehearsal, she would have played her role differently in the final performance.

After tonight there would be no more performances for her. Fitting, perhaps, that her last play was a tragedy.

With nothing left to do but take her bows, Hannah stood poised in the shadows offstage. She tried to contain her nerves, but she was impatient to move on to the next chapter of her life.

At first, when Hannah had returned to Chicago with Mavis in tow she had craved the escape of her profession. Needed it as much as breath itself. In the end, she'd only found loneliness. Guilt.

Regret.

Unwanted memories slid into her mind, playing out as strangely real as the last moments of the play. She'd been so angry at Beau for his high-handed treatment of her. All because he'd chosen to ally himself with her father. Looking back now, she realized she'd felt betrayed by them both. Yet it had been easier to forgive her father than Beau.

Why was that?

Because she'd allowed fear and pride to dictate her actions. She'd overreacted, jumped to conclusions and had cowardly disappeared before the final act.

Well, Hannah would make it right. All she had to do was find Beau and then ask for his forgiveness.

With that thought, Hannah leaned slightly forward, her eyes searching for the woman positioned in the wings off the opposite end of the stage. Mavis waggled her fingers at her, and then pointed to their packed trunks behind her.

Tonight they would leave the theater forever.

Hannah's hands started to shake again, threatening her outward calm. A deep, driving urge to leave now, before the play was complete, washed through her. Hannah roped her fingers together and clutched her palms tightly against one another. In this mood, her mind wandered back in time, back to that dismal night in her father's parlor.

Why hadn't she asked Beau about his church? Why hadn't she loved him enough to support his dream?

Because she'd been afraid. Afraid she'd turn into an

Amelia. And because of that fear, she'd allowed pride to rule her heart.

Unable to bear her own emotions, she shifted her gaze toward the audience. Hannah squinted deep into the shadows until her gaze focused. Countless faces stared at the stage with their usual rapt attention.

Tonight, however, their willingness to accept the lie grated. Why were so many hungry for an illusion? Hannah no longer wanted the deception herself.

From this day forward, she wanted nothing but truth in her life.

Taking a deep breath, Hannah turned her attention back to the stage. The actor playing the Norwegian prince, Fortinbras, had just demanded Hamlet be carried away in a manner befitting a fallen soldier.

Hannah sighed in relief. A few more minutes and she would be free.

At last, Hamlet's body was carried offstage.

A hushed pause filled the theater.

Then…

The audience surged to its feet. Applause thundered. And the curtain began its slow descent. Chaos instantly erupted behind the delicate veil between audience and actor.

"Places, everyone," yelled the director. He turned to Hannah and motioned her forward.

Hannah wove her way through the labyrinth of rushing humanity, gliding toward her spot on the far edge of the troupe.

Once in place, Hannah rubbed her tongue across her teeth before turning her head to seek out Mavis once more.

Hannah's breath backed up in her lungs.

Mavis was gone.

In her place stood...

Beau.

With greedy eyes, Hannah looked at him. He'd grown thinner, a bit worn, but was still the most beautiful man she'd ever seen. For once in her life, she ignored pride. She ignored obligation. And broke formation in a run.

"Hannah," said the director. "Where are you going?"

She flicked her wrist at him. "I'm through."

"You can't do this," he called after her. "You must take your bows."

Speechless with frustration, she turned back. One step, two, and then she hesitated, poised between her past and her future.

She chose the future.

Shooting the director an apologetic shake of her head, she swung her back to the stage and rushed toward Beau.

Eyes focused on him, and him alone, she ignored the director's howl of outrage.

With each step, Hannah noted the conflicting emotions on Beau's face, love overriding everything else.

She picked up the pace, but was suddenly jostled by an actor on her left. Beau's eyes filled with alarm, but Hannah caught her balance and continued forward.

At last, he smiled at her.

Fear gripped her in response. She couldn't lose him again.

Lord, fill me with a humble heart, she prayed. *Fill me with the courage to ask his forgiveness.*

How easy it would be to allow pride to keep her from admitting her share of the guilt.

Hannah pressed her lips together, realizing she'd missed the point all along. What did it matter if they lived in a church in the meadow or in a mining camp or a saloon? Life with Beauregard O'Toole, wherever it took them, would hold the perfect blend of Christian grace, charity and hope.

With a shake of her head, Hannah smiled at her astonishingly handsome costar in life.

Golden, spectacular, filled with charm, Beauregard O'Toole was everything she wanted in a man. Three priorities ruled his actions. God. Family. Ministry.

She stopped in front of him, suddenly unsure where to begin. She looked at his chiseled, handsome face. What if he didn't want her? What if she'd misread the love in his eyes?

A knot of anxiety twisted in her stomach. The noise of the theater became a dull drumming in her ears.

He reached for her hand, bent at the waist and dropped a kiss onto her knuckles. The gesture brought tears to her eyes.

Everything would be all right. As long as they were together.

"You were breathtaking tonight, my dear." His voice was a little shaky, and the most beautiful sound Hannah had heard in the last six weeks.

He rose slowly, deliberately, and then sent her a suave half smile. "How I've missed you."

Pressure built in her chest and stole her breath. "Oh, Beau, can you forgive me?"

"It is I who needs to be forgiven." The sorrow in his eyes was real. "I've been a stupid, stupid man, ignoring the blessing right in front of me. Well, I see you now. And I see my mistakes. I should have asked you to marry me before I spoke to your father."

"I should have given you the chance to tell me about your church."

He shook his head.

She gave him a wobbly smile.

The noise increased, making it hard to speak without shouting. Hannah looked around, tugged him farther away from the stage and into a private nook under the rigging.

"I'm leaving the company tonight," she told him once they were nestled in the quiet alcove.

His eyes met hers, and in them she saw what she'd missed in her father's parlor. Beau was prepared to treat her as his equal. "Mavis told me."

She made a watery sound in her throat. "Did Mavis also tell you we were starting our search for you?"

"She did."

Ah, Mavis. The dear old woman was better than any godmother in a Grimm's fairy tale.

"You never let me explain about my new church."

His gray eyes blazed so brightly with conviction, the heat of shame warmed her face.

Hannah lowered her head. "I'm sorry," she whispered.

He placed his finger under her chin and applied pressure. As her chin rose, Hannah had to fight the urge to look away from his face. But she forced herself to keep her gaze locked with his.

"I didn't accept the position in Greeley," he said. "I turned your father down that night in his office."

In the face of his declaration, it was remarkable Hannah's knees didn't give out. As Beau had once done to her, she'd judged him without knowing the complete facts. Yet he didn't hold her mistake against her. He'd come to find her, with love shining in his eyes.

Oh, Lord, thank you.

"I… You're going to continue traveling as before?" she asked.

"No." He smiled. "God has a different plan for me, for us."

Hannah blinked. "Oh?"

"I'm starting a new church, outside of Denver, right next to—"

"Charity House."

"Precisely."

A sense of rightness filled her. "That's wonderful."

"Marc planted a seed months ago," Beau said. "One I nearly let die. The orphans at Charity House need a spiritual shepherd, as do their mothers and others like them."

"It makes perfect sense."

"Although the Rocky Mountain Association won't offer any support or assistance, your father will. Actually, he's been giving me advice in the initial planning stages."

Her father giving Beau advice on a church designed to open its doors to all people? Oh, how far they'd all come.

"I would have been here sooner, but I wanted to have some stability to offer you first."

"Oh, Beau, my home will be wherever you are. I will follow wherever you go. So, you see, I don't need stability."

"Maybe I do. Maybe I need to know I can give you more than a vagabond life."

She cocked her head. "What if God uproots us?"

"Then we go. Together." His eyes glittered, and he tugged her hand against his heart. "You said you were coming in search of me? Where did you plan to start that search?"

"In Greeley. I wanted you to know I would support you wherever God leads."

He stared at her with awe and love in his eyes. "Will you consider coming back to Denver and assisting me in my new adventure?"

Her heart dropped to her toes, bounced, then hung suspended for a split second before settling back in place. "*Assist* you?"

His eyes never left her face, but a charming O'Toole grin slid on his lips. "I need your help."

"My help?"

"Starting a new church is too big a job for one man to accomplish alone."

"Too big a job?"

His grin turned into a full, heart-stopping smile. It was a weapon against which she had no defense.

"Are you going to keep repeating my words?" he asked.

She cocked her head at him, searched his eyes. Beauregard O'Toole was up to something. "Are you going to ask me the right question?"

"I'll need a helpmate to start my church."

"A helpmate."

"A wife," he blurted out. "I need a wife." He shook his head. "That had to be the worst proposal ever. Second only to the last one, when I *told* you we were getting married. Hannah, I—"

She placed her finger against his lips. "I kind of like this most recent proposal of yours. In fact, I think it's going rather well."

"Do you like it enough to say yes?"

"How can I? You haven't actually asked me a question."

He lowered to one knee. Threads of light from the stage cascaded in his hair. Her golden knight. No, better, her rebel preacher.

"Hannah, will you marry me?" His voice came out grave. "Will you assist me in doing God's work? Will you stand by me, no matter where life takes us, even when I'm an arrogant son of an actor?"

"How could I refuse such a lovely offer?"

He slowly rose to his feet and placed both hands on her shoulders. "Is *that* a yes?"

"No."

His face fell. Apparently, he wasn't in the mood for teasing.

"It's an ab-so-lutely."

He abandoned restraint and pulled her into his arms. "That's more like it." He pulled back and gave her an arrogant wink. "We'll get married right away. No arguments. I'm not going to risk losing you again."

"You know, Beau." She turned her head at a saucy angle. "Sometimes your arrogance is really rather appealing."

"I'll remember you said that."

"Well, remember this. I'll marry you, yes. Under two conditions."

"Two?" He set her away from him and studied her face for a long moment. Then he smiled. "Only two?"

Apparently, he *was* in the mood for teasing now. "One." She pointed her finger toward the ceiling. "We get married right away."

"Makes sense to me." He regarded her with a triumphant look. "Since I already said that."

Enjoying herself immensely, she pursed her lips. "You scoundrel."

He gave her a careless shrug. "I'm working on my arrogant streak."

Hannah rolled her eyes and tried not to smile. "You still have a ways to go."

Ignoring her comment, he touched a strand of her hair, twirled it around his fingertip, then looked back into her eyes. "What's your other condition?"

She took a deep breath and forced a serious expression onto her features. "We adopt Mavis."

He stared at her. Blinked. Stared at her awhile longer. "Isn't she a little old for adoption?"

Up went her chin. "I think she's the perfect age."

"Hannah Southerland, you are an eccentric woman, and I love you with all my heart." He punctuated his words with a soft kiss to her lips.

"I love you, too, Beau." This time she didn't have to feign her serious expression.

He cupped her cheek in his hand and smiled.

"So, what do you say about adopting Mavis?" she asked on a wispy sigh.

He kissed her on the nose. "Done."

"I knew you'd see things my way."

A single eyebrow shot up. "Now who needs to work on their arrogant streak?"

"We'll work on them together."

He laughed and pulled her into a tight hug. "It'll probably take us a lifetime."

"I have the stomach for it, if you do."

He laughed again.

"I love you, Beauregard O'Toole," she whispered in his ear.

"I love you, too, Mrs. O'Toole."

"Mrs. O'Toole?" She pulled slightly away and lifted her head.

"Just checking to see how it sounds."

Mavis chose that moment to join their happy twosome. With a gnarled finger, she poked Beau on the shoulder.

He released Hannah and looked down at the scowling woman. "May I help you?"

"Are we getting married or not? Yes or no, boy?"

Beau pivoted and kissed Mavis on the cheek. "I say, yes!"

Mavis snorted. "'Bout time."

Beau reached out a hand to both women and pulled them against him. "What say we make our final exit and start our life together right away?" He looked down at Hannah with love shining in his eyes. "Yes or no, woman?"

A lone tear slipped from her eye. "I say, yes!"

Epilogue

Hannah and Beau's wedding day arrived on a snow-filled morning in late November. Beau had requested the ceremony take place at Charity House. Hannah had immediately agreed.

Of course, once her friends at the orphanage took over, the simple ceremony in Marc's study had turned into an elaborate affair that required an additional three weeks to organize.

Beau, being Beau, hadn't complained.

Hannah, being Hannah, had resolved to make the celebration well worth the many delays.

With that silent promise in mind, Hannah spent all morning preparing for the big event. Determined to impress her groom, she took special care dressing, paying particular attention to her hair. Confident she'd done her best, she pinned the last ribbon in place, brushed a barely noticeable wrinkle from her skirt and strolled to the window overlooking Charity House's backyard.

The cold mountain air seeped past the window casing and whispered across her face. Taking a moment to settle her nerves, Hannah dragged the coolness into her lungs and took in God's splendor before her.

The sun shone in a cloudless sky, soaring over a world washed clean with snow. A gentle breeze swirled a transparent, frosty mist along the top layer of flakes. Off in the distance, the western peaks wore a heavy blanket of glossy white.

Hannah squeezed her eyes shut and prayed for her future with Beau.

Heavenly Father, I pray You mold me into a good and decent wife. Bless my marriage to this wonderful man and make us better together than we could ever be apart. I pray this in Your Son's name, Amen.

Opening her eyes, she returned her attention to the yard. She traced the perimeter with her gaze, noting with joy how it backed into the empty lot where they'd soon break ground on their new church. She would always remember the look of admiration in Beau's eyes when she'd told him she'd sold some of her Chicago property to buy the land and materials needed for the building.

If she squinted, Hannah could almost see the church in her mind. God's house would be sturdy and tall, with an impressive white steeple and a long line of eclectic members seeking refuge. A—

The door swung open and hit the wall with a thud. She jumped away from the window and spun quickly around. Her shock turned to pleasure as she caught sight of Laney entering the room.

"Oh, *Hannah.*" Laney gasped, her words coming out in a rush of pleasure. "You're beautiful."

There was no time for a response. One breath, two, and Hannah was pulled into Laney's tight embrace.

Overwhelmed with joy, Hannah clung to her new friend, her sister in Christ.

One more solid squeeze and Laney released her. "The guests are all assembled in the parlor. We just need—" she stretched out her hand "—the bride."

Smiling, Hannah reached out, as well, but a deep-pitched clearing of a throat had her dropping her hand and peering toward the masculine sound.

"Father," she said in surprise. "I thought you were waiting with Beau."

"I was." He moved deeper into the room with his usual air of authority. "I would like to speak with you first."

He sounded so formal. So distant. So like the father she'd always feared. But then he smiled, revealing a dimple in his left cheek, and Hannah immediately relaxed. Praise God, the cold man of her childhood no longer existed.

"I'll leave you two to talk." Laney squeezed Hannah's hand and quickly left the room.

Alone with her father, Hannah stood very still, very attentive. What had he come to say? Would she know how to answer?

Seeming in no hurry to speak, he scanned the room and then flicked a glance out the window. Moving closer, he rocked back on his heels and studied the pristine scenery with a blank, unreadable expression.

Anxiety churned in her stomach. Had the venerable reverend changed his mind about supporting her marriage to Beau?

She held her breath as he turned to face her again. But when their eyes met, Hannah saw nothing more than nervousness staring back at her. Not judgment. Not second thoughts. Merely the genuine unease of a father releasing his daughter to another man.

That knowledge gave Hannah the courage to break the silence herself. "I'm grateful you agreed to perform the ceremony, Father. It means a lot to Beau and me."

"I wouldn't have missed it." He pulled in a deep breath, released it slowly. "You make a beautiful bride, my dear. Just like your mother on our wedding day." Tears formed in his eyes.

Love and hope blossomed in her heart. "I...thank you."

"I have something for you." He stuck his hand into one of the inner pockets of his coat and pulled out a small velvet-coated box.

At the sight of the familiar container, Hannah willed her own tears into submission with a hard swallow.

"Oh, Father," she said, curling her fingers into the soft velvet. "You don't have to do this."

"I want to."

The look in his eyes stole her breath. It was the look of fatherly love. The look she'd craved all her life but feared would never come.

"Go on, Hannah. Open my gift."

With trembling fingers, she flipped back the lid, and gasped at the emerald pendant winking up at her.

"It was your mother's," he said, his voice storming with emotion.

Blinking rapidly, Hannah concentrated on the necklace. On the black velvet box. On anything but the fresh ache in her chest. "I remember," she whispered. "She only wore it once a year, on Easter Sunday."

He smiled. "The stone reminded her of spring, renewed life and—"

"The Resurrection."

"She would want you to have it." He cleared his throat. "*I* want you to have it."

His softly uttered words staggered her, and the muscles in her throat quivered, making a response impossible.

Silently, she handed him the necklace and turned to face the mirror. "Will you help me with the clasp?" she choked out.

"Of…course."

She lowered her head and waited.

He hesitated. Then, with unsteady fingers, he fastened the pendant around her neck.

When she lifted her head, she caught his gaze in their shared reflection.

A lone tear slid down his cheek.

"I'm forever grateful the Lord brought you back to me," he said on a shallow breath.

Hannah squeezed her eyes shut and then faced him directly. It was time she set aside the last of her foolish pride. There could be no more excuses now. After years of deception and misplaced loyalties, Rachel no longer stood between them.

Lifting her chin, Hannah gave her father a shaky smile. "I love you… *Daddy*."

A strangled sound whipped from his throat, and he roped her tightly against him.

"And I you, my beloved daughter."

The hug was short. But when he stepped back, another tear trailed down his cheek.

The reflex to scrub at her own eyes came fast, but he lifted his hand and wiped her face with the pad of his thumb.

"Our time is up, Hannah," he said softly. "Your groom is waiting."

As if on cue, Laney reappeared in the doorway. "Is the bride ready?"

Hannah inhaled deeply, touched her fingertip to the emerald pendant growing warm against her skin. "Yes."

Her father pivoted on his heel.

"Father, wait."

He turned, a question in his gaze.

Lifting to her toes, she placed a kiss on his cheek. "Thank you."

With pure delight in his eyes, he gave her shoulder a quick pat and then headed down the hallway that led to the back entrance of the parlor.

Arm in arm, Laney and Hannah made their way to the front of the house. At the sound of voices lowered to muted whispers, Hannah stopped midstride. Much to her surprise, a surge of nervousness swept through her. She hadn't been this anxious before, not even the first time she'd graced the stage as a leading lady.

Happiness overwhelmed her to think her life would now be guided by the Master Director, the Ancient of Days—her Heavenly Father.

Laney gently unwound their arms. "This is where I leave you, my friend."

Swallowing, Hannah nodded.

With a quick smile and a backward glance over her shoulder, the other woman disappeared into the room. Stomach twisting into a dozen knots, Hannah peeked around the corner after her.

Every orphan was in attendance, grinning from ear to ear and, of course, fidgeting. She counted at least ten adults lined against the outer wall. Thankfully, it didn't take Hannah long to locate Mavis sitting on the floor amidst a group of the younger children. Several had managed to climb onto her lap.

As though she sensed Hannah's eyes on her, Mavis looked up and winked.

Hannah winked back, and just like that her nervousness melted away. She was among friends. People who loved her. People she loved in return.

Feeling more confident, Hannah moved into the center of the threshold and met her father's gaze. His tenderness, his quiet acceptance silenced her remaining apprehension.

Chin up, Hannah finally turned her attention to her groom. Their gazes locked. A low buzz filled her ears, and everyone else in the room faded.

In the span of a single heartbeat, a thousand words passed between them.

Beau. *Her Beau.*

So handsome, so upright. With him, her life had found its pulse.

In pure O'Toole fashion, he sent her a quick, captivating smile. And the breath backed up in her throat.

With his charming brand of arrogance firmly in place, he stretched out his hand and summoned her to him.

Her heart took a quick tumble.

And then…

She simply…

Sighed.

Notching her head a fraction higher, Hannah squared her shoulders and began her ascent toward the man of her dreams. Her best friend.

No matter what hardships arose, no matter what challenges God brought their way, they would face them together. Two cords linked as one.

Bucking tradition, Beau abandoned his post next to the reverend and hastened down the makeshift aisle to meet Hannah halfway across the room.

Surrounded by the adults and children of Charity House, he took her hand and cupped it protectively in his. A dozen happy thoughts ran through Hannah's mind as Beau swept in a low bow and touched his lips to her knuckles.

When he rose, his eyes locked with hers again. "I'm yours, Hannah Southerland. Heart and soul, forever."

She had to gulp several times in order to regain her voice.

"I'm yours, Beauregard O'Toole," she pledged. "No matter the place, the circumstance or the season, I will always stand by your side."

Grinning, he lowered his forehead to hers. For a long moment they simply stood unmoving, neither speaking, both breathing deeply.

A hush filled the room. Hannah heard a rustle of clothing as everyone leaned forward in anticipation.

Finally, Beau stepped away and aimed his beautiful, silver gaze at her. "Then I say we get married *right now*."

Forty-some voices lifted in a cheer of agreement.

Twining his fingers with hers, Beau led Hannah down the last half of the aisle toward her father and the place where they would pledge their lives to one another.

Sealed in marriage, Hannah and Beau would no longer be two transient people drifting from place to place, waiting to hear God's clear direction for their lives.

Secure in His plan, they were home. Home, at last.

* * * * *

SPECIAL EXCERPT FROM

Love Inspired.
SUSPENSE

*An Amish widow and a lawman in disguise
team up to take down a crime ring.*

Read on for a sneak preview of
Amish Covert Operation *by Meghan Carver,
available July 2019 from Love Inspired Suspense.*

The steady rhythm of the bicycle did little to calm her nerves. Ominous dark blue clouds propelled Katie Schwartz forward.

A slight breeze ruffled the leaves, sending a few skittering across the road. But then it died, leaving an unnatural stillness in the hush of the oncoming storm. Beads of perspiration dotted her forehead.

Should she call out? Announce herself?

Gingerly, she got off her bicycle and stepped up to a window, clutching her skirt in one hand and the window trim in the other. Through her shoes, her toes gripped the edge of the rickety crate. Desperation to stay upright and not teeter off sent a surge of adrenaline coursing through her as she swiped a hand across the grimy window of the hunter's shack. The crate dipped, and Katie grasped the frame of the window again.

"Timothy?" she whispered to herself. "Where are you?"

With the crate stabilized, she swiped over the glass again and squinted inside. But all that stared back at her was more grime. The crate tipped again, and she grabbed at the window trim before she could tumble off.

Movement inside snagged her attention, although she couldn't make out figures. Voices filtered through the window, one louder than the other. What was going on in there? And was Timothy involved?

Her nose touched the glass in her effort to see inside. A face suddenly appeared in the window. It was distorted by the cracks in the glass, but it appeared to be her *bruder*. A moment later, the face disappeared.

She jumped from the crate and headed toward the corner of the cabin. Now that he had seen her, he had to come out and explain himself and return with her, stopping whatever this clandestine meeting was all about.

A man dressed in plain clothing stepped out through the door.

"Timothy!" But the wild look in his eyes stopped her from speaking further.

And then she saw it. A gun was pressed into his back.

"Katie! Run! Go!"

Don't miss
Amish Covert Operation *by Meghan Carver,*
available July 2019 wherever
Love Inspired® Suspense *books and ebooks are sold.*

www.LoveInspired.com

WE HOPE YOU
ENJOYED THIS

LOVE INSPIRED® SUSPENSE
BOOK.

Discover more **heart-pounding**
romances of **danger** and **faith** from the
Love Inspired Suspense series.

Be sure to look for all six Love Inspired
Suspense books every month.

Love Inspired. SUSPENSE

Any day she could see Sammy was a good day. But she was pretty sure Jack was about to turn down her nanny offer. And then she'd have to tell Penny she couldn't take the apartment, and leave.

The thought of being away from her son after spending precious time with him made her chest ache, and she blinked away unexpected tears as she approached Jack and Sammy.

Sammy didn't look up at her. He was holding up one finger near his own face, moving it back and forth.

Jack caught his hand. "Say hi, Sammy! Here's Aunt Arianna."

Sammy tugged his hand away and continued to move his finger in front of his face.

"Sammy, come on."

Sammy turned slightly away from his father and refocused on his fingers.

"It's okay," Arianna said, because she could see the beginnings of a meltdown. "He doesn't need to greet me. What's up?"

"Look," he said, "I've been thinking about what you said." He rubbed a hand over the back of his neck, clearly uncomfortable.

Sammy's hand moved faster, and he started humming a wordless tune. It was almost as if he could sense the tension between Arianna and Jack.

"It's okay, Jack," she said. "I get it. My being your nanny was a foolish idea." Foolish, but oh so appealing. She ached to pick

Sammy up and hold him, to know that she could spend more time with him, help him learn, get him support for his special needs.

But it wasn't her right.

"Actually," he said, "that's what I wanted to talk about. It does seem sort of foolish, but…I think I'd like to offer you the job."

She stared at him, her eyes filling. "Oh, Jack," she said, her voice coming out in a whisper. Had he really just said she could have the job?

Behind her, the rumble and snap of tables being folded and chairs being stacked, the cheerful conversation of parishioners and community people, faded to an indistinguishable murmur.

She was going to be able to be with her son. Every day. She reached out and stroked Sammy's soft hair, and even though he ignored her touch, her heart nearly melted with the joy of being close to him.

Jack's brow wrinkled. "On a trial basis," he said. "Just for the rest of the summer, say."

Of course. She pulled her hand away from Sammy and drew in a deep breath. She needed to calm down and take things one step at a time. Yes, leaving him at the end of the summer would break her heart ten times more. But even a few weeks with her son was more time than she deserved.

With God all things are possible. The pastor had said it, and she'd just witnessed its truth. She was being given a job, the care of her son and a place to live.

It was a blessing, a huge one. But it came at a cost: she was going to need to conceal the truth from Jack on a daily basis. And given the way her heart was jumping around in her chest, she wondered if she was going to be able to survive this much of God's blessing.

Don't miss
The Nanny's Secret Baby *by Lee Tobin McClain,*
available August 2019 wherever
Love Inspired® books and ebooks are sold.

www.LoveInspired.com